The Wilder Sisters

Books by Jo-Ann Mapson

The Wilder Sisters
Loving Chloe
Shadow Ranch
Blue Rodeo
Hank & Chloe
Fault Line (stories)

The Wilder Sisters

A NOVEL

Jo-Ann Mapson

HarperFlamingo

An Imprint of HarperCollins*Publishers*

Grateful acknowledgment is made to Jennifer Olds for the use of her poems, "Requiem," previously published by Event Horizon Press in *Rodeo and the Mimosa Tree*, copyright © 1991 by Jennifer Olds, and "The Howling Wind (Desire)," copyright © 1998 by Jennifer Olds.

HarperCollins books may be purchased for educational, business, or sales promotional use. For information please write: Special Markets Department, HarperCollins Publishers, Inc., 10 East 53rd Street, New York, NY 10022.

FIRST EDITION

Designed by Nancy Singer Olaguera

Library of Congress Cataloging-in-Publication Data
Mapson, Jo-Ann
    The Wilder sisters: a novel / Jo-Ann Mapson. —1st ed.
        p.   cm.
    ISBN 0-06-019116-3
    I. Title.
PS3563.A62W55   1999
813'.54—DC21   98-41175

99 00 01 02 03 ❖/RRD 10 9 8 7 6 5 4 3 2 1

To my mother, Mary Catherine,
my sisters, Leslie Ann and Carol Jeanne—
and to the members of my tribe:
Phyllis Barber, Earlene Fowler, Cynthia Gregory,
Terry Karten, Jennifer Olds, Rachel Resnick,
Ruth Salter, Nancy Scheetz, Deborah Schneider,
and the irreplaceable Alexis Taylor:
women of words, courage, and spirit

Blood thins. Men die.
Love could still make her into something,
but first
it would have to find her.

—*Jennifer Olds*
"Requiem"

Acknowledgments

Newport Harbor Animal Hospital in Costa Mesa, California, generously took me behind the scenes and demonstrated how to manage a veterinary clinic with care and grace; Sharon Cummings educated me about Greyhound Rescue operations and gave me time with her elegant, fortunate dogs; Jimi Kurzmack and Roni Piastuch were my second home and support in Albuquerque; as always, the state of New Mexico provides inspiration and history; C. J. Mapson advised me as to the medical world and western myths; Dennis Hallford taught me about CAT equipment; Marie Loggia gave me the lowdown on dirt bikes; Lois Kennedy, MFCC, tendered vital life support; Mark Secor, DVM, once again generously offered specific veterinary and chiropractic information that helped make this story accurate; Ruthanna Bridges ministered to my horse, Tonto, when I was unable to be there; Don K. Pierstorff continues to provide unconditional fatherly love and sage advice. Continued thanks and appreciation to my agent, Deborah Schneider, to my copy editor, Sue Llewellyn, to my editor, Terry Karten, and to her assistant, Megan Barrett, who challenge me to reach beyond my known grasp.

And to Stewart Allison: *Contigo pan y cebolla*; I could say thank you forever, and it would not cover all you have done for me this past quarter century. Now it's your turn.

The Wilder Sisters

1

An Echo from a Former Life

I used to love my children," Rose Wilder Flynn said as she held the
mare's bound tail aside so the vet, his gloved and greased arm sunk
up to the shoulder inside the horse, could palpate the horns of the
uterus for signs of pregnancy. "Sesame Street Band-Aids, scout meetings, classroom cupcakes with the little colored jimmies. Once upon a
time, Austin, I did the whole nine yards for them."

Austin Donavan, DVM, rotated his arm inside Miss Winky, Rose's
five-year-old quarter horse. "I believe you. It's easy enough to love
them when they're small."

"I should have had a passel of kids instead of stopping at two. Yes,
with three or more offspring, my odds would definitely improve."

"How's that?"

"Because at any given time one of them is bound to need a loan, a
ride somewhere, or a babysitter."

Austin smiled. "I suppose." A faraway look came over the vet's face
as he pressed forward and down, gently palpating and massaging. Miss
Winky, who had earned her nickname for advertising her business end
when she was in season, tolerated the inspection with dignity, probably because her upper lip was caught in the bind of a humane twitch.
The device, which looked like a nutcracker pinching Winky's upper lip,
in reality was releasing endorphins so she wasn't in any pain. Rose
scratched the mare's neck with her free hand while murmuring words
of encouragement. It was not exactly the kind of treatment Rose herself received when she saw the gynecologist, but why not calm the
horse down if it made Austin's job easier?

He turned his face toward her. The vet was clean-shaven and unsmiling, and though it appeared he was looking directly at Rose, she knew he was concentrating on the mare. They stood no more than two inches apart, their boot tips touching. Over the healthy scents of alfalfa and nervous horse, Rose could detect the soap Austin had used that morning to wash his face. Nothing fancy, but compared to his usual stink of alcohol, soap smelled like cologne. Then he smiled, and Rose's heart fluttered for a single beat. *Oh, let it be!* Winky hadn't caught on the first attempt at breeding, back in March. They'd tried again late in May, July, and August. Pregnancy in maiden mares could be detected as soon as thirty days after breeding, if the exam was performed by an experienced vet. Rose crossed her fingers. "Is she?"

"Knocked up like a cheerleader," he said. "I can feel it along the bottom of the left uterine horn, about the size of an orange." He withdrew his arm and rolled off the lubricated sleeve, throwing it into the back of his pickup. "Barring unforeseen circumstances, you'll have yourself a foal next summer, Rose. Going to trailer her up to your dad's?"

"Yes. Soon." Maybe, if she got her way, this very weekend.

"I'll set up a vaccine schedule, and you give it to Shep or your father. Meanwhile, start her on supplements. I'll fetch you some samples from my truck."

Rose unwound the string from the twitch, put it away in the barn, then using a garden hose, washed the mare's butt clean of the slippery lubricant. She turned Winky out into the small arena that took up most of her backyard. Cut loose, the nervous horse squealed once, kicked at the fence, then resumed her usual behavior, which involved standing at the rail, gossiping to Max, the elderly bay gelding who technically belonged to Rose's absent daughter, Amanda.

Dr. Donavan set the patient file on the seat of his truck and flipped through the boxes of medical supplies. Rose had seen him give them away to patients who couldn't afford proper veterinary care. His thick brown hair was cropped close, almost down to a burr. It looked as if he'd given himself the haircut with the same kind of shears Rose used to clip her horses. Over his ears some gray was beginning to creep in. They had known each other almost all their lives, and had been friends for the last ten. Rose remembered a time when Austin's hair was long enough to touch his collar. At the time she'd been too young for him to notice, but she'd always had in mind that there'd come a day she'd run her fingers through that hair. Now it was gone, and the moment for that had passed, too.

"Lately I've been thinking about children," Austin said. "Now that I'm into my fifties, sort of wish I'd had a couple."

The question that immediately came to mind was, *What stopped you?* Every resident of Floralee, New Mexico, believed the reason Austin Donavan had remained childless was his wife's—well, Leah was his *ex*-wife now—vanity. She was extraordinarily pretty—cover-girl material, people often remarked. Rose would never come right out and ask, but she suspected that some kind of infertility issue was going on there and had been a contributing factor to the Donavan divorce. She wished she'd thought twice before complaining about her own kids. Trying to make light of her words, she said, "Oh, come spend a week here. The collect calls will convince you otherwise. Everyone seems to think I have a built-in mother compass when it comes to my children's whereabouts, and at the end of the month, I get to pay for telling them I haven't a clue."

Austin laughed, and Rose relaxed. She rolled up the hose, hung it over a nail protruding from a side of the barn where the horses couldn't get to it, and walked out of the arena and into the small yard, where a clothesline was strung between two trees. She bent over a wicker laundry basket half full of dry clothes and began folding. Indoors there was a washer-dryer in working order, but somehow hanging laundry out to dry made the last little bit of summer linger in her clothes. She hated to see it end. With its ninety-degree dry air and indigo sunsets, summer was Floralee's finest season. Actually, fall wasn't half bad either, when the light glowed off the Sangre de Cristo Mountains and the trees began to turn, or spring, when the air was briefly filled with the scent of lilac; she waited all year for that, too. And people could bitch all they wanted about winter, but crisp snowfalls and *farolitos* lighting the way into town made Rose love that season, even walking home in wet shoes. The only time of year she could do without was mud season, when snowmelt and spring rains turned the porous red earth into a kind of quicksand, and tempers short enough that New Mexico's crime rate, already fairly high on a national average, hiked upward of 25 percent.

"The phone bills sound bad, Rose, but when you get old, won't it be nice having your kids around?"

She turned and gave him a rueful smile. "When they were babies, it seemed like the most natural thing in the world, sacrificing my breasts so they could fill their little bellies, or rocking a colicky infant until the sun came up. Mothering came as natural to me as breathing. I'm telling you, Austin, I loved my babies like a three-star general. Now I doubt they'd give me the time of day."

Austin peered over his wire-rimmed glasses. The bulk of his calls involved tube-worming the parasitically infested, cleaning geldings' sheaths for lazy owners who ignored the loathsome task until it caused an infection, or fretting himself into the morning hours over what might be causing a particular animal to colic. The wind lifted his collar. "All right. What's all this confession leading up to?"

"Begging for time off."

"I guess everyone deserves a vacation. How long?"

"Three weeks?"

He sighed, and Rose could tell he was going to say no.

"I was planning on having my stretch marks surgically removed, joining a witness protection program. A woman needs a little down time for that."

"You know I can't do without you for that long, Rose." He closed the technical manual he'd been consulting and held out the inoculation schedule. "I've said this before, but I feel the need to remind you: I'm not your priest. You don't have to justify your feelings about your kids to an old drunk like me."

"The hell I don't." Rose tucked the card into the back pocket of her faded Levi's. "Every time you drive up I'm wracked with guilt over how those kids left these animals. I don't see why I can't take your books with me along to Pop's ranch. It's September, not foaling season. I want to put my feet up and watch the sun set. Stare out at the mountains and think of nothing."

Austin nodded. "Wouldn't mind a little of that myself. Now, where's my buddy Max?"

At the sound of his name, the gelding brayed. He was a smart old horse, and he always recognized the noise the vet's truck made long before Rose saw it coming up the gravel driveway. Austin had been seeing to Max since the animal came to the Flynn house as an eight-year-old ex–schooling horse. Rose had grown up on a breeding ranch. She knew there had to be a reason anyone would sell a gelding that young and handsome at such a low price. Amanda, twelve at the time, and horse-smitten, a state that preceded boy-crazy by three incredibly short months, swore she could not take another breath on this earth without Max for her very own. Philip, Amanda's father and hero, had caved in to her demands and purchased the horse over Rose's objections. Amanda possessed the attention span of a goldfish and always would, but Philip had been father-blind to his daughter's shortcomings. *You're awfully cynical for a mother,* her husband had often pointed out. Philip traveled weekdays during their marriage, staying in hotels and enjoying room service on a sales rep's expense account. He'd come home on weekends when the kids were as far from the house as possible. *Rose, with all your free time, can't you keep this place picked up?* Though his words still echoed in an uncomfortable way, they no longer mattered. Philip was dead. Two years ago Christmas, some liquored-up vacationing skier from California had broadsided him on Highway 84. The drunk driver had better lawyers than Rose could afford, and no amount of money was going to bring her husband back. She accepted the insurance settlement and parlayed her job from part- into full-time. Amanda was twenty now, running around the country with some tattooed drummer whose hairstyle resembled that of a puli dog. The boyfriend smelled like bad cheese, and his clothes never matched. He'd made enough of an impact on Amanda that she'd adopted the same fashion stance. Given the state in which she'd left her room, it was clear that Amanda and dirt were destined to have a long-term relationship.

Not surprisingly, over the past two years, Max's back problems had emerged. He was going on eighteen, getting up there in terms of horse years. It was Rose who had to deal with the medical situations and find the money to pay for them. Austin was trying out different therapies, but vet care wasn't the only expense. Max needed special shoes that cost more than Rose had ever paid for a pair of her own. If he wasn't regularly schooled, he nosed the gate open and "exercised" himself, across the road toward the highway. While Winky made a temporary pal for Max, companionship wasn't enough. The fact was, if you owned a horse, it deserved a consistent relationship. Most vets wouldn't, but if Austin needed to assess the animal's problems firsthand, he'd sometimes take Max for a couple of laps around the corral himself. Then again, Austin Donavan wasn't most vets, Rose thought as she watched him kneel down and put his hands in the dirt in front of him. "Austin?" she asked. "Have you taken up yoga?"

Without looking up at her, he lifted one knee, plucked a piece of gravel out from under it and flung the offending stone away. "Sometimes if I get down on all fours, I can look at the world the way an animal does."

"Really? And how is that?"

"Well, for one thing, it's all hard ground down here. Imagine if you've already got a sore back. When there's only gravel between you and the open road, just moving forward can seem like a trial."

Rose wondered if he meant she should shovel her driveway down to dirt. If she did that, when the snow fell and the road froze over, Max could slip and break a leg, or she could.

Apparently Austin hadn't learned everything he needed to down there, because after awhile he stood up, brushed off his knees, and climbed onto the horse's back. He executed a few diagnostic transitions from the walk to the trot. Rose hoped that in addition to diagnosing Max's problems Austin was also giving her vacation request serious consideration.

Austin sat a horse the same way Rose's father did. His long skinny legs hung loose, his barely two handfuls of muscled butt straddled the thousand-pound animal with ease. He didn't need a saddle; his body melded to the horse's back. Rose climbed the fence and settled herself on the top rail. Watching him, she believed she understood the origin of the centaur myth: Some early literate woman had been rendered speechless beholding this very sight.

She said a silent prayer that the gelding wouldn't pitch her boss into the sand. Lately—if one could call the last five years lately—her life had felt so unpredictable. Things that generally moved along in a plodding, predictable fashion went strangely awry. There were entire weeks she felt on edge, and usually they centered around her children.

What Austin said was true. Rose could blame her daughter, but it wasn't going to accomplish anything. Neither Amanda nor her brother Second Chance stopped by the house much at all these days, finding life outside Floralee far more intriguing than in it. Second Chance raced motorcycles and seemed to have made a parallel career of breaking girls' hearts. Sooner or later they tracked down his home phone number and called Rose in the wee hours of the morning. *Is Second*

Chance there? they'd whimper tearfully at two A.M., and when Rose sleepily explained she had no idea where he was, they tried to unload on her. *He promised he'd:* call, write, pick her up from work—the list had no end.

Rose's son had a face so handsome girls threw themselves at him, but even if he looked like a man, he was still a boy more enamored of motorcycles than women. *There are two sides to every story,* she told the girls who telephoned. *Don't get me wrong. I believe he let you down, and I'm sure sorry about that. Go back to college, honey. Join a church group, and date somebody with both feet on the ground.* Beware of the entire male race. She never actually said the last part out loud, but sometimes she thought it. She lay awake in her bed until the sun came up, wondering how on earth her two genius offspring had made such bona fide messes of their lives. Those times her children did show up, they spilled detergent on the tile, swiped money from her purse, inferred that she was one step away from housecoats. Second Chance delivered Max a pat on the muzzle and threw the ball for Chachi, his Jack Russell, who literally bounced off the walls with joy until the last long toss, which sent him running so far on his stubby little legs that by the time he retrieved it, her son had lost interest or driven away. The curmudgeonly dog then tore the ball to bits and returned to his life's work, which consisted of digging to China in what remained of Rose's front yard. Austin had suggested filling the holes with water, but that only awakened in Chachi a latent love of mud, so Rose left the front yard in ruts. Let the neighbors think she was one of those women who allowed everything go to hell when the husband died. Maybe she was.

In the years since Philip's death, her daughter had come to hold her mother responsible for loosing such anarchy on her well-ordered world. *Maybe Daddy wouldn't have been working all the time if you'd paid him more attention,* Amanda had accused. Rose understood Amanda's grief better than she did her own. *Oh, honey. Your father was in the wrong place at the wrong time,* she patiently explained. *People die, Amanda. Never the ones who deserve to, and never when it's convenient. It's one of life's more mysterious lessons, just like men getting craggier and more handsome as they age, and women, no matter how generous our souls, how polished our wit, just growing old.* Second Chance had inherited his grandfather's tact. Instead of hurling accusations at his mother, he took things out on himself. He rode the most difficult dirt-bike tracks at record-breaking speeds. He broke bones the way some people bit their fingernails. Rose couldn't remember the last time she'd seen her son without a limb cast in plaster. She prayed for her children so often that she wondered if God was growing weary of her appeals.

"I don't know," Austin said, frowning in the direction of the horse's neck. "He's still tender on his front end, Rose. But I can't find any trace of lameness there, and he isn't navicular. How is he for you at the lope?"

"Max never had what you call a rocking-horse canter. Amanda all but tore his legs apart with that barrel-racing. He's a willing horse. There's times I'd go so far as to call him stoic."

The vet reached up under his glasses to rub his eyes before he resumed the trot. "Half the horses I treat have been barrel-raced into lameness. The others have been run hard and turned left team-roping. If you're going to blame one group you're going to have to blame them all."

"My father brought me up to treat animals like first-class citizens," she explained to Austin. "He doesn't say it outright, but his silence speaks volumes. Pop believes I failed to educate my children in the basic Wilder family tenets, which means I misfired as a mother. Well, my therapy group says it's good to share my views," she added, aiming her words to the horse as well as the vet. "Max isn't big on feedback, though he makes a superb listener."

"Therapy? Since when did you start going in for that New Age crap?"

Rose smiled and ran her fingers through her dark, curly hair, which was cut in layers to fall just at the top of her shoulders. "Since never. I made that up to see if you were listening."

Austin looked skyward as if seeking divine assistance. Slowly he shook his head from side to side. The tenderness in his fifty-five-year-old face elevated him from an average man emerging from a year of grief to nearly handsome. When Leah walked out on him last fall, Austin, only an occasional drinker, had fallen deep into his cups and stayed there all year. With a duplicate set made from the keys he misplaced all over the office, Rose had let herself into his house every week. While the vet slept off his drunken sorrow, she packed his fridge with food. She couldn't help but stop now and again to admire the Donavans' kitchen. Saltillo tiles, a six-burner restaurant cookstove, a Swedish stainless-steel dishwasher that ran whisper quiet, the adobe oven tucked into the wall so a woman could make bread the traditional way. How she could cook in this room! she always thought. Any meal put together here would have to turn out right. Her Pyrex casserole dishes looked small sitting there atop the oven mitts surrounded by so much silence. Knowing how deeply enmeshed Austin was in his drinking made her gestures seem pitiful, but Rose had never been one to give up trying just because a situation was difficult.

Austin's drunkenness made for another country, one Rose didn't care to visit. She'd yank off his boots and cover his skinny shoulders with a blanket, but she wouldn't mop up vomit or drive empty bottles to the dump. He needed to get sober and stay that way. As much as she ached for him to go there, she could not draw him a map. She delivered macaroni and cheese with toasted bread-crumb crust, potato-topped shepherd's pie, lasagna with hidden grated vegetables. Sliced and served cold, it tasted as good for breakfast as it did for supper. She fed the man, and she waited.

Her official job title was bookkeeper, but to Rose there didn't seem to be any good reason she had to lose two good men in her life as a result of alcohol. Leah's divorcing him had caused Austin to forget so many things. He forgot that the animal population of Floralee depended on his expertise and generous heart. He forgot that he had friends who also were hurting. Rose and Paloma, Austin's receptionist, put their heads together and hired substitute vets anxious for extra cash to fill in so the practice didn't fall completely to pieces. On the days Austin made it to the office, Rose handed him his appointment schedule and reminded him that the coffee decanter was right there on his desk. He always nodded politely and said thank you. Periodically they heard the clank of bottles hitting the trash can, an indicator that Austin's dipstick had hit the full mark. He'd take tentative steps back toward an orderly life; then a call from Leah's lawyer wanting more alimony, or somebody reporting they'd heard she was whooping it up in Santa Fe, would trigger a backslide and he'd drink again. Nobody mentioned his slips. The unspoken Floralee code went something like this: You can shoot a horse that rears up, but people are only human.

The gelding appeared anxious to move beyond the trot. He began twitching his ears, and his long black tail kinked up. "Max," Rose said sternly. "Try anything funny, and I'll climb down off this fence and brand your ass myself."

Austin smiled. "You're what my daddy called a *pistola*, Rose Ann. I can hardly believe some of the things that come out of your mouth."

"If I'm boring you, tell me to shut up."

"Mrs. Flynn, nobody could call you boring around me and get away with it." He dismounted, untied the lead rope he'd fashioned into a makeshift rein, laid it over the horse's back, and faced his patient.

The basic tenets of chiropractic medicine—align the spine and court good health—seemed far too simple to work. Needles Rose understood. Pain, too, because it was a wake-up call that couldn't be ignored. Healing often hurt more than the original injury, but that kind of pain was good for you. It forced you to listen. It tore your heart out by the roots. Then it was up to you to plant what remained back in the earth or leave it uprooted to rot. But the sight of Austin's beat-up hands caressing the old gelding's backbone, his tobacco-brown eyes shut deep in concentration, that moment when doctor and patient found a connection—oh!—this was arcane business, sensual in a way that made her flinch deep inside her belly. While it felt natural to sit by the cages of the dogs and cats in the hospital, to stroke furry heads, hold on to paws, and soothe the anxious, this felt beyond intimate. Yes, the way Rose felt when she watched Austin adjust Max embarrassed her to death.

"Okay, then. Here we go." Austin planted his bootheels firmly in the dirt. He laced his hands around the horse's massive black crest. In order to achieve maximum release, he had to heave his weight forward into the gelding's left shoulder while pulling down on the animal's neck. He shut his eyes and appeared to travel deep inside himself, past his wife's walking out, past the year's worth of bottles stacked up in his living room, past the mundane business of human survival into the peculiar, compelling realm of man knowing horse. It made the hair on Rose's arms stand up, and though there was no good reason for it, her nipples stiffened beneath her T-shirt. Then, as the vertebrae moved under his hands, there came the sound of machine-gun fire, followed immediately by an equine groan of profound relief. It had been so long ago that Rose wasn't sure if what she was hearing was an echo from her former life or the longing for similar noise in this one, but the sound her horse made was eerily close to that of male orgasm.

Austin unlaced his fingers and stepped back. "You've been waiting for that for a long time, haven't you, boy?"

The horse shook his head. His lower lip drooped, revealing long yellow teeth. The gelding rubbed his muzzle along the vet's faded blue workshirt, nudging and pushing until the man had to take steps to catch himself or go right over. Rose watched Austin reach up and tenderly stroke the horse's neck. Max's ears flicked with pleasure, and he lipped an imaginary handful of oats from the vet's open palm. In the background, now that somebody else was getting it, Winky squealed for attention.

At that moment Rose knew that here was exactly what she needed—someone to hold on to her like that, someone whose primary desire was to deliver relief she couldn't seem to provide herself—and that the man she wanted to do it was Austin Donavan. *It's never going to happen*, she scolded herself. *Leah ruined him forever. Everyone knows that. But can someone please explain to me why it is men can't drive the damn speed limit, make a little sense when they talk to us, and not drink? Maybe we don't grow old as gracefully as they do, and not all of us are blessed with physical beauty, but underneath, where things count, can't they see that a woman's heart stays as passionate as ever?*

Asking questions like that was like wondering if she should dye the growing streak of gray hair under her left ear black. Eternal, with no right answer, and certainly not intended for women like her sister, Lily, to whom she had not spoken in five long years. Sit any decent male down in a chair, and have Lily walk by. Even the most educated of men would be transformed into a Tex Avery cartoon wolf—eyes bugging out, tongue lolling on the floor, his entire vocabulary suddenly reduced to a primal whistle. Well, at least Austin was safe. He loved only alcohol, and Lily had long since moved on to more lucrative pastures—Southern California, the land of frozen yogurt, drive-bys, big bucks and aerobic everything.

And it wasn't as if Lily didn't deserve Rose's silence. The two sisters had spent a lifetime arguing, but what Lily'd done that had zipped Rose's lips shut had happened at Second Chance's high school graduation party. The Wilder clan—cowboys, ranchers, and rednecks from way back—was used to shenanigans and found the humor in almost every situation, but Rose's mother's side of the family did not. Mixed in with the white was a concentration of Spanish and Indian heritage, and in the State of New Mexico, the amount of blood one could claim set one's station for life. The Martínez family were formal, as reserved as they were religious, and descended from a wealth so quiet it was detectable only in their perfect manners. When Lily's present—an exotic dancer hired to "entertain" the new graduate—called out Second Chance's name in a well-oiled voice, every member of the Martínez family except for Mami had made polite excuses, left behind their cards and gifts, and gotten into their cars and driven home. Lily apologized, but the party Rose had planned for so long was spoiled. *I'm sorry* were just a couple of the overworked words her sister hauled out when they suited her purposes.

The vet latched the corral gate behind him and wiped the sweat from his forehead with a bandanna. A fine sheen of Max's horsehair marked the butt of his Wranglers, which he wore cowboy tight. Before Leah left, they were starched with a crease so sharp a person could cut herself on it. The right back pocket was the spot where most Floralee men's jeans bore a circular imprint from their Copenhagen cans, but Austin didn't smoke or chew, never had. He ate oranges. In a single spiral reminiscent of DNA, the peels littered his dashboard, curling into a stiff, fragrant potpourri under the constant bake of the New Mexico sun. No matter how much he scrubbed, Austin's fingers probably smelled of horses and oranges. The scent of his truck cab reminded Rose of childhood Christmases, when fruit in her stocking was a big deal. A wistful smile crossed her face. She wished she were ten again, snuggled up to her father on the bench seat of his old pickup truck as they rode fenceline looking for breaks to repair. She let the daydream carry her back to a place where she could almost feel the sun dappling her arm hanging out the passenger-side open window and the comforting clove-and-spice scent of her dad's pipe smoke filling the cab of the truck.

Austin was staring at her. "The way you look right now I'm almost afraid to ask what you're thinking. You planning on how best to murder the kids?"

"I'm afraid it's more desperate than that."

He fluttered his fingers in a let's-hear-it gesture. "Spill."

Rose scraped her bootheel against the fence rail. "Just taking a bath in memories, Austin. You turn forty, that's allowed."

"Well, soak until you prune up, lady, but remember I need the payroll taxes figured before I incur penalties. And I have other patients to see. Mind if I duck inside, use the facilities on my way out?"

He always asked, and she never refused. "There is one small matter," she said, pausing to frame the request in less obsequious terms. "If you have two seconds."

Austin had been making notes on Max's chart, but now he tucked the pen behind his ear. "Not Chachi's anal sacs again. Rose, dammit, I—"

"Please. He's dragging his bottom all over the yard. It's painful to watch. He needs them expressed."

The vet swore softly and threw his papers into the truck. "Paloma can do this. Even you can."

"Chachi snaps at everyone but you. The last thing I need is a lawsuit. Plus, if he bites my right hand again I can't type, and you know what that means for the payroll taxes."

"That's blackmail, woman."

"Call it logic and you'll feel better."

Dr. Donavan set his handsome jaw as he snapped on a pair of surgical gloves. "Forget worrying about lawsuits," he said in neatly clipped syllables. "People around here don't sue. Your kids'll hit bottom, and when they do, they'll straighten out whether you love them according to the books or otherwise. The only problem I can see that's unfixable in your life is that damn designer dog."

She fetched the Jack Russell from his favorite napping place, a rut that stretched beneath the porch steps, where the red earth was always cool. Chachi, generally chock-full of attitude, growled at her until he saw the vet. Then he began to shake and try to make things up to her. "Relax," Rose told him. "This will be over in two seconds."

"About two seconds longer than I'd like," Austin grumbled.

"Oh, stop it," Rose said. "I owe you, all right?"

"Come to think of it, a casserole might even the scales." He worked his magic, and there was minimal growling. Set free, Chachi flew across the yard, barking indignantly. Austin went up the steps into the house, and Rose unpinned the rest of the dry things from the clothesline and folded them into a neat pile.

A few moments later, she carried the laundry basket into the house. She watched Austin's back strain against his shirt as he finished rolling up his sleeves and bent to wash his hands at the kitchen sink, which she suddenly remembered was full of her few good bras and lacy panties, soaking in sudsy Woolite. From where the vet stood, it probably looked like leftover dishwater. Men weren't picky. To them water was water, soap was soap. Austin's hands were always a wreck, cut up from slipped scalpels, bitten by his patients, the nails on those thick, short fingers of his chewed to the quick. "Austin—" she said, but he'd already thrust them into the water and brought them right back out full of wet lingerie.

"Well," he said, holding on for just a moment before dropping the slippery garments back into the sink. "I expected you were soaking a pot or something. Hope I didn't wreck anything."

The expression on his face was such a mixture of befuddlement and longing that Rose wanted to cry. Nasty underthings were Lily's department. She favored French imports. Rose was practical. Strictly Jockey for every day, but every once in awhile she'd drive down to Albuquerque, hit Nordstrom's, and stand in front of the dressing-room mirror assessing her untouched body, lightly running her hands over imported lacy bra cups. Was that a crime?

Austin faked a halfhearted glance at his watch. "Running late again. Adios, Rose. Don't forget my taxes."

It only took a few days' sobriety for the man to come springing back to life. Then it seemed as if he couldn't wait to take off running from it.

2

Chasing Sheep

Some 846 miles away in her dollhouse-size condominium, Lily Wilder bent to blow out the aromatherapy candle on her bedside table. The scents of sage and cedar lingered in the corners of her bedroom. In the dark the smell reminded her of late fall in Floralee, the only time of year she didn't feel like running away. Nights got cold enough that Pop lit a mesquite fire in the patio *chimenea,* and the trees all turned the colors of really great eye shadow. One of the stable pups would roll over at her feet and show her his precious milk-fat belly. She'd rub it, sing to him in the little Spanish she knew, and believe that under this gaping blue sky, her one true love was just around the corner.

But this wasn't a New Mexico fall, it was summer in Southern California. Financially, ecologically, and spiritually the state was a wreck. Thanks to air conditioning they had pickled the smog into some nearly breathable concoction. It was past midnight, but Lily wasn't sleepy. She pinched the burned candlewick down with her fingernails and sloughed the ash into a saucer. Her bedroom suite came from the Santa Fe collection at Sears. *Phony-wannabe-lodgepole,* she thought every time she pulled the covers up. Despite its practical origins, it reminded her of her mother and the unique style Poppy Martínez Wilder left in her wake wherever she flung down her causes and gallery openings long enough to decorate. Mami had whitewashed pine with a ratty old paintbrush long before that kind of thing became fashionable. She'd draped brightly striped Guatemalan fabrics over threadbare chairs, and nowadays you couldn't walk into a hotel without seeing that style utterly done to death. If Mami got bored or sad, all it took was one of her wistful smiles, Pop made a few calls, and in less than an hour, the courtyard filled up with artists, horsemen, the smell of barbecue, and the sound of music. Jeez, how long since Lily had been to a halfway decent party?

A Veloy Vigil print of a white coyote stared out at her from the oystershell walls. In its place her mother would have hung her O'Keeffe. Lily's mother was a beguiling blend of Navajo, Hispanic— *European* Spanish roots—and enough white mixed in that she felt comfortable in all three worlds. She knew Maria Benitez and R. C. Gorman well enough to get invited to their Christmas parties. She'd had a fling with that National Book Award writer who taught literature at UNM. She rescued greyhounds and had her private pilot's license and her own plane. In the high cheekbones Lily and her mother resembled each other, but Lily's skin tone was more like her father's. Lily had tried her hardest to step into her mother's high heels, but on nights like this? Screw the career, the accomplishments, all her cultivated wildness. She worried that she had only ended up looking like a well-dressed slut. For sure her sister Rose's assessment would go something along those lines. Rose, who lived in T-shirts and denim and comfortable, ugly shoes, had probably sloughed off her tits five years ago, saying, *What good are breasts unless you're nursing a baby?* The few traits Lily'd mastered of her mother's were a longing for fine things, impatience about their absolute unavailability, and being a deadeye at spotting imitation. Her desire for solid men pretty much went without saying, but there were times Lily wondered if Mami had maybe roped the world's last best male in Chance Wilder. Men like Lily's father seemed like affordable housing—relics of a distant, simpler era.

In the Ralph Lauren sheets on her bed a few feet away slept Southern California's handsomest and most spoiled cabinetmaker. At first Lily found it cute that Blaise refused to eat anything green, even though that left out pesto on Krisprolls, which were Lily's dietary staples. Then, as the relationship progressed, she discovered that he also shunned food from cans, which meant she actually had to *look* in the aisles when she race-shopped for those ecologically backward manufacturers who packed in glass or plastic. But food wasn't all there was to a person, and on the plus side Blaise was a fairly good dancer. He didn't hate horses, even if he didn't ride all that well or care to improve, and that counted for a lot because Lily loved horses. Six months earlier, at the start of things, Blaise had proved to be a major stud pup: He could go three times a night when he was in the mood. *At last,* Lily thought, *I've found a man who can keep up with me.* She relaxed enough to take her photo album down from the shelf, and to point out Shep Hallford, her father's ranch wrangler, a man she loved as much as she did her pop. When Blaise put a finger to the darker faces interspersed among the paler ones and asked, *Who are these people? Do they work for your father?* Lily, sure of Blaise's reaction, explained her family's complicated bloodlines and history. *But you look white,* he'd said, and at the time Lily remembered forcing a laugh and saying, *Yeah, well, things are hardly ever what they seem,* and hadn't that turned out to be a prophetic thing to say? She did look white, whatever "white" meant. With a surname like Wilder and enough makeup and tailored clothing, she looked as generic and rootless as anybody else in California, an exterior that had propelled her far in the business world. *An awkward moment,* she'd told herself. *It doesn't matter.* But lately Blaise ran out of pocket money, and she had to pay for their dates. He'd rather stay home and watch *Seinfeld* reruns than take her dancing. Just being in the vicinity of horses, he said, made him itchy. To Lily he was starting to sound maybe a little bit selfish. *Oh, face up,* she scolded herself. *More than a little.* That little problem Blaise had with eating had evolved to include nibbling on Lily, which was more than a little annoying. She practically had to perform backward handsprings across the carpet for any attention. On the horns of this dilemma the double standard held as true as ever. Kneel and purse your lips, and the man became hard in a nanosecond—truly engaged for as long as it took to make himself happy. Then he sort of conveniently forgot about Lily and fell asleep.

Oh, what was the use of sleep, really? Lie down in the darkness and shut your eyes for eight hours. If the mystical antidote to daytime graced her—rare these days—bad dreams were likely to follow, or thoughts of quarterly tax payments, or orders she needed to write on medical products she no longer felt she could totally stand behind, or the egomaniacal surgeons she needed to fly twelve hundred miles to take out to a five-course dinner they didn't have to pay for. All this to keep her in the winner's circle, to play hardball with those bad boys infected with MBA-itis. Such thoughts rose up like guffawing armies of nocturnal hyenas. Hyenas made her think of Buddy Guy, her overweight Queensland heeler, banished to the laundry room because he did not approve of men sharing Lily's bed. One guy she dated before Blaise had enjoyed both Lily's company and a trip to the emergency room for stitches on the first date. The thing was, she loved sleeping with Buddy Guy. In fact, she worshipped her bad doggie more than any male on the planet. She would rather have his chubby blue-gray hide snuggled next to her than anyone, even Michael Jordan, who— face it—was a god in a mortal man's skin. Buddy could sit up and beg, which in males was incredibly rare. He could play dead, which was not. Buddy had every single toy she'd ever bought him, squeakers intact, and he had learned to *put them away* in his basket. That was miraculous in those sporting the male appendage, though she'd had Buddy neutered when he was nine months old. Also, Buddy liked kissing. He'd slobber and lick until Lily yelled, *No more!* and even then try it one more time just in case she didn't mean it. She lay down and put her head against her pillow, even though sleep was definitely out of the question.

Some days, she mused, her blood jittering in her veins, *it seems like Krisprolls are the only thing that fills me.* As she shut her eyes, she wondered if one of the chemical components of semen could possibly be caffeine.

Meanwhile, in the laundry room, the reek of Outdoor Fresh Bounce dryer sheets abounded. Buddy had shredded the entire box of forty and chewed through the laundry basket as well. In its weave he could smell the ghost-aroma of Lily's sweat-stained workout clothes, an odor that panicked him into thinking he might never see her again. Plastic was wonderfully satisfying, however, and chewed into tiny pieces it went down the gullet like butter. Buddy was bored, pissed off at not getting to sleep in the big bed, and he didn't like the way the cabinet-maker had put his hands all over Lily during supper. In his wicker-and-flannel Dingo Den, Buddy tried to sleep, but when he closed his eyes, deep in the primal sections of his brain a nebulous idea of chasing sheep reared up. Buddy had never seen sheep and wouldn't know one if it fell out of the dryer's lint trap, but he desperately wanted to guide a herd into the proper field. Moonlight crept in through the garage window, illuminating the front quarter panel of Lily's creamy white leased Lexus. Buddy didn't like the look of the windshield wipers, set at an angle like that, ready to swoop down like cabinet-maker's hands. He got up, stretched all four legs, then sauntered non-chalantly over to the car. Wipers still there, still dangerous. He strained until he could take hold of the driver's-side victim in his teeth. Oh yes, rubber. He knew it well. A close relative of plastic.

His five-hundred-dollar private obedience-training course disappeared in a flash of instinct. For three or four minutes he became a feral dog, fierce to his bones, tearing the throat from a marauding wildcat. There. His precious Lily would never have to worry about sudden movements from that bastard again. Any minute now she'd open the door, throw him a biscuit, and shower him with praise.

"Later, baby. Got to get to the jobsite. Thanks for the shower fun. Hey, don't make that Mexican pig dish again, *por favor*?"

Lily stood dripping in the shower stall, already late for her first appointment. Had she heard that right? Blaise dissing *posole*? Her family legacy, a recipe with more than two ingredients, not to mention made from scratch? "Excuse me?"

"You know, with the pork and the swollen corn? Last time you made that crap it gave me the runs. I was up all night, *señorita*."

She wrapped a towel around her hair. "Don't try to talk Spanish to me, Blaise. Coming out of your mouth it sounds racist."

"Oh, lighten up. You know I dig your brown sugar. Both kinds." He covered his wide mouth with his palm, and *woo-woo*ed like a cartoon Indian.

They shared a moment of profound silence. Seemingly of its own volition, her still-wet hand closed around the tall white cylinder of Paul Mitchell mousse and aimed it like a shotgun at the arrogant carpenter. One French-manicured finger fired. It struck Lily this was exactly what her mother's ancestors should have done generations back to every smiling white face that walked into Floralee to claim the land and shame the culture out of the people. But at this moment all Lily wanted to do was obliterate the half-assed picky eater, even if it meant she had to go to work with flat hair.

"Catch." She threw him a towel. "From now on, Blaise, make your own damn dinner. And when you go, leave your key on the counter."

He sputtered and wiped at his eyes. "Come on, Lily, you know I didn't mean it like that."

"There isn't any other way to mean it," she said. "I want you out the door in five seconds, voluntarily, or Buddy will be delighted to escort you."

Blaise took a step toward her. "You're a fucking bitch."

The words stung, but Lily continued to point the can. "Maybe I am. But I'm armed."

He backed out of the bathroom and down the hallway. As soon as she heard the front door shut, Lily sat down on the toilet and cried her brown eyes out for exactly five minutes, since that was all the time she had to spare. Then she dressed in her copper size 6 Dana Buchman suit, blow-dried her long, dark hair, tugged on her dreaded pantyhose, kissed Buddy thirty-five times (once for each year of her life), filled his dish with gourmet biscuits, and ran out the door. She drove onto the 5 freeway, pasting dollar signs in the pupils of her red-rimmed eyes, and merged with the unrelenting traffic. Immediately some balding control freak in an orange Dodge Viper cut her off. She pressed the button for the windshield washer, which had worked fine yesterday, and received only a windshield scratch for her efforts. How much would that cost to fix? She sighed, lifted her car phone and punched in the code for her messages.

Ms. Wilder, I've got a ten o'clock gallbladder scheduled for OR number four. Nothing special, but I'd like it if you observe . . .

Wouldn't it just figure. Dr. Help-Me-I-Can't-Do-This-Procedure. Exactly what she needed on a Friday morning when the rest of her life had gone completely to hell. Usually her Fridays ended at eleven o'clock, and she drove out to the stables to ride for three hours. Rent-string horses weren't the same as owning your own, but she'd made friends with a sweet little paint gelding, and the guy who ran the rentals usually saved him for her. Now, instead, she could look forward to freezing to death in the OR. Three months back Dr. Help-Me had some old lady split open from sternum to pubic bone, then got hung up on the phone with his attorney. The anesthesiologist hadn't smoked the patient deep enough, and she'd sat up in the middle of the procedure. Lily'd had to break scrub—violate the sterile field in order to keep the patient's guts from spilling out onto the floor like a hara-kiri victim's.

Her job was insane—surgeons pulling down a jillion dollars a year, Lily doing half their work, making a fraction of their salaries, fielding their constant innuendo. *Why's a pretty package like you still single? Are you a lesbian? Why won't you go out with me?*

Because I don't date freaks, she wanted to answer. *Have me arrested.* But she had to grin and bear it and keep those orders coming in, even to the point of observing surgery. Lily Adrienne Wilder, aka the LAW: top gun in laparoscopic sales in Southern California. She crept along in the traffic, painting a picture of the Floralee ranch house in her mind's eye. How good it would feel to sit on the wraparound porch in one of those falling-apart rockers, a cold drink in her hand, and stare all day at the Sangre de Cristos. Rum and Coke—now there was an autumn beverage, the rich, deep shade of a bay horse's mane. She remembered family picnics at Ghost Ranch, stuffing herself on her mother's tamales, Pop puffing on his pipe—Captain Black, White Label—that sweet-smelling smoke getting tangled in her hair as he told her story after story under the sky. How she missed that wide-open blue, blue sky with the impossibly white clouds scudding across it, that catch-in-your-throat sky. Back then, there was all the time in the world to get to Happily Ever After. Then, as her last resort, because it hurt her as much as it cheered her up, she recalled every detail of the best sex she'd ever had, which wasn't sex at all, but making love, to Tres Quintero, her high school boyfriend, their clothes strewn along the banks of the Rio Grande. Tres had gifted hands, that magic middle finger, and the instincts of a cougar. What could compare to the feel of a man's callused hands on your body when the calluses came from real work? Or getting your butt as tan as your shoulders? Rose told her that only sluts sunbathed nude. *Damn Rose anyway. Philip dies, and she won't even let me say I'm sorry. That stripper thing was supposed to be a joke. Not to mention happened a million years ago. I need a drink,* Lily thought. *It's eight o'clock in the freaking morning, and I want a pitcher of martinis, delivered intravenously. Either that, or to do my last nine years over.*

The patient was thirty-five years old, five years under the Fat, Fair, and Forty adage that seemed uncannily to support gallbladder disease in Caucasian American women. But her ultrasound showed serious thickening of the organ's wall, and she presented the typical profile:

intractable pain penetrating all the way through to her upper back and right shoulder, an indulgence in and intolerance to a high-fat diet. Lily stood to the surgeon's right, watching the amiable anesthesiologist explain what he was doing in an attempt to soothe the patient.

"This surgery's very common. One hour and we'll have you back out there with your husband. Here we go now. Some patients say they experience a taste in their mouth from the anesthetic similar to garlic. Do you? Okay, then I'd like you to begin counting backward from one hundred." At the corners of his surgical mask Lily could see the man's mouth turn up in an honest smile. She liked the gas docs. Their egos came in size medium.

The patient's smile faded as the anesthetic began to take effect. She had only gotten to number ninety-eight. As her lids lowered, Lily wiggled her gloved fingers and said, "Bye."

Meanwhile Dr. Help-Me fumbled with the trocar, probing the surgical cavity a little too enthusiastically for Lily's taste, and nearly dropped the laparoscope. Lily waited patiently, not even bothering to look at the monitor screen. The videotape was a formality; these days a cholecystectomy was a breeze, finished off with internal staples. Thanks to her company's innovative products and health care's primary concern being cutting the expense of patient care while rewarding physicians with incentives, the days of lengthy incisions and weeklong hospital recoveries had become historical footnotes. Thanks to their regulations, she had to stand here and watch.

"Favorite Hawaiian island," the anesthesiologist said, posing a discussion subject, something he and Lily often did because it gave them something to talk about when the surgeries were routine.

"Kauai, I guess."

"What's wrong with Maui?"

"Give me a break. Who wants to fly six hours to bump elbows with tourists?"

"I admit Maui's gotten a little touristy, but the golf courses are to die for. And restaurants. It's got the best eats."

"Hawaiian vacations are about island wilderness and beaches," Lily insisted, "not five irons and four-star dining. Um, doctor, do you really want to use that approach? I think the one we practiced might give you a better view."

"I'm fine here," he said, switching to her suggestion.

"Yes, you're doing great," Lily said, crossing her fingers. And he *did* seem to be getting the hang of things. Her neck was cramping with tension, and she tried to relax. She glanced up at the clock, assessing his time. He was almost on track.

"Australia's got wonderful beaches," the gas doc said.

"Never been there," Lily answered. She couldn't afford it.

"Try it sometime."

"I don't know. I think that long a plane ride might kill me. I get antsy after six hours."

"Take a Xanax and upgrade to first class."

Easy for someone who made all that money to say. "Tranqs don't do much for me except make me hyper."

"Really?"

"Yep. Like putting hyperactive kids on Ritalin. Exact opposite effect."

Dr. Help-Me looked over at them. "You know, Wilder, I bet you'd look pretty good on a topless beach."

Definitely better than you would, Lily thought. No way was she going to venture into sexual harassment territory while he had one of her laparoscopes in this woman's abdomen. "How about we just finish up here and call it a day?" she said. "There's all weekend for swimsuits."

"I thought you were going to take me to lunch. I might want to approve that order, but I really can't make a decision on an empty stomach."

Lunch. Two hours of his knees poking hers under some trendy café table. But if he came through on this order, she'd earn a seven-hundred-dollar bonus, and that second territory she wanted might be within reach. "I guess there's time to grab a quick bite."

He gave her a wink. This Portly Short, a set of jowls on him like a bulldog, and *married*, not that that small inconvenience seemed to have made a dent in his overinflated ego, winked. "Your technique's really improving," she said, hoping a little flattery might redirect the heat.

"I graduated from USC, didn't I?"

Probably at the bottom of the class. Lily mustered up a response: "Go Trojans."

Finally Dr. Help-Me clamped the last staple and yanked her company's instruments free. The scrub nurse shut down the taping equipment, and Lily heard the whirring sound of it rewinding. "By the way," he said. "You're both full of it when it comes to beach vacations. Hands down, it's the Cook Islands. Otherwise you might as well go roast hot dogs at Huntington State Beach with the masses. Well, she's finished. Clean her up and send her to postop."

The assistant surgeon stepped in as Dr. Help-Me strode toward the OR doors. "Lily?" he said. "Our lunch?"

The assistant surgeon cleared his throat. "Doctor? Could you step back here a moment?"

"Are you deaf? I said, she's ready for postop."

"No offense, sir, but I—"

Lily turned to look at the patient. The woman's color had gone as pale as bone, shocky, really, and her abdomen seemed more distended than could be due to the pumped-in gas used to inflate the cavity. What was the problem?

Then her pressure dropped, and the anesthesiologist began to scramble. Frantically he forced air into her lungs. "Oh, my God, Charles, I think she's bleeding out."

Dr. Help-Me pointed a finger. "I'm the surgeon here."

"Then start behaving like one!"

He yelled out an order for plasma, and Lily's knees felt as if someone had loosed them from the hinges. The smoke doc was right on target: That was exactly what was happening. Dr. Help-Me had probably sent a staple through the aorta. Contrary to what the general public believed, the aorta did not end at the heart but, like a tree trunk, extended down the abdomen and then branched into major arteries serving all the organs. This one-hour routine surgery was going to end in a funeral.

Lily swallowed hard, watching them try to save her, never once looking away. Those were her instruments; this was her job. And that was—or had been—a woman's life.

When situations turned critical, the OR became increasingly frantic, and now the patient had a real incision, but this last-ditch surgery was nothing like that television show on Thursday nights. Lily couldn't understand why Blaise had loved to watch it. Medical scenarios made for compelling anecdotes, but those episodes were about actors reenacting real-life tragic events. She bowed her head, wanting to say a prayer, but beyond *Santa María, madre del Creador,* a phrase she'd memorized at the age of eight only in a futile attempt to please her grandmother—who always favored Rose—she couldn't remember the words.

The heart monitor was flat, and had been for forty-five minutes. The sound of surgical gloves snapping off filled the air. The patient lay dead on the table, the airway tube sticking out of her mouth like an albino snake.

The anesthesiologist ripped his mask from his face. "Call it, Charles. Just fucking call it so we can get out of here."

"Time of death," the surgeon announced. "Eleven fifty-two A.M."

Lily filled out her paperwork with trembling hands. It wasn't the first time that a patient had died in her presence, but this time it shouldn't have happened. Her company would throw this fiasco to the corporate lawyers, and probably nothing would come of it besides a cash settlement, but Lily would never be able to forget it. The bottom line was that the inept surgeon would still get paid, not to mention go on to operate again. He could live with killing people even if Lily could not.

She turned off the radio and drove the speed limit all the way out to the stables. Once there, she couldn't seem to make her legs stop shaking. What in hell was she thinking, going riding in a straight skirt? She waved to the rental guy, turned her car around, and stopped at Cook's Corner, the last of Orange County's true roadhouses. Now it was a trendy place to go country-and-western dancing, frequented by a few authentic bikers and far too many aspiring ones. She and Blaise had danced there a couple of times. She ordered a Corona and fries. At the furthest picnic table out behind the saloon, she sat pinching the greasy potatoes into inch-long segments, feeding them one by one to the crows. Like teenage boys dressed in dark clothing, they fought and scrapped over every single piece. They tore feathers from one another to get to the food, but half the time they didn't even eat what they'd won. She wondered if they had avian MBAs, or drove Dodge Vipers, or called their girlfriends fucking bitches.

There was a time in her life, not so very long ago, when leasing the luxury car, owning her own condo, and pulling down 150 grand a year seemed like the perfect plan. All that college, which at the time seemed so annoyingly tedious, had finally parlayed into something functional.

She had a fat 401K, a stock portfolio with bloodlines like one of her father's best horses, investments that were paying off her mortgage. From her family's viewpoint she was successful and had moved up in the world. How many thirty-five-year-old women could say that? Certainly not the one lying on the morgue table. Lily shuddered. But the last couple of years, what with Rose not speaking to her, Southern California going down the toilet—the crowds, the cost of living, and men like Blaise—as her pop used to say, *Lily, my darling, this does not look like a path even a mule could hack.*

She watched the assortment of leather-clad bikers down their bottles of American brew. They didn't fool her into believing they were outlaws. Leather and sunglasses and those imposing, pointless silver chains: They wore uniforms as blatant as any Catholic schoolgirl's. One tough old broad, as weathered as beef jerky, stood under an awning by the creek entrance selling jewelry. Her skin under the leather vest was so tan that Lily wanted to walk over and deliver a lecture on melanoma. Not today, though. Today she couldn't even tell herself what to do. Speaking of uniforms, her pantyhose were causing rivers of sweat to run down her thighs. And her crotch—well, didn't that feel like the loneliest rainforest on the whole spinning planet? She looked at her calves and noticed a run creeping upward. She had frozen her pantyhose, soaked them instead of washing them, dripped them dry all over her damn bathroom, but from costly Anne Klein to supermarket L'eggs there wasn't a brand that lasted more than twenty-four hours. They really should market the evil things as a single-use, disposable item. She wanted to strip them off and throw them in the creek that ran alongside the bar, but that would be unfair to the little bit of natural water California had left to offer.

At home she sat on the couch hugging Buddy Guy, ignoring the jingling telephone. She had turned the answering machine way down, so whoever kept calling was reduced to a whisper. Probably telemarketers. They were relentless in their pursuit to get her to subscribe to the *Orange County Register.* Like a silver charm fallen off a bracelet, she fingered the key Blaise had left on the counter. She left her mail unopened; it was all bills, anyway. The sun descended in a blaze of orange and violet she knew was due to smog. Lily's own private term for California sunsets was the "southern lights." Maybe food would help, she thought, and nuked a Lean Cuisine penne dinner. She took one sniff, gagged, and fed it to Buddy. She poured herself a glass of costly Merlot, which after one sip, tasted sour. "Good" wine versus ordinary wine was like comparing racehorse manure to that of an old nag; call it what you want, it was still the same old *caca.*

Summer was definitely not fireplace weather, but had that ever stopped the Wilders from enjoying a meditative blaze? She didn't have any of those Duralogs, however. Struck by an idea, she ran around the condo gathering up her pantyhose. Buddy, certain this was a new game, ran alongside her. When she had them all in hand, and was sure there were no more hiding in drawers or the hamper, she took them outside and deposited them in the barbecue. She lit a match and threw it in. In a whoosh that singed her eyebrows and caused her to crow-hop backwards, the stockings ignited. The flames leapt up, caught a drooping palm leaf, and raced up it. Lily clapped a hand over her mouth as the fiery frond bent under its own weight and touched the wooden shingle roof of her condo. She couldn't bear two disasters in one single day, so she punched 911 on her cordless and waited for the firemen.

Being handsome and growing a mustache seemed like requirements for the firefighting profession. The four men who answered her call extinguished the flames rather quickly, and the cute red-haired one issued Lily a ticket for burning trash without a permit.

He took her aside. "Miss?"

"You don't have to say it again. I know it was a reckless thing to do." She waved the citation. "I have my ticket here to remind me." In the background Buddy Guy yipped and scratched behind the garage door.

The fireman smiled and touched the corners of his mustache. "I'm glad no significant harm was done. I was wondering if you might want to go out sometime, have a drink with me or something."

He was ten years too young for her, handsome beyond his potential for intellect, and all she wanted to do was throw him down on her bed and screw her way out of this miserable day. But there was Buddy to think of, and she thought maybe she should allow at least a week to elapse between boyfriends. "Thanks, but maybe in another lifetime. These days I hardly ever get thirsty."

"Too bad. See you around?"

Lily hoped not.

Around midnight she got up out of bed, hungry, opened the refrigerator, and studied its contents. The Tupperware container her sister had given her one Christmas was half full of the *posole* she'd made for Blaise last week. When Lily popped the lid, a fierce stench met her nose. She replaced the lid and threw it in the trash. Then, as she turned to shut the fridge door, an urge overcame her, and her hands began grabbing anything and everything that could possibly rot. Out went the fat-free peach yogurt, half a head of lettuce, some questionable cottage cheese, three pears not quite ripe enough to eat. When she was down to individual jars, Lily opened the sun-dried tomato pesto and sank down to the kitchen floor. She ate it off her fingers until she caught sight of her reflection in the glass of the oven door: pathetic, single, and looking like she was going to stay that way. Buddy Guy sat hopefully at her feet. Her chubby blue dog never begged, but he was always grateful for whatever came his way.

"What do you think, *amigo*? Should we have an adventure?"

Buddy Guy woofed, and she offered him the last fingerful of pesto. Never a picky eater, and always eager to use his tongue, he lapped her hand clean.

"Okay, then. Go find your toys."

Lily packed her good jeans and her little Calvin Klein tops. She tore her closet apart until she located her old English riding boots, which needed a good polishing. She left behind every vile vial of makeup, left hanging in the dry-cleaning wrap the costly suits that graduated from taupe to charcoal to funereal black. She dug through the drawers in her office until she found her maps, then drew up a plan that would include two days' driving. She finished packing the Lexus just as the sun was coming up.

Gazing to the east, she could hardly wait to put miles between herself and this moment. *Look out, Floralee,* she whispered. *Your prodigal daughter is on her way back.*

3

She Wanted Money

After dashing home for lunch, running errands that included buying cups for the complimentary coffee in the front office and toilet paper for the restroom, Rose drove the red Bronco up the oval driveway toward the territorial-style adobe that housed the veterinary office. She navigated the wide curve around the small patch of green lawn, shady under the single gambel oak someone had planted decades before. Beneath the tree various brave and heroic police dogs were buried. Small brass plates marked their graves: Kit Carson, Tecumseh, and Hobson's Choice. On patriotic holidays people left little American flags, poking them into the earth. Sometimes passing schoolkids stole them, but otherwise no one ever bothered to take them down. The sight of the fading Stars and Stripes flapping in the breeze always touched Rose's heart, made her feel American in a way that voting failed to.

Employee parking—a wide swath of gravel—was located behind the building. Rose dutifully parked there, but rain or shine she walked around to the front of the building to enter, because the back door led through the freezer room. Inside, stacked like so much kindling, dead pets awaited pickup for mass cremation. In a separate refrigeration unit, various animal corpses were scheduled for necropsy. Since the days when she could toddle upright, Rose had brought home abandoned magpie nestlings and nursed them with eyedroppers. Orphaned kittens grew fat and happy under her care. The cool scales of garter snakes didn't repel her the way they did other girls. Horses trusted her the same way they did Pop, sensing that Rose's consistently quiet nature was something they could rely on.

Animal lives were so brief. She understood that not every client passing through Austin's veterinary clinic would receive a clean bill of health or necessarily make the exit. Responsible doctors sometimes had to cut into corpses to find answers, but the blood-and-guts stuff gave her the shudders. It haunted her the same way Philip's accident did. In the freezer room once, she'd encountered—spread out on a tarp—what looked like miles of intestines from some poor horse who'd died of sand colic. On the back counter Austin had a collection of enteroliths he'd removed from various equines whose owners could afford the surgery. The "stones," which formed around undigested material in a way similar to the creation of a pearl, graduated from the size of a child's fist all the way up to a pygmy boulder. Like colic, an enterolith blockage was a painful way for a horse to go. Or there might be dog brains packed in dry ice, waiting to be sent to the county to rule out rabies. Rose had worked at the clinic seven years, and in that entire time she'd only used the back door twice.

She passed the bulletin board offering free cats and ads seeking homes for puppies, parrots, boa constrictors, whatever animal some-one once had to own but it seemed could no longer be bothered with. In the front office she nodded hello to Paloma, who was on the phone. Three people with dogs were waiting on the wooden benches for the low-cost vaccination clinic. The tile floor smelled strongly of antiseptic and faintly of cat pee: Business as usual.

Rose's office was upstairs. Halfway up, the narrow hallway snaked to the left into a long, windowless room used for storing purged files and cleaning supplies. Rose stepped inside and shut the door behind her. She set the case of toilet paper on the supply shelf. Going in there to dump files—a task she tried to work on a little on each day—she enjoyed the aloneness, the utter quiet. Also, depending on where she stood, she could unobtrusively eavesdrop on the treatment rooms, the front office, even the kennels. She knelt on the floor to riffle through the file box. All summer she had carefully weeded through the manila fold-ers, removing onetime and deceased clients from active status. Each day she tried to get through another letter of the alphabet, but so far she was only up to *B*. In her hands she held the Brannon file. She remembered the horse, a flea-bitten gray Mrs. Brannon had rescued from an abusive situation. Sultan had lived five happy years in that family's care. One day the Bronco was in the shop, and Rose had begged a ride home from

Austin. Along the way his pager went off. They stopped to take a look at the silver-tailed gelding, too elderly to withstand the costly colic surgery. Austin gently suggested that to end to his suffering they put the animal down. Mrs. Brannon took the news stoically. Austin had stroked the horse's neck before he depressed the plunger of the syringe. Later, in the truck, he'd pulled over to the side of the road and turned his face away from Rose. That was the first time she had seen him cry.

Downstairs she could hear Paloma contending with Mrs. Ortega, who had her house dogs, a pair of yappy Chihuahuas—not to be confused with her ranch dogs—groomed weekly.

"Did Maria give you any trouble?"

Paloma didn't have to answer the question because Mrs. Ortega wrote and acted out dialogue for her pets.

"Maria says, *I wouldn't do that. Jose and I were good little* cachorros, *yes, we were. We got our toenails trimmed and our* tutus *cleaned and now we're fresh and pretty for Mami.*"

Rose could imagine the patient expression on Paloma's face. Mrs. Ortega was the widow of one of the richest ranchers in the state. She managed her late husband's assets with a shrewdness that impressed even Chance Wilder. Best of all, she paid her bills immediately and in cash. As far as Paloma was concerned, she could dye the bug-eyed, trembling little pooches lime green. Rose made it up to the letter *C* on the files before she quit. Tomorrow she'd deal with another letter. She left the supply room and headed upstairs.

At the top of the landing, directly across from one another, were their offices. Austin's featured a shower and half bath. The vet he'd bought the practice from had been open twenty-four hours a day and had probably spent a lot of nights here. Since his time, however, Floralee had grown to support three vets, two of them large-animal, Drs. Zeissel and Donavan. The OPEN TWENTY-FOUR HOURS sign that used to hang out front under the beams now hung here on the wall. Austin said it was the happiest day of Leah's life when he took the sign down. The Floralee vets traded off being on call. Beneath the sign was a double-bed-size futon sitting atop twenty equally spaced crates. Inside the boxes were photographs, winter ski clothes, and books. Next to the bed sat a Mission-style armchair. Austin insisted this setup was necessary if he had to stay the night with a tough case, but no one bought into that lie or called him on it. The books beneath the futon were his dearest possessions. The man was a fool for the classics, a voracious rereader of Steinbeck and Hemingway, an anomaly in the days of television tabloid shows, talk radio, and the three newspapers serving Floralee. The real reason Austin had moved these things in was that Leah had thrown them into the driveway the day she kicked him out. At first she wanted their house to herself. Eventually, when she left Floralee for a larger playground, Austin moved back into his home. Anyone else would have returned the books to their rightful places, but not Austin. If his bookshelves at home were bare, maybe that meant one less thing to dust. If the matched set of Mission chairs suddenly stood solo—well, perhaps he didn't feel compelled to invite people over. The furniture that stayed here seemed to Rose like a testament, not just to Austin's fractured marriage but also to his inability to move forward from Leah to trust another woman.

At the opposite end of the stairway, Rose's office was neatly organized. Her pine desk featured stacking in and out boxes; her paperwork was date-coded and her blotter free of doodles. A donkey-tail cactus hung above her desk, prickly and green, its healthy appendages nearly glancing the top of her computer monitor. On the left-hand corner of her desk two matching picture frames held photographs, one of the kids riding double on Max, and the other, a closeup of Philip, taken a few months before the accident. Her late husband had been hiking at Bandelier with his buddy Mike. Philip's hands grasped the ladder leading out of the ceremonial kiva at the upper ruins. Emerging from the darkness, he was smiling, looking directly into the camera lens, his eyes open so wide that those dark blue circles surrounding the iris stood out, reminding Rose of the doomed O-rings on the Challenger space shuttle. Every time she looked at the picture she couldn't help but feel he had been thinking about something important, some thought she'd never get to hear, information that might change how she lived the rest of her life. He and Mike trained all year long for the autumn run. They ran the trails to the kiva, then took the four hundred feet of vertical ladders at a clip that would stop anyone else's heart. Mike could recite the results of the last decade's Super Bowls, explain which individual plays had led to magnificent upsets, but otherwise he wasn't much for recalling details. Usually Rose felt comforted by the photo, but lately the broad smile had the opposite effect.

Philip's customers had expected him to be upbeat as he hawked his company's industrial product line, which included all manner of adhesives, power tools, and saw blades. To Philip, smiling was a work thing, and in his leisure hours he'd had few grins to spare. She ran her finger over the glass and frowned at the dust. Somehow, the last time she'd cleaned, she had missed his picture.

For a long moment she stood staring into nothing. Had her marriage been happy? She'd always assumed so. Then why was it that the longer Philip was gone, the more it felt as if a weight had lifted off her chest? In that airy space that remained, she felt a flutter of panic, as if at any moment she might run out and charge herself a diamond necklace just to obsess about something different. Quickly she ordered her thoughts to redirect themselves. Her computer was calling to her, humming almost imperceptibly, as the earth was rumored to do in nearby Taos, the town where Philip had died. Rose had to concentrate to hear it, but the sound was real, all right, a drone in her ear that made her feel impatient and restless. She leaned forward in her chair and began to juggle numbers into the Advanced Veterinary Systems program she had badgered Austin into ordering. It printed out checks, set up appointments, tracked inventory, and offered a way to store client records that would take up virtually no floor space. Unfortunately, Paloma had an aversion to computers and Austin, understandably, needed concrete proof of all things, so basically she did her job twice in order to make everyone happy. *Someday*, she vowed, *we will get this office running properly*. Until then Rose picked up a pen and started in on the payables. She liked the envelopes stuffed, stamped, and licked, ready for the post office one day early.

Rose had become a bookkeeper the way some people became manager of a store: She'd been standing there when the other lady quit. Compared to grooming dogs and working the reception desk, her earlier position, how hard could bookkeeping be? Pay the bills, figure the taxes, assist in the trenches when blood ran. It was similar to being a wife. You didn't necessarily have to *love* every little thing you did, you only had to keep things running in the face of disaster.

The intercom buzzed and Rose picked up. "Yes?"

"How's it going up there with the paper and stuff?"

"My head's above the waterline. How's it going down there with the furry stuff?"

"A little more interesting than I like it."

Paloma was the queen of understatement. "Uh-oh. You need an extra set of hands in the clinic?"

"I need a wheelbarrow is more like it."

"Don't tell me somebody brought in another dead Rottweiler."

There was a pause on Paloma's end. "A drunken veterinarian dragged himself in as best as he could. He kind of parked his truck, too, if you can call leaving it in the middle of the lawn parking. A little while ago he was barking."

Rose was sure she had misheard. "You mean barfing as in vomiting or barking as in dog?"

Paloma sighed. "Either way, it sounded a lot like a certain ex-wife's name to me. Will you hold him down while I put him out of his misery?"

Rose closed the file she had been working on. "I'm on my way." She hung up and checked her watch. There were still things to be grateful for: She wasn't going to be called into the hospital to identify Austin's body. This time he had waited until the afternoon to get smashed. The only clients likely to come by at this hour were picking their dogs up from grooming. If there was an emergency, Dr. Zeissel could cover. She wondered if Austin had made it to any of his appointments, and then prayed he hadn't driven drunk anywhere except from the bar to the clinic, a few short miles of back road with very little traffic.

A man could break your heart in a number of different ways, and Austin had them all down pat. He lay slumped against the wall of the room adjoining the small animal surgery. These were the quarters Paloma referred to as the "main brain" of the hospital. On the counter, the Vet Test 8008 printed out blood panels on presurgical patients. Austin was dressed in the same clothes as yesterday, and they were fragrant with alcohol and sweat. His cheek was scraped as if he had been dragged across asphalt, and he was minus yet another pair of glasses.

"*Hola, guapa,*" he crooned to Rose as she stood in the doorway. His hands lay slack in his lap. "Wanna come over here and make a sad man happy?"

Paloma shook her head, her long black braid swaying. "What we'd both like is to make a stupid man get smart, but that is beyond our powers. What's it going to take, Austin? You going to have to wrap yourself around a tree before you stop this crap? Rack up another DUI?"

Austin cocked his head at Rose. "You hear how she talks to me?"

"Hey, you don't like how I talk to you, fire my ass."

Rose crossed the room and knelt by his side, offering him her arm. "You're lucky she talks to you at all. Let's get you upstairs and into bed."

"I don't wanna go to bed."

"Why not?"

"It's lonely in there by myself."

She and Paloma exchanged a look and laughed.

"What's so funny?" He rubbed his mouth, as if that gesture would somehow clarify his slurry speech.

"Hush, Austin. Get to your feet or we'll both quit."

The two women struggled but finally managed to upright the man. It was a good thing he didn't weigh more than 150 soaking wet or they would've had to leave him to snore on the tile—which, now that she stood out of breath at the foot of the stairs, didn't seem to Rose like such a bad idea.

All the way up—Paloma pushing, Rose pulling—Austin muttered the words of wisdom drunks feel are essential to share with the sober world. *Love is a sick joke; trust a stray dog before you trust a woman; the only reliable comfort is found in bottles and bars.* Rose had heard this litany so often she could recite it herself. Then Austin started in on Leah in particular, as if the tall, black-haired woman hovered there in the stairwell, an apparition he could not reach but ached to touch.

"Built her a goddamn kitchen the Mayo clinic could have used for surgery. Did she ever so much as dirty a pan in it? Bought her a twenty-thousand-dollar racehorse. She sold it and spent the money on a lawyer. Closet full of designer clothes, turquoise jewelry..." A tremor entered his voice. "Tell me what I did wrong. Didn't I fuck her enough?"

"Yeah, that's it," Paloma said. "Some girls need it three times a day."

"I was good for twice."

In the background a chorus of howling from the kennels started up, and Paloma said, "Hear that, Austin? Not even the dogs believe you. Save it for your pillow."

They shoved him facedown onto the futon. Rose sat down on the edge and tugged off his boots. She looked up at Paloma, who was rubbing her crucifix with her thumb and forefinger, mumbling. Ask her outright, and she'd deny wasting prayers on Austin.

"Myself," Paloma said, "I prefer a chubby boy, one who don't feel the need to Rogaine the bald spot. That kind, you fill his belly, love what hangs underneath it every once in awhile, and everything stays nice and calm."

Rose dropped the boots to the floor and was confronted with Austin's socks, which had holes in the heels because, just like the rest of him, his feet were skinny. "You make it sound simple."

"It pretty much is, so long as you don't marinate it in alcohol."

"Some people have a hard time finding their way to calm, Paloma."

"Especially if they enjoy *loco*."

Rose shrugged, thinking of the nights when the enormity of the loss of Philip caused her to shake with fear until the sun rose in the sky. Sometimes she had a drink, just to quiet the racing of her heart, but she could never lift the bottle without thinking, *This is what killed my husband*. "It's just taking Austin longer than most people. He'll come around. I know he will."

Paloma laughed. "Sure, in about fifty years, if his liver holds out. By the way, here are his keys."

Rose held out her hand. "Thanks. I'll lock them in the safe after I move the truck."

"Don't forget to reset the combination. He has a memory for those things."

"I won't forget."

Austin stirred in his sleep, the arch of his foot coming to rest against Rose's palm. Absently she ran her thumb over the skin.

Paloma *tsk*ed. "Let go, Rose."

"What do you mean? I'm holding his foot, for God's sake."

"You can't cork every bottle in the state. Let him sink to the level of the gutter he wants so bad to lie in. Stop throwing him floats. What you see in that sack of misery is beyond me." She turned and padded down the stairs, where the world spun on its proper axis and nobody was tanked unless it was due to anesthetic.

Smarting a little from Paloma's words, Rose sat for a long time on the end of the bed, studying the vet's whiskery face against the pillow. Even in sleep his expression was stubborn. His lips parted slightly, and moved the way they might if he were kissing a child. The wings of his shoulder blades lifted and settled with each heavy breath. Did drunks dream? Rose could hardly lay her head down on the pillow at home without entering some complicated dreamworld where she argued with Philip over the children or tried and failed to outrun faceless strangers. Sometimes she saw her daughter in profile and called out to her in a strangled voice, but Amanda, having long ago turned a deaf ear to her mother's wishes, never heard. In her late thirties Rose had thought about having another baby because her life suddenly felt so empty. An infant in one's arms certainly presented an all-encompassing task, but all that longing turned out to be about was throat-clearing for grandparenthood. If that ever happened, Rose would face it alone. She pressed her fingers to the pulse in Austin's foot. Like the Achilles' tendon, the arch of the foot was such a vulnerable place. From time to time she thought that if the human heart rested there instead of bracketed inside the rib cage, people might be a little more careful of what they did with it. Austin's blood beat solidly, like the trot of a well-trained horse. Her fingers tightened protectively; then all of a sudden the idea that she was sitting here comforting a drunk made her skin crawl. She let go and stood up. Austin's arm dangled from the mattress and his fingertips grazed the floor. For no reason other than that he was unable to stop her, Rose rubbed her knuckles against his scraped cheek. He moaned in his sleep but didn't rouse.

"I'm warning you," she whispered. "There are people here who care about you, but they are quickly losing patience." Then she went downstairs to move his truck.

Two hours later Austin was still asleep when she switched off her monitor and headed for home. Paloma walked out back with her, and they stood by their cars, talking in the fading sunlight.

"Why don't you come home with me for supper? Nacio's making rabbit with that *mole* he brought up from Oaxaca. I can set out a third bowl. Afterward we can play cards."

Her friends suffered these attacks of kindness once or twice a week. Rose carefully chose when to say yes and when to decline. "Sounds wonderful, Paloma, but I've got the dog to see to, the horses to feed, plus I'm in the middle of a really good novel. Bring me some leftovers on Monday?"

Paloma's forehead wrinkled in concern. "You better not be coming back here to check on you-know-who. I'll know if you do; I have co-dependent radar."

Rose laughed. "Cross my heart, swear to the Virgin."

Paloma seemed satisfied as she drove away in her silver Dodge Ram. Rose opened the door to the red Bronco, a '68, practically an antique. It was one of her father's old ranch vehicles, and she'd driven it since she was sixteen years old. Wouldn't win any beauty contests, and parts for it were difficult to locate, but it ran like a top and had four-wheel drive for the winter snow between home and the three miles to the veterinary office. Philip had driven a decked-out Ford Taurus, totaled in the accident. Rose had thought about buying a new car, but in the end decided it made more sense to save the insurance settlement for a larger crisis. When she spent money these days, it was on repairs to the barn or toward the horses' keep. She was counting on Winky's foal to bring in a little extra cash, planning her future one day at a time. In some ways it felt as if her life were regressing back to a simpler time, and that only concentrating on horses would make it manageable. She drove home without the radio, listening to the sounds of early evening, birds calling, the fall wind whistling through the trees, on which the leaves were already beginning to turn.

She parked next to the barn and checked the mailbox. There was nothing but ads and the electric bill, and these she set down on the kitchen counter. Chachi sat up on his rear legs, his white paws held up; begging was the only trick the Jack Russell had ever mastered. Rose praised him, threw him the dog cookie he expected, and changed into riding breeches.

She checked on Winky, then buckled a bareback pad on Max and walked him down the dirt road toward the open prairie behind her house. The air smelled of sage and distant weather. She could hear the faint sound of a motorcycle, which made her wonder where her son was, if he'd broken any new bones this week, and when she'd see him again. Eager to stretch his legs, Max snorted, and Rose could feel the restrained prance in his gait. Winky whinnied at being left behind, but Rose didn't want to pony the nervous mare alongside the gelding today. She extended the trot, taking in deep breaths, smelling the earth as it turned up beneath his hooves, a perfume as complex, insistent, and deeply New Mexico as incense. Her thigh muscles unknotted themselves, and her calves hung loosely, gripping his barrel. A magpie shot by her shoulder, then another, scolding the first. Rose could smell rain coming, feel that subtle damp-ness penetrating her shirt collar, and see the almost imperceptible change of color in the sky. She strained her ears and thought she heard thunder. Moments later, to the east, she caught a glimpse of lightning arcing toward the earth. Farther north, on Pop's ranch, she could sit for hours watching a storm roll in. It was the best show in town. The horses would mill about, then turn frisky as colts when the first fat drops began to fall on their backs. Later, if the rain was heavy, instead of standing miserably in the downpour, they could have the shelter of the barn. Once she got Winky moved up there and settled in, she'd feel better. Rose intended to keep a hand in the mare's pregnancy, but Winky needed the kind of supervision her father's wrangler was famous for providing. If any potential problems arose, Shep would spot them. At the ranch Rose was convinced everything would go right with the foaling.

Austin hadn't said yes or no to her vacation request. She wondered if he'd woken up yet, felt his pocket for his keys, and then realized they'd once again been taken from him by the women he paid to keep his clinic running. For an educated man, the vet wasn't terribly smart. Rose toyed with the crazy idea that if he could just move past the alcohol, Austin could maybe find comfort in regular life, rides like these, the passage of days, having sober, ordinary conversations with a woman who was named Rose Ann instead of Leah. She imagined explaining all this to Lily, who would sit there listening to all her reasons and then systemat-ically shoot holes in every one. Lily ran on cold-blooded logic. Pop often remarked that she thought like a man, which probably meant that Rose thought like a woman, inferior for sure. Oh, the hell with all of it! Lily wasn't here, and Rose could always drive up to the ranch for the weekend. There was nothing keeping her here. Trailer Winky, bring Max along for the ride, and throw Chachi in the passenger seat.

She leaned her body forward, shortening her reins the way she'd learned as a child. Beneath her she could feel Max's flanks trembling with anticipation, awaiting her leg cue. The moment she grazed his right side with her heel, he exploded into a riotous canter. Smiling, Rose let him blast along for a few strides. He was aging, and would run out of gas soon enough, *But, oh,* she thought, *such a willing animal.* Rose felt her whole body relax and slacken, her lungs soar open so that the clean breath of all that rain-washed air seeped into her cells, feeding her heart, causing the muscle to beat slower and deeper than usual, every hard thud echoing in her blood. The lightest of rains peppered her face, and she shut her eyes and enjoyed every drop. At times like these she was grateful Amanda had abandoned the horse.

"Hey, Mama."

Rose set her book down on the couch and looked up to see her daughter standing in the back doorway. Chachi roused himself from a pile of cushions and barked once. "Amanda?"

"Great watchdog."

"He tries." Her daughter's long brown hair was twisted into those grubby ringlets her boyfriend favored. They shrouded her pale face so that her kohl-rimmed eyes looked sunken and haunted. The overall effect was like something a cat might throw up. Amanda's clothes were damp, as if she had walked a little way in the rain, like maybe someone had cowardly dropped her off in town rather than drive up to the door. As she stood up, Rose forced herself to smile, to say nothing she would regret. "Well, this is a surprise. Towels are in the hall closet if you want to dry off. Are you hungry? I could heat you up some lentil soup. That's what I had for supper."

Amanda shook her head no. "Caleb's band was opening for a concert in Santa Fe. I thought since we were in the area I'd—you know—drop by, see how you were doing, maybe spend the night."

"This is your home, Amanda. You're always welcome."

Amanda reached down to pet Chachi, who was so delirious to see her he kept performing his begging trick over and over. "Chachi, that's enough," Amanda said. Then, casually, "So, how's Max doing?"

Oh, no. She wanted money. Periodically Amanda pointed out that since Max was technically her horse, she had the right to sell him. No matter that she hadn't contributed a dime to his upkeep, and as if an old horse would bring anything more than two hundred dollars from the dog food people. In the kitchen Rose put the kettle on to boil. She took down the boxes of tea bags, plunked Sleepytime into one cup and Mandarin Orange Spice into another. She deliberated, measuring the effect of each word before she said it aloud, certain that Amanda's agenda would unfold in time as long as her mother didn't push. "Your horse seems very happy here, despite his back troubles. Doctor Donavan sees him every couple weeks, and I exercised him today. Max, I mean," she added quickly, hearing the unfortunate double-entendre in her words. "We got a nice ride in before the rain started coming down so hard. Weatherman says it's supposed to clear up by tomorrow."

Amanda picked up the book her mother had been reading. "Mother, are you reading *romance* novels?"

Rose flushed. "What's so terrible about a happy ending now and then? It's a nice break from real life."

"What's that supposed to mean?"

Rose poured the hot water, then brought the cups in and set them on the coffee table. Talking to her daughter was like learning chess; she constantly had to project several possible moves into the future or find herself cornered. Amanda stared into the unlit firebox of the wood-stove. She had her knees drawn up to her chest under one of those import store dresses, a dull green material with a pattern that looked like hopelessly tangled vines. Her Birkenstock sandals stuck out under the hemline. Funny how such an expensive shoe always looked two steps away from the trash. "Nothing earth shattering. I like to read about things working out. It gives me hope."

Amanda sighed as she picked up her cup. "You are so clueless," she said. "There is no such thing as hope."

"Wow. That's a pretty cynical thing for a girl of twenty to say. May I ask what contributed to your opinion?"

Amanda blew across the surface of the tea. "It's just how I feel since Daddy died." She took a drink, her eyes blazing, daring Rose to try to convince her otherwise, just aching to engage her mother in battle in order to exorcise her own sorrows.

Rose picked up the paperback and threw it into the wastebasket. She took her teacup and stood at the open back door. Outside the sky was black, and the rain moved across the yard in characteristic September monsoonlike sheets. As was typical of mares, Winky brayed at the sight of one of her humans, but Max remained quiet. One of her neighbor's horses called back, and the equine chorus began. In bad weather they could go on for hours. *And people complain about the coyotes making noise*, Rose thought.

"Mom," Amanda said with that same superior tone in her voice. "I just meant you should widen your reading scope. There's way more meaningful stuff to expose your mind to. The *I Ching*, for example. And Camille Paglia. Caleb's turned me onto all kinds of great books."

As relieved as she was to see her daughter alive, not visibly pregnant, and not wearing handcuffs, Rose tuned her out. She concentrated instead on the drumbeat of the rain on the barn roof. Here was a girl who could never get above a D in her English courses because the teachers were "out of it," and the books they assigned were "boring," lecturing her mother about literature via a reggae drummer. Reggae wasn't even that popular anymore. What Rose would give to do her life over, graduate college instead of getting married at eighteen, earn credits for something as pleasurable as reading books. She sipped her tea silently as Amanda prattled on. Then Rose noticed the shadow of a figure coming up the side of the yard. She knew who it was before she heard his voice call out.

"I want my keys back this minute! I'm not kidding."

Austin had walked here all the way from the veterinary office. He knew she'd change the combination to the safe because she'd done it before. He could have called, saved himself the walk, but Austin was smart enough to know that if he pleaded his case in person, Rose might soften. In the past he'd broken her down as if she were a shotgun. He knew just where to press to find her trigger.

"Rose! I know you're in there. Let's not drag this out."

She didn't move. It occurred to her that humble people knocked, hat in hand, and asked forgiveness. It also occurred to her that she was not dealing with a man who understood the power of humility.

Amanda got up and stood beside her mother. "Who's that screaming out there? Should you call the police?"

She touched her daughter's arm. "No, honey, it's only Doctor Donavan."

"What's his problem?"

"Me. I locked his keys in the safe at work."

"Why?"

"He was drunk when I did it."

"Mom, he looks really steamed. Maybe you should give them back."

Steamed wasn't the quite right word for it. Austin looked drowned, furious, and he was standing there letting the rain pelt him like any minute he knew Rose would rush out there with a towel. Not this time. No matter how much she ached to.

"Dammit, Rose, my boots are full of water. I could catch pneumonia."

"Come inside. I'll give you a towel."

"I don't want a fucking towel, I want the keys to my truck!"

He wasn't completely sober or he wouldn't have used the F word. "Not tonight, Austin. Tomorrow I'll be glad to give them to you."

"Then you're fired!"

She kept her voice deadpan. "Okay, I'm fired. Goodnight. Have a pleasant walk home." She shut the door.

"Mama," Amanda cautioned. "He sounded like he meant it. Maybe you better apologize. You need your job."

Rose's heart sank. Her instincts were right: This was going to be about money. She wondered if the absent Caleb had put Amanda up to this. She sat back down on the couch and waited to hear what it was her daughter wanted.

Amanda opened the door. "He's taking Max! Mother, are you just going to sit there and let him steal my horse?"

Rose craned her neck to look out the window. Sure enough, Austin had thrown a halter around the old gelding's head and tied the lead rope into a makeshift rein. She watched as he managed to pull his skinny butt up onto the animal's back. The horse was so wet that Austin nearly slid off the other side, but he caught himself on the fence, swearing; then away he went, riding into the rain, still enough of a horseman that he managed to post the trot. Winky heaved herself at the fence and neighed as if Austin were absconding with the other half of her heart. Locked into a separate stall, the mare wasn't going anywhere. Eventually she'd quiet down and snuffle her oats, then angle her elegant muzzle across the fence in an attempt to swipe Max's portion. Rose fetched her book from out of the trash. Of course the story was going to end happily, but somehow, while she was reading, she could lose herself pretending that she wasn't certain of the outcome. "Austin's just borrowing him, sweetie," she told her daughter. "I wouldn't lose any sleep over it."

4

Whatever Your Wild Blue Heart Desires

It was the billboard just outside Winslow, Arizona, advertising the vasectomy reversal that caused Lily to start crying. It should have been echoes of the flame-war conversation she'd had via car phone with her boss, Eric, who insisted that a leave of absence meant she was job hunting, not that she needed a break. Paranoid, that about described Eric. And a definite possibility for tears was turning on the windshield wipers and yet again scraping the hell out of the driver's-side glass with what remained of the wiper assembly she'd forgotten to have replaced. One expected those kinds of things to be the proverbial straw that broke the indefatigable camel's back. Lily was hardly the crying type, but within the last week she'd done it twice. Breaking up with yet another boyfriend was just cause, but a billboard? All she knew was that miles from anywhere, here was this advertisement for men who could take back a final decision regarding fertility, and suddenly this lonely howling came bellowing up out of her gut and did not go away. Buddy Guy freaked; he kept pawing her, trying to get her to stop. Eventually she reined it in, but damn whoever had put up that billboard straight to Satan without a soft drink! As if driving long distance wasn't tough enough without being reminded that her internal clock ticked louder than any other timepiece on the planet. She scolded herself: *You had your chance to become a mother. Get over it.* But of course following one of her own lectures was never as easy as delivering it.

She switched on the CD player, and the car was filled with Lyle Lovett crooning his Texas-size heart out to Julia, whom all the boys had fantasies about. Think of what might fit between those lips, and how easily it would fit there—that explained male fascination with Julia, who'd already left Lyle's ass in the dust and bought herself a fifty-acre ranch in Taos. The one commodity northern New Mexico did not need any more of was beautiful women. Just by looking at the CD covers, Lily could tell Lyle would kill in bed. He would positively *shred*. He possessed all the attributes Lily felt essential to a lover: He was skinny, indicating agility. Forget muscle-bound hulks; thin guys had stamina. His lyrics were laconic, which meant he conserved his energy, plus they were intelligent, which meant that after incredibly great sex, if he was able to talk, he'd have something to say. And the way he sang—his voice burned through her speakers as if he were holding back a passion as powerful as a draft horse's. *Oh, Julia*, Lily thought. *You dumb little rich starlet. You didn't know what you had when it lay right there in your bed.* Then, after a few more miles had peeled away under her tires, Lily had another thought: *To be fair, neither did I, eighteen years ago. Well, Julia, one of these days I hope one of us smartens up.*

Her stomach cramped, and she swore she could feel dozens of her eggs go bad as she passed the vasectomy reversal sign. She flipped it the bird and gunned the Lexus's engine, taking it all the way to ninety. Lily'd been pregnant once, accidentally, at eighteen. She hardly ever allowed herself to think about abortion as anything but a necessary medical option. Trouble was, with her medical background, she knew far too much about the various stages of gestation to ease her guilt. The embryo hadn't even been the size of a watch battery; nevertheless, it haunted her. If she had gone through with her pregnancy, she'd have a nearly grown child now. She supposed that just to punish her the baby would have been a girl, precociously prepubescent, her little body bursting with enough hormonal madness to turn Lily's hair prematurely gray. On the positive side, her daughter would have had half her handsome father's genes. Tres Quintero: What kind of father would he have made? If they'd stayed in Floralee, a dependable but frustrated one, because just like Lily, Tres had ambitions larger than staying in a small town. On the negative side, Lily's daughter would have a mother in the nuthouse because she'd had to forgo a career, an aunt who didn't speak to her mother, plus a grandmother prettier than the granddaughter could ever hope to become. On top of all that, like some bizarre mix of ice cream flavors, Lily's daughter would have to wrestle with the complications of culture. While Lily's Spanish and Indian blood was diluted enough to dismiss, Tres Quintero was dark skinned. His facial bone structure screamed out his surname. All her life Lily had run from her roots, hoping to avoid the politics that accompanied it, wishing to blend into some larger, more anonymous mainstream where she would be judged on her actions, not the traces of her blood. Marrying Tres—which he would have insisted she do—even at eighteen he was the kind of guy who believed it took two people to make a mistake—would have shut down all her paths. Repeatedly Lily assured herself she'd done right not telling Tres, going through the procedure alone, yet she couldn't help imagining what gorgeous eyes any baby of his might've had, or how their mingled spirits would have melded together to create one remarkable child. *Postpartum blues have to be a snap compared to this,* she thought, and took a swig of the juice she'd bought at the Stop and Go in Flagstaff, next to the motel where she'd spent the night. Her mouth puckered and she nearly choked. The sad fact was that without the addition of vodka, there wasn't a whole lot to recommend grapefruit juice.

In less than a hundred miles she would cross the New Mexico state border. She felt curious as to how that might affect her after all these years. The Albuquerque airport was an aeronautical anomaly, with beautiful tile floors and leather seating. She flew in there all the time when she visited surgeons. The terminal had airflow and art on its walls, not recycled jet fuel exhaust and fading travel posters of faraway beaches. The cool southwestern beige, aqua, and touches of coral eased the traveler's bleary eye. Whoever had designed it must have understood territorial architecture, because cramped coach seats and dreadful airplane meals were instantly forgotten the moment one stepped from the jetway into the high-ceilinged terminal.

Driving to New Mexico offered another transition entirely.

Gallup, the first big town she would come to, was in close proximity to any number of trading posts she liked to shop: There was the Outlaw, seven miles east, in Church Rock, built in the old bullpen design, and Pinedale, with its enviable collection of dead pawn, just off that little road that ran parallel to I-40. Or in town, and by appointment only, but worth it, Tanner Indian Arts. Her bare wrists just *itched* for silver bracelets. In her mind's eye she designed herself a pair of custom-made cowboy boots with eighteen rows of feather stitching on the deerskin shafts. If she was going back to the homeland, arriving dressed like a native made sense.

Buddy would flip out if she left him alone in the Lexus. Since the Dairy Queen incident in Flagstaff, they'd already had a long talk about car etiquette. Buddy had felt certain the college kid handing Lily her Reese's Peanut-Butter Cup Breeze was out to carjack her. The poor kid, his face a battleground of acne scars, was only doing his job, handing her the concoction upside down, which was DQ's shtick, proof that their ice cream was so thick and creamy it defied gravity. Like a wild dingo high on crack, Buddy lunged, and the kid dropped her money between the drive-through window and her car, where the wind blew it swiftly across the parking lot. He'd nearly cried, and Lily'd had to beat Buddy into submission with her Los Angeles–to–Orange County *Thomas Guide*, which—later on, when she'd thought he was quietly napping—he'd shredded into packing strips.

"Even for you that was an all-time low, Buddy Guy," she reminded the blue heeler she had named after her favorite blues guitarist, an enthusiastic man who'd never become famous on his own but had played with all the greats—Jimi, Stevie, Robert Cray. "Because of what you did, that boy probably had to quit his job and go for pet counseling. He's destined for a career in the lawn furniture department at Wal-Mart, all because of you, you evil, twisted, fang-boy love-puppy cutie-pie. Give Mama a kiss."

Buddy's pink tongue hung amicably out of his square jaws, giving every appearance of a satisfied smile. Lily rubbed his head, which was shaped like a diamondback rattler's. The hair on the very top of his noggin was stiff from leftover Breeze. Lily had only wanted a few bites. Buddy was more than happy to take care of the rest. His approach to Dairy Queen dining was methodical. After he scarfed the larger quantities, it became necessary to tilt the milkshake cup up on his muzzle, thereby furthering his ability to ream the waxy crevices with his tongue. Sure, there was some loss with drippage down the sides of his neck, but sacrifice was inevitable. Also, it was necessary to take the cup past the wax all the way down to the paper; the job simply wasn't finished until Lily yelled at him for making disgusting noises and threw the empty into the backseat, the graveyard of her past meals. He looked up at his mistress with his crazily mottled face. Lovingly, taking her eyes off the road for only a second, she delivered him a smooch. "Buddy," she whispered, "even though your marble sack's empty, you just might be the only male on the planet I can handle who's got one."

Out of all that gibberish, Buddy understood only his name, but that was enough.

Lily decided to stick to I-40, cross the Continental Divide in a routine manner. The yellow cliffs of Gallup were pretty wonderful all on their own. She could always buy jewelry in Floralee. Plus if that hippie dude John was still working the Floralee Post, all she had to do was wear her tightest Calvins and her lacy black DKNY T-shirt with nothing underneath, and John would bury her in affordable dead pawn up to her stiff brown nipples.

When her car phone rang a second time she regarded it suspiciously. Continued fallout from Dr. Help-Me? Eric, eager to go another round on her still-unapproved leave? She'd promised to be back in six weeks. The time was more than due her. She had accrued vacation up the yin-yang. If Eric forced her to return to the OR any sooner, she knew she would lose it. She hadn't slept well the last several nights for thinking about that poor dead gallbladder patient. *Ty can pick up whatever calls come in,* she told her boss. *I left instructions even a chimp could follow.*

The nice thing about car phones was that if the conversation took a bad turn, one could always claim poor reception and hang up. Into the mouthpiece she said, "Lily Wilder."

"How's my business girl? Haven't heard from you in a while, so I thought I'd better check."

"Pop? Oh, Pop. I'm fine. I am *so* glad to hear your voice. Where in hell are you? You'll never in a million years guess where I am. Go on, try. Fifty bucks says you won't."

She listened to his creaky chuckle and waited. Obviously her father had no idea how many dollars per minute a car phone could rack up. "Well, Little Bit, your mother and I are in Austin, Texas. What you might call a true college town. As far as the eye can see there's nothing but coeds in tank tops and young boys driving automobiles they didn't pay for. They've got restaurants galore. A person could live here and eat out a different place every night of the week."

"Did you see the statue of Stevie Ray Vaughn? Did you take a picture for me?"

"No, I didn't, and no, I didn't, but just now I do believe my wallet feels about fifty dollars fatter."

"Why is that, Pop?"

"Because I know exactly where you are twenty-four hours a day, every day. You're my daughter, which means you're in trouble, aren't you? Pay up."

Lily grinned. She should have narrowed the parameters considerably before she made the bet. "There's a little trouble. Nothing major. It'll pass or it won't. I'm not sweating bullets. But Pop, listen, I'm about seventy-five miles from Gallup."

"Alone in your car? You'd better be carrying your .357."

"I've got Buddy here beside me." She held the receiver out and told her dog to speak. He was more than happy to oblige. "What do you think of that?"

"Sounds like a dog, all right. What a thoughtful daughter you are, coming to pay your old man a visit. Sad thing is, I won't be home for a week or so. I'm settling some horse business down here, and your mother, God bless her, is busy making new friends or saving greyhounds. Every night it's dinner with that professor who wrote those horse books or some whacked-out artist who can't eat anything normal. I swear, my stomach's a wreck. Raw fish, pasta in cream sauce, or some greasy French stuff that will likely bring on my gout."

"Order Caesar salad. Ask for the low-fat dressing, and you'll be fine. I practically live on it. When you get back home I'll cook you some real food, Pop. And we'll trailer out and go riding in the mountains, maybe even camp a few nights. How's that for something to look forward to?"

Her father sighed. "About one step beyond wonderful. No bullshitting around now, Lily. What in the devil is going on with you that your work can spare you like this? Did you get yourself fired?"

She bit a hangnail and stared at the passing landscape. In some ways she was thankful it looked so desolate. It kept too many people from relocating. New Mexico's total population was just over a million and a half; Los Angeles County alone was over nine million. Nine million! There wasn't anything in the world there should be nine million of, unless it was tax-free greenback dollars nestled in her bank account.

She might just have to extend her leave to forever. "Everything's taken care of, Pop. Have fun in Texas, and go see that statue. It's supposed to be very cool."

"Sooner or later you and I are going to sit down and talk, *entienda*?"

The phone crackled and buzzed. "Yes, Pop. Love you to pieces, but I'm losing reception. Gotta go. Bye now."

She pressed the phone's End button, and Buddy gave her a questioning look. "That wasn't a lie," she said. "There was some static on the line. Besides, holding back a little is not the same thing as lying." He licked her elbow and nudged her with a slimy nose. "Buddy, quit acting like a shrink." She rummaged in her purse on the seat and, one-handed, unwrapped a berry-flavored PR bar. "Eat your snack and take a nap."

As Buddy worked on his treat, Lily wished like hell she could clear the dead bugs from the driver's side of the windshield. When exactly had some *vato* decided to decimate her wiper? And furthermore, why? That pointless violence, it was just *so* Orange County. Car envy, road rage, whatever you wanted to call it, ran rampant in Southern California. She wondered if she had left her steam iron on back at the condo, then decided no, that was panic-attack syndrome rearing its ugly head—yet another of the state's perks to which she had nearly succumbed.

In Albuquerque she bought lunch to go at the Owl Café, parking at the far end of the famous burger joint's lot. It wasn't very crowded, and the waitress who brought her takeout order comped Lily a handful of stale cookies for Buddy. Lily changed the CDs in her cassette and sat sharing her salad with Buddy. She ate whatever was green, and after he finished his chile verde burger, Buddy took care of the croutons. "What a great deal we have going here," she told her dog. "Why did it take me so long to see it? You're the only guy for me, forever."

Buddy licked the Styrofoam platter clean of ranch dressing, and Lily threw it in the back seat. She started the Lexus and the CD player clicked into Tish Hinojosa's voice bleeding through the speakers, as honest as the river she was singing about. Each separate note traveled down Lily's spine like a piece of ice some boy had slipped down her blouse. Even though she had forgotten most of her Spanish, she shivered at the emotion emanating from the lyrics, and Buddy began a primal whine. "You're right," Lily said, switching tracks until "San Antonio Romeo" replaced the Rio Grande ballad that was reminding her of how broken her heart felt now that Blaise was on the past boyfriends roster. "We don't need to hear that, do we? He wasn't worthy of either of us. Say it out loud with me, Buddy: *We deserve better. We deserve better. We deserve better.* She patted his head and straightened his collar so the bone-shaped tag with his name on it was centered beneath his chin. "Only a couple more hours, dingo mine. Then you can chase horses and pee on every sage bush your wild blue heart desires."

Floralee was north of Santa Fe, but not quite as far north as Taos. Off 518 the town was accessible by a twisting, partially paved road that seemed to be in a constant state of resurfacing. Lily waited behind a line of cars for the flagman to wave her along. She passed sleepy old ranch houses that had been handed down from family to family over the years. Cottonwood trees swayed in the breeze, and curious backyard horses peered over fences. Willows spilled lacy canopies of shade. In the neighboring towns it seemed that very little had changed since her childhood. Floralee, on the other hand, she knew would feel different than last time she'd been here. Over the years word of mouth had slowly leaked out: *Buy property in Floralee. Good riding, nearby fishing, more bang for your buck. Historic haciendas and two excellent restaurants. I'm telling you, Floralee's about fifteen years away from being another Taos.* As Lily drove past the Kiwanis sign, she saw that the whispered rumor was having an effect. The single gallery that had supplied the town with posters and local art had been joined by a couple of rivals. Just down the block, the general store with the saloon doors still offered homemade tamales, but they had tripled in price. The ¡Andale! roadhouse had a fancy new bay-shaped window and looked more like the bakery next door than the down-home watering hole featuring second-rate bands every weekend, where Lily had worn out more than one pair of shoes. The tack shop facing the small plaza had mutated from a practical sportsman's' outfitters to a thinly disguised gift emporium. Each crumbling adobe storefront had been tidied up very carefully, maintained to appear old and quaint. Colorful wildflowers grew in haphazard plantings, contrasting nicely with the brown clay—a New Mexico staple—but there was something deliberate even about their placement. Even the old hardware store had been repainted and now wore a mantle of subtle hipness. The whole effect put Lily in mind of one long bed-and-breakfast so expensive that no one in this town could afford to stay there.

Disgusted, she sped up the two-lane main drag and made the sharp right turn, heading east toward her parents' ranch, passing a clutch of rural mailboxes in various shapes and sizes. Farther along a metal windmill worn to the color of pewter by the elements spun lazy circles, making that wonderful unique whirring noise she'd never heard duplicated anywhere else. Lily opened the car window and took a deep breath, inhaling the comforting balm of newly cut hay and deeper, more faintly, horse manure. The apple tree out front of El Rancho Costa Plente was heavy with fruit. The only car noise Lily could make out came from her Lexus. There were no competing sounds other than birdsong and her tires crunching across the gravel. She shut the engine down in front of the two-story adobe with the shining metal roof and sat listening to the silence.

"Look, Buddy," she said to the heeler as she pointed a finger at the outbuildings. "You were born in that barn right over there. Here comes your mama now."

The emerging pack of dogs barked a collective warning, showing off their various stations in the herd hierarchy. Jody Jr., the old blue heeler bitch who had mothered so many of the ranch pups, walked among her fractious offspring, hackles lifted, but somehow she managed to make threat displays come off regally. As she spied Lily, she began slowly wagging her long tail. Pop didn't believe there was any good reason to dock puppies' tails, no matter what was popular. To him dogs were working animals, and whatever God-given attributes they'd been born with they ought to be allowed to keep, including testicles. Lily worried a little about that, since Buddy was no longer in possession of his. Well, Pop would just have to get over it. Lily stretched her arms above her head and turned her neck from side to side, trying to erase the hours of driving from her sore muscles.

Shep Hallford, her father's ranch foreman, sat on the fence, packing his cheek with a fresh plug of Red Man. His expression didn't change when he saw who had just stepped out of the fancy white car.

Lily, however, grinned and ran over to him, wrapping him in her arms, hugging him as hard as she could. Had Shep allowed such things, she would have covered him with kisses and sat in his lap. Instead, she stepped back and said, "Hey, Sheppie. How's it hanging?"

He nearly smiled. "Well, well. Look what the cat drug in. Haven't seen you around in a pile of years. California crack apart and fall into the ocean?"

"We can only hope." Lily leaned against the post-and-rail fence, which was as old as she was and remarkably sturdy. "What's up with you, old man? Fathered any new children recently?"

The weathered old cowboy spit tobacco juice onto the dirt. "These days I'm sticking to horses. Shorter life span, plus you don't go to jail if they need killing."

Lily laughed, and Buddy came bounding up, relentlessly chased by the other dogs. He tried to scramble into Lily's arms and she took hold of his front paws. "Rule number one, Buddy. You've fight your own battles here. Mama can't help."

Shep craned his neck and stared at the dog's hindquarters. "Unless my eyesight is going, I'd say your dog appears to be toting a couple of empty suitcases."

"I had him cut."

Shep clucked. "Your father will not be happy to hear that."

"Hey, my father didn't have to bail his blue ass out of dog jail everytime he attacked my dates, either. One little incident cost me upward of five hundred bucks. Trust me, a no-nut version of Buddy is preferable to having to put him down."

Shep didn't seem convinced. "We'll see what Chance has to say. You sticking around awhile, or is this one of them drive-by things?"

"Sticking. It was either come home or check myself into the nuthouse."

"Around here some days it's pretty hard to tell the difference." He slid down off the fence, his faded Wranglers and flannel shirt unable to hide the fact that he'd lost weight. "Boyfriend troubles?"

"I've quit liking boys."

"Ha. That'll be the day. Well, sane or not, I'm glad to have you. I'm getting so old and stove up I can't ride all these damn horses by myself anymore. Your pop's always gallivanting off to one place or another. Starting tomorrow you can help me work."

He ambled off in the direction of the bunkhouse without saying good-bye. Lily watched his back until he ducked into the doorway. Shep had worked here all her life. He was like some cautious uncle who knew all her secrets but was loathe to step into the fray. A man of few words, each one he chose to share was direct, and always good advice. She'd wear herself out riding whatever horse he asked her to, just not tonight, while the sun was going down, and she felt so deliriously road weary. She needed groceries, a bath, and a sunset, *pronto*.

Lily used her key to let herself in, set down her purse and keys on a table covered with mail, then stood in the Great Room, looking around at familiar sights. One entire wall was covered in river rock, surrounding an open fireplace so large five adults could stand inside it. Twin Stickley couches, a Mission-style chair, and a coffee table constructed of pickled pine were carefully arranged facing the hearth so as to appear casual, but Lily knew how Mami had planned everything, choosing a particular grain of leather, rejecting all but just the single piece of pine. The east wall of the room was covered in framed pictures of Lily and Rose, cataloging their lives from birth to young womanhood. Some were pastel studies, others charcoal sketches, portraits executed by artists to whom her mother had endeared herself. Professional-quality photographs snapped in the early days of careers by names that had gone on to shine in the art world were present, too. A few of the more casual shots had been taken at horse competitions, and in those pictures Lily, astride a Wilder-bred horse, was wearing her trademark half smile, breeches the color of skin and tight little tops that barely contained her budding breasts. Lily thought of her business suits, the unwritten rule that professional sales-people couldn't wear anything sleeveless, and looked again at the tank tops and sports bras. Mami didn't seem to care what her daughters did, so long as they didn't outshine her. Still, how Lily's outfits must have driven her father nuts. Her youthful boldness made her smile until she came to Rose's pictures, when her amusement caught in her throat and stuck. Here were her sister's babies. Rose, looking tired but determined in a hospital bed. Philip standing alongside her, smiling way too hard to be happy, his gaze fixed just outside the camera's range. Philip—Lily knew more than one tale on that man she could tell Rose, but it wasn't right to speak ill of the dead. Better to concentrate on the living, such as her niece and nephew, whom Lily couldn't have loved more if she had birthed them herself. Their pictures were here, too, Amanda gap toothed in elementary school, and Second Chance, already handsome at twelve. Rose's family had always seemed sacrosanct, a tribe Lily would defend to the point of death. She'd sat in the waiting room when Rose gave birth to her son, had acted as godmother when the boy was baptized Second Chance after their pop instead of Philip after his father. When Amanda came along, Philip had been off fishing in Mexico or some damn thing, and Lily experienced the singular privilege of holding her sister's hand while she labored and gritted her teeth, pretending the whole business didn't hurt like hell. Lily would never forget Rose lying on that delivery room table, barely twenty-one years old, scared breathless, or herself at sixteen, in awe at the sight of Amanda's full head of hair coming into this world.

On the west wall, Mami's O'Keeffe hung alone in a *nicho* carved deep into the plaster. It was a small painting, one of the flower series, made all the more captivating because so little attention had been called to it. More than anything in this house, that painting reminded Lily of Mami's power, which at times seemed to exist as its own separate force of nature. As she'd often done when she was a child, and pissed off at something her mother'd made her do, she reached out an index finger and touched the canvas. *Take that,* she used to whisper when she committed the unforgivable sin of Touching the O'Keeffe. Just thinking the words made her smile.

Buddy sighed at her feet, and Lily turned away from the pictures. She fed and watered the dog and then, in the downstairs bath, stripped off her clothes and ran the shower. Under the fine spray, she shampooed her long hair and hummed, wondering how Rose might react if her sister were to show up at her house tomorrow. She would still be pissed; however, two years of widowhood might have tempered her anger, made her see that life had a larger picture than one stupid prank. That silly high school graduation present to Second Chance was history. So what if the Martínezes got a little huffy? They'd needed to let their hair down for generations. Besides, nothing was ever going to get them over Mami marrying Chance Wilder, a Colorado cattleman possessing no New Mexican blood whatsoever. That was a mortal sin if ever there was one. Somewhere in all these years surely Rose had developed a sense of humor.

Lily wrapped herself in her dad's terrycloth robe and rolled up the sleeves. In the kitchen she heated up a pan of tomato soup and searched the cupboards for Krisprolls, but among the gallon cans of hominy and mammoth bags of tortilla chips, she found none. She took some cheese from the fridge and grated it onto toast. "Shopping tomorrow," she told Buddy, who seemed thrilled with the available dog food, which was some special blend Mami used to feed her rescued greyhounds. "Provisions are required."

Taking her mug, she settled in the swing on the porch that wrapped around the house, sipping her soup. Across the yard, Buddy was working out herd hierarchy with a half-dozen other barking caste members. Various good-looking horses neighed and lingered around the fenceline, hoping that Lily's presence meant another meal or carrots. Shep's light burned from inside the bunkhouse, and Lily smiled. She'd bet money the wrangler was reading *Leaving Cheyenne* for the jillionth time.

For so long Lily'd imagined doing this, sitting here and staring at the Sangre de Cristos as they purpled in the growing dark. She thought about painting her toenails exactly that color. Surely Mami had that shade of polish upstairs in her bathroom. Lily had always appreciated color peeking through her nylons. When she was surrounded by men, toenail polish reminded her that at her utmost core, the place no man could ever reach, she was absolutely undeniably female. Little touches of femininity—imported lingerie, diamond earrings, a silver ankle bracelet worn under her hose—these things kept her moving through the most full-blown, messed-up bitch of a workday. Stockings made her think of the firemen and the whooshing blaze she'd started. If she didn't pay the ticket, they'd come after her, if they could find her. In some ways her life felt like always being on call for jury duty. What an idiot idea that bonfire had been. Nevertheless, beneath her brief shame she felt excitement at having taken a metaphoric stand. Pantyhose might become a thing of the past, she thought as she admired her mountains—and they *were* her mountains. Just like Georgia O'Keeffe thought of El Pedernal as hers, Lily loved these mountains enough to claim possession. She dared anyone, even Georgia's ghost, to try to take them from her.

The fall air cooled quickly. Crickets chirped, which meant that in six weeks, maximum, the first frost would hit. Already the oak leaves were turning among the golden aspen and thin slivers of willow. The gambel oaks would eventually glow orange against the mountainside. Lily lit some stubby piñon chunks in the *chimenea* and inhaled the smoky perfume. A few of the hardier no-see-ums hovered around her, working the last of the season, but Lily had never been the one whose skin they sought. Rose was the sister with sweet blood. Out of doors in the summer, within ten minutes Rose was a mess of bites and slathering calamine on her raw skin. Lily ran around half naked and hardly ever got bitten. She missed her sister fiercely. There was no one else in the world she could sit next to in the dark without saying a word and know that she understood exactly what Lily was thinking. Shep came close sometimes, but Lily's logic annoyed him. Not even Buddy was telepathic like she and Rose could be. A person could hate her sister forever and underneath the anger she'd still take a bullet in her name. Lily pictured them as young girls, their coltish bodies dressed in matching white nighties with pink ribbon drawstrings at the neck. They sat up in the dark in Rose's double bed long after they were supposed to be asleep, tracing designs on each other's back. It was one of their secret games, drawing on each other, then allowing five guesses as to what it was they'd drawn. Rose, no artist, usually sketched predictably, easy-to-guess things like horses or sunflowers. Lily got all sidetracked with the narrative end of things, creating steep mountain passes, the swift current of the Rio Grande cutting into the earth, details that stretched all the way down to individual rocks before she got to the horses. Often Rose fell asleep with Lily's fingers still at work.

It was time to go indoors, make up one of the beds, and let this day be finished. The drive had exhausted her, but she sat stubbornly on the swing, hugging her arms around her chilly shoulders, unwilling to give up the wide-open space and lengthening shadows for an indoor bed. This ranch nourished her. It wasn't about money, though it made enough to keep her mother in a private plane and designer clothing. It was that everything here felt timeless and solid. The horses snorted in the corral, the embers glowed in the *chimenea*, Buddy's occasional snores reminded Lily that time was passing, this was real life, and when she woke up tomorrow it would still be here, but she couldn't shut her eyes on it, not just yet. Finally she dragged a sleeping bag down from the camping closet and snuggled in, zipping the soft flannel high up around her neck. She lay back in the porch swing and gave it a push that set it to gentle rocking. *I'm home*, she thought pleasantly, one hand grazing the top of Buddy's head as he stayed close, curled up beneath the swing, protecting his mistress.

* * *

Lily's day began at sunup, when Shep nudged her shoulder and said, "Time to ride, Sleeping Beauty." Lily opened her eyes to a cup of coffee brewed so strongly that one sniff seared her sinuses and caused her to gasp. "I have to take a shower," she complained, but her father's wrangler would hear none of that. "No point when you're going to get dirty all over again. Throw on your trousers and boots. Let's get to work."

Shep allowed her enough time to brush her teeth and put on a T-shirt, then he directed her through the barn, pointing out horse after horse, chattering instructions all the while. Lily nodded and began bridling each animal with its own particular bit and gimmicks. Riding rent-string horses in Southern California, she'd forgotten how many varieties of bits there were, and how many buckles and straps and martingales were needed to fine-tune an animal in training. By midmorning, she'd lost count of how many horses she'd exercised, and her thigh muscles were humming. Shep indicated a particular horse; Lily saddled it and rode. While he explained the work he'd done previously, Lily moved the horse through his gaits: walk, trot, canter in hand, transitions, again the trot, then cool the horse down with a long walk. Other trainers employed a hot-walker, which cut time, but for Shep Hallford it was the old-fashioned ride all the way, a trademark of what you got when you bought from El Rancho Costa Plente. Whenever Lily suspected lameness, she called out to Shep, and only then would he mount the horse and ride a few laps, his head bent at a peculiar angle, frowning as if the beat of the horse's hooves against the arena sand would tell him what he needed to know. During those brief time-outs, Lily caught her breath, drank from the water hose, and occasionally shook her head in awe of Shepherd Hallford on horseback. Her father's wrangler was on the downhill slope toward seventy, but on a horse his age couldn't have mattered less. The old man didn't *ride*, he more or less tried to stay out of the way while encouraging the horse's innate talents to surface. He dressed like a redneck and eschewed proper grammar, but place him on the back of any decent equine and he couldn't hide the fact that his riding history ranged from hunt seat to dressage to third-level grand prix.

Shep's schedule was to start out working the easier horses, older ones who weren't used for anything more strenuous than trail riding, and then those already broken to saddle. After a couple hours of that,

he moved Lily to the newest horses, animals in training her father was
looking to sell and wanted in top shape to show at a moment's notice.
These horses were green-broke, only ridden a couple of times, a little
unpredictable, and a far cry from exactly tame. Of course these were
Lily's favorite mounts. Faced by a fractious personality, the haughty
spirit of a young animal, she'd be happy to fall off horses all day long.
The first time she got thrown that day, she lay on her back squinting
up at the sky, trying to figure how this particular horse had managed
to get the best of her. "What was it? My leg?" she asked Shep. "Have I
completely lost my chops?"

"Nah. That one's sneaky," he answered. "Throws me every time.
Which is why I let you ride him."

"Thanks buckets, Shep. What would happen if we took him out of
the Pelham bit and tried a mechanical hackamore?"

"You know how I feel about hackamores."

"So? I know how to use one properly."

"Suddenly you're a bitting expert?"

"Well, golly gee, Shepherd, what the hell difference does it make if
it's the wrong choice? I'm lying here in the dirt, and the horse thinks he
won. Let's try it before he starts telling all the others."

"Yes, ma'am." Shep changed the bridles and Lily legged the surprised horse into a trot. A hackamore looked deceptive, as if it were no
more punishing than a halter, but there was metal underneath. Lily'd
learned that the lightest hands were required for this type of tack to be
effective. She fed rein out and watched her horse's ears flick upright in
surprise. His wonder was eventually replaced by a begrudging trust,
and Lily took her feet out of the stirrups and rode in lazy circles.

"You ride like a sack of potatoes," Shep teased her from the fenceline.

Lily threw her head back and laughed. She didn't give a damn what
she looked like riding. She'd gained the horse's trust in just under a
half hour. From now on, she'd do whatever was necessary to avoid
breaking her neck. No horse was going to get the better of her. She
could tell Shep admired her way with animals, even if it'd kill him to
say so out loud.

By noon her calves were throbbing from teaching green horses the
concept of yielding to her leg, and she could feel the bruised skin
inside her breeches already swelling. Most of the horses knew what she

wanted, but it was in the animal's deeper nature to resist. As far as the equine population was concerned, nothing beat standing around slapping tails, hogging the waterer, and ignoring humans—that is, until mealtime rolled around. Lily had a little bit of a headache since all she'd had for breakfast was Shep's coffee. She hoped the mild throbbing in her left eye socket wasn't thinking of becoming a full-blown migraine. She dismounted and stood in the shade of the barn, her legs wobbling slightly from work. "Shep, if I'm going to ride another horse, I need pesto and Krisprolls. Nothing else is going to cut it. I think I'll ride Georgia into town, pick up some groceries. Feed us both."

Shep knotted the horse's reins in his fist. He scratched his nose and thought a while. "I ain't hungry. But if you have to go, seems like driving your fancy car would be faster."

"Absolutely not," Lily said. "I want to wave hi to everyone I pass. Let them know who's back in Floralee. I've been anticipating doing that every single minute since I got here. First, however, I plan to change into my French bikini."

Shep began taking the tack off the horse she'd ridden. He didn't speak.

"Ha ha, Shep. I was kidding."

He didn't smile. "You ask me, your father was too easy on the both of you. Rose wanders around acting all dreamy, you talk bold just so you can raise a little hell. I reckon it'd take a whole roll of duct tape to shut you up. But so long as you're hell-bent on taking a break, pick me up a spool of fencing wire at the hardware. Tell them I want the same kind as last time, and to put it on your pop's account." He handed her a cloth backpack. "This ought to hold it."

"Will you hang on to Buddy for me?" All morning the blue heeler had lurked under one of the ranch trucks, peering out anxiously. Whenever he ventured forth a couple of inches, one of the ranch dogs came over and snarled, and back under the truck Buddy went. He had an oil spot on his head so large it looked as if he'd been marked by Jody Jr. as cootie dog deluxe.

Shep looked at the heeler and said, "Lily, that dog of yours puts me in mind of a nancy boy. Have you had his hormones checked?"

"Cut him some slack, Shep. Buddy's a city pooch. He understands concrete, not dirt. Give him a week, he'll get the hang of things. You be good, Buddy," she called out to her dog. "You mind Shep."

"He'd best stay parked under that truck," Shep said.

Lily unsaddled the horse she'd been riding and led Georgia, a stunning flea-bitten gray Morgan mare, out of the barn. She brushed Georgia's back and threw a bridle over her, then checked her feet for stones. Satisfied, she pulled herself up and felt every one of her sore muscles complain, but the cure for that was more riding. She started down the road bareback, passing the landing strip where her mother's plane would eventually once again be parked. She legged the horse into a brisk trot as soon as they came to the road. Lily began to post, rising gently, sitting a beat until she found a rhythm comfortable to them both. Georgia's ears flicked back and forth, listening to Lily's leg. She was such a trustworthy horse that Lily fed her a long, loose rein, and every now and then, shut her eyes and sleepily let the horse lead the way.

Outside the hardware store the decorative hitching-post rail had been recently painted Santa Fe blue. Lily dismounted and untied the knotted reins, securing the mare with a single slipknot. That way, in case of disaster, the horse could pull away without tearing her mouth. Lily brushed the worst of the horsehair from her crotch before she entered the store. There wasn't much she could do about how sweaty she smelled, but this was a hardware store, for Pete's sake, not Nordstrom's. Who cared what she looked like so long as she bought something? The screen door banged shut behind her. Several old men stood around discussing serious plumbing issues. All they needed was a couple of pickle barrels and a checkerboard and they could have modeled for a Norman Rockwell painting. On and on they chattered, slow and deliberate, as if she were no more bothersome than a housefly. Lily tried not to act Californian about having to wait, but it was killing her, plus she was starving.

"The wax seal," one of them was saying. "That's the ticket."

"Yeah, get that little honey off-kilter, might as well go back to outhouses."

"Those new water conservation jobs seem like the plan. You get many complaints on those, Bill?"

"Can't say that I do. Can't say that I don't, either."

The men laughed.

"What can you say?"

"Expensive."

"Necessary."

"Only come in white, so women don't much care for them."

There was hardly any subject discussed in New Mexico that didn't eventually bear heavily on the issue of water. Who got it, how much was used, and where it was being diverted and for what purpose. Lily tapped her foot and studied a box full of mousetraps. She scanned the shelves behind the counter, where dusty keychains shaped like chili peppers and aluminum flashlights abounded. In a long row, jars of salsa with gold labels sat waiting for some tourist who needed a length of rope to tie suitcases to a luggage rack to buy them on impulse. Bottom line? This was guy heaven, she was a girl, therefore invisible. Her stomach growled and her head ached.

"Haven't had much luck with the push-button handle assembly," the first man said and Lily couldn't help it, she sighed loudly.

Behind her she could hear the footsteps of another customer approaching. He cleared his throat, and the plumbing debate ceased. The men looked clean through Lily to whoever stood behind her.

Well, dammit all, no way was she going to lose her place in this mythical line due to her gender. She stepped forward and slapped her hand down on the counter. "Hey, I might have been gone from town awhile, but that doesn't mean I'm transparent. All's I want is a roll of fencing wire for Shep Hallford. He said you'd know what kind, you can charge it to my pop's account, and I'd appreciate getting it before I'm eligible for social security."

A hand touched her shoulder, and she spun around angrily, expecting a fight or, worse, additional plumbing facts. Instead she looked straight up into soulful brown eyes surrounded by lashes so long it was criminal they'd been wasted on a male.

Just saying his name made her throat ache. "Tres?"

"Sugarbush," he said, low and easy, using his pet name for her all those years ago. The endearment meant exactly what it sounded like, and Lily's face burned with equal portions of pleasure and shame. "Tell me I'm not dreaming."

"Unless I am too, you're not."

A pretty, dark-haired, very young woman stepped up beside him, locking a possessive hand onto his forearm, the arm attached to the hand that was just barely touching Lily. He placed his hand over the young woman's and patted it, but he did not stop looking at Lily, who had unconsciously tried to smooth her hair, which she was certain looked as bad as the rest of her. "It sure is good to see you. When did you get back into town?"

Lily wrinkled her nose and stared at the young woman. What was she? Seventeen? For God's sake, who did Tres think he was? Woody Allen? "Apparently not soon enough."

Tres turned to the girl and smiled an embarrassed smile. "I'm sorry. This is Leah. Leah, I'd like you to meet an old friend of mine, Lily—" he stopped and gave her a questioning glance.

"Oh, it's still Wilder." Tres wanted to know if she was single. She supposed that counted for something, but she couldn't say what, exactly. Leah was dressed in pressed jeans and nice boots, wearing one of those fancy embroidered denim jackets that cost a criminal amount of money and no one who actually lived in the West would be caught dead in. Lily became painfully aware of the chill of her sweaty T-shirt with the damp stains under her breasts and perspiration stripe down her back. Leah flashed a smile reminiscent of Buddy Guy just before he had lunged for the postal worker foolish enough to knock at Lily's condo door. Lily grabbed three jars of the salsa just to put something in her hands. She turned and walked toward the door because she couldn't bear to say good-bye.

"Hey, lady," the man behind the counter said. "Don't you want your wire?"

The way the man spoke the word it sounded like *war*. Lily nearly lost her balance turning back to get it, but she recovered with grace, letting the door slam behind her to tell Tres Quintero what she thought of grown men who dated children.

She tried putting the salsa jars into the cloth backpack she'd brought along for the groceries she'd planned to buy, but they were glass jars—Blaise's container of choice, she reminded herself, feeling the slight pang of sorrow she knew would dog her for at least a year— and no matter how quietly she rode back to the ranch she knew the jars would clatter together and eventually one of them would break. There was a trash can on the hardware store's porch, out of which stuck some old newspapers. Lily had her hands in the trash can pulling out sheets of newsprint when Tres and Leah exited the store carrying a brown paper bag full of God knows what they needed.

Leah looked long and hard at Lily before she spoke. "It was nice to meet you," she said. Tres opened the passenger-side door of a truck, Leah got inside, and Lily hoped the first time she tried to wash it that jacket would lose half its beads, fade, shrink and get lost in the wash.

"Maybe I'll see you around," Tres said before he closed the driver's-side door and started the ignition.

Lily just stood there with the moldy *Floralee Facts* smudging her arms with ink. She could have driven the Lexus, but no, she had to ride. She could have taken five seconds to change clothes, run a washcloth over her face, but no, this was Floralee, a town so small she never expected to see anyone who mattered. But the world was just chock-full of awful coincidences like this one, just aching to test her sanity. She didn't say anything at all to Tres or that well-dressed little twit, but she did watch their truck pull away, drive down the street, and veer to the right, toward the mountains, where she remembered that Tres's parents once had a cabin.

They're probably headed back to their love nest, Lily thought. *What a shame it would be if Tres pulled a groin muscle. That kind of injury can take forever to heal.*

5

Mere Hours Away from That Seventh Star

It was six-thirty A.M. when Rose cleared away the breakfast plates, surprised to see that Amanda had eaten both her eggs, three pieces of toast, and all the bacon. Her daughter's appetite was typically bird-like, and she rarely got up this early. Amanda complained that her mother sneaked fat into everything in an attempt to make her obese. However, not this visit. Rose tried to think of all the reasons why that might have changed. Amanda and Caleb had been bumming around the West for months, and musicians weren't typically the highest-paid members of the work force. Maybe Amanda'd learned to tank up when the opportunity presented itself. Perhaps it was some elaborate show staged for her mother's benefit, and later on she was planning to throw it all up. Or maybe, just maybe, she wasn't eating only for herself, a notion that made Rose feel as though she'd swallowed a rock. Beneath those baggy import-store clothes, who could tell what was going on?

"Know what I was planning to do today, before Doctor Donavan stole Max?"

"Go factory-outlet shopping, Mom? No thanks."

Rose ignored the jibe. Only once had she suggested they try that, and Amanda's derisive laughter had made her determined never to bring up the subject again. "Drive up to Pop's ranch and spend the weekend. It's so pretty up there this time of year. He and Mami are out of town, and the view's so spectacular from the porch. It's early yet, but some of the leaves are turning. You could come along if you want."

Amanda shook her head no.

Rose's fingers itched to get at the dreadlocks, to pour conditioner over each ropy strand, and even if it took hours of separating and combing, return the lovely brown hair with red highlights to its original shine.

"Look, Mom, even if I wanted to, I couldn't. The band plays in Flagstaff tomorrow night."

Rose knew there were a dozen things she could have said: *You're not in the band, you're only the girlfriend; you could come for a couple of hours; what is the true purpose of your visit to the mother you cannot stand?* But all she said was, "It's a long drive to Flagstaff."

Rose ran hot water over the plates and scrubbed the egg spots so they wouldn't dry caked on for life. No way was she going to make things easy for Amanda—ask what was going on or offer her money. They had been down this road before, and it always ended in flames. "Would you drive over with me to Doctor Donavan's? Somebody has to ride Max back here."

Her daughter sat looking out the window, leaning on her fist, which was tucked beneath her chin. "Why don't you just hitch up the trailer?"

Rose set the clean plates into the dish drainer. "I was thinking you might like to ride your horse back. It's only a couple of miles. But I can put him in the trailer if you don't want to."

Amanda made a face. "What*ever*, Mom."

Which, if she didn't say another word, Rose had learned meant yes. She let out a careful breath. "Okay. Just let me take a quick shower, and then we can get going."

In Austin's driveway Rose parked the Bronco in front of the adobe retaining wall surrounding his house. The wooden door set deep into the clay bore a carved likeness of the Virgin of Guadalupe. It reminded Rose of Santa Fe's historical district, the old adobes along Acequia Madre, which ran parallel to Canyon Road. She wondered if Austin had built the house with such attention to detail to please Leah, something along the lines of, *If I'm going to move you all the way out here in the Floralee boonies, I promise I'll make things as luxurious for you as I can.* If everyone suffered from such good intentions the world would be a much nicer place in which to live. She opened the gate latch and walked into the courtyard, where more weeds than flowers were blooming.

Rose left Amanda at the barn seeing to Max, who ran loose in the arena with Jewel, the quarter-horse mare Austin had bought several years back from Rose's father. Shep had pointed at the long-legged foal not long after she was born, remarking that one day she was going to make a wonderful riding horse, a real beauty temperament-wise, and that he hoped she'd end up with someone who'd appreciate her talents. When Rose's father sold Jewel to Austin, horse and rider seemed like a perfect match. Austin had a quiet hand, Jewel was as responsive as they made them. He hadn't ridden her in the Floralee parade this year, or lately much at all, it seemed—not that it was any of Rose's business what he did with his mare. She opened the front door of Austin's house and nearly tripped on the black-and-white blur that came flying around the corner. Bijou, his long-haired border collie, was eager to welcome any visitors. Rose petted the high-strung animal she could never look at her without feeling a pang of sympathy. How close the collie had come to losing her life! Six months back, first thing in the morning, a stranger had marched into the clinic dragging the collie behind him, tied to a length of filthy rope. It was obvious even to Rose that the dog had a broken front leg, but the man wasn't standing there anxious for help, he was demanding the dog be put down. Paloma tried to explain that the injury wasn't hopeless, but he stood firm: He wanted her euthanized. "How can you be so heartless?" Rose had said without thinking. She started to explain that if he wanted to put the dog up for adoption there were several organizations she could refer him to, but he began yelling at her about his constitutional rights, and it all got very scary until Austin interrupted all the commotion when he laid a file on one of his surgical patients down on the counter. He hopped the reception counter and untied the dog from the rope, scooping her carefully into his arms. Never once had the collie whimpered or tried to bite, and Rose knew the leg had to hurt. "Consider this dog no longer your responsibility," Austin had said, adding, "There's no charge for the leg." The man balked and one last time demanded she be put to sleep, as if the only thing that would satisfy him was seeing the still form of the troublesome pet. Rose would never forget the look Austin delivered. There was a fierceness present in his face that went even further back than divorce court. Certainly this was about taking care of a mistreated animal, but his own feelings of abandonment seemed also to be at stake. "I'd like you to leave my place of business at once," he icily informed the man, who recognized that the warning would soon be backed up by a fist. They never saw the man again. Austin had sedated the collie and set her leg—it was a simple break—nursed her back to trusting men by taking her everywhere he went, on calls and to lunch, errands, what have you. Austin might have forgotten to feed himself, but Bijou was never neglected. In fact, she was so grateful to have a kind home she'd do anything the vet asked of her, including wait forever for him to sober up.

Rose stooped down and petted her. "Hey, Bij. How are you?"

The dog lay down, looked up at her, rolled over, looked again, and then played dead, pausing between each trick, checking Rose's face for approval.

"Good girl," she told her every time, scratching the patch of white chest hair that grew between her front legs, the broken one healed so nicely she didn't even limp. Faintly, from down the hall, Rose could hear the sound of the shower come on. Well, ambulatory was progress. "Morning, Austin," she called out extra loud while she poured kibble into a grateful Bijou's dish. Austin didn't answer, but Rose hoped her voice had pounded another spike into his hangover. She went out back to check on Amanda.

Her daughter was just pulling herself up onto her horse's back. Despite the rotten hair and the shapeless clothing, Amanda still looked graceful on horseback. Rose watched her gently leg Max forward at the walk and circle him to check for lameness. If a person could still be kind to animals, there was hope. Amanda was her old self murmuring encouragement to her horse. *If I could blink my eyes and erase the past two years*, Rose thought, *I'd have my daughter back*. But wishing didn't accomplish anything, and the past was a door better left shut. As she watched the old horse give in to his affection for Amanda, her eyes threatened to spill over with tears witnessing that unbroken bond. Rose had learned to hold those kinds of emotions in. All it took was some hard swallowing and a series of deep breaths, and no one but her own self could tell how close she'd come to crying. On bad days it happened to her as often as a couple of times. On good ones she remained dry eyed and busy. Mostly she tried to put her sorrow in perspective by telling herself that this, too, would pass, that this undercurrent of sadness would eventually deposit her on a different shore. But Philip's death had torn a hole in her life she hadn't managed to stitch up. Behind her she heard steps and knew that Austin was standing there watching the both of them. She could feel his eyes on her, examining the situation with a clinical eye, formulating his prognosis.

"Bye, Mom," Amanda called out. "Thanks for the munchies and letting me crash."

"I'll see you back at the house. We'll have lunch, okay?" Rose waved and headed toward the Bronco. The screen door slammed back against the frame as Austin stepped onto the porch.

"So," he said. "Your prodigal daughter returns. I hope to hell you didn't give her that horse."

Rose thrust her chin up in the air and continued walking.

"Hold on there, Mrs. Flynn. I believe we're good enough friends that you can spare me a minute."

"What do you want, Austin? To steal my car, too?"

He came around to the driver's side and laid his hand over Rose's, which was clutching the chrome door handle. "I'd like a chance to explain."

Austin was dressed in his jeans, an unbuttoned clean blue work shirt plastered damply against his shoulders where he had missed with the towel when he was drying off. He had his old glasses on, and either he needed a shave or he was growing one of those trendy goatees. It didn't look half bad on him, but it wasn't a style commonly seen in Floralee. "Fine," Rose said. "Apologize for stealing my horse so I can get back to my weekend. I don't get paid for this. Actually, I don't even have a job since you fired me last night."

Austin took his hand away. "I did?"

"Yep. And then you stole my horse. I think it's still legal to hang people for that in this state."

"Forget about it. I was out of my head."

"What's new about that?"

He frowned. "I had almost a week of sobriety down. I was doing good. You know I was."

Of course she knew. For every sober day in a row Austin had, Rose marked her calendar with a little star. When he accrued seven stars, she made him a plate of cookies for a reward. Austin would eat amost anything except coconut macaroons, but he preferred Rose's oatmeal-

and-raisin cookies. This last time he'd been only hours away from the seventh star. She'd already bought the bag of raisins, which was sitting on the counter at home, just waiting to be folded into the batter.

"Want to know what set me off?"

"Not really. I just want your word you'll climb back on that wagon."

He opened her car door, and Rose started to pull herself up into the high seat until he took hold of her arm. "Leah," he said, breathing the word out like cigarette smoke.

Austin's face pinched with pain, and Rose could see tears gathering in the corners of his eyes. Any minute now they'd fog up his lenses, and she'd feel so sorry for him she'd get the urge to go bake him a coffee cake. But today it just made her angry. Leah wasn't dead; they were divorced. "For crying out loud, Austin, why can't you let her go?"

He gave her butt a push, and she sat down hard in the seat. "Just can't. I know I disappoint you. I'm sorry."

She took his whiskered chin in her hands. She meant every word she was about to say, and several others she wasn't brave enough to try out loud. "It isn't me you need to worry about disappointing. Think of your reputation, your clients. More importantly, your liver."

He reached up, encircled one of her wrists with a rough hand. They knew each other so well they touched each other all the time. Yet now that Rose's feelings had shifted, there was this continual sense of newness whenever his fingers met her skin. In a strange way this kindling of passion reminded Rose of grief. Both these very different feelings imparted a glistening edge to everything: the sound of birds singing first thing in the morning, the clarity of drinking water she poured into a glass, a shaft of sunlight streaking across her horse's back, the autumn leaves clinging to the trees, even though soon enough that same tree would shrug them loose and away they'd blow in the wind, to crumble and be lost forever. Austin's ordinary touch now felt intimate to her, and caught off guard by such a visceral response, Rose accidentally bumped her purse, which fell to the ground and spilled its contents into the red dirt. Her face burned as Austin bent down and began picking up each item and handing it to her.

"I've always thought that you could just about draw a psychological profile of a woman by looking through her handbag. Let's see what we've got here. Lipstick, now that's stock in trade, but whatever shade it is, it hardly shows, 'cause our Rose Ann doesn't like calling attention to herself." He picked up a Tampax Slender Regular and grinned. "The Girl Scout in her is always ready for emergencies."

Rose couldn't help but smile.

"And look here! We've got some sugarless gum in the wintergreen flavor, which just happens to be my favorite, and a little bottle of hand cream. Carmex for chapped lips, sunscreen, bug repellent—yes sir, you can tell this purse belongs to one true New Mexican. Let's see what's on her grocery list. 'Pasta, tomato sauce, poblanos, chicken, milk, bread crumbs.' Sounds like some kind of dinner I'd appreciate even if her wild-haired daughter does not. We've got a hairbrush for her curls, and three pens. Why three? In case one of them goes dry and somebody needs to borrow the second."

She laughed, and Austin picked up her billfold.

"What's this? One wide-open wallet. Rose, you should keep this thing snapped shut or all your credit cards could fall out. Let's just check how much mad money she carries."

Rose knew there was $110 inside. She'd gone to the bank yesterday, withdrawing grocery and gas money. Because she hated balancing her checkbook, she paid cash as often as possible. But when Austin separated the halves of the bill compartment, not even a stray dollar could be seen.

Rose laid her forehead down on the steering wheel and groaned.

Austin gently touched her shoulder. "I didn't mean it about firing you. Do you need a raise? For God's sake, Rose, don't cry on me. Tell me what's the matter, and we'll fix it. Look at me, dammit."

She couldn't bear to. If the money was gone, there was only one place it had gone: into Amanda's ratty macramé purse. The facts spoke for themselves: Her daughter was a thief, she was a rotten mother, and now she was a rotten mother $110 in the hole. "I have to go."

Austin pulled her from the cab of the car and marched her inside his kitchen. He sat her down at the table and measured out coffee for the pot. His hands were shaky, and he spilled some on the counter, but didn't stop to sweep it up. Eventually his grip on the measuring spoon steadied enough that he got coffee and water into the pot and it dripped down into the decanter. Neither of them said a word until he'd set the mug in front of Rose. All she could think when she raised the Mimbres pattern china to her lips was, *I bet Leah picked out this pattern. It's so beautiful. I can't imagine why she left it behind. Myself, I have supermarket dishes, Corelleware, unbreakable, affordable, and completely forgettable. Here I am, sitting at a custom-made table—I don't know what kind of endangered wood—drinking imported coffee in the kitchen of an entire house designed for Leah Donavan, the woman who does not love him but whom Austin cannot forget. It's a Leah museum. I'd drop a dollar in the donation basket, but thanks to my daughter, I don't have a dollar to drop. I'd better get myself out of here before I start punching out windows.* But instead of moving, she sipped, swallowed, and thought about how every single day of her life she stepped blithely through the most painful situations making ordinary motions like normal people did while inside her heart was screaming like a coyote with his leg caught in a trap. Rose was a lot of things. She was a widow, the daughter of a difficult mother, a mother of two difficult children, a bookkeeper to a heartsick alcoholic who had no idea how she felt about him. People expected that she would behave in a predictable, dependable manner. No matter how many times they disappointed her, *she* couldn't let them down.

"Two minutes after I buried Philip, I should have put a personal ad in the paper, gone out on dates, gotten married right away, given those kids a father figure. That's where things went wrong, Austin. It has to be."

"So why didn't you?"

Her cheeks flamed, and she looked Austin in the eye. "One, because I'm an idiot, and I figured my children needed my undivided attention. Plus I clung to the outdated notion that love had to figure into the mix."

"Two?"

"Well, gee, Austin. Maybe nobody asked me!"

He put his thumb to the rim of Rose's cup, smearing the pale lipstick imprint. "Love only thrashes you around, Rose. It's overrated. Marriage might work out better if people went into it for more practical reasons."

"Name one."

"Safe sex partners."

"No sex is safe. Name another."

"Shoot, I don't know. Somebody to eat dinner with's as good a reason as I can come up with. Who doesn't mind watching reruns. To bring you soup when you're sick. Hell, maybe nobody should get married, maybe nobody's really happy."

"My parents have been married forty-five years. My dad still brings my mother flowers. She walks in the room, and his eyes light up like it's the first time he saw her. Is it a crime for a woman to want that?" She made herself swallow more coffee against her closing throat.

Austin frowned. "Let's see, wasn't there a literature professor awhile back?"

"So she had one little dalliance! Men do that all the time and no one condemns them. She ended up back home with Pop, and that's what matters."

"Did you do that with Philip?"

"Fool around? Of course not. I took vows. Did you do that with Leah?"

"Why bother when she did it enough for both of us? Besides, who wants to take a broken-down vet stinking of worming medication into her bed?"

Only me. Rose sat back in the chair, biting her tongue. Austin thought of her as his friend. He confided in her. How could she ever explain what she felt for him without forever altering—possibly ruining—their friendship?

Austin rubbed his face and sighed. "What in hell did I say wrong this time?"

There was no common language in which to discuss what she needed to say, and thanks to Leah, he would probably never be able to hear. "Never mind. I'd better go home and see if the little thief is still around. Maybe if I'm lucky, I can get half my money back. Thanks for the coffee."

Austin walked her to the car, held the door, and when she was safely belted in, leaned over and gave her a kiss on the cheek. Instantly Rose's hand flew up to touch where his mouth had been. "Thirty-four, twenty-two, thirty-six," she said.

He laughed. "That's about what I imagined, but why are you telling me your measurements?"

"I'm not, you idiot. That's the combination to the safe where your stupid truck keys are." She started the engine and pulled the door shut. He stepped back.

"Thanks."

"Don't thank me, Austin. Just don't drink anymore."

He held up his coffee mug. "I'm working on it."

Rose shifted into reverse and raced home.

"Amanda?" she called into the kitchen. "I need that money, Amanda. No matter what you think, I'm not made of the stuff." Chachi sat in the middle of the floor with his head cocked and ears flattened, staring at her. If she raised her voice any higher, he would creep under her desk and hug the wall, develop an attack of colitis, require an enema, which would involve another visit to Austin, and that Rose could not bear right now. In Amanda's room, where the unmade bed and the mess of discarded clothing and books reminded her why she rarely opened this door, she did not see her daughter. She wasn't in the bathroom either, but her towel was on the floor and the soap lay in a gooey mess at the side of the sink, not two inches from the soap dish. *Face it*, she told herself, as she picked up a book of poetry and scanned a page, the words barely registering. *There is no note, no conscience, no nothing.* Exasperated, she walked out to the barn where Max stood nosing his empty hay chute, whinnying at her when she unlatched the gate. Winky's was full, and she was making a great show of eating. *That child sat here eating my food, stole my money, and couldn't even bother to throw hay to her horse. I'd've given her money if only she'd asked. Not $110, but something.* Rose measured out the alfalfa flake and threw some vitamins and sweet feed on top of it, drizzling the whole mess with blackstrap molasses. She licked her finger and replaced the cap on the bottle. It wasn't even close to lunchtime, but maybe she'd go inside fix herself a bowl of ice cream. No, a banana split. With caramel sauce. Cherries. Why the hell not? Everyone had had a stressful morning.

Cooking always made her nerves settle. Rose rolled chicken in flour and chile powder, fried it to a crisp, and assembled all the ingredients for Mexican potato salad: black beans, yellow potatoes, peppers, and bacon bits. When she got to the ranch, she'd add the dressing: It was a blend of mayonnaise, shallots, pickled chipotles, Lawry's salt, a scant tablespoon of bacon grease, and whatever amount of milk necessary to thin the mixture. Shep'd grown so thin since the prostate surgery that she always liked to bring him a meal. Sometimes it seemed he anticipated her visits. She'd drive up, and there would be Alfred, her favorite horse, spit-shined and ready for saddling. She wrapped the chicken in foil and loaded up the cooler. Chachi danced at her feet.

"Relax, I already said you get to come along."

Winky stepped nervously into the trailer after she watched Max do it. Rose double-checked the hitch. Half an hour later, moving at a leisurely pace, they pulled into the circular driveway under the swinging metal sign announcing El Rancho Costa Plente. At the fork in the drive, Rose veered right, parking behind the barn instead of in the driveway. She unloaded Winky into the arena. At once the mare began braying her presence, and the other horses, skittery at changes, neighed back. Max nickered to old friends, and that seemed to calm Winky down a little. For a second Rose stood watching her mare, hoping that this show of anxiety would pass quickly, that Winky wouldn't pass her tentative nature on to her colt. Shep had some herbal supplements he called "Arab medicine," which he gave to horses who had trouble settling down. The nickname evolved from his primal dislike of the notoriously high-strung breed. Winky didn't have any Arab in her, but she was finer-boned than most quarter horses. Her coat was a lovely dappled gray, and the stallion Rose had bred her to was also gray. *She's going to throw a perfect, calm, healthy colt,* Rose insisted to herself. *Beautiful, too,* and fetched the cooler from the Bronco. She called Shep's name as she walked around the bunkhouse. There was a fancy white luxury car parked in front. Prospective buyers often came along when her father wasn't here. Shep could show horses and deal as well as Chance. When Shep didn't answer, Rose figured he was out on horseback somewhere. She hustled Chachi up the steps and opened the screen door. At once a chubby blue heeler flung himself at her dog and bared his teeth. The scrappy Jack Russell, essentially a big dog in a small dog's body, returned the favor, and the dogs began to tumble and fight.

Rose dropped the cooler on the floor. "Chachi, *no!*" She grabbed a broom from the front hall closet and began smacking the blue heeler on the butt. "Let him go, you bully!"

The heeler whimpered and backed off, and Rose took hold of Chachi's collar. He strained, barking nonstop, and Rose could barely keep him in hand. She held the broom in front of her, bristles facing out. Her plan was to shut Chachi in the downstairs bath and shoo the rowdy ranch dog out of the house, but when she opened the bathroom door, standing in front of the mirror, pinning up her hair, she saw her sister, Lily.

Lily removed a hairpin from her mouth. "Hi, Rose."

Rose's heart ached at seeing her after so much time apart. "Lily?"

The blue heeler scrambled into the bathroom and squeezed himself behind the toilet. "What's going on out there? Did I hear barking?"

Rose pointed. "That strange dog was attacking Chachi. What are you doing here?"

Lily laughed. "That strange dog is mine. Buddy, you knock that crap off." The blue heeler cowered behind the porcelain. "We're on vacation."

"You can't take a vacation here," Rose said.

"Why in hell not?"

"Because *I* need a vacation. That's why."

"Really." Lily stabbed the last pin into her French twist. Rose thought her sister looked like Audrey Hepburn, if Hepburn had fancied tattoos and had sex partners that approached the triple digits. "So take one, nobody's stopping you."

"I was planning to take it *here*."

"Good thing it's a big house."

The two sisters eyed each other. Neither one was about to back down. Rose let Chachi go, and he snapped twice at Buddy, then ran out of the room and huddled under her father's desk. "Look, we can't both be here at the same time. It's as simple as that."

"Why not, Rose? Because it offends your precious morals to have your bad sister in the same room with you? Because you can hold a grudge longer than the Ayatollah Khomeini, who, by the way, is dead? How mature. Let me just pack up and check into a motel, because Rose always gets her way, doesn't she?"

"That isn't true, and you know it." Here she was, forty years old, and still Lily could reduce her to tears. If only Rose knew how to play the game. Amanda she could sometimes handle, but Lily? No way. "Besides, what about your job? Or did you get fired?"

Lily smiled. "Not yet, but the day is still young. Does that make you feel better, Rose? Knowing your sister's in career misery? PS, I also recently broke up with yet another boyfriend. Guess this is turning out to be a red letter day for you."

Rose bit her lip. "Actually, it's a major relief to know something goes wrong in your life once in awhile. Somehow I always picture you out there in California living the high life. You were the one who always got her way. You dressed nicer, too."

"Horse manure."

"No, it's true."

"Well, I'm glad we got this part over with." Lily stepped forward and embraced her sister. "Still, you could at least *pretend* to be sorry about my boyfriend."

"I am sorry, Lily. Was he 'the one'?"

"Hell, no. But I sure tried to believe he was. Oh, well," she started to say, and both sisters recited in unison, "They come and they go, but mostly, they go."

Their laughter rang out in the bathroom. It had felt so odd to feel her sister's arms around her that Rose could only pat Lily's back awkwardly.

"I know you don't believe me, but I was sorry about Second Chance's graduation."

"I figured you were."

"So you finally forgive me?"

"Me? Only about four years ago. The Martínezes? Never."

"Jeez, why didn't you say so?"

"Must be that stubborn Wilder streak."

"No kidding. Rose, I'm so sorry about Philip. I would have come home for the funeral if you'd let me."

Rose felt sorrow choke her throat like an old tradition. "I guess I should have. I hardly remember that time. Everything is such a blur. It's funny, Lily."

"Funerals are *funny*?"

"No, of course not. I know I should still be sad, but I hardly miss him at all. I mean, I miss certain things, like the way he always took the trash out without me asking, having someone to cook for, going out to dinner or the movies, and somebody warm next to me in the sheets, those things I miss. But it's as if Philip's dying left this huge chunk of ice inside me. A glacier or something. I've tried to move past it, but so far no luck. "

Lily looked away, as if Rose's confession made her uncomfortable. "What have you tried?"

"The usual. Grief group, also known as pity party. Working hard.

Riding the horse Amanda had to have and then left behind. I pray."

"All that holy crap isn't going to heal you. You need to get laid."

Rose sighed. "Isn't that just like you."

"What?"

"We're together less than five minutes and already you're bad-mouthing my faith and talking about sex."

Lily took her sister's hand. "No, I'm talking about getting laid. Major difference. Hey, are you hungry? I bought this weird salsa at the hardware store. Apparently no one in Floralee has ever heard of pesto."

"Well, actually, I brought along some food."

"What?"

"Nothing much. Fried chicken, potato salad, fruit, and I made some tortillas."

"That's my sister, Rose, all four food groups. Come on, let's go find Shep. We can set a place for him, then talk dirty and watch him turn red."

Rose followed her sister from the bathroom into the living room, where her cooler sat in vaguely the same place where she'd dropped it, only now there were tooth marks on its aqua-and-white handle. Chachi and Buddy lay side by side on a Storm Pattern rug. As Rose looked from one dog face to the other, she tried to match the fang marks to the owner. It appeared that sometime in the last few minutes, these boys had formed an alliance, a canine bond approaching that of siblings. The inherent code was, "No matter what, never rat each other out." To Rose it paralleled herself and Lily a little too closely, a partnership that seemed way too good to last.

6

Sparrow at the Gate

Lily half expected her sister to fold the lunch napkins into swans. When they were teenagers, Rose had always felt compelled to pretty up the ordinary. Their grandmother had made such a big deal over it, as if the ability to tie a really terrific bow and embroider French knots was going to carry Rose through life. Lily, whom Grandma had never quite approved of, didn't bother to compete. That lacy kind of house crap was utterly impractical, on a par with the way hotel maids were paid to fold the toilet paper roll into a pleat. Of course, Mami defended Rose, calling her needlework *style*, and frequently pointed out that Rose naturally possessed what Lily had to work to attain. Well, newsflash, nobody at this table was a teenager anymore, paper swans didn't erase heartache, Lily had mastered style, and Rose, in her faded jeans and ratty blue T-shirt, had about as much élan as a gym towel. Not to mention that her hair could use a good colorist and a shaping from somewhere other than Supercuts. There was something about her sister, however, that Lily found hard to define. The way Rose moved, her easy smile, that uniqueness even in the way she spoke—what could you call that—grace or grief?

"Hey, Shep," Lily said, passing the platter across the table. "Look here. Rose saved you the chicken's titties. Wasn't that thoughtful of her?"

The old horseman loaded up his plate with potato salad and eyed the platter suspiciously. He made a face and shook the salt shaker over his chicken breast. "A chicken only has one tit."

"Too much salt will kill you," Lily warned.

He set the shaker down with an audible thump. "Well, I hope it does. If nothing else, I want to go out with a good taste in my mouth."

Rose pointed with her fork, which rested in her fingers like a paintbrush. "The corporate world sure hasn't taught my sister any manners, has it, Shepherd?"

"Ha," Lily said. "You think manners is what business is about? You should see me in a suit. I can haul ashes just like a big boy. Half of them think I have a dick."

"Count me in," Shep said. "You came out of your mother kicking and screaming, and as soon as you could manage a fist, you were whaling on the local boys, sending them all running to their mamas in tears."

Lily spit the mint leaf into her palm and took a drink of her lemonade. "Somebody had to prepare them for the real world. Dispense a few calluses."

"Yes," Rose said, "Somebody always has to be the bully."

Lily stuck out her tongue. "I wasn't a bully, I was a leader."

"So was Hitler."

Shep set down his fork. "Girls . . ."

"Apparently," Rose said, "we have different vocabularies."

"That's because we inhabit different worlds. Like to see you do my job. You'd be crying within the first ten minutes." Lily turned her face to the ranch foreman. "Come riding with us this afternoon, Shep. It'll be like old times."

He stood up and took his plate in hand. "Hell, no. I'm going out back and finish my meal in peace. The dogs have got to be better company."

He threw his napkin on the table and beat a retreat for the door. Chachi got up to follow, then seemed to think staying close to the chicken offered better odds. He lay down, head on his paws, brown eyes wide and begging. Buddy sidled in closer to Lily and sprawled across her bare feet. "Well," Lily said. "I guess we've been royally dismissed."

"What did you expect? I don't understand why you tease him like that," Rose said. "Poor guy had his prostate out last year. He couldn't make a fist if he wanted to."

"His prostate? How was I supposed to know that? Bantering's always kind of been a tradition with Shep and me. Is he all right? I swear, no one in this family ever tells me anything. "

"Bantering's cruel. Shep's fine. And some traditions should be done away with."

"What's this? Sister Rose, who sends Arbor Day cards, bad-mouthing the tried and true? I wonder what earth-shattering thing she'll try next—white shoes after Labor Day?"

"Shut up, Lily."

"You shut up first."

They finished lunch in a silence that dripped with the weight of unspoken argument, truly like old times. Lily took bites of everything but left most of the food on her plate. Her sister ate all of her chicken but picked the black beans out of her salad and left the chunks of potato sitting in the dressing. Now Rose was clearing away the leftovers, packing the chicken in foil and putting plastic wrap over the salad. Lily watched, impressed by her sister's efficiency. She never tore off so much as one centimeter more of the wrap than she needed. Rose wound that seal around the bowl like Betty Crocker. Lily left open jars sitting on the counters, generally forgetting them until they smelled funky, which was when she tossed them out.

Rose stood at the sink, her back to Lily. She sighed, and as her shoulders dropped, Lily had to admit, even her gestures of defeat possessed elegance. Rose turned, and Lily could see that her mouth was set in the old familiar hard line that meant incipient sermon. Her sister took a breath. "I'd still like to ride the horses. But maybe we could not talk for awhile."

"Fine with me. You don't have to get all snooty about it."

A quarter mile into the trail ride, Rose was explaining about Max's chiropractic adjustments, and how since she worked for Dr. Donavan, he gave the horse free treatment. Lily's suspicions were aroused, but she figured she'd let Rose chatter on a little longer, see where all this was leading.

"He says it helps him to practice, and that's payment enough. It's a great deal for me, and kind of him to do it. He has a way with Max."

"He must," Lily said. "The Max I remember used to kick the snot out of anything vaguely veterinarian."

"Max is going on eighteen. His kicking days are long gone. And even if he wasn't, Doctor Donavan really is that good with animals." On she went to explain about the rescued border collie he'd taught any number of tricks. This man wasn't a veterinarian, he was a magician.

Lily could smell the real reason lurking beneath that Swiss cheese logic. Her sister was hot for the vet, downright hormonal. Of course, she would never come right out and admit it. Privacy was all with Rose. Lily'd bet a year's salary the vet had no clue Rose was even interested.

"Have you ever let him adjust you?" Lily teased.

"He only works on animals."

"Last time I checked, women were animals. Particularly Wilder women."

Rose made a sound of disgust. "Lily, if you don't want to hear about my horses, just say so."

"Rose Ann, I *love* hearing about your horses. It just occurred to me that perhaps the reason you mentioned Doctor Donavan seven hundred times in the last hour might be that you were interested in more than his chiropractic skills. So?"

"Oh, for Pete's sake! I don't know why I bother. How about let's just enjoy the scenery?"

"Okay by me." Lily nudged the old horse up the gradual incline of the trail that wound behind the ranch. It was soft, red dirt all the way, beneath the wind-rustled pines and the clatter of cottonwood leaves, the air cool thanks to yesterday's rainstorm. They climbed five hundred feet in silence broken only by birdsong and the horses' occasional grunts and nickering. When they rested the horses, Lily stared down at their father's property. All 240 acres seemed like a small speck in the larger sea of muted blue-green grasses. The Wilder land stretched north, toward the Colorado border. Every now and then a farmhouse broke up the acreage, the glint of sun arcing across a metal roof, the soft red of barn siding worn down to wood by the elements. If a California developer saw all this, he'd get an immediate erection, picturing how many lots he could cut, how many cheaply constructed houses would fit there, and the size of the pockets he was going to need to stuff all his dollars inside. Lily tried to imagine the ghosts of her mother's ancestors dancing across this land, the drumbeats of old songs echoing around a campfire where *Diné* women nursed babies. At some point, they had to feel the approach of the Spanish conquerors who'd come on horseback, an army of soldiers cresting the hills with equal amounts of rape and religion in their arsenals. They were

Mami's ancestors too. How could a person ever reconcile such oppos-
ing halves? Mami rarely talked about her heritage, but Grandma had
made it her life's work. Once she started in, Lily turned her mind off
and dreamed of horses. Rose, ever diligent, listened politely.

"It's amazing," Rose said, rambling on about the damn horse. "The
adjustments work so well I hardly have to Bute him anymore."

Lily let simmer what she wanted to say. "Bute's decent medicine,
though it has its drawbacks where long-term use is concerned. I take it
myself every once in awhile."

Rose gave her a look. "Why? Are you going lame?"

"Very funny." Lily looped the reins over her left fist. "For migraines.
Don't tell me you've never had one. They're supposed to run in families."

"Describe it for me."

The debilitating headaches had on one occasion caused her to
write out a will.

Whoever finds this note, please return Buddy Guy to Pop's ranch.
He's been a good dog, and always made me feel safe. He bites,
though, so you'd better tranquilize him first. Maybe with one of
those darts they use to knock out mountain lions. I also recom-
mend a muzzle, better get leather; Buddy can rip through those
Velcro jobs in nothing flat. Send my good jewelry to my bitchy sis-
ter, Rose, even though she'll never have the nuts to wear it the
way it should be worn. My stock portfolio should probably go to
my niece and nephew, but for God's sake, get a lawyer to hold it
in trust until they acquire some sense, like say around age forty-
five. And bury me in something comfortable but flattering, like
my camelhair coat from Bloomingdale's, and my Calvin Klein
jeans with the rip in the ass. No pantyhose, no matter what
Mami says! In fact, no underwear at all. Well, that's that. I can't
say I'm happy to leave, but anything is better than how my damn
head feels. Adios, cruel world.

She'd lain down on her bed, one arm around Buddy, waiting for
eternity, only to wake up the next morning with a stiff neck and so
much dog hair up her nose that she spent the day sneezing.

"Migraines are the tractor pulls of headaches. Sometimes, at the start, I see purple and yellow spots about a foot out from my field of vision. If I take the Butalbital, lie down with a cold cloth on my forehead, think of nothing, it usually goes away. I don't know about horses, but Bute makes me feel absolutely pliable. I do believe I could win a gold medal for sex on Bute."

Sister Rose looked intrigued by that comment. "Did you ever just take it for—you know—that particular effect?"

"Of course I did. Somehow it doesn't work unless you have the headache too. Weird recipe, huh? Total waste of a side effect, since moving a limb while in the throes of migraine invites agony. But if, say, I'm in some endless meeting with surgeons, or driving in stop-and-go traffic on the freeway and I can't get to my pills, well, imagine whoever's driving the tractor is dragging an eight-hundred-pound spike through my left eye. And the wretched beasts can last for hours! I had one once that went on for two days."

Rose looked over at her sister. "Except for the feeling sexy part, that pretty much sounds like every single day before Amanda left home."

"I can't believe she's running all over hell and gone with a reggae musician. How could you let her go?"

Her sister reached down to straighten out Alfred's reins. She scratched the gray gelding's neck affectionately and shrugged. "Maybe you can tell me how was I supposed to stop her."

"Didn't you take her to a shrink?"

"Sure. After Philip died I got us all counseling. Second Chance pointed out the *P* encyclopedia on the psychologist's desk, and Amanda refused to waste her nights healing our family when she could be spending them with boys. Seemed kind of ridiculous for me to sit there explaining my kids' behaviors and writing checks, so—" and here Rose forced a smile "—eventually I let her flunk her classes, get tattoos, pierce her belly button, stay out all night, sleep with boys, and learn for herself. Of course I'm still waiting for that last part to happen. She passed through town the other day. Lifted a hundred and ten dollars from my purse."

"You're exaggerating!"

"I am not. And it wasn't the first time."

Lily yanked Max's head away from a low-hanging branch just seconds before it would have smacked him between the eyes. "Wow! For a chiropractically adjusted horse, he just zones out sometimes, doesn't he? And what about Second Chance? Is he depraved, too? Did I set him on the road to ruin with my hired stripper?"

Rose ran her fingers through her curly hair, lifting it from the back of her neck. This part of the trail was hot and windless. The sun beat down with an intensity that would sunburn her shoulders. "It's still motorcycles. Lately dirt bikes on the circuit. He wins money occasionally, and his picture shows up in the Albuquerque paper. I never know where he is until he calls home."

Lily thought of the carnage she'd witnessed in emergency surgery due to motorcycle accidents. "Hope to God he wears his helmet. I miss those little monsters."

"Me, too, but they're grown up, Lily. Sooner or later I had to let them go. And try like hell not to feel like a failure about how they turned out. If I had my way, they would have said good-bye waving college degrees, with my blessings. Things hardly ever work out the way one plans."

"Don't you worry about them?"

Rose's expression clouded over, and Lily was shocked at the equal portions of beauty and sadness her sister's face could hold.

"Every single day. I look at their baby pictures. Try to remember the good times. I light candles for them at church every week."

Lily wanted to scream. A long time back, when they attended mass on Sundays alongside Mami, Lily had lit votives and stared into the twenty-five-cent flames, matching their intensity with her own. She'd lit as many as ten candles at a time, hoping to incinerate her larger sins. Holding up her hands, palms forward, she had felt the heat emanate from the flickering wicks. Was that the holy presence or merely by-products of combustion? Candles in some old church didn't amount to faith, but there was this thick, collective feeling of *otherness* embedded in the adobe walls. If faith was real, she thought it would inevitably find its way inside her. The Virgin Mami worshipped exuded a powerful kind of female peace, but it was difficult to sustain belief when hardly anything one prayed for ever worked out. How did Rose manage? And it wasn't like Lily had spent *all* her childhood prayers asking for a leopard Appaloosa. She asked for Grandpop to survive lung cancer, which he hadn't, Grandma to like her—fat chance—and enough food to fill the belly of every starving baby on the planet. From reservation statistics to those heinous commercials on television, all that infant hunger haunted Lily and made her doubt God. The biology she'd learned in college turned out to be like one giant eraser scrubbed over all that hokey-smokey seek-and-you-shall-find stuff. She couldn't exactly call herself an atheist, but at this stage in her life, religion kind of boiled down to the Golden Rule, except in the business world, where all rules had a brass exterior covering a lead interior. Rose had never stopped believing, but Lily felt done with a capital *D* when it came to the Catholic Church. "Prayer," she said. "Hmm. Usually I just pour myself a drink."

They stopped at the stream to water the horses. Alfred sucked noisily, taking in long, slow drafts that traveled down his neck in rippling swallows, but all Max wanted to do was splash around, act like an idiot, make a mess. Damn horse was into his second childhood. The feeling of the cool water dampening her pants legs cheered Lily up. Every wet rock and cottonwood tree seemed worth the blisters she'd feel tomorrow. The stream was clean and cold, and the gently swirling current beneath the horses' hooves would grow swift enough in winter to carry off a tub of lard like Buddy. Blue sky peeked through the turning leaves, that impossible shade that made New Mexico famous, turning the heads of painters, photographers, and people whose broken hearts felt exactly the same color. Lily wondered if Blaise was dating somebody new by now. Her fussy carpenter was such a charmer she couldn't imagine him sleeping alone for longer than two days. She wondered if he'd pick a blond this time around. It wasn't that she wanted him back, because she didn't, but that didn't make letting go any easier. *Maybe if I wish him happiness some will boomerang back to me,* she thought. *Nah, that kind of thinking is bullcrap, and besides he really hurt my feelings. I want him to suffer a little while longer, at least long enough for me to feel better than he does.* The chill air in the shade felt bracing. But the best thing about the landscape was that there wasn't anyone with an M.D. in sight.

Rose began to guide Alfred out of the stream and back onto the trail when Lily reached a hand out to stop her. "Let's dismount. I need to lie down after all that food."

"Okay." Rose slid out of her saddle and loosened Alfred's girth. She ran her irons up the stirrup leathers, just as they'd been taught to do. Lily did the same. A little ways from the water, they ground-tied the horses and let them graze on the small amount of grass. Rose kicked away rocks under a cottonwood until she'd cleared a smooth patch of dirt wide enough for both of them to sit. Lily pulled off her shirt and hung it on a branch. She sat down, naked from the waist up, sweat cooling on her body, smelling like the earth.

Rose clucked, sounding exactly like Mami.

"What? We're in the middle of Egypt, and you're going to lecture me about partial nudity?"

"I can't believe you don't wear a bra."

"Give me one good reason why I should."

"You're thirty-five years old. How about support?"

Lily flexed her pectorals and her petite breasts lifted. "See that? Weights. Sixty reps in the morning and the same at night. I have muscles to hold my tits up, I don't need to be tortured every day of my life by ridiculous underwires."

Rose pursed her lips. "When you go braless, it makes you look . . . I don't know, cheap."

Lily howled with laughter. "Cheap is one thing I *know* I am not. If anything, I am expensive. Besides, I always wear one to work, and—" she leaned over and yelled in her sister's ear "—I'm on vacation!"

Rose grabbed a handful of sticks and cottonwood flotsam. She pelted her sister until the downy white fuzz was floating everywhere. Laughing, Lily pulled the fuzz from her hair, flinging it back at her sister. They graduated to tickling, at which Lily, the wirier of the two, was unparalleled. She wrestled Rose to the dirt and grabbed the hem of her T-shirt. "So show me your great supported tits," she taunted her sister.

Through her laughter, Rose gasped for breath. "No, stop it!"

"Come on. I want to see what wearing a bra every second of the day has done for the great Rose Wilder Flynn."

Lily pulled the shirt up, and just as quickly Rose yanked it back down.

"No fair. I didn't see anything except that ugly white bra."

Rose pulled the shirt over her head and unsnapped her bra. Lily quickly grabbed her clothes. Rose's breasts spilled forth, larger than Lily's, nowhere near as toned, but still nicely shaped. "Happy?"

Lily studied the pale striations marbling the sides of her sister's breasts. They weren't unattractive, exactly. She looked like a woman who'd used her body for its designated purpose. Sure, they rode a little lower than Lily's, but Rose's bosom still looked like a place some man could rest his head, find comfort and passion, and maybe if he was smart, be moved to tears of gratitude. If the wonder vet was smart that way, it might be him.

"Now you've seen forty-year-old tits. Stretch marks and all. Give me back my clothes."

"I will in a second." Lily checked the tag on the bra. It was cheap and American. The support argument was pointless if the garment hadn't been manufactured in Europe, where clothing designers understood lingerie. She handed it back. "How can you wear this ugly old thing?"

"It's comfortable."

"Comfort isn't everything. If I ever stop working out, mine are going to drop like a set of water balloons. You look good, Rose. So whose lucky fingers have fondled your nipples lately? That chiropractor vet?"

Rose blushed as she reassembled her clothing. "For God's sake, Lily."

"It's been two years. Nobody since Philip?"

"I've been busy."

"Nobody is *that* busy. You need to get laid, Rose. Just set your mind to it and it'll happen. Let's do a drive-by on this Doctor Donavan. I want to check him out."

Her sister's face was somber. "Let everything be, Lily."

"If I do that, you won't have sex until the next ice age. Come on, you know you want that vet."

"It might be for the best, considering he's still in love with his ex-wife, Leah."

Immediately Lily thought of Tres Quintero at the hardware store, with that eleven-year-old Leah at his side. Could it be the same person? Nah, too long odds. Maybe it was infectious, a plague, the Leah virus attacking the state of New Mexico like that hantavirus scare a couple of years back. "Leah? What kind of loser-chick name is that? A Leah when you could have a Rose? I'm sorry. The hell with him, then. You're young, and you have a generous heart. You have a really good butt, too, and you can cook fried chicken to make Shep Hallford cry. It's insane to let all that talent go to waste." She peeled the bark from a cottonwood twig bearing three yellow leaves. "You know, Rose, I'm going to pester you about Philip until you tell me everything, so you might as well give up and get it out of the way."

Rose lay back in the shade of the tree. "If there is one subject I do not want to discuss, it's Philip."

"I'm your sister."

Rose sighed. "He's gone, I'm alone, that's that." On the last two words, her voice had risen half an octave.

Lily leaned over her sister, touching her cheek with the yellowest leaf on the twig. Quoting their grandmother, she whispered in a voice that came out spookier than she intended, "From fate and death, no man escapes."

Anger flashed in her sister's brown eyes. "Oh, spare me, Lily. Who's ever died on you?"

Lily thought of the gallbladder lady, that airway tube jutting from her purpling lips, how she'd never kiss her husband or her children again. The sixty-four-year-old man who'd rescheduled his surgery so he could climb one last mountain with his grandchildren, and died on the table when his heart gave out. The kid with the brain aneurysm, the pyloric stenosis baby with the one-in-a-million allergic reaction to anesthesia. Lily's job was about saving lives, but behind every miracle lurked the potential for so many things to go wrong. When they did, she was supposed to pack it all up inside her Hartmann briefcase and fit it into a clinical graph that excused any company failures that coincidentally happened to erase peoples' lives.

"I don't know what made me say that. It just came out of my mouth from nowhere, this terrible echo of Grandma. She used to scare the hell out of me when she said things like that."

"Me too."

"I always resented her favoring you. That's such a mean thing to do to sisters. Why do you suppose the old witch was so divisive?"

Rose shrugged. "I went to church with her while you went fishing with Grandpop. Rather unladylike to prefer worms and tackle over a chance to confess your sins and say eternal penance."

Lily smiled. "All those years she scolded me for every little thing. All I could think of to do was refuse to speak Spanish to her. I knew the language so much better than you did. You totally murdered the grammar."

"I tried. Would it have killed you to make her happy with a few *Abuelitas* now and then?"

"Well, damn, Rose, at the time I sure thought it would. As a kid, didn't you ache to fit in out there in the world, not just in various *nichos* in Floralee? She was always trying to dress me in clothes made from tablecloths! For bedtime stories she told me folktales about mothers drowning their children. Jeez. Sometimes I felt my entire life was supposed to be one long-drawn-out apology for not having more Spanish blood running through my veins. It made me nuts. Watching Mami haul it out like a nail file, use it when she needed it, then tuck it away the rest of the time—was that any better?"

Rose was quiet, dragging a stick across the dirt. "It wasn't about your Spanish, Lily. Grandma never got over Mami marrying a white man. Whenever she looked at you, she saw her own daughter again, and the feelings of helplessness made her go extra hard on you. It wasn't fair. Still, I think that's how it was."

"Plus you were a goody-two-shoes, and I preferred to run barefoot," Lily added.

"Yes," Rose allowed. "That was some of it."

Lily lay down in the crook of her sister's shoulder, pressing her face against her Rose's arm. She let the leaves and sticks drop from her fingers. "Draw a picture on my back, Rose."

"That old game?"

"Yes. Please. Come on, I want to guess."

Rose sat up and brushed the dirt from herself. Lily turned on her side. She felt her sister's index finger, warm against her bare skin, begin to trace an outline. She closed her eyes and let her mind buzz in that sleepy suspension that accompanies sensual concentration. In two seconds she could tell Rose was drawing a horse, but no way did she want her to stop. "Keep going," she encouraged her sister. "I don't get it yet." She felt her fingers trace the almond-shaped ears pricking forward inquisitively, shape a long, Roman nose, capture the graceful curve of equine neck. Rose added nostrils, mane hair, a shock of forelock. Then, with her fingernail, she drew a crooked star where most horses had a blaze. Lily grinned and opened her eyes. "Sparrow. I miss that old pony something fierce. She went everywhere with us, didn't she? If there's a heaven, Sparrow will be at the gate nickering."

"If you *go* to heaven."

"Oh, I'll be there." Lily sat up and reached for her shirt. "Your all-forgiving God loves sinners and whores best. Bet I get in before you do."

Rose slapped at a bug bite on her shoulder. "I swear I'm an insect magnet. Does that look like a mosquito bite to you? Hope it wasn't a spider."

Lily touched the raised welt, already swollen to the size of a nickel, the color of window putty. "I don't know about you, but I've had enough of nature for one day. Let's go get you some calamine lotion and me some wine."

Rose gazed longingly up the trail, and Lily could tell she wanted to press on, even though there wasn't enough light left in the day to go any farther. "We can do this again tomorrow, Rose. It's not like this trail's going to disappear."

"Days like this don't come along that often."

She clucked to Alfred and began making her way down the path. Lily understood what she meant. The delicate balance of anything going well was so easily broken. "There'll be others."

The horses were full of energy on the ride home. Within the last half mile of the ranch, they began to hear faint whinnying travel up from the common arena. Their horses answered back, their deep, barrel-rattling neighs causing Lily's legs to throb and her crotch to feel wonderfully ticklish. Pop's horses liked nothing more than every member of the herd in his designated place. Rose was quiet, rubbing her bug-bitten arm as she rode ahead of Lily. Lily felt bad that she'd pushed her sister about the subject of Philip, but she had a feeling the rift between them wouldn't heal until that subject had been laid wide open. At the mere mention of his name Rose shut down. How could she ever tell her the things she knew about that man?

They untacked their horses, and Rose got out the Fiebing's saddle soap and the sponge. Lily brushed saddle stains from the horses' backs, checked hooves, and fetched each gelding a bucket of oats while Rose polished bridles. Various dogs milled around their feet, angling for a handout, but Buddy wasn't among them. Lily turned the horses out into the arena, and after some initial threat displays involving boundaries, they both rolled and got properly dirty, transforming back into ranch horses. As she locked them into the common arena abutting the open barn stalls, Shep rode T.C. into the ring.

Shep's saddle was padded with a couple of layers of yellowing sheepskin, commonly referred to as "cheaters," the mark of a *dengue,* or sissy rider who lacked the chops to stay in his seat longer than an hour. Lily wondered why he was using them. Whenever Lily asked

Shep any horse questions, he generally worked things around so she was forced to answer them herself, which was how she'd learned 90 percent of her equitation. As to which horse breed was the best, and which ranch horse was Shep's favorite, he always shook his head and said, *Honey, all they are is horses,* as if preferring one four-legged beast over another was a waste of his time. For awhile Lily'd taken that as sage advice. But factor in that whenever Shep rode for pleasure he chose T.C., and that the riotous gray gelding splattered all over with black leopard spots was the only Appaloosa to be found at Rancho Costa Plente in all its years of existence, that nobody besides Shep ever rode him, and Lily knew the old wrangler had a soft spot for this horse. She leaned against the fence and watched him work the animal through his paces.

T.C. was twenty-five years old this year, ancient by horse world standards. But Shep swore he knew a man down in Tijeras whose Appy mare had lived to the ripe old age of forty-two and spent her last years on his porch. Every morning he cooked up a gallon of oatmeal and hand fed her. Whatever supplements Shep gave the old gelding had worked a kind of Geritol magic. His spotted coat was as shiny and thick as a five-year-old's. He had more weight on him than Shep did, actually, and Lily wondered again about the prostate surgery.

She sighed with pleasure as her father's wrangler used his leg to coax T.C. into the side pass, a basic dressage move, where the horse fluidly, leg crossing over leg, walked sideways until Shep cued him to stop. After making a figure eight crossing the ring this way, he moved the horse into a collected canter, lapped the arena twice, and began to execute flying lead changes. The horse's dark gray forelock lifted and fell against his beautifully shaped head, which was held so exactly that— were this a horse show—any judge worth his salt would award him extra points. The animal was entirely focused, and so far as Lily could tell, hadn't missed a single cue. As Shep alternated asking for the right and left lead, the horse's hooves cut into the arena sand, throwing up spray just like the wake on a boat. Lily shivered. After five minutes Shep halted the horse, reached down and patted his neck affectionately, as if they were the only two breathing creatures on the planet. Lily saw Shep's lips moving, speaking to the horse as he walked him, cooling him out before putting him away for the night. She wondered what it was a taciturn old man said so easily to horseflesh that he found difficult to speak to humans. She would have given her eyeteeth to know.

Lily never grew tired of watching the world of her father's ranch. Sometimes she wondered why it was she'd left. For sure she had better luck with horses than she did with men. It was dusk now, and she needed to get a sweatshirt or give it up and go indoors. Slowly Shep dismounted, placing a hand against his lower back as if he'd strained it. Picking up fifty-pound sacks of grain will do that to you, Lily guessed. He hated using the wheelbarrow and was always too proud to ask for help. She'd say something to Pop, or for as long as she stayed, make sure to move the grain herself. She waited for Shep to come back outside, sit on the fence, and smoke a cigarette, but he didn't. Maybe he was in the bunkhouse, lying on a heating pad. After awhile she latched the gate behind her and went up to the house.

Rose had already gone upstairs to her old room, the first one at the top of the stairs. Lily could hear her bumping around, probably tucking her sheets into hospital corners, plumping pillows, changing into some regulation nightgown appropriate for a forty-year-old woman. Lily hadn't remembered to pack a nightie. She got into one of Pop's old work shirts, poured a glass of wine, and took it upstairs. Rose sat on her bed, clipping her toenails. "Stop. We'll get manicures and pedicures tomorrow," Lily said. "Have a real girls' day."

Rose looked up. "You spend money on yourself like that every week?"

"Sure. Where is it written that women need to go through life wearing hair shirts?"

Rose gathered the clippings in her palm and tipped them into a wastebasket. "I guess I let all that go when Philip died."

"So pick it up again. You're not a hundred years old, Rose. There's time for another man in your life if you want one."

"Easy for you to say."

"What's that supposed to mean?"

She made a face. "I'm forty."

Lily winked. "And at your sexual peak."

"I'm afraid."

"You're supposed to be."

Rose set the scissors down. "Lily, you're pretty, you have an education and more than a little nerve. What do I have to talk to a man about? My kids? Which coupons I clip?"

Lily pulled a Nancy Drew out of the shelf above the bed and flipped its yellowed pages. "Mami never throws anything away, does she? All you have to do is tell him he looks nice, Rose. Ask him questions about himself. They love to answer. Just be yourself. Everything'll unfold from there."

"Maybe I don't want another man." She pulled her knees up to her chest and laid her face across them.

Lily's heart went out to her sister, but Rose also pissed her off. All her life Rose was the "sensitive" one, the one Mami treated delicately. Lily was expected to "shape up." Did Rose think she was the only woman on earth who'd had her heart broken? "That's fine, too. Whatever you want. Let Doctor Donavan pine away for his ex-wife until the cows come home," Lily said. "Like I care. I'm going to bed. Good night."

"Do you think I'm feeling sorry for myself?" Rose asked stridently. "I'm not. I'm just being practical."

"The hell you are. You're chicken. Pleasant dreams."

"Lily?"

"What now?"

Rose looked near tears. "I had a good time today. I'm glad we made up."

"Me too. See you in the morning." She let Rose hug her good night.

Out on the porch swing, Lily rocked and thought about Tres Quintero. On guys like Paul Newman or Richard Farnsworth, every wrinkle looked rugged, every silver hair glinted with sexual health. Tres Quintero seemed to be aging like that. His handsome face at thirty-six was different from how it had looked at eighteen, but it was still compelling to look at, however briefly she had done so. Lily touched her upper lip where her own fine wrinkles made the skin feel loose, dusty. The dry air of Floralee required slathering on the moisturizer. She understood where Rose was coming from. Going back out there time after time wasn't just scary, it made a woman world-weary. But if a person gave up on love, all that was left was money and horses. Horses got old. You had to constantly break in new ones. Money went hand in hand with paying taxes, and what remained wasn't any fun if there wasn't somebody to spend it with you.

In the gravel driveway in front of the house, Buddy was performing some odd little dance, trying to get Lily's attention. He looked like a doomed helicopter might look, had important blades been shot off by the enemy, and fatal impact imminent. Chachi sat calmly observing the show. Lily figured Shep had fed the little beggars along with the ranch dogs, so she ignored his antics, curled up in her sleeping bag, and waited for the wine to deliver her to dreamland.

"I've decided we're going shopping," she said at breakfast.

Rose set her spoonful of blueberries back into the dish of milk. "The outlet place?"

Lily snorted. "Those places are a total rip-off. Nothing under size twenty-four and ugly colors. We're going to Santa Fe."

"Maybe you can afford the shops there; I can't."

Lily poured herself a cup of coffee and added cream. "There's all kinds of shopping, including window. Come on, Rose, it's civilization."

"Everything's changed," Rose said. "Mediterranean restaurants. Year-round tourists. Unbelievable traffic. Cerrillos Road is the biggest eyesore ever invented."

"I'll take my chances," Lily said. And then her pager went off. They could hear it trilling from the confines of her purse.

"Philip had one of those things," Rose said. "He wore it clipped to his belt as if he couldn't breathe without it. It always managed to go off at the damnedest times."

"Really?" Lily said, thinking that there were a lot of things Philip couldn't seem to get along without, and how it was likely that they paged him, sometimes pretending to be customers, and probably met him for long, slow afternoons in really nice hotels. Well, if Philip was dead, what good would come of telling his widow what a cheating s.o.b. he was? "It's probably nothing. Let me check my messages and then we can blow town. Dress nice, Doctor Flynn."

"Doctor?"

"Yep. Today you are going to be Doctor Flynn of the Santa Fe Medical Center, and I am going to take you to lunch and explain how you cannot live without my company's medical products. Then we are going to eat a really good meal, starting with appetizers, and charge it to my American Express corporate card. Next we'll shop LewAllen and LewAllen for some silver trinkets, ogle whatever walks by in trousers, and decide if it is worthy of Wilder women's attention."

"I don't want you to get in trouble."

"Rose!" Lily took her bowl away, ate a few spoonfuls of the blueberries, and then pointed the spoon at her. "This is how *regular* people live *regular* life. Corporations expect it. It's like golf for men. They build greens fees and expensive booze into the budget. Now go take your shower and leave off worrying for ten minutes already."

Lily recognized the flashing number right away; it was Eric, her boss, calling from California. She punched in her blocking code so he wouldn't know where she was calling from. Then her calling card number, the secret access code that was the same as her PIN number at the ATM machine, finally his number, and then she waited for him to answer. "What now, Eric?"

"The personal relationship you've developed with your clients is in peril, Lily. Get your ass back here and smooth plumage."

"Haven't we been through all this already?"

"Ty's doing a really good job, better than I thought he could. I've been thinking maybe I should give him half your territory."

Lily scratched Buddy's head, which was resting on her knee. "Nice try, but you forgot I have a brain and Ty can't find the john without a detailed map."

"You want the truth?"

"Well, I like it a whole lot better than this lame bullshit."

"There's been a dip in your sales, and if you aren't back by the end of the week, I'm going to have to replace you. Understand that's not what I want to do, Lily, it's just the way things are. Policy."

Lily covered the phone with her hand so Eric wouldn't hear her laughing. "I've been gone what—four days? I have two massive bonus checks coming from orders I placed *last week*. How can my sales be dropping?"

"Where are you, Lily?"

The connection sounded like her boss was in a wind tunnel. She bit her thumbnail and straightened a painting on the wall above her father's desk. It was new, but its subject was the same: Poppy Wilder, nude, artfully draped in a blanket. Artists waited in line to paint her even though she was sixty-two. Lily wondered how warped her own psyche must be, having seen so many nude photos and paintings of her mother from such an early age. That had to leave scars. "On vacation, just like I told you."

"Physically, where might that be?"

"This great little town, Eric, just north of None of Your Business. If this isn't life or death, I'm hanging up."

"Wait." She could hear the nerves in her boss's voice fraying. "There's a rumor going around that Manhattan Instruments might be staging a buyout."

"Rumors are rumors. No reason to panic."

"That means we might not have jobs next month."

"Good. Aren't you tired of working? I am. Maybe I'll start a new career as a waitress."

"Right, Wilder. I can just see you scaling down to an '89 Tercel and a studio apartment. Yeah, that'll happen."

"Stranger things have."

"What if it's true? You know the first thing they'll do is clean house. They'll bring in new people, and we'll be out on the sidewalk."

"Then dust off your skateboard. I wouldn't fret this, Eric. Worrying will give you an ulcer."

"If I were you, I'd cancel your leave and get over to every account, reassure the docs, bring doughnuts, CYA big time."

"But you're not me."

"Hey," he said, "Fair warning. You don't believe me, log on to the Internet and see for yourself." He hung up.

Lily groaned, switched on her laptop, which she never traveled without, waited forever for the damn AOL link, and hit the graph icon at the top of the screen. Her company's stock was up. Every fifteen minutes the exchange updated the figures, so it was a trustworthy indicator. A rise could mean great things, or it could mean an impending buyout. Rumors like that flew all the time, though. She clicked on *Reuter's*, didn't see anything besides some new Michael Jackson baby stories, clicked out, then noticed she had an e-mail flag.

"I miss your sweet little box. Give me another chance, baby," Blaise had written. Two whole sentences. He'd even spelled the words right.

She thought of the good sex they'd enjoyed on those rare but memorable occasions he hadn't drunk so much he lost his erection. She tempered this memory with the numerous times he'd embarrassed her in front of clients by talking stupid, or kicked Buddy out of the bedroom, or—for a really pleasant memory—called her Squaw, which roughly translated to the *c* word. She logged on to Mail Center

Controls, put a block on his incoming e-mail, and then deleted him and decided there was time to wash her hair.

They paid five bucks to park the Lexus in La Fonda's lot, walked around the plaza once, then ducked into the Plaza Café, ordering lattes to go. While their drinks were being made, Rose stood at the cashier's island, chatting with the hostess, who had gone to school with Amanda. She was a pretty girl, Indian, but in Lily's opinion she could have stood about three grand worth of orthodontia. Rose insisted on paying for the coffee, and Lily thought it was pointless to argue over five dollars, so she let her.

"Coffee," she said, taking the cup in her hand. "If we can only find pesto, this day will be perfect."

Outside the fall wind blew, and there was a huge line—it stretched almost to the plaza—for the O'Keeffe museum. At first Lily thought perhaps that was what the commotion was about, but then she saw a stream of people advancing from the opposite direction. It was a film crew, everyone wearing surf-company shorts, expensive sunglasses, and acting as if Rolexes and attitude meant they owned the town square.

"Wonder what that's all about," she said, nudging Rose.

Rose pried the lid off her coffee and sipped. "They're always filming something or other here. It's gotten so trendy to have New Mexico as a background in your movie. I think lots of stars just want to hang out where the sky's not smoggy. It makes money for the city, but just like nuclear energy, the fallout left behind is ours to clean up." She pointed in a southeasterly direction. "There's no ugly blue sign to warn you, but that shop second from the end is a Gap."

"A *Gap*?" Lily was furious. The only chain business in the plaza had always been—and always *should* have been—Woolworth's. Now going-out-of-business signs plastered every window. She snapped her head to look where Rose had pointed and saw the reason for the film crew, the move-your-ass-this-is-important attitude of the photographer's assistants. Dressed in something from the late great Versace, walking their way, leading a brace of six greyhounds, was their mother, Poppy Wilder.

Rose dropped her coffee. Lily felt the hot liquid splatter her ankles, but no pain registered. She took a firm hold of her sister's arm. Just look at the woman: She qualified for the senior discount, but that body filled the gray evening dress the way cognac spilled down the bell curve of a brandy snifter. Not to mention her racehorse neck, ancestral cheekbones, the waist-length black hair with the silver streak spreading out from her widow's peak. Add to that some nervous, elegant dogs, and Rose and Lily were immediately cast out as understudies to the star who never got laryngitis and wore shoes two full sizes smaller than they did.

"You want to skip the manicures?" Rose said.

"Sure." Lily threw her coffee into a trash can, and the sisters raced toward the nearest establishment that served alcohol, which just happened to be La Fonda hotel.

7

Shoes

Rose stared down into her tumbler of ice. A few minutes ago there had been several dollars' worth of rum and Diet Coke in the glass. Now it was sloshing around inside her belly, warming her from the inside out. Lily had ordered the drinks. "They've been away a couple of weeks," she told her sister. "You know how Mami gets restless. She probably flew the plane back alone."

"I don't care," Lily said, peering down from the Bell Tower Bar on the hotel roof. It was the perfect spot to observe the sunset, in addition to the plaza spectacle, now proceeding down toward Paseo de Peralta. "I'm just not ready to see her."

"Why not?"

"Because Mami will give me that look, and then she'll want to know every little detail about my life. Then she'll start in with the hocus-pocus and I'll lose it, Rose, I swear I will. It'll be worse than when I saw Tres Quintero in the hardware store."

"You saw Tres? Why didn't you tell me?"

Lily stirred her drink with her finger. "It was one of those moments I'm trying like hell to forget. Talking about it only makes it worse."

"And you expect me to talk to you about Philip!" Rose sat back against her wrought-iron chair. The bar wasn't crowded. Only a few tourists speaking another language sat in the alcove by the trademark bell. From this distance she and her sister could be anyone, but Poppy Wilder knew things sometimes even before they happened. Fear of her mother's premonitory abilities had kept Rose's sex life in check until

100

she married Philip Flynn. The extent of Rose's ESP reached far enough for her to be sure it was only a matter of time before Mami discovered them.

Her mother walked the elegant hounds back and forth across the plaza grass. Camera flash glinted off her hair, causing Rose involuntarily to reach up and touch her own. This probably had something to do with shutting down dog tracks, as Mami was death on greyhound racing. Austin treated several pets that had been retired from the track, and Rose had heard the horror stories: Dogs that didn't place in the money or broke a toe ended up dead, with their left ears cut off so they couldn't be traced back to a breeder. She thought greyhound racing was shameful, too, but nobody was champing at the bit to take *her* picture in an evening gown. Mami's beauty had always struck Rose as a lot like the state of New Mexico itself. Take your basically rocky, water-deprived land, beat religion into it, throw in the persistence of culture, endow it with chiseled cheekbones, and watch it give birth to art, whose main purpose was to disturb, provoke, and above all commemorate. The best her daughters could do was stand back in awe.

Austin's remark about her mother's extramarital affair had struck something deep inside Rose—she didn't quite know what. Instead of listening to Lily, Rose found herself thinking of ways to justify the eccentricities of her parents' marriage. Her mother was at ease with the rich and famous, and because of this her causes flourished, so she was always raising money for one thing or another. To that end her photograph was often in the paper, which made it difficult to think of her as belonging exclusively to their family—her mother, Pop's wife. Sometimes it seemed as if the union had endured because Pop willingly took a second chair to Mami, yet in the early years, as far back as Rose could remember, there had been tight-lipped silences and occasional absences. Rose believed wholeheartedly in the sacredness of vows. It wasn't morally right to look outside your marriage for happiness, but it was certainly human to try to make yourself happy. Rose had just never expected to exercise that particular argument using her own mother as example.

The photographer handed his camera to an assistant. Mami was laughing. He kissed her cheek. Rose's heart skittered in her chest. Maybe *nobody* was happy within the confines of marriage. Then, for no reason at all, she thought of Philip and got mad at herself that she'd more or less sat with her hands in her lap the entire length of their marriage, allowing him to make out the budget, say when they could afford a vacation (usually fishing, camping—something he wanted to do), choose a new car without asking her input. When he'd died Rose felt as if someone had dunked her face first into ice water. Over the past two years she'd learned the ropes, even if sometimes they felt like barbed wire in her hands.

"Can you believe that smart-ass waiter is ignoring us?" Lily said, holding up her hand like a second-grader who needed permission to go to the lavatory. "You'd think they could lay out a few chips and salsa if the service is going to be this slow."

Rose shrugged. "It's La Fonda. What did you expect?"

"I don't care if it's the freaking White House, Rose. How much can a bowl of chips cost?"

"A fourteen-ounce bag goes for $1.79 at the market where I shop."

"My point exactly." Lily waved her napkin at the waiter. Her sema-phoric antics were amusing the people at the next table. "So glad someone is getting a thrill out of all this," she remarked.

"Look at the greyhounds," Rose said. "Aren't they beautiful? They look like echoes of one another, almost coordinated in size and stature."

"The blue one's kind of cute," Lily offered, "if you like bony."

Blue was the color everyone associated with greyhounds. Racing had all but bred it away, believing blue to be unlucky. Their long narrow muz-zles pointed this way and that. A makeup person touched a powder puff to the blue dog on the far left. "I wonder what shade of powder matches a dog," Rose asked.

"Probably eye shadow," Lily said.

The animal wrangler stood behind the makeup lady, every now and then shaking a rattle that made the dogs prick their ears and look his way. Thin, in a cowboy hat and faded jeans, weathered in the face, he was as about as Santa Fean as they came. Rose tried to imagine what amount Californians would pay him for handling these utterly docile animals. Probably enough to cover his winter rent, keep him in beans and rice until spring. In the end the photo would go on some fundrais-ing poster for a soirée to which only important people would be invited. Mami would make an entrance late in the evening, leading one of the dogs, looking so gorgeous that she would touch everyone's hearts, and their wallets would fall right open.

The waiter arrived, and Lily begged for chips as he set down their second drinks. "I have hypoglycemia," she told him.

"Really. Can you spell that?" he said as he turned away.

"That was friendly." Lily rested her face on her arms, spread out on the table in front of her. "Maybe we should go back to the ranch."

"We just got here. What about my free dinner?"

Lily pulled her cell phone from her purse. "I'll phone Pasquale's."

"If they don't have any reservations, we could always eat at the communal table."

The rum appeared to be having its effects on Lily, who pushed away her second drink. "By then I'll have sobered up."

"It's pretty hard to get a table at Pasquale's unless you know God," the waiter offered, setting a teacup-size bowl of tricolored tortilla chips down on the table. The salsa container he placed alongside it reminded Rose of Amanda's old doll dishes. It couldn't have held more than two tablespoons. "Harry's Roadhouse. Down toward Lamy. Half the price and twice the atmosphere. Interested?"

He spoke to Lily alone, as if Rose were her imaginary friend.

Lily gave him double-stink eyes, cold enough to stop his heart. "Wait a second. I was *invisible* for the last ten minutes while I was desperately trying to get your attention, I was too stupid to spell a valid medical condition, and now you want me to go to dinner with you? I'm confused. I thought you were here to serve, not annoy. FYI, pal, I am not *remotely* interested in anything you have to show me except a few more chips than this."

The way he studied Lily, it crossed Rose's mind that the waiter could be a writer. Frequently they bothered people just to catalog their reactions. It seemed you couldn't throw a rock in Santa Fe without hitting one. They worked the galleries, bussed tables, or gave massages while they waited to be discovered, and resented every customer who walked in the door. Of course, to be fair, that pretty much described artists, too.

He pocketed his order pad and smiled. "So, do we have a date?"

"In your dreams." Lily dunked a twenty-dollar bill into the dregs of her drink. She took Rose by the hand and led her toward the elevator. "This town has definitely changed."

"I warned you."

The drinks, the chips, plus tax—Rose figured Lily had stiffed the waiter for at least three dollars of the tab, not to mention leaving no tip. Embarrassment factor aside, she thought her sister had behaved like a hero. She was smiling when the elevator let them off in the hotel lobby, immune to the flash of the tourists' cameras angling for a shot of the O'Keeffe painting next to the registration desk. More than anything, it resembled a slice of burned toast. Rose could look at that any time she wanted in her own kitchen. "Okay, Lily. You said you wanted to go shopping. I know just the place to spend your money."

The narrow streets off the plaza sloped down toward Water Street. On various corners shrubs of pale green native sage gave off a faint perfume. It was a lovely fall day, warm enough for sunscreen and a hat. The sisters blended in with the constant swarm of visitors. "If we run into Mami, we run into Mami," Rose said. "Let's just not sweat it."

She waved hello to various shopkeepers she knew, and made Lily stop in front of the Raven Gallery window display so she could look at the new Kit Carson jewelry display. His silver work had ushered in the "new" New Mexican trend—zoot-suited coyotes, Grateful Dead guitar-playing skeletons, cacti studded with coral where the blossoms should be. "Oh, look at those," Rose said, pointing to earrings featuring a coffee cup with two gold beans dangling beneath.

"Buy them," Lily urged her.

Rose laughed as she pulled her sister away. "Sure. Right after I win the lottery."

At Chelsea Court she opened the door expecting to give Lily a thrill, because Ginny, who ran the place, sometimes brought Rio, her red Queensland heeler to work with her, along with the greyhound she'd adopted from Mami. Ginny's clothing line was distinctly non–Santa Fe, so tailored it reeked of class. Her stock was upscale but not entirely unaffordable. On a shelf in her closet Rose had a black cashmere sweater from this store that was five years old and still looked as nice as the day she'd bought it—on sale. Ginny hugged Rose and said hello. "It would have to be the one day I leave Rio at home," she apologized.

"That's all right." She introduced her sister, and the two women talked heeler stories for a few minutes.

Behind them a customer was flipping angrily through the racks, her arm full of things to try on. Rose was wondering what had upset her when she realized that the customer was Leah Donavan. Rose studied her beautiful, bored face and tried to imagine Austin kissing it.

While Ginny rang up a customer's purchases, Rose touched Lily's arm and whispered, "That's her."

"Who?"

"The ex he can't get over."

Lily walked over, stood alongside Leah, and began collecting her own assemblage of try-ons. Periodically she turned to Rose and flashed a wicked smile.

Don't you dare, Rose mentally begged her. She wished she'd called out to Mami, because surely that would be easier to endure than whatever Lily was up to. When her sister ducked into the fitting room, Rose saw two choices before her: She could sit on the couch and wait for Lily to come out and model or more likely make a scene, or she could walk over to Leah Donavan and say hello first. Fueled by her rum and Coke, she opted for the latter.

It was easy to see why Austin couldn't forget her. Some women were put together better than others—finely boned in the face, elegant hands with tapering fingers, legs so long regular pants had to be let down to touch their ankles. *The rest of us console ourselves by being good cooks,* Rose thought. "Leah?" she said, and extended her hand. "Rose Flynn. I wonder if you remember me? I work for Austin."

Leah's anger dissipated, replaced by a brief, automatic smile. "Oh. You're the girl who does the books, right?"

Rose nodded. *I am that forty-year-old girl, indeed.* "That's a lovely jacket," she said, pointing to a hanger Leah was holding. On it hung a sage green silk blazer studded along the lapels with bugle beads. "It almost looks like an antique. Ginny finds such unique things."

Leah held it up, reconsidering. "I was thinking of putting it back."

"It seems perfect for you."

"Yes, but Austin hates this color on me." Leah set down her armful of clothes on a sale table and slid the jacket on. She stood in front of the three-way mirror and looked at herself, carefully assessing the angles. Rose knew before she'd tried the jacket on that it would look good, but Leah's dark hair, her olive skin, even her burgundy nail polish complemented the jacket as if it had been designed for her. It fell to mid-thigh and made her blue jeans look formal.

"Austin's wrong," Rose said, and meant it.

Leah buttoned the jacket, looked over at Rose, and this time her smile was genuine. "Ginny," she called out. "Put this on my account. Hold all the other stuff for me, will you? I'll be back."

Then she was gone, wearing the jacket as if it had belonged to her for years. The shop door's old-fashioned bell tinkled as she pulled it shut. Lily tapped Rose's shoulder. She was dressed in the very same jacket, and all it did was make her look short and slightly anemic. "Ginny," she whispered mockingly to her sister, "hold the earth for me, will you?"

"Like poking fun at her's going to accomplish anything."

"Hey, at least I wasn't telling her how great she looked."

"She did look great. Why should I lie?"

"Oh, Rose," Lily said. "You're so naive. I've half a mind to force you into buying those earrings."

"Sure. Then next month when my mortgage payment's due, I'll seal them in an envelope and send them to the bank. I'm sure they'll love that."

Their next stop was LewAllen and LewAllen, where Lily pored over the jewelry cases while Rose read a pamphlet on custom-designed silver charms. Her eye was immediately drawn to one called "Homespace," which featured a tiny adobe compound carved into the cylinder-shaped bead. "We all need a Sacred Homespace," the copy read, "a place to rest our weary souls." "Stand Up and Look Over the River," was the name of another, which basically translated to, "Lift your head out of the sand, you dodo." Amanda would choose that charm, Rose knew. In all endeavors, including theft, her daughter looked forward. Lily didn't believe Amanda had taken the money. What Lily knew about motherhood could fit in the Bell Tower Bar's salsa dish.

Lily smoothed a length of variegated purple rock climber's rope across the counter. On each end were S-shaped silver clasps, which could be removed to slide charms like the ones Rose was admiring over the rope. From a box with tiny separate compartments, Lily selected letters to spell out Buddy Guy. Each charm cost ten dollars. Lily said, "Plus I want a dog bone charm on either side and a couple of those ones with hunks of turquoise, too, separating his names. A dog that has never let me down deserves this collar."

"Absolutely," the clerk agreed.

Over the store's piped-in music came that song Rose always switched off when she heard it on her car radio. She didn't know the title, and she didn't care to, but the girl who sang it was named Jewel, just like Austin's horse. In a voice that sounded husky from crying, the singer tried to explain to a man who didn't want her that they were meant for each other, that their being together was larger than trying to stay apart. Standing alone at the store's window just now, and plenty of other times, say five miles from anywhere riding Max, deep in her marrow Rose felt drawn to Austin Donavan exactly that way. It was as if an invisible hand had been placed against each of their necks and were slowly guiding them one toward the other, toward the never-ending near misses. Mami insisted that God had a plan for every single person, and that occasionally he erased and penciled in new events, but that most of them were written in that really soft black pencil that smudged to unreadability if you tried to change your answer. Rose couldn't believe that Philip's death had been part of a larger plan. They'd married when she was eighteen. After twenty years and two kids together, God needed him back? If a person looked hard enough, reminders of inevitability were everywhere, even in these foolish silver charms.

All that belly-warming rum and Coke began to turn on her. Rose knew she'd better sit down, or better yet, breathe some fresh air. Maybe what Paloma had been warning her all along would happen had happened. But she couldn't fall in love with a drunken vet who would never love her back. That was downright stupid.

The final figure on Lily's invoice horrified Rose, who couldn't imagine spending that much money on a necklace for herself, let alone a dog. "I'm going to duck into the cathedral for a minute," she said.

Her sister sighed impatiently.

Rose pointed her finger. "Don't go making that noise at me. Nobody asked you to come along. I can light a candle all by myself."

"I just don't get it. What has God ever done for you, especially recently? Your husband croaked, your kids are all screwed up."

Rose knew Lily was right about her children, but it still stung to hear anyone talk like that. "I can't explain faith to someone who doesn't have it. Either you feel the presence of God or you don't."

Lily tucked her receipt into her purse and waited for the clerk to box up the dog collar. "You're not getting me inside a church."

"Nobody asked you. I'll meet you outside in half an hour."

A wave of calm cloaked her shoulders as she shut the door behind her. She closed her eyes and inhaled the reassuring bouquet of incense, beeswax, and history. Commingled with all of that, and impossible to isolate, was the scent of human beings rendered humble enough to kneel and ask for guidance. By the etched windows at the south side of the church she dipped her fingertips into the holy water font and crossed herself. Philip's memorial service had been held in a mortuary. Floralee's church was small, nothing as fancy as the cathedral, but Philip wasn't Catholic, and Rose knew that any formal religious fussing would have made him angry. As soon as Shep dug the grave, Philip was buried on her father's property, adjacent to Grandpop and Grandma. You could do that in parts of New Mexico, just dig a hole and throw your relatives in. Afterward Mami held a reception—coffee and biscuits was all Rose could remember. It seemed that everyone in town showed up to tell her they were sorry. When their friends and coworkers shook her hand, Rose could see in their eyes just how relieved they were it had happened to her and not to them. In all the shock Rose still couldn't comprehend why he'd ended up in Taos when he said he was going to Colorado.

She opened her purse and took her olivewood rosary out of its cloth drawstring bag. Rubbing the crucifix between her thumb and forefinger, she thought of her children, her father, her mother, her sister, and then Austin, Paloma, and all the animals and people she'd loved in her life, past and present. She asked for enough water to go around so that people and animals wouldn't go thirsty, and the trees, grasses, and perfumy sagebrush would continue to thrive. She knew it was selfish hoping for the Bronco to endure another winter but sent her appeal up anyway. She bent her neck so that her forehead touched her fingers, interwoven with the beads, and recited the rosary beginning with the Our Father, then three Hail Marys, another Our Father, followed by ten Hail Marys. Then she said the Glory Be, and her favorite, Hail Holy Queen. It wasn't a by-the-book recitation, but she was pretty sure God didn't mind. She kissed both sides of her crucifix and sat back in the wooden pew. The cathedral was named for Saint Francis of Assisi, who had embraced lepers, lived in poverty, and made peace treaties with wolves. The lives of the saints made every option seem unlimited. The realm of possibility was boundless. Rose felt that her own life had come to a place where *many* things were possible, but day by day those options narrowed.

To the left of the main altar was a nave bearing a carved wooden gilt *retablo*. Above the crucifix stood a statue of the Virgin. Rose left the pew and wandered over, knelt by the bank of votive candles burning in glass cups nestled inside an iron frame. Only a few were lit, their wicks flickering low in the shallow pools of wax. She stuffed a dollar in the collection box and lit four candles. She made the sign of the cross, then left the church to meet her sister, passing by the confessional, a part of the Catholic religion she had jettisoned along with the church's absurdly out-of-date views on birth control. Here they were letting all manner of divorced people annul marriages with children, and they couldn't accept condoms or the pill. Maybe the pope needed that silver charm, "Stand Up and Look Over the River."

Lily stood outside the church in the shade of a tree. She tapped her foot while she talked on her cell phone. "Because I don't want to drive all that way. Why can't you just rent a car? Hold on a second." She held her palm over the mouthpiece. "It's Pop. He wants us to come pick him up at the Albuquerque airport. How am I supposed to fit his luggage in my Lexus? Tie it on the roof? Plus I'm still a little buzzed from those drinks."

Rose took the phone from her sister. She could hear the weird background static that meant Pop was calling from an airplane. "Lily has a point, Pop."

"Listen to me, Rose Ann. This has been a long couple of weeks, I'm tired, and I don't relish arguing over a one-way rental with those brainless counter folk at Avis. Besides, seeing you two in the car together is a sight I cannot miss. Come on down here and fetch your old man. He'll spring for a steak dinner at the establishment of your choice." He told her the flight number and then said adios.

Rose handed the phone back to Lily. "Let me drive. I'm sober."

Lily tossed her the keys.

Passing through town and leaving behind the crowds and traffic, Rose was shocked at how responsive the Lexus was compared to her Bronco. She set the cruise control. At the freeway exit for the town of La

Cienega, she could keep quiet no longer and fronted her question with a request. "Don't be a smart aleck and don't tease me, okay? Just tell me what you thought of her. Your basic impression. That's all I want to know."

Lily had her bare feet planted on the dashboard. She was admiring Buddy's collar, which she'd looped around her wrist several times, turning it various ways so the silver caught the sunlight. It positively shimmered. "The ex-wife? Your basic supermodel material, unfortunately. Who gives a damn if they're divorced?"

"Austin must," Rose said. "At least once a month they tangle, after which he falls down drunk."

Lily yawned. She looked out the window, then back at her sister. "There's no point in wasting your time until he's finished with her. Trust me, Rose, I know from experience. She looks great in clothes, but is there a brain in her head?"

"Probably. Austin would never marry a stupid woman. He reads all this literature and stuff."

"Renaissance men," Lily said, "are the most difficult breed."

They drove along for several miles, not speaking. Lily offered a PR bar to Rose, who declined. Lily ate the bar herself and threw the wrapper in the backseat. She shut her eyes. The nearer they got to Albuquerque, the more prominent the red dirt and rocks became, until the sparse trees and green brush nearly disappeared. Rose thought of the time she and Philip had camped high up in the mountains without the kids. Amanda was enrolled in a summer horseback-riding program that had cost more than Rose thought they could afford; Second Chance, eager to earn money, was working on her father's ranch. Rose sat alongside her husband while he fished a stream that in the middle of summer still ran icy from snowmelt. She recalled listening to the wind move through the trees, not motivated enough to read the book she'd packed. At night she pan-fried Philip's catch rolled in bread crumbs and butter, assembled a salad from greens she'd brought to the campsite inside a cooler. She'd convinced herself that one of the best things about a long-term marriage was a couple's ability to spend long, quiet hours together without asking each other a million questions. They'd stayed out three days, time enough to recharge Philip's batteries before he left on another weeklong sales jaunt. In her mind's eye, Rose visualized the starkness of her husband's profile by the light of their campfire. Philip rarely shaved when they were camping, so his chin was grizzled with whiskers. He looked stern, but she was sure he had been thinking of nothing more complex than which bait had proved itself useful. Had she the luxury of living that moment over again, she would have pushed her shoulder into the quiet, forcing the night to move in a different direction. Instead of being satisfied with the companionable crackle of the fire and basking in the stars of the night sky, Rose would have asked her husband straight out to tell her what was in his heart. She wouldn't have let him rest that night until he told her. Then, at that moment, she had been so sure she knew him. Now, years later, she only knew for certain that she had been terribly mistaken.

"I'll tell you one thing about Philip," Rose said to her sister.

"What's that?"

"To him, smart never mattered. What he really found threatening was imagination."

"Imagination? What makes you think that?"

Rose took one hand from the steering wheel and bit her thumbnail, considering. Lily thought things out before she spoke. Too often the truth came bubbling up from Rose's gut, and after she'd spoken she had to analyze what she'd said in order to understand it. "I don't know, except that I know it's true. Do you mind if I open the sunroof? I never drove a car with a sunroof."

Lily pressed the button, and the panel retracted. A warm breeze above them blew lightly through their hair. "Did you love him, Rose?"

"Of course I did."

"Did he love you back?"

They were near enough to the airport now that Rose took the car off cruise control. When her foot hit the gas pedal, the car lurched forward. "He married me."

"You didn't answer my question."

"Well, do you think Tres felt as strongly about you as you did about him, way back when?"

Lily pressed the button for the CD player. Lyle Lovett's "Good-bye to Carolina" boomed out of the speakers. "I love everything about that song," Lily said, "except for the part about leaving the puppies behind. A woman singer would never let a lyric like that go by without rewriting it so it had a happier ending."

Rose set her turn signal indicator for the airport exit. Read between the lines, and the answer to both questions was exactly the same.

"Rose," Lily said, when her sister pulled into a parking space. "I have to ask you something. Did you and Philip ever socialize with the vet and his wife when they were still a couple?"

"Floralee isn't exactly a metropolis. Between church functions, Mami's parties, sure, I guess we bumped into each other from time to time. Leah's father was one of Philip's customers. He sold him saw blades and adhesives for their furniture shops. They have one in Taos now, as well as Santa Fe."

Lily's face hadn't changed expression. She fastened Buddy's new collar around her neck and admired herself in the rearview mirror. She pressed no further, but Rose had an uneasy feeling that her answer had only given Lily more questions.

The rating of men in airports was a Wilder woman tradition. Both Lily and Rose had spent considerable time in this terminal, waiting for Pop to come in from horse country. Sometimes it was Virginia, other times Kentucky, but more often than not it was Texas. He had a special fondness for a breeder down in Austin, and had bought several mares from him over the years. One time he had flown home with a horse in tow. They had to meet a cargo plane, then calm the animal enough so they could trailer it home. Pop took the wheel and Lily rode shotgun. Rose was ready with the syringe of sedative in case the already anxious horse got antsy. After that nerve-racking ride, Pop had settled for ground transport, even though it meant waiting the better part of a week, and patience wasn't his long suit.

In the terminal's leather seats, the sisters slouched and read the *Cosmo* they bought, quizzing each other on "How Sexy Are You?" or "Fifteen Ways to Drive Your Man Wild in Bed." Lily read their horoscopes aloud. Despite her outwardly calm demeanor, Rose was an Aries, fiery at the marrow. Lily was a Leo, the fiercest of cats, and it was true that if you fought with her, she left marks. October promised to be memorable for them both. Then, bored with printed matter, like so many times in the past, they took to watching men. Over the years this male-gazing had led organically to the rating of them.

They tracked a man in an off-the-rack business suit with a red striped tie strangling his pale, slightly double-chinned neck. He carried a brown leather briefcase, a notebook computer, and, under one arm, *USA Today*. On his feet he wore those incredibly expensive walking shoes, and he was eating a Big Mac as he made his way from one gate to another. "Could be generous in bed," Rose said, beginning the game. "Since his feet don't hurt."

"Ha. Could also mean incipient bunions," Lily countered. "Plus, way ugly suit. He's what, fifty? By that age, every man should be able to afford one really nice Brooks Brothers, or if he has an ounce of class, a DKNY or even an Armani. I think he's cheap. The shoes were a gift from his wife. She thought they might loosen him up, make him amenable to trying new sexual positions, but no such luck."

"Maybe he saves his money for his wife. Buys her really nice negligees and jewelry instead of suits that no matter whose label you stitch on them essentially all look the same. Why buy a good suit if he got this far without it? He's ten years from retirement. He wants to spend his money on their mountain cabin. He put a whirlpool tub in the bathroom like she always wanted."

Lily sighed. "Rose. Did you *look* at this guy? He's carrying a newspaper you can read cover to cover before you finish half a Big Mac. He's dull and couldn't find a clitoris with a compass."

Rose laughed, even though she thought Lily could have said something besides clitoris and still made her point. They turned their attention to an Indian guy coming down the jetway. Early forties, maybe, though it was hard to tell because he had such terrific skin. He was dressed in a tight, faded blue T-shirt that showed off his pecs. He wore Wranglers the color of lake water, and expensive snakeskin cowboy boots. Over his shoulder he carried a round cardboard tube with a makeshift handle attached to either end, and on top of his waist-length braids sat a black felt cowboy hat with a cattleman's crease.

"Be still my heart," Lily said. "Whatever is inside that tube is worth money. He's coming to Santa Fe to chat up a gallery owner or drop off new work. Nicely worn clothing, totally casual, which indicates a level of comfort and self-assuredness."

"No suit," Rose chided.

"He's got it in his carry-on should he need it. And if the gallery owner doesn't like his stuff, five other places are dying to show him. And as I know from vast experience, and my sister only from hearing secondhand, this is definitely a man to invite to eat crackers in your bed. Nothing fancy, but you'll go to sleep with a smile on your face. Let's ditch Pop and introduce ourselves."

"You're the one who needs glasses," Rose said. "The hat is straight off the rack, and the crease is embarrassing. But I can forgive him the hat if only for the boots. They're Lucchese, Lily. He knows where a girl's magic button is. It's the first thing he looks for. And he knows all those Indian tricks like the Kickapoo twist and so forth. If I were in the market, that's the style I'd pick."

Lily sat up straight in her chair, giving her sister a shocked look. "Rose Ann!"

"What? Because I got widowed I'm not allowed to think about sex?"

"It's just that I'm so impressed. So I know it wasn't a fluke, do that guy." She pointed toward a medium-tall, skinny man of about fifty. He was graying at the temples and carried a leather backpack. He wore little wire-rimmed glasses, a nondescript flannel shirt rolled up to the elbows, Levi's jeans, and Birkenstock sandals with red socks. Trade in the sandals for Dan Posts and he could have passed for Austin's brother.

"Well," Rose said, her eyes tracking the man as he stopped to buy some tea, not coffee, from the cart vendor who was making a killing since airlines never stocked anything but icky Lipton's. "Here we have a man who is far too intelligent for whatever crappy job he does to make a living. He's so overeducated he's still paying off student loans. Divorced, I bet."

"Why?"

"Again, the shoes. He thinks they make him look hip. They remind him of college, when girls asked *him* to go to bed if he so much as looked twice at them. He lives on frozen dinners and nine-grain bread he buys at Wild Oats. He has two daughters, a single one he worries won't settle down and one who married wealthy, to a guy that makes more money than he does." She stopped.

"Jeez, I didn't ask for a biography," Lily said. "What's he like in bed? Not my type, but he's pumping out the pheromones like sweat."

To go there wounded Rose the same way that song in the jewelry store made her want to switch off the radio. To imagine this man with the red socks in her bed blew out every candle she'd lit, erased the prayers she'd whispered in church. What the hell, why not say out loud what vexed her dreams and occupied too many of her waking hours? "It would be difficult to get that man into your bed, Lily. He has some overblown idea that he's a romantic, that there have to be hearts and flowers before so much as one button comes undone. The art of the chase is what he lives for. He treats a woman like his own personal yo-yo. This man would put you through all kinds of tests before turning down the top sheet. He'd make you say 'I love you' first. He'd let you sweat a couple weeks before saying it back, that is, *if* he ever got around to saying it. He's still furious that his wife left him, *and* he resents Mommy for whatever she failed to do for him. The reins are in his fist, and he'd let the bit slice your tongue in half before he'd give you an inch."

"Whoa." Lily fanned herself with somebody's leftover *Albuquerque Journal*. Her lips came up in a smirk, giving her cheekbones just the faintest hint of blush. "My, my," she said. "I'm coming by your work tomorrow to take you to lunch. I have to meet this veterinarian who has infected you with heartworm."

Before Rose could say, *You will not*, Pop was there, grinning around his pipe stem, his arms full of flowers. "My girls," he said, as if they were still teenagers, kissing them each one on the cheek. He was carrying three bouquets, yellow roses—always available in Texas—tiger lilies, and a nosegay of coral poppies, their petals deceptively frail.

8

The Rose Tattoo

From the passenger's-side floor their father picked up a FedEx box that had gotten wedged between the console and the seat. A McDonald's wrapper stuck to its edge. He rattled the box as if it were a Christmas gift. "Anything important in here?"

Lily grabbed it and peeled away the wrapper. "Only about five thousand dollars' worth of laparoscopic instruments."

"If they're so all-fired expensive, maybe you should lock them in the trunk."

"You know what, Pop? I haven't lost any of the company's products so far, so why don't you quit worrying about it?"

"There's enough trash in her backseat to choke a landfill," Pop said, handing Lily his carry-on bag. "Your sister have a policy against throwing things away?"

Rose was just standing there by the car, her hands full of flowers. She set them down on the hood and raked up empty cups and a few Styrofoam salad containers into an empty shopping bag. "There. Now it's clean. Pop, you sit down and *cállate*, or I swear we'll drop you off at the bus station."

Whoever had peed in his morning Cheerios had done a thorough job of it. Lily wondered if that someone was Mami. They weren't even out of the parking lot, and already Lily wanted to charge him for the ride. She strapped herself into the driver's seat and started the car. "Rose, where did you put that parking receipt?"

"On the dash."

Lily held the ticket between her teeth while she maneuvered into the long line of cars waiting to pay so they could exit the airport. It was rush hour, the congestion typical for California driving conditions, but seeing the endless pairs of brake lights ahead of her in Albuquerque pissed Lily off.

In the backseat, Lily heard the sound of Rose carefully wrapping the flowers in an old newspaper. "I hope these last until we get home," she said.

Lily, growing increasingly weary of creeping along in the traffic at fifteen miles an hour, hoped the flowers were edible. Ten miles later she'd had it. "I vote we stop for dinner and let this thin out."

"There's that Australian restaurant that serves kangaroo and ostrich," Pop offered.

Rose groaned. "Does every meal out with you and Mami have to be an adventure in courage? How about someplace ordinary?"

Pop turned so he could look at Rose in the backseat. "Courage. Now that's an area you could work on, Rose Ann."

Lily checked the rearview mirror. The embarrassment in Rose's face made Lily want to slap her father. "Pop?" she said. "Isn't Mami the one we should be consulting about living the bold life?"

Her father clamped his teeth down on his pipe stem. "Sass from the daughter who can't buy an American automobile to support our failing economy is just what I need to round out my day."

"Hey. I support the snot out of America by paying way too much in taxes. When somebody American designs a car that isn't as ugly as sin and has the features of this one, I'll be first in line to buy it." She checked the rearview mirror again, and winked when she saw her sister looking back.

Just past the upscale community of Rio Rancho, Rose said, "By the way, Pop, it turns out my mare's definitely in foal. Austin says it looks like she'll deliver next summer."

"Good news. I was starting to wonder if she was barren."

"Why does everyone always blame it on the mare?" Lily asked. "Stallions shoot a blank now and then."

Pop ignored her. "Make sure to give her the proper supplements. It's a known fact that only forty to sixty percent of pregnant brood-mares deliver viable foals. The high rate of miscarriage and still birth is largely due to protein, vitamin and mineral allotments, plus the necessary vaccines. I can't tell you how many sad stories I've heard that didn't have to happen."

"Well," Rose said. "I guess that shouldn't be a problem, since I moved Winky up to your ranch."

"You're going to dump her on Shep?"

"Of course not, Pop. I'm entrusting her to *you*." She paused, and Lily savored the expression on her father's face. It wasn't often either of them could render him speechless. "Of course," her sister continued, "I'll pay for her feed and vet care. And drive up every weekend to do my part."

Chance Wilder was a proud man, and the offer of Rose's money left him chagrined. But he had held the door wide open. He absolutely deserved everything she'd said. *Good for you, Rose,* Lily thought. *Smack them in the crotch with your lunchpail once in awhile.*

Finally he said, "That sounds like a sensible plan. We can work the money issues out later."

Rose unbuckled her seat belt, leaned forward, and kissed him on the cheek. Lily smiled. She knew he'd die before he'd accept a dime of Rose's money. She also knew that her sister would find some way to make him take the money, even if she had to make a donation in his name to an orphaned horses fund.

"How about this place?" Lily said just south of Santa Fe, when the sign for the Wolf Creek Brewing Company appeared on their right. The place was new enough that no Wilder held an opinion, so she pulled on to the wide curving exit and parked the car behind the restaurant. It smelled good, which when you came right down to it was the sensory equivalent of a billboard. They walked inside and found a table near a window.

Pop chatted up the waitress, ordering *carne adobada* for all of them. The spicy dish was the house specialty, but after a few exploratory pokes into the meat with her fork, Lily stuffed the complimentary tortillas with her vegetables and dipped the makeshift burrito into salsa. They talked about her father's new mare, a dark bay whose paper name was Dulcinea's Bailador. "This might be the last horse I buy for awhile," he said, tearing a tortilla in half before smearing it with butter.

"Why?" Lily asked. "Is business slow?"

"No more than usual, but Shep's making noises about retiring. I don't want to haul in somebody new just yet. Rancho Costa Plente can afford a slow season while he makes up his mind."

"I'd be glad to help out," Rose said.

Her father patted her hand. "And I'll call you if I need you."

Rose had sat quiet most of the meal, occasionally glancing up at her father, as if seeking the approval he generally withheld. It was as if their father spoke only to Lily, when Rose was the one with horses. Why was it that one on one, the man behaved like a complete teddy bear, but put his two daughters along either side of him and at once things turned prickly? All around them in the restaurant happy families and groups of vacationers sat enjoying themselves over various microbrews. The laughter was way up there on the decibel scale. Lily had no doubt the out-of-staters imagined that if they lived here year round, their lives would be meaningful in a way that people who were allowed to start over fresh savored, saw as a turning point, a landmark from which to chart a better life. She couldn't blame them. There was a presence here she never found in California, not even walking along the edge of the Pacific Ocean in the wintertime. There, even next to the roaring waves, she felt that the sand underfoot was constantly shifting, and all those earthquakes made her nervously anticipate the next, larger tremor to come. Here her feet dug happily into solid earth, and the sun beat down baking the adobe. Sometimes home was as simple as believing that what was under your feet would hold you. "Hire somebody part-time," Lily said. "Shep won't feel threatened. He loves ordering people around, or me, anyway."

"I'll think on it," their father said.

Which struck Lily as odd, because Chance Wilder hardly ever took time to decide anything unless he was buying a ten-thousand-dollar horse.

"Lily," he chided at the end of the meal. "You left more food on your plate than you ate."

"Can I help it if they serve portions large enough to feed a family of five?"

"You don't eat right."

"I'll take my leftovers home and feed them to Buddy."

"You spoil that animal."

"Have me arrested."

Her father reached over and lifted the edge of Buddy's collar, which Lily was still wearing around her neck. "That necklace you're wearing's a tad on the showy side, wouldn't you say?"

Lily flashed him a smile. "God, I hope so. It cost buckets of money."

Rose covered her mouth to stifle her laughter. Pop took out his wallet, picked up the check, and headed for the cashier.

"I'm sorry we didn't get to have our private dinner," Lily said.

"There's still time."

True, but Lily had imagined sitting alone with her sister in some fancy restaurant where, after a glass of halfway decent wine, Rose would spill her innermost secrets. "I know. I'm just tired."

"Me too. This has been a long day. "

"Plus I didn't get to buy any new clothes."

"Now that's what I'd call a tragedy," Pop said, returning to the table with a toothpick in the corner of his mouth. "Come along, girls. Let's go home."

It had rained while they were eating. Wide, reflective puddles filled the dips in the parking lot asphalt. The evening air smelled scrubbed clean. *One of those typical hard, brief, swift-moving rainstorms must have passed through on its way to Texas or Oklahoma,* Lily thought, *and I missed the whole thing. Damn.* Pop lit his pipe, and the cloud of aromatic smoke drifted by her, mingling nicely with the odor of recent rain. All around them the gently sloping hills were covered with grasses beginning to brown in anticipation of the coming winter. Lamentably, certainly, but inevitably, this part of Santa Fe was just beginning to be developed. Lily wondered who would settle here. New Mexico's blend of cultures imparted to each distinct community the feeling that the history of the Old West hadn't taken place all that long ago. One great thing about life in a state possessing a frontier mentality was the determined way newcomers sent down roots. Yet if smalltown hardware stores stocked men like Tres Quintero, no matter where a person traveled to in an attempt to start over, the past followed.

Rose took hold of Lily's shoulder. "You look as if you're plotting your next battle."

There it is—proof that sisters can read each other so keenly they might as well have walkie-talkies implanted in their brains, Lily thought. "I was only wondering whether it's ever possible to take a step backward and not regret it, Rose. Do you think that's asking for trouble?"

"I don't know," her sister said. "Look at us. All that time we didn't talk. What a waste."

Lily brightened. "No kidding. We can't let that happen again, even if we only stay friendly to team up on Pop."

"He's not all bad," Rose said. "Though he's in a foul mood today. You should let him drive the Lexus home. You know he's dying to."

Lily whistled, and their father, who had been walking several paces ahead of them, turned at the sound. "Catch, Pop," she said, and threw him the keys.

After Santa Fe, there were so few city lights he turned on the high beams. Lily dozed against the backseat, inhaling the gentle decay of the floral bouquets. The roses smelled the strongest, but there was a sharp undercurrent of her lilies, too. Only the poppies were scentless. Idly she listened to her father and sister's conversation.

"Well, Rose Ann. I haven't heard from my grandkids lately. How about you?"

"They call home all the time," Rose lied.

Lily understood exactly why she would do such a thing. If she could keep the remainder of her answers simple, Rose might come out of the discussion with her dignity intact.

"And how are they doing?"

"They're both fine. Probably they'll be home for the holidays."

"Second Chance winning lots of races?"

"He sure is."

Their father sighed. "He's damned athletic, but a high school diploma isn't going to make him his million. My offer still stands to pay for his schooling."

"He finished that one year of community college," Rose said. "He might decide to go back someday and get his degree. Or maybe he'll be a mechanic. If it's got a motor, he can fix it."

Wrong move. Rose was letting let Pop suck her into an argument she couldn't possibly win. *Surrender now,* Lily wanted to say. *Wave the white flag or you'll end up using it for a hankie.*

"It's been my observation that the longer someone stays away from school the more difficult it is to return."

In the short silence before Rose answered Lily felt the sting as sharply as she imagined her sister did.

"You never went to college."

"I inherited my father's business, which was a going concern."

Lily thought that comment hit below the belt, considering that all Second Chance had inherited from his father was his watch.

"And Mandy?"

"What *about* Amanda?"

"Does she have any plans?"

Lily watched her sister turn her face to the window. It was pitch dark outside. Lily would have told the old busybody to lay off. Rose could not. What bothered Lily more than his incessant poking, however, was hearing the echo of her own questions delivered only a day earlier, when the sisters were riding up into the mountains.

"Listen, Pop. Over the holidays you can talk to Amanda yourself."

"At her age you were married and a mother."

Rose's laughter came out soft, but there was a brittle edge to it Lily felt alarmed by even if her father didn't notice. "Which is a life choice I certainly would not wish on any daughter of mine."

Apparently Pop had no desire to move the discussion in that direction because he shut up. Too bad, because Lily was dying to hear his views on the subject. Rose's, too. Maybe tomorrow she would pin her down. She relaxed against the leather seats, wondering if it was Saturday or Sunday. Forgetting the date was how she knew she was truly on vacation. The remainder of the drive home she drifted in and out of sleep. Her father and sister kept their voices low, but dulcet tones didn't mask the tension.

By the time they arrived at the ranch, it was nearly midnight. Pop insisted they walk over to the barn and check on Winky. Rose held a flashlight while he felt the mare's legs and looked at her teeth. The neighboring horses began to stir at the change in routine, and pretty soon Shep came out of the bunkhouse in his flannel robe. He stood there looking at the sisters and his old friend and employer without speaking.

"Shepherd," Chance said. "Anything going on I should know about?"

The old cowboy thought a minute. He scratched his head. "Only that most people are in bed about this time, which is directly where I'm headed."

Lily laughed. "Get to the point already, you chatterbox."

Shep returned to the bunkhouse and the sisters watched the light inside his room go out.

"A man of few words, but always the right ones," Rose said.

"Oh, he's just got a wild hair because I woke him out of his beauty sleep," Chance answered. "He'll be fine tomorrow."

Rose clicked the flashlight off, and they waited a moment for their eyes to adjust to the darkness. The mare stood quietly, nosing her empty feeder. Her large eyes glistened as she regarded these humans, some familiar, others not. Rose reached out a hand and stroked her neck. As if he felt her fingers, too, from a few stalls away Max neighed. The sound of a dozen questioning nickers erupted, and the complex smells of feed, various liniments, saddle leather, and tack oil made the entire scene so intoxicating to Lily she wanted to pitch her tent right there.

"Listen to the horses," she whispered. "It's like this perfect small town where everybody knows everybody else. Jeez, what I wouldn't give to grow a mane and tail and register to vote."

"I swear, the damnedest things come out of that mouth of yours," Pop remarked.

Lily kicked at the hard-packed dirt. "Oh, poop. I just say what I feel."

"Which is why you're always on the verge of getting into trouble."

"Safe's boring," Lily said.

"Rose, did you notice how that sister of yours always has to get in the last word?"

"Of course she did," Lily snapped.

The three Wilders walked toward the puddle of yellow light illuminating the porch swing. In Lily's temporary sleeping berth, Chachi had made his bed in the discarded sleeping bag. The Jack Russell roused enough to wag his tail. A few of the ranch dogs came out of their sleeping places and tagged along for awhile, grumbling at Chachi, then returned to the barn. Buddy was inside the screen door, whimpering and begging for a million neck scratches to make up for how long Lily'd been gone. Lily opened the door, bent down, and fastened the new collar around his neck. "Buddy boy baby," she said. "Don't you look handsome?"

"For God's sake," her father said. "It's even uglier on him that it was on you."

Lily covered Buddy's ears. "Don't listen to that cranky old man."

Rose, still on the porch, turned in the direction of her car. "Thanks for dinner, Pop. I have to be at work in the morning, so I'll take off now."

"That's insane," Lily said. "It's too late to go. Catch Monday flu and we'll go riding again."

Rose shook her head. "Can't. If I'm not there, the bills won't go out."

"Then sleep here, get up early, and go to work in your jeans. It's not like you have to impress the CEO."

"Really," Rose said, stifling a yawn. "I'm not that tired."

Lily pulled her inside and aimed her toward the stairs. "You're not awake enough to drag a horse trailer two inches, let alone fifteen miles. We'll see you in the morning. Hey, something to look forward to: I'll let you fold the breakfast napkins."

Rose glared at her, but she went up to bed.

Downstairs in the Great Room, Pop had set a fresh pot of coffee and two mugs on the pine table. He'd changed into his pajamas and robe. Lily had put on her sleep shirt (a red-and-black flannel of his), and added a pair of his socks, too. "Nice shirt," he said when she walked into the room.

She modeled for him. "It's not Ralph Lauren, but it's comfy."

Pop closed the screen in front of the stone fireplace, where the logs burned steadily and would continue to do so for a couple of hours. He lit his pipe, and the sweet odor of burning tobacco filled the room. As Lily collapsed on the couch, Buddy jumped up beside her.

"Animals don't go on the furniture," Pop said, sitting down beside her.

"They do where I live," Lily answered. "I should have made you rent a car. I'm whipped."

Pop leaned forward, took hold of Buddy's right rear foot, lifted it, and peered underneath. "Your dog lose something in a fight?"

"Trust me, his neutering needed to happen."

He poured himself a mug of coffee, added cream, and leaned back against the cushions. "Talk to me, daughter."

"Why should I? You're not very nice to my sister."

"Sometimes Rose needs a little push."

"Half the time all she really needs is a hug."

"I'm not the hugging type."

"You used to be."

"You're both all grown up. Go find boys to hug you."

"Rose could be sixty years old, and she'd still be your daughter needing reassurance."

He fingered the fancy charms on Buddy's collar. "Philip dying was a shock, but you and I both know that marriage wasn't the love match of the century. Is it a crime for me to want to see her move on?"

"Of course not. I want that, too. Just don't be a prick to her, okay?"

"I'm not, whatever that's supposed to mean."

Lily sighed. "Yes, you are. I don't think you realize the state Rose is in. Amanda stealing her grocery money, does anybody even *know* where Second Chance is, I mean, in case of an accident? She prays all the time, lights candles like they're going to blaze a path that will show her the way out. It's scary."

"Amanda stole money?" Her father sipped his coffee and scratched Buddy's ears while the dog panted happily. "Those two never had to work a lemonade stand or wash cars for pocket money. I bought them horses and motorbikes, even when Rose asked me not to."

Lily kept quiet, hoping he'd go on, and in a few minutes he did, picking up the conversation as if there had never been a lull.

"You know, Philip and I went more than a few rounds before the accident took his life. I never entirely trusted that man, but Rose Ann loved him, and I wanted her to be happy."

"I didn't trust him either. She's got a mammoth crush on that vet she works for."

"Saw that one coming a long time back. When it comes to men, Rose picks them the same way your mother did."

"What's that supposed to mean?"

Her father mimed tipping a bottle to his lips.

Lily pulled a throw pillow over her face. Pop's drinking problems were little more than stories to her. Though he'd been sober since she was nearly ten years old—almost twenty-five years—Lily had pushed the memories of the time he was not from her mind. On Sundays Mami went to mass and Pop to his AA meeting. When her mother drank wine from a long-stemmed goblet at dinner, her father's glass was filled with water. The way things were delivered enough information for her. She breathed deep into the pillow until the scent of her mother's hand lotion embedded in the fabric made her pull it away from her face. "The best thing for my sister would be a senseless affair.

It's like candy for the heart. Short, sweet, and makes you believe in yourself again."

Pop set his pipe down in a granite ashtray. "When your mother stepped out on me, I like to've died from that particular brand of candy."

Lily set the pillow down. "Oh, Pop. I'm sorry. You know I didn't mean it that way."

"Happened a long time ago. Don't worry about it. I've made my peace."

"Well," she said and paused. "Since you brought it up, how *did* you forgive Mami? I mean, she didn't exactly try to hide what she did."

"Had to. For years I had my arms around a mistress, only mine took the shape of a bottle."

Lily recalled vague snatches of overheard conversations, her father's bellowing voice reaching her all the way through her closed bedroom door, under that pillow, too. Her mother's voice, sometimes tearful, sometimes rising in pitch into Spanish, and the tense family breakfasts that followed. "Just like that? You forgave her?"

"What would you recommend?" he said quietly. "That after twenty-some years of marriage, I was supposed to send packing the only woman on earth who still manages to fascinate me? When a man loves a woman as strong as he is, the balance of power's always an issue. I sure as hell didn't want to live out here all alone playing cards with Shep. Besides, I wasn't always such a Boy Scout myself."

He crossed his legs and his pants leg rode up, revealing the rose tattoo on his ankle. Numerous times when she was a child, Lily had rubbed it with her thumb, as if the faded red and green ink might erase with her efforts. "Please, please, please," she whispered, begging for the story behind the indelible emblem. Over the years he'd told her various segments, but the intriguing parts had never quite added up to a satisfying whole.

"I woke up one morning in some old lady's dirt garden in Mexico," her father said wearily. "First thing I saw was a shotgun in my face. She had been cultivating what appeared to be a right sturdy crop of carrots up until the time I landed there. Anyway, she dog-cussed me in nasty-enough Spanish that I was motivated to move along. As I was crawling my way down the road toward civilization, my leg began itching, and when I stopped to look it over I noticed this rose on my ankle. In due time it became clear that I had a good case of the clap on my equipment, too. No memory of how I acquired either traveling companion. One stayed with me until I saw a doctor, the other has been with me for life."

Lily's found her father's mysterious past continually amusing. "Wilder legends," she said. "They're endlessly versatile. What's the lesson for me this time?"

"I don't know. How about, 'One way or another, whatever you do in the pursuit of love leaves its mark on you'?"

"Ha. You don't have to tell me that." Lily wondered where Tres Quintero was at this particularly witchy hour of the night. Blaise, she knew, would be whooping it up in one bar or another. Her reputation was going to suffer if she spent many more nights like this one, deep in conversation with Daddy. "I've tried to talk to Rose about Philip, I mean, about what he was really like, but she doesn't want to hear it."

"Which is why I'm always nudging her, only you call it being a prick. Get Rose mad about one thing, she generally goes to fixing whatever's wrong elsewhere. I'm hoping that will hold true where the vet's concerned."

"Pop, you don't understand. Rose still believes in *love* love. Fairy-tale endings, Hollywood movie happiness. Fidelity, romance, crap that can never come true."

He cocked his head and studied her. "Little Bit, have you listened to a word I've said tonight?"

Lily sighed. "Look at me, Pop. I mean take a good long look. I'm not so ugly that I crack mirrors, am I?"

"You're the spitting image of your mother thirty years ago. Sometimes I see you out of the corner of my eye, and I have to stop and remind myself what year it is."

"If I'm so damn pretty, why have I been in the dating game twenty years? Why am I still flying solo?"

Pop set his pipe down in a glass ashtray. "You didn't want to marry that boy you loved in high school. He was your equal. You walked away from him to explore the world."

"You brought us up believing we could have everything if we wanted it bad enough and worked hard to get it."

"Didn't exactly work out like that for Rose, did it?"

"No. And I guess if I end up an old maid that's your fault, too."

He touched her cheek. "Everybody makes choices, Lily. You give up one adventure to take on another. You put yourself exactly where it is you want to be. Whatever your sister does has to come from her. She has to believe it's her idea. If you insist on worrying, worry about yourself."

Lily looked at her dog, and as if he understood the cloak she kept pulled tight around her heart, Buddy sighed, too. "I took a leave from work because I needed to see my hometown."

Her father set his mug down on the table. One of the logs made a loud pop in the fireplace. "Floralee's pretty in autumn."

Lily rubbed Buddy's ears, which were velvety soft and spotted with blue and gray hair. She hugged him close and nuzzled his face. Instead of his usual dog breath, she could detect a faint odor of cookies, which meant Buddy Guy Lock Picker had probably figured out how to open the pantry door. "You don't know what it's like out there, Pop. Sometimes I think I should quit this job and go work in a coffee shop. Nobody tells you that in order to make the big bucks you have to pay with your spirit."

"That bad?"

"Sometimes it is. And this last guy I dated? He put on a great show for a couple of months. He wowed me in bed. Then one day I woke up, and here was this cold-blooded snake lying next to me and scales all over the damn pillow. First thing I did was check my ankle for a tattoo."

Her father laughed and Lily joined him.

"Anyway, crap like that, I can handle. Not Rose."

"You're both strong, intelligent women. That puts you at somewhat of a disadvantage, but not out of the game entirely. Somewhere out there, I know it, there's a man sitting with his head in his hands, wondering where the hell our Rose Ann is, and would she please hurry up and fill his life with her down-home cooking and generous loving and her gentle way with horses. He might be Austin Donavan, or he might turn out to be somebody else. When it's time, she'll find him."

Again the fire crackled, and one of the logs slipped in the grate, sending off a shower of sparks. When they had burned out, Lily snuggled up close to her father. In time she felt his strong hand gently close around her shoulder. "I thought you didn't hug."

"Only when absolutely necessary."

Buddy woofed, and Pop thought that was pretty funny. "Are we going to talk some details about your job?"

"Pop, when I can say two words without crying, you'll be the first to know."

They sat silently looking into the fire, and for the first time in a long while, Lily felt sleepy without needing any wine.

Rose took off before any of them got up. Lily awoke to the sound of the Bronco's tires on the gravel and the horses whinnying a protest over one of their own leaving the corral. She knelt on the bed and parted the curtain so she could peer out the dormer window. Rose's old trailer was hitched up to the Bronco. Max's tail hung over the door. Rose had bound it with Vet Wrap so the long hairs wouldn't catch on anything. She'd done everything herself even though Shep or Pop would have been glad to help. Lily squinted, watching her sister's car slowly move out of her field of vision. *Well, fine, then,* she thought. *Go already. I'll catch up with you later.* She fell back into the sheets to sleep another hour. All the way down to her bones she felt tired. As she drifted off, she wondered if she was getting sick. Then it occurred to her that this was what *not* working like a crazy person did to her. It made her appreciate old, soft worn sheets from when she was a kid, and clean air coming in a window she could leave open all night and still feel safe. It made her feel all those simple but necessary pleasures that had been absent from her crowded California life, even in a bed designed to fit only one person.

Lily stood on the porch still wearing her sleep shirt, clutching her second mug of coffee, feeling completely without ambition. She couldn't get started today. In the arena Shep turned horses out to exercise. She noticed the mounting blocks in the center of the arena and pointed.

"What are those for? Are you giving riding lessons?"

He continued to move horses without looking over at her. "Little Miss Have to Know Everything."

"I asked a simple question."

"No, I'm not giving riding lessons. I'm an old man. Seems reasonable to me that at this stage of my life I can get a permanent leg-up without having to explain why to you."

Sheepskin on his saddle and having to use the mounting blocks—Shep must have been so ashamed. *Sometimes,* Lily thought, *my mouth should not be allowed out in public.* "Sorry."

"Come on over here," Shep said. "Got something I want to show you."

Lily minced her way barefooted across the gravel to the fence. She watched Shep place an old stock saddle on the ground, whistle her dog over, then praise Buddy Guy when he agreed to sit on it. He shooed the dog away, lifted the saddle to the fence, steadied it, then when he patted the seat, the dog leapt up. The blue heeler remained seated, even when Shep kicked the bottom rail of the fence and set it wobbling.

"Impressive," Lily said. "At home, if there's so much as a sonic boom, he hides under my bed."

"Hang on, I ain't done yet." Shep told the dog to get down, then moved the saddle to the swayback of Pablo, one of the oldest horses in her father's stable. Pablo was too old even to ride, but Chance had a soft spot for the last remaining horse from his father's era, so he got hand-fed and babied, and would until the day he died. Shep patted the saddle seat a second time. Buddy ran a lap around the arena, then jumped up on the saddle. Lily stood there open-mouthed. Buddy didn't know horses from hat racks, but with soothing words and a horseman's patience, Shep had somehow convinced the dog that riding Pablo was safe. "What did you feed him? Steak?"

"Didn't feed him at all. I don't cotton to bribery."

"Get out. Without bait, I can hardly get Buddy to sit."

"That's because you hold stock in the reward instead of the animal. Your dog wants to please you so bad he buys into your foolish thinking."

Foolish thinking. Lily thought of the money she'd spent on dog training and wished she'd given it to Shep instead. Every time the dog got the urge to leap off the slow-moving gelding, he looked to the old cowboy for reassurance. A barely perceptible nod was all it took, and Buddy returned to cowboying. All his life he'd been searching for a man he could trust. Of course, so had Lily. Buddy didn't intend to bite whoever she brought home, he simply wanted to protect her from those evil boys who were always wanting to jump her bones. From Buddy's point of view, orgasm probably sounded like an SOS. It had been so long since she'd had one, Lily decided, hell, maybe it *was* kind of a distress call.

While the old horseman spat tobacco juice into the dirt, Buddy calmly rode the horse around the arena. No doubt life aboard Pablo beat having the ranch dogs bare their fangs every time he walked by, not to mention the endless butt sniffing. Lily was so fond of the old horseman she couldn't imagine life without him. But doctors didn't exactly rip prostates out for the fun of it. Still, that kind of cancer had a pretty high cure rate. Surely if they hadn't got it all Pop would've told her. He was just getting old. Poor man. For as long as she'd known him, Shep had reveled in the company of ladies. He always had one or two telephoning him, and rarely spent weekends at the ranch. Lily wondered what sex must be like for him now, if he was okay with having a penis that was only good for peeing.

"I can't believe you got him to do this in three days. And he never bit you?"

"The thought never even crossed his mind."

"I wish I had my camera. Make him do one more lap, Shep."

The old man clucked and Pablo, reacting to the decades of training echoing inside his brain, picked up the pace to a jog almost slower than his walk.

Lily thought of the one time she'd seen Buddy Guy, the musician, in person, at the Long Beach Blues Festival. Up on stage, the black man's eyes were shut and his large-toothed grin open wide as he picked an electric guitar painted with polka dots to match his gaudy shirt. Buddy Guy was the link between the masters, guys like Robert Johnson and Muddy Waters, John Lee Hooker. He'd played with Hendrix. The late great Stevie Ray Vaughn had learned his licks from Buddy Guy. She loved how sometimes in the middle of a song he cussed his own playing, stopped, and started over again. *Here's how Stevie would have played it*, he'd say. Maybe he wasn't a sharecropper making history on three strings, but he was humble enough to bow to larger talent. He played his heart out. "Damn Right I've Got the Blues!" Lily had envisioned the same eagerness in Buddy the pup. He came from her father's best stock, memorable dogs like Jody Jr. and Maromero, but he wasn't going to do anything greater in his lifetime than ride this horse.

"Rides a damn sight better than that one-trick Lassie," Shep told Lily, who stood at the fence rail wiping tears from her eyes. "All he needed was to get out of that crazy state and run on real dirt. He's looking right smitten with old Pablo. Got a feeling from now on you're going to have a hard time convincing him to walk anywhere."

"I bet you're right. Shep?"

"What?"

"Rose and I saw Mami in town. Did she come home last night?"

Shep pursed his lips, shook his head no.

"Any idea why?"

He halted the horse and lifted Buddy off the gelding's back. "Go on to your mama now, Bud. I got horses to see to, fences to mend."

"Dammit all, Shep. You never tell me anything."

He looked at her over the top of the saddle. Behind them, a huge orange horse transport trailer was pulling into the driveway. In there with a dozen other animals was Pop's new mare. "I'll tell you something. Go change out of that ugly nightie and into some riding britches. Then you can help me get that new animal settled in."

Several hours later, Lily heard the whine of a twin engine plane overhead. She leaned against her rake and watched the amber and white wings of Mami's plane tilt from side to side as she squared herself for the landing. Shep shaded his eyes against the glare but said nothing. Her father stood in the open corral, watching. To Lily it felt as if their collective will and not her mother's skill brought the plane down properly on the runway at the eastern boundary of the property. When the plane was safely landed, Shep continued working Rose's mare on the longe line. Pop dipped a kerchief in the stock tank to clean some of the dirt from his face.

A few minutes later, Mami drove up in the Suburban. The vanity plates on the car read *RSQ GRYS*, and stickers of greyhounds in the back window explained the plates. Lily had finished prepping the stall the new horse would live in after it completed a week of quarantine. She hung up the rake she'd been using inside the barn. Her father brushed straw from his pants and walked over to greet his wife. Mami got out of the car, opened the rear door, and released two of the greyhounds Lily had seen her posing with in Santa Fe.

Pop let out a groan. "Somehow I thought you might change your mind."

Mami gathered their leads in her hand and stood tall. To Lily she looked as imperious as Cleopatra. "Chance, I told you they're going to California as soon as I can get their papers straightened out."

"They'd better be. First I have to give up my seat on the damn plane, next thing I know you're probably going to kick me out of bed."

Mami made a face. "*Egoísta*. You know that will never happen."

Lily recognized the root of the Spanish word her mother had used. It translated roughly to "selfish," but it didn't accurately capture her father's stance. If the plane had been a four-seater instead of a two-seater, he still might have opted for a commercial flight to avoid competing with her beloved dogs.

"Come on over here and help me with my luggage," Mami said. "And while you're at it, could you kiss me? I missed you. Aren't you glad to have me home?"

Lily marveled at how the woman could make a pair of worn-out blue jeans and a man's white shirt look like Chanel. To describe her mother as fit was to gloss over the Martínez heritage, whose strength and solidity rose from generations of roots so deeply crisscrossed they could neither be dug up nor dismissed. Even when she admitted she was wrong, Mami's resolve did not waver. She swung her long black hair over her shoulder and shone her wide smile on her husband. At once his bad mood began to dissolve. Lily observed the grateful way each moved into the other's embrace. As Pop pressed a hand to the small of her back, Lily bit her lip. All her life she had wanted a man to need her that way, to love her so much that her presence was like the sun coming up, there every morning to warm everything, waking the world from sleep, keep things growing. It struck Lily that maybe she loved people the same way her mother loved the greyhounds, preparing and feeding exquisite meals, making certain to provide top-notch vet care, but it was as if a corner of her heart seemed held in check, as if she believed every situation would turn out to be temporary.

"Hey, Mami," she said when her parents were finished kissing.

"Lily!" Her mother handed the dogs' leashes to Pop and hurried over to her daughter. They were exactly the same height. Mami was sixty-two years old and Lily was thirty-five, but of the two, Lily was the one who looked her age. Unconsciously she began to brush the cedar shavings from her sleeves. Mami placed her hands on Lily's shoulders and kissed both her cheeks. "Look at you all messy with horse dirt. I can't believe we missed each other in Santa Fe."

So they were busted. Somehow she and Rose had been found out. "What were you doing there, anyway?"

Poppy Wilder put her arm around her daughter. "Shooting an

infomercial the Greyhound Rescue League is hoping to air on cable television. That took most of the afternoon, and then there was a reception at the Frank Howell Gallery. I had to shake some hands and have a glass of wine, because those people give generously to rescue. I thought about coming home last night, but I don't like to fly when I've had anything to drink. I left the plane at the Santa Fe airport and spent the night at the Inn of the Anasazi. They were very understanding about letting me keep the dogs in my room."

"I guess the phones were all out of service at the hotel."

Mami reached over and tweaked Lily's nose. "You know, I'm glad to see you even if you insist on giving your *ama* the third degree." She waved hello to Shep. "Come inside, Lily. We'll have a cold drink and get caught up."

"What do you want me to do with these dogs?" Pop asked. "Stand here posing in case a photographer comes by?"

Mami took the leashes from his hands. She kissed Pop's cheek and he smiled. Behind him, Rose's mare ran wide circles at the lope, her nostrils flaring pink with the effort. The elegant hounds followed Poppy toward the house. "Coming, Pop?" Lily asked.

He gestured to the arena. "I'll be in later when I've made a dent in this work."

"I'll remember that," she said under her breath.

Despite their reputation for being high strung, the greyhounds weren't nervous at all, not even with the ranch dogs' greetings, which included Buddy's incessant barking behind the screen door. Lily told him to pipe down, then shut him outside while Mami folded blankets into makeshift beds and placed them in the room's sunniest corners. She poured water into dishes, set them on the floor, then switched the television on to a talk show. "I hope you don't mind background noise. These dogs are straight off the track. They'll need constant chatter for a couple of days in order to settle down."

Lily sat down near the blue dog, which was taller than the others. It laid a paw on her and looked up with soulful, doe-brown eyes. She stroked its neck and studied the numbered tattoo inside its left ear. "So that's why Pop had his knickers in a knot. You kicked him off the plane for pooches."

"There's a weight safety limit for the plane. I couldn't let these dogs down, not with all they've been through."

Lily didn't care to hear the details, which always broke her heart. "I'll take your word for it. Do they really have homes?"

"Not just yet. There's a woman in California who has the most wonderful setup, though. I'm betting she'll keep them until they're adopted. I'll call her, and in a few days fly them over. You could come along if you like. I'd love to spend some time with you."

Lily petted the blue dog. "This one's not leaving."

Mami kicked off her flats and sat down on the couch. "Now what makes you say a thing like that?"

She looked into her mother's face, where the truth lay as obvious as her cheekbones. "Gut feeling."

Mami laughed. "I thought Rose would be the one to inherit my second sense. Please don't tell your father just yet," she said. "Let me break it to him."

Lily rolled up her sleeves and tied the tails of the workshirt at her waist. "He already knows."

Poppy Wilder put her feet up on the coffee table. She pressed her lips together and looked up at the O'Keeffe on the wall in front of them. Several minutes passed, during which time Lily petted the blue greyhound and watched the black-and-white one nose around, investigating the house. Compared to the stocky blue heelers and border collies around the ranch, these two looked like malnourished aliens. Lily understood how they felt, not certain they could trust this sudden luck. "What is it about greyhounds?" she asked.

Her mother shook her head. "*No sé.* I only know that I look at them and this desire to shut down all the tracks overwhelms me. If every litter born from this moment on was allowed to simply be loved and appreciated as dogs, not to have to run for their lives, that would make me happy. I'm sorry I can't explain it better than that."

"That's passion," Lily said. "You don't have to explain it any better than you did."

"I must," her mother said. "Otherwise the tracks will never shut down."

"Maybe that commercial will help. By the way, who was the director? Looked like you two were old friends."

"His name is Robert Turney, and we are friends, to *greyhounds*. Are you home for a visit, or have you made a life change?"

Lily bristled. "That's a strange thing to say."

"Oh, I don't think so. For some time now I've felt you *descontenta* out there in California. I prayed to the Virgin to make you happy, and she told me to be patient, that you were coming home. I didn't think it would be before Christmas, but here you are."

First Rose, now Mami. All that God talk drove Lily nuts. "You can tell your Virgin that the only reason I'm here is I needed a vacation. That's all."

"Lily, I don't presume to tell the Mother of God anything. I listen to what she has to say."

Either faith was a whole lot simpler than it was made it out to be or it provided the most convenient excuse in the world. "I'm curious," Lily said. "What does the Virgin say about Rose and this vet?"

Poppy stroked the black-and-white greyhound, who had come over to the couch for reassurance and laid its muzzle on her thigh. "If you really want to know, I'll tell you."

"I do."

Her mother touched the elaborate silver crucifix she wore on a chain around her slender neck. One of her artist protégés had designed it for her, and she rarely took it off. "That in another lifetime she and Austin were lovers. There's no escaping what's going on with those two. Nothing for us to do but sit back and watch and eventually pick out some wedding china."

"Really, Mami?" Lily sighed. "Just once I wish you'd offer a motherly perspective instead of hiding behind the Virgin. I can't speak for Rose, but I'd kill to know what you alone think, to hear that kind of advice."

Color came into her mother's cheeks. She opened her mouth to laugh but seemed too stunned to do that. "*Enamorada,* what is happening to your sister is already in progress. There's nothing you or I can do about it, not really. Just like I know you are here for good. Whether you admit it to yourself or not, it's something that is and cannot be altered."

There was no use arguing. Her mother was like that New Age philosophy, coming from basic logic, inseparable from religion, sprinkled liberally with star barf and frosted with a complex Spanish credo. "There's nothing good to eat in the house," Lily said. "How come you can throw a party at a moment's notice but you never have any decent food?"

Both greyhounds had come to her mother and stood before her. She nuzzled their fine-boned faces. She was going to have a hard time letting either dog go. What was two more dogs in the pack, anyway?

"How about you make a shopping list and I can go to the market for you?"

"That's a wonderful idea," Mami said.

Which was the first normal mother thing to come out of her mouth so far. Lily said, "Okay. Let me get some paper and a pencil."

She had to drive out of town to find a real supermarket, but the good news was the larger the market, the more likely the possibility of her beloved California Krisprolls and pesto. Lily parked the Lexus in the lot of the Taos Smith's Food King and walked in through the automatic doors. She studied the community bulletin boards with their perpetual ads for rental properties and used farm equipment. Four hundred dollars a month for a guest house on an estate near Angel Fire, provided you'd agree to feed and water horses. In California you couldn't rent storage space for that. She could live on her savings for a long while with rent that low. Not that she was planning to run right out and call, but Lily did jot the number down on the back of her list. *It doesn't hurt to pipe dream,* she told herself.

"Excuse me," she said to the girl at the deli counter. "Do you know where the pesto is?"

"Try aisle three," a male voice behind her said. "That's where they keep the spaghetti sauce."

Lily turned to say thanks and was looking into the baby browns of Tres Quintero, who in addition to hardware stores, apparently also frequented markets. "Are you stalking me?"

"Today I am."

He appeared to be alone. "Where's your supermodel?"

He gave her a puzzled look. "What are you talking about?"

"You know, *Leah.* As in, 'Hi, I'm Leah and I have fabulous clothes.' That Leah."

He smiled. "My stepdaughter is back at Stanford."

"She didn't look like a stepdaughter. Actually, I think she was pretty old for a stepdaughter."

He held up his hands. "Trust me, Leah's the one good thing I got out of the divorce. Stanford's term begins later than anywhere else."

"Stanford? For real?"

"Yep, I'm so proud of her I tell everyone I know. You got any kids, Lily?"

Lily had to grab hold of the deli case and lean over the cheeses to stay on an even keel. *No child except the one I aborted, the one who never leaves me, yours. We're standing here by the cold case, and you're grinning over an eighteen-year-old who isn't even your blood. Pesto in aisle three. Tres Quintero, my first lover, unencumbered by females (stepdaughters or otherwise), and you* followed *me here. We're alone in a supermarket with only a shopping cart separating us. Jeez Louise, I completely forget how to talk.* "No, I don't have any kids."

Tres fingered the change in his left pocket. Lily listened to the jingle, a sound so utterly male it made her shiver. He was a left-handed bad boy and he was looking straight at her. "Come on," he said. "I drove all the way from Floralee behind your car. Let's not fight. Did you know I was planning on cutting you off if you headed toward the airport?"

"No."

"Well, I was. You feel like grabbing a bite to eat or having a drink? Let's catch up on the last ten years, Lily. I want to sit next to you. You've been on my mind ever since I saw you in the hardware store. Before that, actually. I had to promise your mother I'd adopt a greyhound to get her to tell me where you were headed."

Lily's best smile trembled at its edges. She wanted the reins back in her fist so bad she could taste leather. She'd say anything to put them back on level ground, to give herself an edge. "The thing is, Tres, I'm just not ever very hungry."

He laughed softly. "Nobody said there had to be food involved. It was just an idea. Tell me what you have in mind, Lily Wilder. Odds are it's pretty close to what I'm thinking."

She took Tres by the wrist, pulling his hand out of his pocket to check the ring finger, to be doubly sure. It was blessedly devoid of jewelry, no pale streak recently uncovered, either, just the naturally dark skin of the digit that lived next door to what used to be her favorite finger in the Western hemisphere. "Cappuccino."

"Looks like a nice day for a drive to the mountains."

"I guess that wouldn't kill me. But it might maim me."

"I've got coffee at my cabin. We could have a picnic of sorts."

Lily laughed. "You and me after all this time ought to be a real picnic. Let's just aim for Folgers in a very public place."

They abandoned the shopping cart there next to the roaster chickens and potato salad that looked past its expiration date and walked toward the exit. "Let me make something perfectly clear," Lily said. "I came here looking for groceries, not trouble."

Tres pulled his keys from his pocket. "To be fair, I believe I was the one looking for trouble."

"Do you think you found it?"

Tres touched the tip of his left middle finger to her lips. "That remains to be seen. Do we really need to take both cars?"

"You better believe it," Lily said, grabbing her keys so tightly that a small bruise appeared on her palm.

9

Legítimos Polvos Chuparrosas

When Austin appeared in her office doorway that Monday, Rose
looked up from the computer and felt her heart betray her in one
single, irregular beat. Thank God its rhythm wasn't audible, and that he
couldn't read her mind, because instead of checking inventory she had
been mulling over a dream she'd had at the ranch. There in her old bedroom, beneath the shelves of childhood mysteries and teen novels that
made a nurse's career sound romantic, Rose had dreamed she and
Austin were riding double on Max. They sat bareback, Rose in front, her
arms loosely embracing the horse's neck. Max wore no bridle, there
were no reins to grab on to, but she trusted that he knew the way.
Austin, seated behind, held on to Rose, his hands inside her shirt, fingers slowly moving up the ladder of her ribs. The dream had endowed
the old gelding with the slow and easy canter he lacked in this life. She
and Austin moved as one at the comfortable gait, but not without distraction. Alongside them loped a single rider: Leah Donavan. Austin
dug his heels into Max's side in order to keep pace with his ex-wife. In
the dreamscape, where the impossible was little more than a challenge,
Rose had leaned back in her seat, arching her neck to whisper in
Austin's ear, *Say no,* and this time he had. His fingers grazing her skin
felt so real that the phantom touch caused her to call out his name:
Austin? And her own voice awakened her. Blame it on *carne adobada,*
Rose had told herself while she drove her horse home and took a five-
minute shower, but the dream continued to pester her.

"Something I can do for you, Austin?" she asked, amused by the irony of her own words. Oh, given the chance, she knew exactly what she'd like to do for him, and it would take the better part of a week.

"Give me a ride downtown? I asked Paloma, but she got all pissed off and told me to walk."

Rose reached for her purse. "Take the Bronco, but make sure that you let it warm up first. Otherwise, sometimes when you pull out into traffic it stalls."

He waved his hand for her to stop. "You don't understand, Rose. I can't drive myself."

"Why not?"

He smiled sheepishly. "I got into a little trouble last night."

She wondered what he'd done, what he'd said to make Paloma angry. "What happened?"

"Nothing, really, except that Billy Ortega stopped me not half a mile from here, and I'd had a few drinks, so he decided to take away my truck."

Billy Ortega had been a year ahead of Rose in high school, a quarterback on the Floralee High football team. He was a cop now, and every time Rose saw him in his dark suit and tall boots, she couldn't help but think that here was a man born to wear uniforms—he did them that much justice. A second DUI was serious business. "Did he arrest you?"

"Well, in a manner of speaking."

"Oh, Austin."

He looked down at the floor. "Billy was nice enough not to throw me in jail right then, but I had to promise to be in Judge Trujillo's chambers at noon. It's half past eleven now."

As of the previous year, New Mexico had a zero tolerance thing going for drunk drivers. Of course, Floralee being a small town, and Austin caring for most of the population's animals, he traveled in its higher echelons. When people like him got in trouble, the consequences were handled "creatively."

Rose let out a weary sigh. "Call yourself a cab."

"Hate to. Everyone will hear about it if I do."

"Maybe you should have thought of that before you had all those drinks." Good Lord, she sounded like his mother! Rose shut down the file she was working on and stood up. "I'll drive you on one condition."

Austin looked visibly relieved. "Name it."

"Tonight you go to an AA meeting."

"I can't do that."

"Why not?"

"People know me here."

"Then you'll go to the one at Our Lady of Guadalupe. And you're going to go every night this week, and the week after that, until you get things under control, one meeting every week for the rest of your life or I will quit my job and you can figure your own damn taxes."

He made a face. "Aw, Rose. All they do at those meetings is smoke cigarettes and tell embarrassing stories. The women are ugly old hammers who all want to kiss and hug you in the name of getting sober, and when they laugh it sounds like they swallowed gravel. Those people grew up in bars and graduated to the gutter. I'm not that kind of drunk."

"Oh, I see. Getting drunk in the ¡Andale! is any more commendable? My father goes to AA. Do you think any less of him because of that?"

"No."

"Austin, I don't care if the women in those meetings ride brooms to get there. If what they do works, it's worth your time. Besides, you'll fit right in. You have a number of embarrassing stories of your own you can share. I can refresh your memory if you don't remember the details."

That shook him up, but not for long. "The church is all the way in Taos. How am I supposed to get there and back if I'm not allowed to drive? It's impractical."

Rose pushed her chair in and picked up her purse. "Simple. I'm going to drive you."

"Do I have a choice here?"

"Absolutely. Me or the cab or your own two feet."

He hesitated only a second before he answered. "You."

As they walked out the front door Paloma made the sign of the cross, rattling off something dire sounding in heavy-duty Spanish. Rose smiled as her boss held the door open for her.

Eloy Trujillo was a fair judge. He loved the law, and the town of Floralee, where his family tree extended back several generations. He also loved his mules, Luz and Oscuro, a stately pair who occupied the field in front of his house and dined as well as his grandchildren. Luz was pure white, Oscuro the glossy bay that comes from excellent breeding, careful diet, and an abundance of tender loving care. They were groomed on a daily basis by Eloy's grandsons, and their health care was entrusted to Austin Donavan, DVM, and nobody else. Now the vet stood before the judge for the second time, and Rose could see that Eloy was having a little trouble managing his conscience. Driving drunk once he could accept. After all, the vet's wife had behaved scandalously, and even the most gentlemanly of individuals could contain the hurt for only so long. But twice? Twice knocked Dr. Donavan down toward the level of ordinary, to criminal. The law was clear on repeat offenses. Austin wasn't going to weasel his way out of this arrest so easily.

"Ever since Billy called me I've been ruminating over your situation, Austin. A broken heart can kick the pins out from under one, yes. But a real man dusts himself off and continues on, or he jumps off the bridge into the Rio Grande. *Qué vergüenza!* You bring dishonor to this town, where you not only have a purpose but also the responsibility to set an example. This time I can't let you off with only a fine, but if I throw you in jail, the animals will suffer. What a bind you put me in." The judge touched his mustache and looked at the New Mexico state flag, which hung limply from a steel pole next to his desk. "I don't care to be pushed into corners."

Austin remained standing, Rose beside him. "I know you'll do whatever you think is fair, Eloy."

"Here's what I've come up with. No driving for one month. You need to go on calls, you get someone to drive you. After that, to work and back only. I'll instruct my officers to stop you periodically, and anytime they ask, you will voluntarily submit to a Breathalyzer test." He shook his finger in Austin's direction. "If there is so much as one *apice* of alcohol in your system, it's straight to jail, no more chances. And you agree to make thirty AA meetings in thirty days, bringing to the court weekly proof in the form of those signed cards."

"As it happens, I'm headed to a meeting in Taos tonight."

With an effort, Rose managed to restrain her smile.

"Excellent. In addition, I think one hundred hours' community service would help to erase this debacle from my memory while eternally fixing it in yours. To that end, the Pueblos can always use some veterinary assistance, and I want you to offer your services free of charge to NMGRA."

"NMGRA? What is that?"

Eloy paused to take a sip of water from the glass on his desk. He set the glass down, and his expression remained solemn. "The New Mexico Gay Rodeo Association. This October they're holding their event in Floralee, down at the sheriff's posse arena. We want to make them feel welcome to spend their tax dollars in our town. It would be very beneficial to our economy. It also promotes goodwill among diverse people. So you will go to that rodeo and make certain their animals receive any attention they require free of charge. *Sabes como?*"

Rose had to admire how quickly Austin recovered his poise. After a few seconds of open-mouthed astonishment he nodded his head in agreement. "Whatever kind of rodeo it is, I guess I can help out."

"Bueno." The judge stood up. "My mules and I are glad this matter could be worked out so easily, as they are needing some veterinary attention before the winter. So if we are all in agreement?"

"That we are."

Eloy stopped at the door, a file folder in his hand. "One more thing, Austin. I don't have to tell you what happens if there is a third occurrence of this trouble. Be assured, if such a thing happens, you will find no mercy in these chambers."

"No, Eloy. I'm guessing I won't."

"Then the next time we meet, it will be in my yard to attend my *mulos.*"

On the drive to Taos, Austin unloaded on Rose, beginning with difficult clients, graduating to medical equipment that needed expensive repairs, eventually getting around to explaining that he'd taken the first drink—which had led to the second—because that day in the mail he'd gotten another request for an increase in Leah's alimony. The underpinnings of his outrage were as sorrowful as they were simple: He missed the wife he'd been court-ordered to write the checks to. Some men just needed to be married. The kind of loneliness he was suffering from wasn't terminal, however. Why, if he'd open his eyes a little wider, all kinds of options were available for the taking.

"You know I'll have to go to court to fight her," he said. "Likely I'll lose."

"Then don't fight."

"How would you like it, Rose, having to pay money every month to the person who wrecked your life?"

She thought of her husband, who'd left her so little in the way of financial security that she'd had to return to full-time work and judiciously clip coupons. Of all those nights she'd sat up in bed afraid to lie down and shut her eyes, to feel how alone she really was. "I'm sure I wouldn't like it at all, Austin. Maybe you could think of alimony like paying off a really poor investment, you know, like a speedboat bought in the heat of the moment."

Austin laughed. "Yeah, a speedboat about covers Leah. Wish she'd move to Europe. God knows she could afford to live there on what I'm paying her."

Rose downshifted to accommodate the road's gradual incline. "Pretend she has."

"Most of the time I can. It's seeing her pop up in my world every so often that knocks me down. You know what Leah's like?"

A dozen answers sprang to Rose's mind, among them: *Yes, a perpetual reminder that I need to lose ten pounds.* "No, Austin. Why don't you tell me?"

"A damned gopher in the vegetable patch."

Rose smiled. "My grandpop used to try to drown gophers with a garden hose. All it did was make the holes muddy. He'd step in one and sprain an ankle, swear a blue streak. I used to wonder to myself, would it be so terrible if he just let them have half?"

Austin looked at her. "What makes you think gophers know how to divide?"

"Um, positive thinking?"

He sighed. "Mrs. Flynn, I'd appreciate the hell out of it if you'd stop trying to cheer me up."

"I'd be delighted to, Doctor Donavan. The moment you stop trying to drag me down I'll do just that."

The rest of the way to town he was quiet, no doubt thinking over his various legal options. *A checkbook was one thing*, Rose thought, *and the money in it, at best, transitional. The problem with this particular gopher wasn't money, it was the half of Austin's heart wedged between the long yellow teeth. That he needed to reclaim.*

* * *

"Buy you dinner at Michael's," Rose said when they arrived in Taos an hour before the meeting convened. "It can't be anything fancy, since as you know, I've recently been robbed."

Austin had been staring out the window. He looked over at her. "You reckon Amanda took that money to buy drugs?"

Rose shook her head no. "My daughter eats too much to be on drugs. I think her problem is that she lacks a moral compass. Amanda sees what she wants in front of her, she grabs it up quick, with no thought to anyone's needs but her own. I tried to set the best example I could, but the minute I turned my back Philip or Pop gave her whatever she wanted. Kind of hard to fight that."

"You seem like a good mother to me. I'm sorry she disappointed you."

"Thanks. I'm sorrier that she took my grocery money." Rose pulled the car into an empty space. "But I bet the *sopas* they make at Michael's will help me forget. What do you say? Will you help me eat a basketful?"

For the first time all day, Austin smiled a smile that was all hers. "Sure. I'll have to pay you back, Rose. I'm tapped clean after paying that fine."

"Don't worry about it. I said it was my treat."

She opened the car door and turned in the direction of the restaurant. Austin stuck his hands in his pockets and followed. The street traffic was light considering the time of day. A slight breeze blew the first fall leaves to surrender in a colorful swirl at their feet. This dusty road led past old churches and a lovingly tended cemetery to the mountains. Austin's troubles were temporary. Rose felt blessed: Her horse was in foal, the trees were turning, and she was about to have dinner with a friend—*Go on, make yourself say it,* she prodded—she had liked for years and now was beginning to love.

Austin held the café door open. "Haven't been to this place in ages. Surprised it's still open."

"Are you kidding? Michael's is famous."

"Is that so?"

"Made it into the AAA guidebook."

"Well, that explains your dedication."

"Stop teasing me and order some juice," she told him when they were seated in a booth by the window. "You need sugar in your system if you're going to make it through the meeting without the jitters."

"How is it you know so much about drunks?"

She unfolded her napkin in her lap and ran a finger down the menu before she answered him. "Let's see, for starters, one killed my husband. I took that a little personally, and then I attended a few Al-Anon meetings so I wouldn't stay bitter and angry for the rest of my life." She bit her lip and waited a moment before finding her voice again. "And what do you know, there happens to be this handsome drunk in my life I'm ridiculously fond of. He doesn't deserve it, of course, but however things are, I try my best to deal with them."

Austin looked at her as if this might be the first time he'd seen her up close without makeup. "What are you saying, Rose?"

Her palms felt damp against the paper napkin. "I think it's pretty obvious what I'm saying."

"I've been under water awhile. I need you to spell it out."

She glanced around the restaurant where couples were tasting forkfuls of each others' meals, laughing over private jokes, chatting easily about how their days had gone. It had never been like that for her and Philip, even though she had wanted it to be. Maybe that kind of closeness was a fable, but it didn't mean a woman had to stop trying. *We have all of us been under water*, she mused, *only some of us were wearing our face masks and snorkels.* "Austin, you're a smart man, figure it out."

He leaned across the table. "Are you sitting here on maybe the worst night of my life telling me that you're *romantically* interested in my sorry carcass? I thought we were friends."

She closed her menu. "I'm going to have the salad and the barley soup. That soup always tastes so good in the fall. When I make it at home it never tastes the same as Michael's. That and the basket of *sopas.* I hope you're hungry. They don't keep well enough to take home."

Austin took hold of her hand. "Your barley soup's a Floralee legend. Whenever you bring me a pot, I try to make it last all week, but I just keep on refilling my bowl until the pan's empty. I asked you a question."

She picked up her spoon and stared at her reflection, which looked sad and bowed in the arc of the metal. She shouldn't have blurted it out like that. Just unpinned her heart from her sleeve and handed it to him. "And I don't think you're ready to hear the answer. So let's eat dinner and get you through that meeting."

"Dammit all, Rose," he said, and then the waiter arrived. Rose ordered her dinner. "Whatever she said, bring that for me, too," Austin said. "Along with some orange juice. Large glass."

When their drinks arrived, Austin drank half his juice down, wincing. "My stomach's full of caterpillars," he said.

"Did you think getting sober was going to be easy?"

"I never expected I was going to want to find out."

"You've been living your life under anesthesia, Austin. Things are going to feel uncomfortable from here on in."

He touched his glass to hers. "Better make sure we toast that good news."

Their food arrived, and they ate in silence. Rose picked at her *sopas.* Austin was so newly sober that maybe he'd forget what she'd said, even though she was sure she'd replay this night in her mind for years. She paid the check, and they walked up the street, into the church, and located the meeting room. On a table by the door all manner of AA literature was stacked into colorful piles, most of it free for the taking. Rose stopped there. Austin said, "What? You're not coming with me?"

"You'll be fine. I'll be waiting for you in the car."

But she did not leave the church until she saw him place his hand on the back of an empty chair. She was that uncertain. Relief flooded her pores when she heard the chair scoot across the floor. *Just listen to what they have to say,* she mentally sent his way. *Nobody's asking more than that.*

She walked around town before returning to the car, remembering the first time she'd gone to an Al-Anon meeting. The sight of that open doorway was daunting. But people said hello; they left her alone when they saw how close she was to tears. While she listened to their stories she began to understand how universal her struggles were, that making it into the meeting chairs was proof of human endurance. Austin would do fine so long as he didn't fight it. And she knew he *would* fight it, with every fiber of his being.

Remember that alcoholism is a disease, she told herself. *It's hard to take the first step. From here on things can only get better for him. A little serenity is better than none.*

She walked back to the Bronco in the kind of autumn evening when the crickets were busy chirping, and the air coming down off the mountains smelled so clean and crisp she wanted to take a bite out of it as if it were an apple from the tree that grew in front of her parents' ranch. The one-of-a-kind craft shops and galleries were open for much shorter hours now that tourist season was ending. Santa Fe had been like this once, historic, charmingly small, more like a territory than its current expansive state, awash in tourists. Everywhere she looked, small changes had come over the sleepy town of Taos. If Taos wasn't exempt from change, then Floralee's days were numbered. JCPenney's was gone, and in its place, a store that sold African art. La Fonda de Taos wasn't as fancy or full up with guests as its Santa Fe counterpart, but in a small room behind the front desk, the strange, chaotic nudes D. H. Lawrence had painted while he lived there still hung on the walls. Rose peered in the window and tried to imagine what life must have been like when the Lawrences and Mabel Dodge Luhan were there, and then Georgia O'Keeffe, Ansel Adams, and Maynard Dixon. Such lasting treasures for the world had come from a circle of talented members of that generation. Their friendships were well known. Were any of them drunks? Had they walked through this plaza agonizing over how to help each other pull their lives together? Rose buttoned her sweater. A few of the shops in the plaza were vacant, and she wondered what outrageous amount they rented for, or if they would stay empty until next year.

Inside the Bronco she put her key into the ignition, tuned the radio to the Spanish station, and sat there listening to Julio Iglesias. All but the basics of the language were lost on her, but Spanish, with its stresses and rolling *r*'s remained a universal tongue in which to seduce women. She often thought that if she had married a man of Hispanic descent, strengthened her bloodline, she would have given birth to children more connected to their culture. Heritage was like faith, it bequeathed a foundation. Grandma had tried to impart the basic tenets, but for every Spanish proverb whose meaning Rose knew, she'd forgotten twice that many. As Mami aged, her roots seemed to become more important to her. Philip was amused by his mother-in-law's eccentricities, but Amanda cursed her brown eyes and begged for colored contact lenses. Second Chance had inherited the most visible trappings of the genes in dark hair and a complexion that tanned to bronze. *At forty, too much of your life is spent on thinking of what ifs,* Rose decided, closing her eyes and letting the music spill over her. If Julio was singing lies, at least they were romantic ones.

When Austin knocked at the window, she startled awake. He got in the car, and she turned the engine over without asking him how the meeting had gone. He'd tell her if he wanted to. Before she could pull out in traffic, however, Austin reached across the seat and shut the engine off. He sat back against the seat cushions and the sound of their breathing filled the car. Before long all that silence began to fog up the windows.

"It's getting late, Austin. Both of us have to be at work in the morning."

He answered that by pulling her to him and kissing her mouth. As soon as Rose recovered from feeling stunned, she discovered that Austin kissed women the same way he dealt with horses: He did not hesitate, there was no fumbling, his mouth found hers the same way he could find a vein in a horse's neck with a silver needle and stick it on the first try. He opened her lips with his own and began to move his tongue at a brisk clip, circling hers, exploring her, making her feel small and surrounded and entirely vulnerable. Lingering on the outskirts of the kiss, she was aware of the scratch of his day's worth of whiskers, his warm breath smelling slightly of coffee, a rough hand at the back of her neck and fingers moving through her hair. It was as if with his mouth he had reached down inside her body, moving insistently forward until with no rest stops or side trips, the kiss landed hard between her legs. She knew this would keep her awake all night, but she let Austin go on kissing her until somehow, in the middle of all that wonderful sensation, she detected just the faintest scent of citrus, and remembered the orange peels on the dashboard of Austin's impounded truck, the reason it was there, and her emotions began to ricochet all over her brain, pulsing inside her veins like adrenaline. *I've been wanting this for God knows how long, I'm so wet I'm aching to pull this man inside me, to take whatever it is he's generous enough to give me, and all I can do is sit here and think, he's imagining I'm Leah.* She pushed him away.

With the back of his hand, Austin rubbed his mouth. "What you said at the restaurant—did I misunderstand you?"

"No."

"Then what is your problem, lady?"

The neon sign of the Taos Inn glowed in the distance, not far from where Pueblo Road joined with Highway 68, the stretch of road where Philip had been hit. The street was congested with motels and hotels, quaint inns, luxury bed and breakfasts. Rose had driven past Casa Europa several times, wondering if the interiors of the rooms were as inviting as the exterior, if the legendary owl still frequented the tall cottonwood tree growing behind the inn that used to be El Buho Gallery. In the off season, their rates were almost affordable. Working people could just walk in, plunk down a credit card, and for the night, enjoy a fireplace, privacy, a bed they could call theirs. Taos was far enough from Floralee that nobody would know if they did. In her place her sister Lily would have already checked in and unwrapped the complimentary soaps, but as much as she would have liked to, Rose couldn't make her heart move at light speed. This thing she'd wanted to happen for so long was happening out of sequence. Austin was supposed to get sober first, be completely over Leah, *then* want her. He watched her in earnest, waiting. He wasn't going to do anything else until she let him know. *I'll kiss him one more time,* she told herself, ashamed at the depth of her desire. *Once won't matter. I won't care who he's pretending I am, I'll do this for me, selfishly, and commit this moment to memory and that will be enough.*

She tilted her chin up and looked into his eyes. Austin moved to meet her. The second kiss started out the same way the first one did, but when she put her hands on his shoulders, the kiss transformed into an expedition. Austin pulled her close. He ran his right hand up her side and stopped just below the swell of her breast. His thumb barely grazed the spot where her nipple pressed against her blouse and her sweater, making contact so precisely it was as if he'd memorized the location, and Rose, a woman with two years' worth of needing to be touched, felt herself dissolving in his hands. In the car's small compartment, they strained to press their bodies against each other until they were nearly on their knees, the seats beneath them impossibly rigid, the stupid gearshift in the way, the AA literature falling to the floor, their elbows bumping in a desperate effort to have skin speak to skin. They broke apart and touched foreheads, gasping simultaneously, and in the back of her mind Rose was inundated with questions: *How come it never felt like this with Philip? Because I was seventeen years old and he was the first man to make love to me? Because I was about to shrivel up from need? Amanda said I shouldn't read those romance novels. Amanda was right.*

Austin rubbed his fingertip across the frown lines wrinkling Rose's forehead. "I'm here for you," he said.

She took hold of his fingertips and pressed them to her lips.

After a measured breath, he exhaled. "I'm here, Rose, like I've always been, to listen to your problems and share a laugh and work at the clinic, but I can't be the lover you want me to be. I'm a wreck and you know it."

There were a million logical rebuttals to that statement, not the least of which was what she felt rise up in his blue jeans as he pressed his body against hers, but Rose couldn't speak over the hole he'd just blasted through her heart. She wasn't going to humiliate herself any further by arguing. She was forty years old, for God's sake; Austin was in his fifties. This wasn't some teenage dalliance that would dissipate by the end of the next school day. Austin was saying things, talking as if he held the corner on rejection. Had he stopped to consider what such a kiss could do to a woman, particularly one so uncertain of her worth that she stood in front of the closet for half an hour each morning, trying to remember which clothes he'd complimented her on the week before so that he'd say how nice she looked again? Was she starved? Oh, so what if she was! Did that excuse him putting his tongue in her mouth and thumbing her breast as if it were his God-given right? She started the car and switched the radio station to English. She tuned in to some big-band instrumental with a complex horn section. Austin didn't complain. Rose put her hands on the steering wheel at ten and two and let out the clutch. Her mouth was stinging with the feeling of his. It filled up with salt. She was holding back the ocean only by the force of her bruised lips. The tide rising up inside her felt angry, too large to control. She kept her eyes on the road. No matter what he said, and even if he didn't say anything, she wasn't going to cry until she was safe in her own bed, with all the lights off, facedown in the safe harbor of the pillow.

On Tuesday morning she was sitting at her computer entering invoices into the AVS system when she heard Austin clear his throat. She looked up, but said nothing. He appeared nervous, which she attributed to alcohol withdrawal, but he was clean, combed, and entirely sober. The good signs outweighed the bad. *Concentrate on that*, she told herself. *Forget everything else.*

"Wanted to let you know I've worked out a ride to those meetings in Taos."

"That's good."

He crossed the room and laid a ten-dollar bill down on her desk.

"What's that for?"

"Dinner last night. That makes us even."

She looked at the bill, old and worn to softness the same as Austin's jeans. The kisses had been a mistake. He wanted to be quit of her, and so here was her money. Rose didn't dare look up. What was there to say that wouldn't make her sound pathetic? By the time she had herself under control, Austin was long gone.

The New Age proponents who found New Mexico so irresistible had created a high profile in Santa Fe and Taos. There were shops galore selling crystals and offering touch therapy, cut-rate Rolfing, a good aura scrubbing, you name it. Rose sat at her computer for an hour thinking about ethics before she took her purse in hand and left work two hours early. "I don't feel well," she told Paloma. "I'm going to the doctor. I'll get to the books tomorrow or whenever."

Paloma touched Rose's forehead. "You seem a little warm."

Terminal embarrassment will do that to you, Rose thought, but she only smiled and waved good-bye. She drove out of town, passing hippie shops, the Overland Trading Company, the river rafting headquarters where Philip used to meet his buddies and take off on weeklong adventures that never included her. He'd come home windburned and rejuvenated, talking about retiring early, buying a custom-made kayak, but never said one word about teaching her to paddle.

Toward the ski basin, the little cafés and general stores thickened in number. Rose passed shops that would earn most of their income in winter when the skiers arrived. She kept driving until she came to a line of adobe buildings where there was a women's collective selling paintings and jewelry, a pottery maker, and a weaver. It was the weaver she was seeking, if she was still here. The old Spanish-Navajo woman made blankets and shawls, but that wasn't all she did. She was also an *arbolaria*, specializing in healing herbs, and rumored to be a *curan-*

dera, a woman who possessed certain powers, a kind of touch therapy no course of study could deliver because what she knew how to do came from her blood. Long ago, when Grandpop died, and Rose couldn't get over missing him, wasn't able to concentrate in school, or even keep her breakfast oatmeal down, Mami had taken Rose here. *Don't tell Pop*, she had cautioned. *Sometimes, Rose Ann, a woman has to look in special places for healing.*

From the outside the weaver's shop looked exactly like its counterparts, a place to shop for locally made handicrafts. Tan adobe walls were cracked by the elements, a yellow cat sat in a window box smashing the geraniums, an empty hammock hung limp. The only movement came from a sun-faded windsock blowing in the breeze. Rose opened the door and let herself in. There was the small wooden counter she remembered, the shelves holding skeins of hand-dyed yarn, multicolored beads of glass and wood, assorted jars of herbs, vials of botanical oils and all manner of religious statuary from magnetic Jesuses for car dashboards to pale blue plaster Virgins suitable for a garden centerpiece. By the light of a south-facing window, the woman Rose recalled from her childhood sat at a loom, pulling colored threads into the fabric of what eventually would become a shawl. She was older now, the age of a great-grandmother. Rose remembered that the woman didn't speak much English, but that hadn't stopped Mami from communicating her needs. She smiled and greeted Rose like an old friend. "*Ya hey,*" she said in Navajo. "*Haash iinidzaa?*"

Rose's languages were so rusty she didn't attempt a reply. It was a relief not to speak, because she knew had she tried to do that, she would have started to cry. She tapped her left breast, just over her heart. "*Destrozado,*" she said, using the Spanish word for "broken."

The weaver's face crinkled with compassion. She got up from her loom and took Rose by the hand into the next room. It was just as Rose remembered it, beeswax candles placed in *nichos* carved into the adobe walls, the windowless space small but in no way confining. She motioned for Rose to undress and lie down on the table in the center of the room. Rose set her purse on the floor. She shut her eyes and listened to the sound of matches striking, smelled the brief scent of sulfur before the light from the candles brightened the room. She unbuttoned her blouse and peeled it away, feeling the candlelight strike her breasts, where beneath the layers of clothing, Austin's hand had awakened in her a feeling so compelling that she wanted it to disappear, to be gone forever, and to take with it when it left, her memories of that night as well.

The old woman handed her a sheet with which to cover herself. Rose let her clothes be taken from her, folded into a small, neat pile atop the wooden bench. She laid down upon the table and tucked the sheet around her. From behind her head came the scent of something sweet and healing, oil of lavender, perhaps, but there was something green mixed into it, juniper or arnica, she guessed. The woman dripped the warm oil onto Rose's forehead in a steady stream. She dabbed it onto her shoulders, at the pulse points in her wrists, the hollow of her throat. She massaged the oil into Rose's skin, working on her neck and shoulders with long, broad strokes. Rose felt her body relax everywhere except her chest. The area around her heart continued to throb, as if it were stuck with a foreign body that was slowly poisoning her. The *arbolaria* pressed her warm palm, fingers splayed, to Rose's chest. She took a deep breath and exhaled. Rose did the same, willing whatever medicine there was in this room to find its way into her body's strongest, sorest muscle. She wanted everything she felt for Austin Donavan to be exorcised. She told herself that she desired the absence of love as much as she had ever wanted anything, for her children to be safe, Philip to have survived the accident, Lily to stop sleeping with so many men, her mother to remain faithful to her father, Shep to gain some weight, Winky to deliver a healthy foal next year, a drink of cool water on a hot summer day, all those things and this, too. The woman's hand rested on Rose's heart as she murmured to her in a dialect of Spanish different from the languages Rose grew up hearing. Rio Grande Valley Indian, she figured from the formality of the grammar. Her speech sounded older, her delivery of each syllable caused her voice to rise in pitch and Rose to concentrate on their probable translations: *chiguata* (woman), *pague* (was that some kind of medicinal plant?), *topil* (authority), *arrollar* (lull to sleep), *dispertar* (awaken?), *dar bau* (she had no idea what that meant), until the hand lifted away from Rose's chest and she felt the skin of her breast chill to gooseflesh. This wasn't like it had been all those years ago with Mami, when Rose had fallen asleep under soft fingers and awakened feeling lighter than breath, so hungry she couldn't wait to eat dinner and they had to stop on the drive home for a sandwich and chips. The woman gently touched her shoulder to let Rose know the treatment was finished.

She left the room. Sleepily Rose buttoned her blouse with awkward fingers. The candles in the windowless room flickered as if generating their own wind. When her legs felt steady enough, Rose wandered back into the room where the loom was. Behind the counter, the woman assembled paper packets, filling them with some kind of white dust. *Oh my God, polvos*, Rose thought, the bewitching powders some people used to attract someone they desired. This was magic, which not only collided head on with her religious beliefs but also seemed a kind of last-ditch attempt only those doomed to failure would attempt.

"*No entiendes, Señora*; I want love to go away, not to come to me," she said in her best Spanish. "*Lo odio.*" When the woman didn't reply, she repeated the phrase in the little Navajo she knew. "*T'oo jooshla.* Don't you see? I hate him, in every language there is."

The woman handed the powders to Rose and took a statue of Saint Anthony down from the shelves. She pointed to a photograph on the wall, mimed the action of taking the picture and wrapping it around the statue. Rose fingered the plastic statue of the balding man holding two lilies and a child. When Anthony preached from the riverbank, the fishes stood on their tails to listen. He was who you prayed to when you needed help finding lost objects. On high holy days, people pinned money to the stoles wrapped around Anthony's neck and it was said that among saints, Anthony particularly blessed the poor. The saint even had his own bread, named especially for him. But there was another purpose for the statue, and Rose knew the drill from her mother's confession. Mami said the day she had met Chance Wilder, she had asked him for his photograph. Instead of carrying it in her purse or framing it inside a locket, with a length of string she had tied his likeness to a statue of Saint Anthony, then tucked the statue beneath her mattress. Within the week Rose's future father was at her side, proposing marriage, begging her to let him fill her up with babies. And the most amazing part of the story—when she lifted the mattress to remove the statue that had done its work, *her* picture was somehow there, too, tied face to face with Pop's. Lily and Rose had laughed so hard when she told them that they lay down on the floor and held their sides. *Do this and your loved one will never desert you*, Mami insisted. Turn Anthony on his head, the same thing could happen, but under the mattress at least your secrets were kept secret.

"*Remedio, por favor*, I came here to be healed," Rose repeated.

"*Sí, sí.*" Within her rapid-fire explanation Rose caught the general meaning: *The cure is to accept when something is meant to be.*

Meant to be. Rose opened her wallet. The weaver lifted the ten dollars Austin had given Rose out of the bill compartment. She fingered it and smiled, and then wrapped it around the Saint Anthony, securing it with a rubber band. Rose let the statue fall into her purse. She handed the woman a twenty, which she accepted.

Outside the weaver's, Rose looked east at the tree-covered mountains. Here and there the blanket of evergreen was broken by trees on fire with autumn colors. In a crooked line, the yellow and red traveled down the mountainside, a reminder that no matter how stranded a person felt in her life, the seasons continued at their regular pace. Lately everything beautiful in the world made her feel just how alone she was. Come winter, the snow would turn the mountains to a bridal white, and the skiing would bring in throngs of tourists. To Rose, only riding horses compared to cross-country skiing, to making first tracks in a snowy field, that in itself a solitary pursuit. But each season someone schussed into a tree or in a macho display of idiocy ventured off the designated trails, got lost, and froze to death from exposure. If it wasn't any one of those things, there was always death by drunk-driving accident, where the lives of innocent bystanders paid the toll, just as Philip had. The drunks, fully insulated, usually bounced.

Friday night, after a week of awkward conversations with Austin—*Sign this invoice, Call that doctor, Where's the payroll checks?*—and working hard to keep her guard up whenever Paloma walked into the room, Rose made her way home. Just as she had every day that week, she stopped at the church to say her prayers. Today, however, after a quick genuflection at the altar to the Virgin and a dab of holy water on her forehead, she fled. At the market she bought five Eternalux candles, two Our Lady of San Juans, three Guadalupes, and a box of twelve vigil candles. She pushed her cart down the aisles, saying hello to people she saw every Sunday in church, to the parents of kids Second Chance used to run with, making lighthearted small talk instead of admitting that she had no idea where her son was. She picked up a bunch of red grapes, a wedge of sharp cheddar, dark bread, and a bottle of Bordeaux. In the checkout line she scanned the tabloids to see what movie star had gotten caught with his pants down this week. Her sister hadn't called in so long she figured maybe Lily had gone back to California by now, to her high-paying job and her condo with the ocean view. Life in California had to be easier than life in Floralee. A person could never feel lonely in that kind of crowd. Rose took her bag of groceries out to the Bronco. It was Friday night, and the streets were hopping. Lovers were going to the movies, out for supper, to hear the last of the seasonal concerts in the park. A low-riding Chevy passed by, its lavender paint job polished to a sheen, its speakers pulsing with music. Rose drove on home and rode Max until it was too dark to make out the road in front of them.

When they got back to the barn, she spent a luxurious hour untangling his long, dark mane with her fingers and a wide-toothed comb. She mixed the old gelding a hot bran mash with dark molasses, and stirred oats into the bucket, smiling when she heard his nearly imperceptible nickerings of pleasure. As she stood listening to the greedy rasp of the old gelding's tongue against the bucket, she wondered how her mare was doing. Tomorrow she'd drive up and check on her, exercise her so she wouldn't lose her gaits, but only in the arena where she'd be safe.

A couple of times Rose threw the ball for Chachi, but after a few retrievals, the Jack Russell let it drop at his feet and returned to digging holes. She went inside and made herself a snack of the cheese and fruit. As she bit into the first red grape, she felt surprised by the explosion of sweetness on her tongue. Considering how much she loved food, the preparation of meals, serving meals to others, watching their faces light up as familiar tastes were savored, it was as if she'd forgotten how good a grape could taste. Deep in her center, all that cooking defined Rose. She loved all facets of preparing dinner, even scrubbing the pots. It wasn't that she wanted to be a professional chef, but if she never got to cook for anyone but herself again there was a part of her she felt might forget its purpose.

She telephoned the ranch to see if Pop was there, if he and Mami wanted to come for dinner on Sunday. Nobody answered, not even Shep, and she hated leaving messages, so she hung up. Her parents were probably laughing around a table thick with friends, interesting people, maybe eating at the restaurant that served kangaroo. In so many ways Mami was braver than her oldest daughter.

Rose lined the candles up along the edges of the bathtub and arranged the votives on the windowsill. She took box matches and lit every wick until the room glowed brighter than it ever had under electric lights. Shadows played in corners where the candlelight flickered against the walls. She drew a bath, dripped in lavender, bergamot, valerian, and poppy oils. She took off her clothes and sank into the steaming water, breathing in the complex, earthy scents. All week long in church she had prayed for strength and felt her prayers fall back into her mouth like sand collapsing down a hole. To show for her efforts she had sore knees and one time, a headache so fierce she wondered if one of Lily's migraines had come to visit. Where was her sister, anyway? She trailed her fingers through the bathwater, carefully shaved her legs even though she couldn't think of a single person on earth who would care if Rose Wilder Flynn had smooth skin or stubble. Every time she thought of Austin she pushed him from her mind, but that didn't stop him from coming back.

After the bath she patted herself dry with a towel and sat on the edge of the tub surrounded by candlelight. She looked into the mirror above the sink. The vertical frown line between her eyebrows rarely relaxed. Her skin was clear, though, and her neck strong, her posture upright. Her breasts still looked nice, didn't they? They still felt good to touch. After two babies and forty years, her slight belly felt earned, womanly. She cupped her hand between her legs, where the dark hair was thick and kinky, twice as curly as on top of her head. Everything was fine except this place inside her felt so lonely that if it could howl, she was sure it would put the coyotes to shame.

Rose tore open the package marked *legítimos polvos chuparrosas*. The paper was stamped with a smudgy likeness of a hummingbird inserting his long, narrow beak into a flower. It didn't smell like anything. On the back, in Spanish, the weaver had written: *Powder of the hummingbird, dried under full moon to conserve the natural flower perfume. Powder your body on a Friday night, after a bath in the alcove, to obtain the grace of true love.*

As she dusted her breasts, her neck, her ankles, her wrists, Rose told herself this was no crazier than answering a singles' ad. If this thing between herself and Austin was meant to be, maybe the powder would hurry it along. She emptied the last fine grains of the powder onto the hair between her legs and shivered when they met her skin. Like insurance, she tucked the remainder of the unused packets into the medicine cabinet. She got into her bed and pulled the flannel sheets up to her neck. Sometimes it felt so good to sleep naked, her flesh clean and raw from a bath, nothing separating her from the bedding.

Between her mattress and box spring lay the statue of Saint Anthony, face down, wrapped in the ten-dollar bill and a photograph of Austin that had appeared in the *Floralee Facts* not long ago. *Austin Donavan, DVM,* the reporter had written, *donates his surgery to save the school's pony from colic.*

Trying to get comfortable, Rose turned until she was lying flat on her back, staring up at the expanse of the ceiling. She couldn't help but slide her hand down her belly and touch herself, there, between her legs, where she ached so much that the emptiness she felt kept her from sleeping. She imagined what it would feel like to have Austin inside her, his fingers touching her instead of her own, or his mouth, the ghost she confronted every time she touched a lipstick to her lips, the mysteries and surprises they would encounter if they lay in this bed together. She told herself that it was foolish to believe she could heal him, and he her. But she had done exactly what the weaver told her to with the statue. She'd lit the candles, taken the bath, rubbed the powder into her flesh, every last bit of embarrassing hocus-pocus.

When it didn't work, somehow she would learn to live with it.

10

Penitentes

"I'm pretty sure there's no Starbucks in northern New Mexico," Lily said at their cars. "Probably we should wait until they build one."

Tres laughed. "I know of one or two cafés where people can drink plain old regular grind and talk over old times."

And get into real trouble, Lily thought, because she was afraid that was exactly what was happening. Tres tucked his keys into his hip pocket and led her up the block to the Loving Oven, where the *i* had been cleverly fashioned out of a rolling pin. Tres sat down in a booth, and Lily took the place across from him. There were no other customers at this time of day, nothing to focus on except the lone waiter setting up tables for the dinner crowd. "Be with you in a minute," he said, and Lily decided she'd just lay things on the line.

"Why now, Tres?"

"Why not now? Damn, it's good to see you. I was worried I'd miss you. Your mother said this was the market you'd probably go to. You look wonderful, by the way."

I look like hell, Lily said to herself. *In my closet back in California I have Italian pumps that flatter my calves, and a black Armani sheath that would leave you breathless. Today, however, I've donned a sweat-stained denim ensemble, just for this reunion. Well, at least the manure caked on the soles of my riding boots is fresh.* She tried to smile. The waiter abandoned his task of smoothing tablecloths and attending bud vases and came over to take their order. "We're not open for dinner for two hours yet," he apologized.

"That's okay," Tres told him. "All we want is coffee."

With a practiced calm, Lily ordered a latte.

It was New Mexico, not Santa Monica. The costly machinery and bottles of flavoring hadn't made their way into the smaller eateries. "Can you tell me how to make that?"

Lily tried to explain. When he took out a pen and began taking notes, she said, "You know what? Just heat up some milk, fill a mug half full of coffee and pour the milk on top."

"Okay."

Tres ordered decaf.

"See what California's done to me, Tres? I'm hopeless. I can't order regular coffee."

"From where I sit you don't look terribly damaged."

Lily leaned across the table. "Oh, but I am," she whispered. "Driving in traffic all day, I want to murder old-lady drivers who can't help getting feeble. If I met those women in New Mexico, I'd respect their age, their background, maybe even let them pass, but in California I just want to erase them."

"I lived in northern California for ten years before I came home. If you don't take public transportation you spend half the day on one bridge or another, tuning the radio for traffic updates. And for some real fun, try being on board BART when it breaks down and you realize you're under water. Claustrophobia."

Lily shuddered.

"What do you do that keeps you in your car so much?"

"I have a great job," she said, explaining how she repped medical equipment, participated in research and development studies, trying to punch up success stories because being negative was such a drag. "Sometimes I'm right there in the room when they save a life. Once, this new mother, twenty-five years old, stroked out following a delivery. There's this new catheter device now that can seal off aneurysms, stop bleeding in the brain. That girl woke up right there on the operating table and started talking to me. Got to send her home to her baby instead of a mortuary. I'll never forget it."

"You're lucky," Tres said. "To you like what you do for a living."

"Hold on there, cowboy. I said it was a good job, I never said I liked it. You remember how bad I wanted to run away from this place twenty years ago?"

"Sure. We both did."

"Why is it when things get tough, the first place I run back to is Floralee?"

"There's comfort in familiar places."

"I don't know. I think it goes deeper than that. Besides making me a lot of money, that job was making me nuts, Tres. It's as if New Mexico's the only place where I feel like my true self. What kind of cake career do you have that lets you hang around here instead of working nine to five?"

He made a face. "You'll find this ironic, but my job was in the medical field, too. I took a personal leave." He adjusted the salt and pepper shakers so their glass cylinders were evenly aligned. "It sounds stupid."

"Just say it."

"Okay. I wanted to do some writing."

Lily grinned. "I remember you filling up those spiral notebooks in high school. You were the only person I knew who actually used every page. You had that cool fountain pen with the turquoise ink. It absolutely killed me that you wrote poems."

"Yeah, I thought I was pretty deep."

"You were deep enough to make me take off my clothes. Is that what you're doing now? Writing poems?"

He shook his head no. "I'm keeping a journal."

"About what?"

"How it felt when my grandfather taught me to fly fish Navajo Lake, in the old days, before the tourists and speedboats ruined it. The change of seasons. Modern-day *penitentes*, you know, your basic New Mexico stuff."

"Penitentes?" Lily said. "Those guys who flagellate themselves and lug crosses to Chimayo? Ick, Tres. That always gave me the creeps."

"It's fascinating," he said. "One of the carvers who makes the statues of the *santos* is letting me apprentice to him. A few Anglos have joined the brotherhood. Spirituality's a good thing."

"Just tell me you're not into the cutting part of it."

He spread his hands out on the table. "As you can see, I nick myself with the chisels, but I promise I don't do it on purpose."

Lily regarded his beautiful, dark hands. She wanted to take them in her own, look them over closely. She wanted to see those carvings, too. "Thank God for that."

"I need some time to consider all my options, decide where I want to go from here. Up there in the cabin, on good days, the answers almost come to me."

"Is all this reorganizing because you got divorced?"

"Nope."

He looked out the window at the passing traffic, and Lily studied the close-up view of his profile. In California he'd be lumped into the category of Mexican, all the subtleties of blood and family dismissed due to the color of his skin. The prominent brow and ancestral cheekbones connected him to this particular region of the state, however. The full lips she used to kiss until they were sore made a part of him hers forever. Stepping back into that time when the whole world was open to the seemed about as possible as stepping forward into something else.

"I expected I'd be married forever, like my parents were. Whatever crossroads I was standing at way back when, I think I made a wrong turn."

Lily imagined their daughter seated with them at this table, a family discussing her education versus a future with some young guy she was head over heels in love with. No way on earth would Lily have known how to advise her. "Everybody has regrets."

"Yeah." The coffee arrived, and they took hold of their cups. "Are you dating anybody special? Has one of those California muscle guys got hold of your heart?"

She took a sip of her coffee and burned the tip of her tongue. "Hey, did you know there's no such thing as a California native? It's true— even the surfers were originally from Cleveland."

"So if surfers are out, what's in?"

Lily peered into her mug, filled with more milk than coffee. "*Mas que nada*. Well, until recently, I was dating this cabinetmaker."

"Hope he at least left you with custom cupboards."

Lily laughed. "I wish."

"So, what did he do that caused him to go from recent to late?"

"Where do you want me to start?"

"The end's usually a pretty good place."

"Blaise was a lot of fun when he wanted to be. We played softball on his construction crew's team. You'll be glad to know I've maintained my stellar pitching arm. We rode horses, even though Southern California has maybe one trail left. He took me country-and-western dancing, which they've turned into some kind of weird religion, I swear. All the couples wear matching shirts! When it came to the important stuff, though, he was selfish. I made myself believe that didn't matter. One day he called me squaw. Then he did it more than once. It's impossible to educate someone who says it twice. So, *adios* cabinetmaker."

"Guess he didn't know any better than to mess around with a Wilder woman."

"Guess he learned. So how about you? Did you go through Hillsborough debutantes like M&Ms?"

"I'm afraid my most successful long-term dating relationship in the last three years has been with my left hand."

Lily laughed. "I'm sorry. It's just such a relief to talk to someone you've shared a past with, someone who doesn't need to be wined, dined, or impressed, isn't it? No stupid games."

Tres took a drink of his coffee. "Whatever game we're playing, at least it's aboveboard. Lily, do you ever—"

The nostalgia flooding his face caused her to hold up her hand. "You would have gotten sick of me. One of us would have felt the other held us back. Bottom line, we were too young."

"Sounds like a lot of good reasons."

"You got married to someone else, Tres."

"Only because I didn't want to be alone."

They were quiet. Lily wanted to run to her car, drive back to California, and quick find some brain-dead handsome hunk to take her mind as far from all of this as possible. "Weren't you happy?"

"Tried to make myself believe I was. What I liked best about being married was just renting movies on the weekend, kicking back in my blue jeans, eating popcorn, reading the paper. Of course, most of the time it was Leah and I who did that. Debbie traveled a lot for her work. Which was where she met the guy she left me for."

"Debbie's an idiot."

"Not really. We're still friends on the days I don't hate her. What made you run away from your job?"

Lily tried to paint an objective portrait of that woman dying during the gallbladder surgery. "Anymore good doctors are rare, it seems like. After the gallbladder lady it felt like my world was one of those Malibu landslides. Suddenly no place but Rancho Costa Plente made sense. So here I am drinking makeshift latte and telling you my life story. Okay, man of mystery, your turn."

At that moment he bumped her knee with his under the table. Lily pressed back. Tres laid a five-dollar bill down, anchoring it with his spoon. Pretending there was no urgency, they walked toward their cars, which were still in the market parking lot. Before Lily could open her door, Tres took hold of her, pulled her close, and held on. A minute later, he kissed her forehead. Kissing at eighteen was like the forest fires that had claimed so much of Bandelier a few years back, Lily imagined. Seventeen years later, people are aware of how long it takes to reforest the landscape.

Thirty-five miles up into the mountains she followed Tres's truck to his parents' old cabin. They parked alongside each other under the tall pines, and he unlocked the door. He laid down a Pendleton blanket in front of the fireplace, knelt and lit the logs in the grate. She set her purse on the table, next to his notebook computer and the stack of paper lying facedown next to the printer. Part of her wanted to go directly to the blanket, just lie down and get this over with. She looked around the cabin at his simple digs: There was a workbench with blanks of cotton-wood and curly shavings. On it a half-finished statue of Jesus was wrapped in a green cloth. One glass, one plate, one bowl were stacked in the dish drainer. The neatly made double bed had a sleeping bag for a bedspread, pulled flat like a comforter. She was disrupting this peaceful den Tres'd made for himself. If she let him back into her heart, even briefly, those earlier losses that haunted her would ache even more. He came up behind her and put his hands on her shoulders.

"I'd better give my parents a call," Lily said. "Where's your phone?"

"Don't have one."

She reached for her purse and retrieved the cell phone, punching in the number of her parents' ranch. Shep answered. "Sheppy, it's Lily. Tell Mami I ran into an old friend and won't be home—" she looked at Tres before finishing her sentence. He held his fingers against her cheek. "For a couple of days, maybe. If it's important, she can reach me at the cell phone number. Please take care of Buddy for me." She hung up before Shep could protest.

"This Buddy," Tres said. "Do I have to beat him up, or can I intimidate him with a few college degrees?"

"Buddy's my dog, Tres."

He took the cell phone from her and threw it on the bed. "Come sit with me by the fire," he said.

"Like all we're going to do is sit," Lily said.

For a long time they kissed. Slowly the revelations that this was familiar territory came to them. Lily shook her head as if she needed to clear it. Tres kicked off his boots. Lily allowed him to pull hers off, first one, then the other, and when he came back to her on the blanket she undid the buttons on his shirt. He looked down and solemnly watched her fingers move against the fabric. When the two halves of the shirt hung loose, she slid her hands inside and shut her eyes, feeling the planes of his chest, the warm skin, the small amount of hair that grew around his nipples.

"There's no way I'm doing this without condoms," she said.

"I don't have any."

"Well, I do," Lily said, and went to fetch her purse. Inside, next to a MAC lipstick in a shade called Desire, she found three. She threw them across the room, and Tres caught them in his left hand.

Back on the blanket, he set them aside. Lily lay down, and he pulled her arms above her head, holding them there with one hand. "I seem to remember you used to enjoy this," he said, forcing her to lie still while he outfitted himself, and then began to enter her inch by agonizingly erotic inch.

Lily remembered, too. How this had felt was a large percentage of why she'd failed to hook up with another man. It wasn't sex, which she felt could be had with just about anybody, it was the entire package. No one else could compete with her past.

At first they took things slow, checking each other's reactions, sighing over every successful stroke and shiver, but later the way they moved teetered on the brink of rough, pushing the boundaries of pleasure right up there next to pain. The edge felt necessary, as if in order to complete the telling of their histories this helped to dismiss their past lovers, and in doing so, allowed this touching to feel different, to belong wholly to them.

The next morning, driving down the mountain looking for a store that sold condoms, Lily was sorry she wasn't repping for Trojan. She stood at the birth control display in the bathroom products aisle of the tiny grocery store and weighed her options. Buying a three-pack, well, that seemed pessimistic. Just like carrying them in your purse, it smacked of one-night stands and low self-esteem. The box of twelve could mean one favored bargains, or expected the current affair to proceed with good sense, to set its own cautious pace. If things fizzled out after one more time, at least eleven USA-made brothers waited there in the box as a kind of consolation. Forget even considering the twenty-four pack. Say she died in a car crash on the way home. No matter what good thing she'd accomplished in her lifetime, sold the most laparoscopes, taught Buddy to play championship Frisbee, won the Pulitzer, whoever gathered up her personal effects and returned them to her family would remember Lily Wilder as a nympho, and a nympho she would forever remain.

She opened her wallet and extracted more of Mami's grocery money to pay for two turkey sandwiches on whole wheat, a gallon jug of apple cider, and most important, twelve condoms. She'd chosen four packages of three each—flavored, fluorescent, ribbed—let her fly-fishing-nature-poet-woodcarver who wouldn't tell her what he did for a living make of her selections whatever he cared to—just so long as he did not impregnate her. The clerk in the general store she'd found at the junction of 150 and 64 was happy to wait on her. October was his slow season. The markup on condoms was over 200 percent.

For the sake of fairness, they gave all the brands a try. Vibra-ribbed Rough Riders caused Lily to philosophize, loudly, on what men assumed women wanted and what amounted to just plain *ow.* Tres countered, stating that Kiss of Mint was definitely slanted toward one partner's pleasure, though he had to concede, they did leave a pleasant tang on her mouth. And the glow-in-the-dark kind that made Tres's erection resemble Luke Skywalker's light saber were responsible for so much silly laughter they both agreed they'd buy that kind again in a heartbeat.

Two days later Tres was at his notebook computer typing when Lily awoke. When she threw her arms around him and started kissing his neck, he peeled her away, put a finger to her lips and returned to typing. Lily walked over to the bench full of wood shavings and chisels. She picked up the statue of Jesus, which now possessed crude facial features, sorrowful eyes, and the beginnings of a beard. Carvings like this could be found all over New Mexico; he could sell it just as it was and make money. But Tres was going for a more realistic finished product. He kept using the word *craft*. Lily drank her cup of instant coffee, day-dreaming how good freshly ground Italian roast used to taste. She imagined the cupboard in California where she kept emergency jars of pesto, and the cute kitchen towels she never used, decorated with embroidered chili peppers, folded over the over door handle. Was she lonely or just bored? She got dressed in order to invoke the universal cure—shopping—which in this case meant driving halfway back down the mountain to the general store.

Around her the cold cases hummed, and an old woman asked the clerk if they had any tripe. *Posole*, Lily thought, and began to gather ingredients: She picked up a bag of fresh hominy, two cans of chicken broth, a fat yellow onion, a head of garlic, fresh oregano, a string of green peppers, and a packet of bay leaves. At the checkout stand, she tucked the twenty-four pack of condoms unobtrusively between the staples. When the clerk picked them up she asked, "Are you sure that's the only brand you have?"

"We got plenty of those lambskin kind."

"Ick. Nothing else in the storeroom?"

"Lady, you bought out everything we had. That there is the last of 'em. I ordered more, but it takes about a week. They come from Los Angeles. It takes the truck awhile to get here."

California—even hundreds of miles away she couldn't escape. They were protection from pregnancy; that was all that mattered. "Can I get two more of those turkey sandwiches, please?"

He fetched the sandwiches from the cooler, totaled her bill, and counted back her change. Lily looked at the dwindling, crumpled bills and coins and felt a small pocket of panic catch fire beneath her heart. Each day that ticked by was like Mami's money, irretrievably spent. Soon she would have to emerge from her comfortable little nest and face real life. During the five days she and Tres had spent together at his mountain cabin, the air had turned from a coppery fall with summer-warm days to thirty degrees at night. Their daylight hours were taken up with hiking and talking, fooling around outdoors. Tres showed her how to tie flies, and she made him let her wear his fishing vest, which hit her mid-thigh, which he found so sexy that it generally led to taking it off. She threw a softball to him and proved that the strength of her pitching arm was intact. Sometimes he worked on the statues, and she was content to sit by the fire listening to his chisel plane away thin layers of wood. Every night was hers. They used every condom in the box, agreeing that plain old LifeStyles, which she'd just bought, was the worst. Tres said it felt like "sex in a wetsuit." Lily dreamed about going to work in a laboratory where she devoted herself to engineering a prophylactic that felt more like skin than skin itself. These days protected sex was essential, but logic counted for zip when you wanted to merge with a man. And despite her vows not to let that happen, Lily wanted to be so close to Tres Quintero that not even atoms separated their bodies. Fine, okay, they'd get blood tests as soon as she could bear to let him out of the bed for longer than it took to empty his bladder so they wouldn't have to worry, but six months, the waiting period from partner to partner, seemed like forever. She was on the pill, but no way was she going to take chances. *If* this was going to last, which was an if of the largest dimensions, she was going to do things by the book.

The windshield of the Lexus was splattered with pine pitch, but until she got the wiper fixed the best she could do was smear it around. She drove squinting up the highway, her pager rattling around in the trunk, her car phone forgotten back at the cabin. She wore Tres's old flannel camping shirt with the sleeves rolled up to her elbows and didn't care how ridiculous that looked. The shirt smelled enough like him that she felt like he was holding her even when he was busy at the computer or hunched over the carvings. Her denim breeches were so dirty she imagined they could probably stand up by themselves. Every night she rinsed out her lacy panties in the sink and hung them over the shower door in his bathroom to dry. When she pulled them over her hips the next morning she told herself, *Just one more day, and then I'll drive back to the ranch and explain to Mami that her two hundred dollars bought one of her daughters a little happiness for once in her miserable life, and hey, what a bargain. No, I won't. I'll go to the nearest bank, wire her the money, sneak back to California, my lucrative career, and my Lilliputian condo, where the jets fly overhead every two hours but if I stand on tiptoe I can see Catalina Island from my deck when the smog lifts, which makes it all worth it. Yeah, that's exactly what I'll do. Sure thing.*

Lies were lies, no matter how you dissected them. It didn't trouble Lily's conscience to fib her way through a sales meeting or dinner with egomaniacal surgeons and their well-dressed, culture-club wives. Unlike Rose the pious, Lily'd break commandments to accomplish her goal. Well, probably not murder, but all the others possessed some level of pliability. She wondered what her sister was up to. She hoped that Rose had taken her advice and hog-tied the veterinarian to her bed. She probably hadn't. For sex outside of matrimony, Rose needed an engraved invitation, a money-back guarantee, not to mention blessing from the Vatican. It was a shame, because life was too short not to have sex like this. She wondered how it was two sisters turned out so differently. Lily, born in the heat of August, socking away IRA-Keogh money, and the minute she could afford to, buying horse property, that leopard Appaloosa, sixteen hands high, and all hers, just chucking it all. Rose, born in one very unwelcome March snowstorm, had opted for motherhood, stuck close to her hometown, sewed curtains with lace edges. In spite of all that icky *domesticity*, it was Rose who had a horse in the barn and another at the ranch with a foal on the way. Lily'd been in the corporate game a lot of years, and her leopard Appaloosa was about as tangible as the drawings she and her sister sketched on each other's backs.

Just like Pop said, love was dangerous business. It could slice your heart down to the bone before showing the glint of the blade. Lily prided herself on knowing when to put up her shield. No way would she end up like Rose, fading away, some beautifully wrapped gift that never found its way to the recipient. Lily knew how . . . *Oh, be fair*, she chided herself. *Rose isn't the only fool in the Wilder family. Believing some phantom leopard Appy was the answer to the gnawing hole inside your heart is just as pathetic. Day hikes by the river, making moony faces to Tres over her homemade* posole, *not even stellar sex constitutes a real future. Nobody, not even smart people, ever stops trying to find their one true one. What happens if you found him, Lily, for the second time, but you aren't* his?

She gripped the steering wheel and bit her lower lip until it went blue under her teeth. They were old friends, using each other. She should have married him right after high school, had that baby instead of aborted it when it was no more than the size of a sneeze. But if she'd never had her career, she wouldn't know what it was like to fly to London, or stay in fancy hotels, or stand at the front of a roomful of surgeons rapt at her instruction on the instruments she sold. And she would have missed every moment of it; IQ didn't evaporate when one procreated. She was thirty-five now, too old to have a baby—well, maybe not too old, but definitely too selfish. How could she remember what a baby needed when half the time she forgot to feed Buddy? She ought to call the ranch again. No, it would be okay. They knew how to get hold of her. Shep would take care of Buddy, maybe even teach him another trick. How could she abandon the beloved blue boy she'd dropped three hundred dollars on a collar for just a week and a half ago? Sexual amnesia, similar to post-traumatic stress syndrome, only this was more about the continual pursuit of relief causing you to do crazy stuff like waste your mother's grocery money on condoms.

"I'm back," she announced to Tres as he stood chopping kindling on the stump outside the cabin. "And I'm going to cook you supper from scratch."

Tres sank the ax blade into the stump and turned to her with a smile. Lily's heart skittered in her chest like it was spilling its rhythm forever. She went into his arms and breathed in all the complex scents of his body: He smelled like honest sweat from hard work, and that shaving gel with the stinging herbal aroma. Best of all, he smelled like her and all the things they'd done together. Another good thing about *posole* was how long it took to cook: You threw all the ingredients into a pot, and then let it simmer for hours.

"All I asked was what your job was," Lily explained. "I don't see how that's prying. Did you get fired? These days everybody does, Tres, that or downsized. Please, please, *please* tell me. It's driving me nuts not to know."

"I wasn't fired."

"Sued?"

"No. Please, let it alone, Lily."

In addition to his job, they skated wide circles around the reasons they had left each other seventeen years ago, but each was thinking about it, and in those unavoidable awkward moments of silence, the other could tell. Lily sighed. "Well, we're running out of topics. What can we talk about that's safe?"

"Tell me about your family. What's Rose up to? How's her kids?"

"Did you know that Philip died two years ago?"

"Yeah, I heard. What a shame."

"Rose was mad at me, so I didn't get to go to the funeral. I planned to crash it until Pop ordered me to stay home. It was probably just as well. I would have told her to save her tears."

"Why?"

Lily shivered, and Tres rubbed her bare arms.

"Because he cheated on her." Lily sat up in bed, pulling the sheet over her shoulders. "I regret not getting to throw a rock at his coffin."

"Poor Rose. Did you know who he was sleeping with?"

"Not for a long time. I think Rose is falling in love again. That's more important than anything that happened in the past, right? The only problem is Austin Donavan seems to still be hung up on his ex, Leah the unforgettable."

Tres smiled. "I know Leah Donavan."

His smile was far too revealing for their acquaintance to be friendly. "Really. How well?"

"Well enough, a few years back. Seemed like a good idea at the time."

She smacked him with the pillow. "You bird dog!"

Tres took the pillow from her. "Hey, don't blame me. One night I bought her a drink in El Farol and she was all over me. It was pretty obvious it didn't matter who I was so long as I had a penis."

"Why, that little succubus!" Lily felt sick to her stomach. Someone— even Rose—could say the same of Lily's sex life. "Was she any good?"

"She cried a lot. That usually doesn't sent men into fits of passion. She seemed confused and lonely. Lots of people believe sex will repair those rips. Doesn't usually work, however."

Lily chewed on that thought for awhile, nervous that his words hit so close to home. "Now you have to tell me about your family," she said. "Unless you worked for them, which would make the topic taboo, and in which case I withdraw the question."

Tres reached for his pants, taking out his wallet. "Well, I have my stepdaughter, Leah."

Lily stared at the girl's senior picture. Premed, valedictorian, she looked like one of Pop's really good horses, beautiful, and possessing bloodlines to die for. Leah wasn't even his biological child, but for the twelve years his marriage had lasted, Tres had been a real father to her, teaching her to ride a bike, helping her with her math, meeting the boys she dated, all that good dad stuff a girl needs to grow up halfway normal. Since the divorce they no longer lived in the same house, but remained close enough that they talked on the phone once a week. Leah, Leah, Leah. Hearing how much he loved her made Lily crazy-jealous. Any baby she might produce now would have a fifty-fifty chance of ending in miscarriage, and then there was Down's syndrome, or it might come out looking like a lab rat since Lily had been on the pill for twenty years, and who knew what that did to a woman's eggs?

"Let's put our clothes back on, go for a walk, enjoy the sunset," Tres suggested. "I think we've told each other enough secrets for one day."

The path they took wound behind the one-room log cabin that had once belonged to his parents. They'd had Tres late in life and were dead now. Lily couldn't imagine having no blood family, none of that eternal extended drama she was constantly plugged in to. Without Mami and Pop, her niece and nephew, the threat of the Martínezes' disapproval, everything would seem so tame. The pines on either side of the cabin made a swishing noise in the wind. It sounded to her ears for all the world like God whispering over and over, "You're nuts, you're nuts." Her stomach cramped. It had been so long since she'd had any pesto or Krisprolls that whenever she thought of them she trembled like a junkie.

They climbed up the mountainside until they found an outcropping of rock flat enough to sit on. Tres put his arms around her. She nestled into the front of his body and he rested his chin on top of her head. He kissed her hair and pulled it behind her ears. They watched the sun blaze out, the sky turn dusky blue and the first stars begin to wink overhead. Under Lily's jacket, the chill raised gooseflesh. She had put herself into an extremely vulnerable position, and just like Pop said, that was where she wanted to be.

She tore another condom off its perforation, took the last turkey sandwich out of the fridge, and went to the old double bed where Tres was asleep in the funky sheets and unzipped sleeping bags. She took off the flannel shirt, dropped it to the floor and got into bed. When he didn't rouse, she gently nipped his shoulder. Then she sat back, holding a sandwich in one hand, the condom in the other.

He opened his eyes and she said, "There are two choices on the menu, sir. Food or flesh. You are the most double-jointed lover I've ever pleasured into unconsciousness, but not even you can eat and make love at the same time."

When Tres smiled, Lily thought he looked like a satyr. His quirky grin caused her to go stupid inside, made her want to reveal to him all her dangerous secrets. He lazily reached out for the sandwich and took a bite, chewed and swallowed. "Good sandwich."

Her mouth formed a little O of disappointment.

"Now, now." He set the sandwich down on the windowsill, grabbed the condom, and tore the wrapper open with his teeth. He slid the rubber onto his erection and wrestled Lily down on the bed. "Did you really think I'd choose food over you, *Cholula*?"

"Maybe."

He began to make love to her again, moving inside her for the second time that day. "You really thought that?"

"Yes. No. Tres, how can I can think straight when you're doing that?"

"I don't want you to think at all except of this." He pressed his hand to the small of her back, lifting her off the mattress, tucking her into him. He held her there firmly, still moving inside her, so artfully positioned that when Lily shut her eyes she felt everything twice as intensely. In a far-off corner of her mind, she imagined herself brick by sandy brick building the astonishing structure of orgasm. No blueprints, no angles, no mortar, just one long impossible arc that spanned years and stacked up higher than she could ever scale. But that was all right; this edifice demanded to be taken apart. To serve its purpose it had to fall to pieces. Who knew what finally tipped her over? The combination of nostalgia and experience present in the boy who was now a man, the first person she'd loved all those years ago who'd learned all this hair-raising technique somewhere else, with other women, but had brought it back to her, his first lover? Pressing up against him, she came once, then after a brief rest, again, and Tres went so high on male pride that now he was coming, too. Lily didn't care. All this good luck made her holler loud enough to rattle the windows. In great gasps that ended in yawns, each tried to catch his or her breath.

After the daze cleared they sat up in bed, taking turns drinking from the nearly empty gallon jug of cider. Tres's back was to the window. The wintry sunlight lit up his brown shoulders. Lily ran her fingers over his chest. Skinny men's bodies stayed hard and muscular with so much less effort. She watched him fold his empty sandwich wrapper into precise, defined lines before setting it aside.

"I could be happy if I got to watch the sun set every day in these mountains. Life without designer clothes wouldn't exactly kill me."

"Temporarily," Tres said. "The older we get, the harder it seems to change what we've become accustomed to."

She turned over on her belly. "Oh, boy."

"Oh, boy, what?"

"Sounds like the build-up to a kiss-off line. You find me too intense, don't you? I was good enough to screw blind for a solid week but not refined enough to take out in public. Break it to me gently, Tres, technically I'm still enjoying my afterglow."

"Afterglows. Plural. Men notice these things."

"Well, if they do, you're the first."

He took hold of her chin, looked deep into her eyes, and she could see he was speaking the truth. "Yes, you scare me. You always have. Back in high school whenever you got mad at me you just about stopped my heart."

"Who cares about high school? I want to know about right now."

"Sugarbush, making love with you feels like riding a freight train full speed through a very tight tunnel. Three orgasms in fifteen minutes? You could say I find it a little overwhelming."

She tried to remember each one, to separate them out, but everything blended together. She placed a hand on his forearm and raked her fingers through the sparse hair that grew there. "I guess I could try to narrow it down to one, if that would make you happy."

"Don't you dare."

"Then what in hell are you getting at, Tres? All of a sudden things are capital S serious. Knock it off."

He scratched his stubbly beard. "Lily, I came here with a plan to take a break from a job I know I don't belong in. To think. Get a little writing done. Carve *santos*. Live on my savings with a woodstove for heat, and make it through the winter subsisting on beans and rice. I have exactly that much money and no more. I can't even afford to buy the condoms unless there's someplace that sells them discount."

What did that have to do with anything? She made a hundred fifty grand a year, give or take a few bonuses. "I'm not asking you to support me, Tres. I just want to keep on doing whatever it is we're doing here. I'll buy the condoms. I'll pay for the blood tests, and then we won't need the stupid condoms."

"Debbie cleaned my clock in the divorce."

"Debbie! I swear, Tres, the name alone should have been your first clue. So start over. Lesser individuals have done that and succeeded." She tipped the jug of cider up and took a drink.

"I'm ass-deep in student loans. Medical school cost a great deal." He gestured around the cabin, frowning. "You're sitting in the only house I'll probably ever own."

In her mind Lily was all set to say, *We could live in a teepee and I'd still want you five times a day,* but instead she choked, spraying cider down her chin, onto her bare breasts, and what came out was, "Medical school? Holy Mother of God. You said you had taken a leave of absence from your *job.* Job means an engineer or a professor of physics or a guy who sells carpet or something. You can't be a doctor."

He put his mouth to the cider creek running down her breast and stopped it with his tongue. "Why not?"

Lily shuddered. "Be a car mechanic, Tres, be a hobo. Just don't put on a white coat and think you run the world, okay?"

She flopped down on the bed, hating herself. *You could cut him some slack, Lily. Maybe he's a pediatrician who worked for an HMO; they have regular hours, make less* dinero, *but in the long run, that's a doable life, except maybe for those annoying Christmas parties.* She turned her head slightly and studied his dark, smooth chest, bare of tattoos, nearly hairless owing to the diluted Indian blood that ran through his veins. She could use a Spanish phrase, and he wouldn't have to run for a dictionary. He'd never call her *Señorita* in a pejorative way. He was so attentive to her needs that it crossed her mind he could be a gynecologist. He ticked all the checks of desirable qualities off the Lily list: When he coughed he covered his mouth, and he did not engage in her single most unbearable male habit, picking his teeth in public. He kept his nails trimmed—surgeon? Not a surgeon, please— and kissed her so hard he bruised her mouth, leaving behind a marvelous soreness that made her remember everything that had led up to it, starting with the coffee and their legs bumping under that café table.

"Please accept my apology," she said softly. "That was a really awful thing for me to say. You're probably a wonderful doctor. I've been on my job too long to be anything but jaded. I promise I'll go into therapy."

"That will be handy."

"Why, Tres?"

"Because I was—still am, I guess, until they revoke my license—a psychiatrist."

Lily covered her face with the sheet. If only it were a little more substantial than one-hundred-thread count, something like a lead apron, something she could hide beneath forever. Through the cloth she said, "Does that mean you've been cataloging every little thing I've done in bed? I've tried very hard to hide all my neuroses and craziness factors. I'm utterly transparent, aren't I? The worst head case you've ever bedded. Admit it."

He pulled the sheet down, palmed her face, and smoothed the dark hair away from her forehead before he kissed her. "There's no hope for you whatsoever. No meds I can think of to bolster your deficiency, no analysis to unknot those convoluted thought processes. I think probably the only avenue open is for you to stay in therapy until the day you die."

She turned onto her side, resting her chin on her outstretched arms, and looked up at him. "That's probably the nicest thing any man's ever said to me."

"Well, that's a shame. You deserve nice things. Every time I make love to you it feels like we've reinvented the wheel."

No man had ever asked Lily to marry him. Maybe no one ever would. But she would treasure Tres's words until she was a wrinkled old lady, senile, good for nothing but shelling peas into a *colador* on the porch. Even if all this ended tomorrow, and—twenty-four pack, there was every chance it would—she could carry what had happened around with her forever. *I had one week of bliss,* she thought. *More than most people get in a lifetime of ordinary lovemaking. More than Rose got, for sure.* She understood her parents' relationship for the first time in her life, Pop allowing Mami her separateness, her airplane, the greyhounds, the artists. Maybe that affair of hers had made them realize how important they were to each other. Just look at the love that had come rocketing back to them. Probably the only way to see if such magic could happen to you was to step out onto the ledge yourself.

She stuck a toe out from under the sheet. The room was chilly. "Will you be my therapist, Tres? Or does sleeping with your patient violate some physician code?"

"Oh, baby," he said. "I wasn't even a very good psychiatrist to strangers."

Lily's heart slipped inside her ribs. She sat up and put her arms around him in an effort to get closer. "I was kidding."

"I wasn't. I couldn't make any money if I set up a practice here," he said into her hair. "New Mexico is full up with shrinks, counselors, *curanderas*, and witches."

"Don't forget shamans."

"Yeah, but usually they're the real thing."

They lay down and looked out the window, neither of them talking for a long while. Lily watched the pine boughs sway in the wind. Somewhere far up the mountain, snow crystals were forming, flaking down onto the higher elevations, settling into the cracks between rocks, covering up anything that could grow in that thin air. "I want to quit my job," she said.

"And do what?"

"I don't know. I could waitress. I have a great ass. Truck drivers will shower me with tips."

"You'd last a week, Lily. You're too smart not to do what you do."

Lily ran her fingers through his thick, dark hair. "But Tres, think of what I'd get in return: Clean air, no traffic, seasons. A chance to be with you."

He studied her face. "Let's go down the mountain today. I'd like to see your family. I want to meet your dog."

She shook her head no. "Let's just have this be about you and me."

"We can't do that. People come with attachments."

"Like food processors? Chop, dice, puree?"

"Yes. In my case, Leah. In yours the Don, Mama Greyhound, Sister Rose, and Buddy."

"Sounds like a band from the sixties. Pop's cool with whatever I do. I have him wrapped around my little finger. I always have."

"He's still your father, Lily. Men have rituals. It has to do with honor. I compliment him on his horses, he decides to overlook the fact that I'm banging his daughter bowlegged. We shake hands, talk basketball, and all is copacetic."

Take all this out in the world? Share it? Allow Mami to see that Lily had lost her toughness? What would Rose say? What if the moment the real world touched what they had, the whole thing disintegrated? "Tres, I spent all my mother's grocery money, and Buddy Guy probably thinks I dropped off the face of the earth. He's made me feel safe the last five years. I owe him some kind of explanation. I'll go. You stay here and work on your stuff."

"How about before Buddy came on board? How did you feel then?"

"Out of my mind twenty-four hours a day. I'm telling you, I have to leave California."

"It means driving three hours to catch a movie. Could you trade in your fancy car for something with four-wheel drive? Live through mud season?"

"I was getting tired of it anyway. Plus some *culo* broke my windshield wiper. It's a Lexus. The dealer will charge me a thousand dollars just to look at it. I'll check the terms of my lease. Maybe I can just turn the son of a bitch in and take a loss."

"A hundred and fifty thousand dollars a year isn't pocket change."

She thought for a long while before answering. Tres was right. She'd have to make do with so much less, maybe never even buy designer labels again. She took a breath and said what was in her heart. "I'm tired of corporate America. Outrageous car phone bills, being tethered to that annoying pager, conferences, expense reports, not to mention pantyhose. I want to take a five-year nap, Tres. And I'd like take it with you."

When she located the courage to look over and see how that news set with him, Lily saw that he'd fallen asleep. Despite the unsettled feeling in her belly, she nestled into the crook of his shoulder and aimed herself toward that last precious pocket of calm. Soon enough, she knew, they'd drive down the mountain, into the consequences.

11

Ven a Mí

"Take Paloma," Rose said, without looking up from the dead files in the storeroom. "She knows how to give shots."

"So do you."

"Paloma's got her Animal Health Technician certificate. I have a high school diploma and really poor judgment in men."

"Dammit, Rose." Austin shut the door behind him. "What's it going to take to move us past that kiss?"

His bootheels struck the creaky planks as he crossed the floor. The veterinarian smelled of a day's worth of hard work. Rose typed his schedule; she knew he'd spent the last eight hours performing a vaccination clinic at the Floralee Equestrian Stables. Clinics were exhausting work: horse after horse, dozens of injections, threading lengths of plastic tubing down uncooperative animals' nostrils, pouring worming medication through the funnel, then having to blow hard on the tube's end to make sure all of the medicine went where it was supposed to and not all over his shirt, fifty-fifty odds at best. Whenever he came back from a stint like that, Austin was a little woozy and definitely parasite-proof. During previous clinics she had helped him float teeth, filing quickly inside a horse's mouth, both of them fancy stepping to avoid getting kicked to death, and there were always a handful of horse owners who, since the vet was already there and they didn't have to pay for the call-out, couldn't resist asking for a little free medical advice on various problems. Austin had to be about to drop from exhaustion. In his shoes Rose wouldn't have wanted to work a rodeo tomorrow, gay or straight. However, that didn't mean she was going to fall for the poor-me routine. Downstairs that sneaky Paloma probably held a stethoscope to the ceiling, listening to their every word.

"We're miles past the kiss," she said. "I'm still not going to the rodeo."

"Paloma's got some big family whoop-de-do going down in Pojoaque all weekend. Nacio's cooking all the food, and apparently every last one of her relatives from Spain will be there."

"I'm your bookkeeper, Austin. That's all I am."

He stood close enough to her that she could feel the heat from his body, and smell the faintly sweet odor of horse manure caught in the treads of his boots. "You're my right arm. What is it you're doing over there, anyway?"

"Filing." She looked up at him for the first time since he'd walked into the room. A good-size bruise in the shape of a *C* marked his left cheekbone. "What in God's name happened to your face?"

"Arab horse took a dislike to it. Are you wearing a different perfume than usual?"

"I don't wear perfume, Austin. Did you get an X ray?"

"It must be your soap."

She pursed her lips, entirely irritated. "You want me to drive you to the hospital? You might have a hairline fracture."

"I've got a hard head. I'll be fine."

"Any double vision? Are your pupils the same size?"

He shook his head. "Tastes a little like blood when I swallow, but that'll go away. Whatever brand soap it is you use, it smells real nice."

Rose tossed the file folders back into the cardboard box. A cloud of dust rose up, and she sneezed, loud and healthy, the same way her sister Lily did. Every time either of them cut loose with a robust *a-choo*, Pop always made a smart remark, as if they weren't feminine. *There go my girls, sneezing like the horses they are.*

"Bless you."

"Thanks." She was too concerned about his cheek to give him the drop-dead look she wanted to. "I think I liked you better when you were mean to me."

"Please come with me, Rose."

"Why should I? You're the one who drove drunk and got sentenced to community service. It's a rodeo, for Pete's sake. You've vetted dozens of them. What is there to do besides stand around and wait for some idiot to run his horse into a wall?"

He lowered his voice. "Don't leave me stranded out there in gay America. What do I do if some nancy boy takes a liking to me?"

And the sad fact was, it wasn't a cliché: The male ego truly knew no bounds. "Oh, my gosh, what if they're just a bunch of ordinary people grateful to have a vet to look after the animals?"

"Hell, maybe I should blow it off, see if Eloy will let me work this off in weekend jail." He held out his hand, trembling visibly. "Look at me. I've got the shakes so bad somebody ought to lock me up."

"Don't try to make me feel guilty, Austin. Won't work. Will not, cannot, did not. You think I give a damn if you go to jail? I don't care if you have a concussion. Ruin your practice, develop brain damage, just leave me out of it."

She tried to pull away when he put his arm around her shoulders, but as thin as Austin was, he was stronger and taller. He knuckled the top of her head and messed up her hair. When he brushed her cheek with his lips Rose could feel the heat emanating from his injured cheek. He should be lying down with an icepack against it. It needed to be x-rayed, two complete views, because head injuries weren't anything to fool around with. Doctors could give you new corneas, a replacement liver, a heart and lungs at the same time, but the brain was still a mystery. Rose pushed him away, but his touch and the kiss had already succeeded in reminding her of what had happened inside her Bronco that night in Taos.

"Pick me up at nine on Saturday morning. Dress casual."

"I said I wasn't going."

"Yeah, but you didn't mean it."

"I have plans, Austin. I'm going riding. Then I'm washing my hair. I might dye it."

Austin reached out to touch her, but she ducked away. "I like your hair the way it is." He dug into his pocket for his keys, and she watched the denim pull tight across his groin. "Here's the keys to my truck. Already fed my animals. Figure I'll spend the night here. Tomorrow morning, all you have to do is honk. If you don't show up, I'll use my extra set and hope no cops stop me. Now I'm going to go read *A Farewell to Arms*. Ernie's happy-go-lucky outlook always cheers me up."

He left the storeroom, and Rose sat down hard on the floor in her black jeans, mentally cussing him. The pants were size six Calvins, one full size smaller than what she usually wore. Until this week they'd been tucked into a far corner of the bureau drawer that used to be Philip's, but she'd lost weight from not eating regular meals, and now they fit her again. She was wearing a new Liz Claiborne shirt, plaid with muted pinks and dove gray, featuring a thin stripe of black that complemented the jeans. Unlike most of her clothes, which were loose and serviceable, this shirt was fitted, the fabric clung close to her breasts, the cut emphasized her waist, and when she looked at herself in the dressing-room mirror she was absolutely shocked at how attractive she looked. The hell with what Lily and Amanda said about the outlet stores, for $19.95, this shirt was a real find. She sniffed the cuff, pulled it back and smelled her wrist. No scent there but her regular old self. Either Austin's sobriety had heightened his senses or he was lying in order to manipulate her into going to the rodeo. Well, if she went, which would only be to check on his possible concussion, she would remain steadfastly out of reach, her newly developed shields all the way up. After that night with the *polvos*, Rose had decided that love and all its trappings were ridiculous, something for young people who didn't yet know better, which she certainly did. She put the candles on a shelf in the kitchen pantry in case of electrical failure, tucked the powders into a drawer, and tried to forget the whole embarrassing episode with the *curandera*.

Upstairs in her office she began to tidy up the week's invoices so she could go home with a clear conscience. Just as she reached for her purse, the phone rang. It was Mami. "Have you heard from your sister?" she asked.

"I thought Lily was at the ranch with you and Pop."

Mami hedged. "Oh, probably she's around here somewhere. Forget I asked. How are you, *mija?* You never call your mother."

You're never home, Rose wanted to say. *You're either in your Cessna 150 flying track dogs to freedom or you're gallivanting around in fancy clothes making infomercials. I'm where I always am, nine to five; you know where you can find me if you want to talk so badly.* Rose knew full well that this line of attack indicated something was up with Lily. Something not quite right. Mami's free spirit would never admit to outright alarm, but deep down she was a mother or she wouldn't have called. "What happened? Did you two have a fight?"

"No. It's just been a little while since I've seen her, so I thought maybe she was with you."

"How long a while? Did you try calling her pager? Her voice mail? The house in California?"

"Rose Ann. *Cálmate.* Your sister is fine. She'll show up when she's finished with whatever it is she's doing. That isn't why I called, so stop trying to distract me."

Mother of God, deliver me strength, Rose prayed. *Help me not to reach through the receiver and strangle this woman who gave birth to me.* "What is it, Mami?"

"I was thinking it's been too long a time since we've had a mother-daughter day. Why don't we go to Ojo Caliente, or Ten Thousand Waves? I love their hour-long botanical facials. Last time I went I met a fellow who gives shiatsu massage; he's very good. Or we can rent one of the private tubs and just soak in our birthday suits and drink fresh-squeezed juice and feel so healthy. My treat."

Mami next to her, naked, that sixty-two-year-old body looking better than her own—now there was a stellar idea. Still, the idea of a man's hands, paid for or not, stroking her back, sounded worth any amount of shame. "I wish I could. Austin's forcing me to go with him to this rodeo he has to work tomorrow."

"I thought the Floralee rodeo was in July."

"It was." Rose didn't miss the subtle dig; her mother believed this rodeo talk was a cover for romance, not community service. "It's a *gay* rodeo, Mami. Austin has to be there all day Saturday since he drove drunk and Judge Trujillo didn't want to send him to jail. I suppose he wants me to stand around so nobody will hit on him. I have half a mind to paste a rainbow decal on his truck and not show up."

"Rainbows." Mami laughed. "Opportunities keep presenting themselves to you, honey. Take advantage. You know what I think. This is fate."

Rose sighed. "Fate is the stuff of musicals, Mami. I don't believe in it."

Her mother made a *tsk*ing noise, and Rose contemplated throwing the phone out the window. "*Enamorada,* it's all right there in your astrological charts. I can show you. In your past lives, you and Austin were lovers, soul mates. Something unfortunate that wasn't supposed to happen occurred, and you two were prematurely separated. Now here you are again, being thrown together to make things right in a cosmic sense. Larger powers are at work. It's going to happen. You should give in, *mija*. Surrender."

Rose ran her finger across the framed pictures on her desk. It was on purpose she didn't have one of her mother. The woman could drive her bats within five minutes. "Honestly, Mami, whenever you want to make your point you fish out some archaic Catholic saint, a Navajo legend nobody's ever heard of, or a Spanish cure that does the opposite of what you ask, and when all that fails, you blame it on star charts. How is it that none of your beliefs ever cancel each other out?"

"What I know is you and Austin were meant to be together."

"Don't you have a dog to fly somewhere?"

Her mother rattled off something in a language that sounded so much like the *curandera's* speech that the hair on Rose's arms stood up. Returning to English, she said, "I would move the earth to make my daughters happy. Rose Ann, you always fight what I am telling you. You know it hurts my heart, so why do you do it?"

Rose held the receiver away from her ear. "I really couldn't tell you. Maybe I'm just rotten to the core."

"Don't talk like that. You're a wonderful girl."

"Mami, I'm forty years old."

"You know, I've never been to a gay rodeo, and neither has your father. Maybe we'll show up."

"Pop probably has a million other things to do."

"We could take you and Austin to dinner afterward. I know this darling restaurant a friend of mine runs."

"Does it serve kangaroo?"

"*Descúlpame!* They served other dishes. Nobody was forced to order the wallaby."

Rose had scored one point. Time to get out of the game before she lost any ground. "I have to go, Mami. I have another call waiting."

"*Adios*, then. Maybe we'll see you tomorrow."

"Sure." *But please God not.* Rose hung up the phone and laid her head down on her desk blotter. There was no other call waiting. She picked at one edge of the heavy green paper until it began to fray. Across the hall she could hear Austin bumping around in his office, then the sound of the shower running. All night she'd fret over the possibility of his intercranial bleeding, which was what had killed Philip. His other injuries were major, clearly, but who knows, maybe they could have been repaired. So he wouldn't bleed to death they had removed his spleen before she got to the hospital. He had anyway, inside his skull. Not even Lily's fancy medical equipment could fix that. An echoey whistle sounded from the shower. After a grueling day's work and a kick in the head, Austin still possessed the energy to whistle.

Rose couldn't help but picture him soaping up every inch of his skinny body. There was barely enough space for one in that tiny shower stall. If two people tried to fit in there, they would be pressed together, unable to make anything but a mutually agreed upon move. She wondered what kind of soap he was using. Probably the disinfectant he washed his hands with in the exam rooms; men didn't care what they put on their bodies. Eventually he'd rinse off, step naked and wet across the tiles, his arm outstretched, blindly seeking wherever he'd left his towel, fumbling for his glasses which would be all fogged up with steam. Out of nowhere, a memory came to her of the last time Philip had returned home from a five-day business trip. Without kissing her hello, her husband had headed straight for the shower. Rose was busy in the kitchen. After she finished scraping the carrots or wrapping the potatoes in foil, whatever task she was doing, she had opened the bathroom door and scooped up his dirty clothes to take them to the washing machine, an action performed a million times, done out of pure habit. It hadn't been her imagination that his shirt smelled like a woman's perfume, or that his undershorts, oh no, this was too awful to remember, too sad to think about. She sat up and rubbed her eyes, sighing deeply. There was no other way to put it, they had smelled like sex. In a shock that rendered her robotic, Rose had stuffed his clothes into the machine and poured in the detergent. That night in bed she waited. After twenty years of marriage, these things sometimes happened. Philip would confess, ask her to forgive him because it was her he was married to, her he truly loved. She knew that. Really she did. Mature people dealt with infidelity, spackled up the holes and clung to the good in their union, treasured the companionship, the mutual support. They moved on from mistakes maybe a little sorrowful from what they'd learned, but always the wiser for it. Philip hadn't said a single word. Rose waited for him to reach for her. As if reclaiming his territory, whenever he got home from business trips, Philip usually wanted to make love. If he had put so much as a fingertip to her body, Rose was going to bring up the clothes, force him to explain, but he hadn't done that either. The husband she thought she knew so well turned onto his side, away from her unspoken questions, and went to sleep. The next morning the phone rang early. When he hung up he said there was some crisis with his northern territory, and after hastily repacking his bag and kissing her cheek, he was on the road again. She had been sitting in this very chair when the phone call came about the accident. She'd pulled on her coat and driven to the hospital to identify his body. Somebody—probably Paloma, she'd never asked—had called Rancho Costa Plente, and by the time Rose arrived at the hospital, Shep was there. She could tell from his fiercely set jaw, the brown eyes that refused to look away, that Philip was dead. Before she could break down crying, Shep had taken hold of her shoulders. *Rose Ann, much as you don't want to, you need to go in there and say good-bye. He don't much look like the man you married, but take it from me, unless you see for yourself that he's gone, you won't find any peace. Go on, now. I'm right behind you.* Shep was right. She'd taken her time saying farewell to the battered body that no longer contained her husband's spirit. She held his cooling hand and told him private things no one else would understand. *Don't worry, I'll make sure Second Chance takes that remedial English class this summer. And I'll cancel your health club membership. But, oh Phil, what will I do about Amanda?* No answers came to her except that it was going to be impossible to fill the gap. *Thank you for the gift of being my husband,* she said, and Shep took her hand, made her leave the room. Later, in the reception area where there were papers the doctor needed her to sign, she remembered feeling her knees buckle. Shep held her up and whispered in her ear, *God don't ever close a door without opening a window.* How peculiar she'd forgotten that incident with the clothes until just now. Put it out of her mind entirely. The depth of her husband's betrayal came flooding over her, howling inside her like a gale-force storm. *Face it, Rose, the last time your husband had sex it wasn't with his wife.* Why was it that the voice of her conscience sounded so much like Lily?

"Stop this right now," she scolded herself out loud, scrubbing at tears that had welled up in the corners of her eyes. She looked up to see Austin standing in the doorway. He was wearing a pair of sweat pants and rubbing his hair dry. He stood there silent, the towel pressed against his swollen cheek. Rose pushed past him and fled down the stairway.

Grand Entry began just before eleven A.M. with a drill team exhibition. A hundred riders maneuvered their horses through a practiced routine of figure eights and side passes at a collective gait that stayed remarkably in sync, save for one redheaded girl on a rearing black Friesian. The sheen of well-groomed horseflesh and polished tack was breathtaking, especially when the single rider on the paint horse carrying in the red-and-gold New Mexico state flag broke formation and cantered the oval arena alone. Rose was reminded of her childhood gymkhanas, where Lily, determined to shine, took the majority of the blue ribbons. Early on, Rose learned she'd never be the pretty kind of rider her sister was. Rose had to work at her equitation, which she had done, but to her riding was strictly for fun. Horses had never disappointed her. Sometimes they colicked, and always they died too soon, but a woman could count on them in every other way. Lately she ended her workdays by having long chats with Max, who at least seemed to listen attentively. When the king and queen of the rodeo, decked out in faux leopard and spangles, respectively, broke from the long line of riders to make a pass around the posse arena, Rose climbed the arena fence and clung there, watching. "Austin, you have to come look at this," she called over her shoulder. "It's like Mardi Gras and prom night all wrapped up into one."

Austin finished rolling Vet Wrap bandages on a quarter horse's front legs. "Invest in leg wraps before you go jumping him over fences again," he told the cowboy. "Horse that nice, you got no business riding without some kind of protection."

"These days protection is the name of the game, isn't it?" the cowboy said.

Austin looked up. "In a lot of ways, I suppose."

"Then how come your cheek looks like you forgot to follow your own advice?" The cowboy laughed, legged his horse into a trot, and rode away.

Austin muttered something Rose couldn't hear and slammed shut the supply drawer in the bed of his truck. He walked over and watched the grand entry exhibition for a few minutes. "I have a king-hell headache already. I don't see how I'm going to make it through this day without a beer."

Rose turned her face to his, slyly checking his pupils, which appeared normal in size, the brown eyes the same ones she always saw behind the lenses. "Have a Coke."

"Already did."

"Have another."

The bleachers were only half full because the rough stock events didn't begin until late afternoon. By then the stands would be packed because everyone, gay or straight, enjoyed watching bull riders full of themselves get humbled with a mouthful of dirt. Garth Brooks clones sauntered by, followed by model-handsome boys who reminded her a little of Second Chance. She wondered where her son was today, and if he might come home for Thanksgiving. She hoped he would. She wanted to hug him and feed him, see for herself he was all in one piece. Since the grocery money incident, she didn't think Amanda would be by any time soon, but with Second Chance one could never tell. He liked surprises. The parade of bodies strutting by looked no different than people who frequented the ¡Andale!, a Floralee watering hole that hosted a live band on weekends. Back and forth everybody walked, searching, hoping that what Pop always said would prove true: *For every pot in this world there's a lid that'll fit it.* But it wasn't only men. A contingent of tough-looking ranch women and their girlfriends sat talking, admiring each other's babies, standing up to cheer when various riders entered the arena. So far as Rose could tell, the only difference between this and a straight rodeo was the occasional same-sex embrace, or advertisements like the woman's T-shirt that read ONLY MY TEETH ARE STRAIGHT.

Behind her Austin had pulled his hat low over his forehead. He hadn't recovered from the announcer's enthusiastic introduction this morning, when he had to walk into the arena and receive applause for donating his veterinary services. The exchange with the cowboy wouldn't sit well, either. Odds that he'd suffered a concussion dwindled by the minute, and Rose was grateful even if he was not. His nervousness amused her. She'd never imagined that being in the presence of a crowd of homosexual men would so rattle his sense of masculinity.

The woman with the thought-provoking T-shirt walked by again. Rose smiled because the slogan was funny, and the woman stopped to light a cigarette. She snapped her lighter shut and regarded Rose for a good long time. "You here with anybody?" she asked, and Rose felt her mouth go bone dry.

Austin's arm came up over Rose's shoulder. "Sorry. This one's all mine," he said, moving in closer, his hand coming to rest on the back of Rose's belt.

"Can't blame me for asking," the woman said. She and her T-shirt moved into the crowd.

Austin let go. "How did you like that, Rose? I notice you weren't too snappy with the comebacks."

She shrugged off his arm. "Actually, it's kind of flattering to discover that somebody finds me attractive, even if it is another woman."

Austin sighed. "I knew you were going to say that. You're attractive. You're also unforgiving. You demand a level of honesty that men can't deliver."

"As far as I'm concerned, there's only one level of honesty, Austin—total."

"Then you're going to be lonely the rest of your life."

"Fine. So what if I am? Why should I settle for less just because men are weak?"

"Never said you should."

"You implied it. That's the same thing as saying it."

They stared at each other stubbornly. Rose wondered what Mami's star charts might have to say about that. The whole argument was pointless since she was determined not to want him anymore. But if she looked away first, it meant that Austin had won.

"Look," he said finally. "How about I buy you lunch? That is, if you think the food's safe. I won't end up with a sudden desire to wear a skirt?"

Rose stepped away from the fence. "If you do, I've got a closetful that are just about your size."

"How generous, Mrs. Flynn."

"I know. Generosity is one of my major faults."

They sat on a bench and ate hamburgers, sharing a bag of tortilla chips. Rose ate half her hamburger and fed the rest to a passing dog. Austin drank his Coke and then asked if Rose was going to finish hers. "Take it," she said, and watched him tip the red can back and drain it dry. The arch of his neck was sleek and clean-shaven. He looked more fit than he had in months. She looked away before he could tell she was watching him.

"I can smell your perfume again," he said, crushing the can and throwing it into a nearby recycling bin.

Her phantom perfume. "Really. What's it smell like?"

"I finally figured it out. Those purple flower vines that grow down by Agua Fria Creek."

"Clematis?"

"If that's what they're called."

"I don't think those flowers have a smell."

"Yes, they do. It's subtle, but there. Unique."

She picked up a stick and dragged it through the dirt. "There's an old horseman's myth about clematis. Pop told it to me."

"What's that?"

"That if you crush the roots of the vine and rub them inside a tired horse's nostrils, he'll revive and go on."

"Interesting. I never heard that."

"Well, now you have."

Austin leaned in close. He lifted her hair and inhaled deeply at the back of her neck. "Yep, it's those purple flowers."

Rose sat very still. Her neck felt all prickly. "I think I'll go to look at the merchandise booths."

"You in the market for some sex toys?"

"Why not? I've heard they're very reliable."

Austin threw his napkins away and caught up with her.

"You don't have to come along."

"Maybe I just felt like being with you."

"Ha. You're afraid to be alone. Admit it."

Austin opened his mouth to argue, then shut it. "You're right," he said. "I'm counting the hours. This place gives me the willies."

"Poor baby. Well, I suppose I owe you for the save back there at the arena fence. Come along, then. We can pretend we like each other. Won't that feel safe?"

He shook his finger at her. "Keep it up, Mrs. Flynn."

She smiled. "You know I will."

There were NMGRA T-shirts for sale, chances to be bought on a basket full of goodies that included an X-rated video, massage oil, personal lubricants, sex toys, and more condoms than it looked like even Lily could use in a lifetime. They passed a booth for gay Christians, where a woman with pale, empty eyes handed out tracts, and to be polite, Rose accepted one. At the pet products booth, she felt safe stopping to look around. Rainbow dog leashes and collars, reasonably priced, but when she looked closer there were distinct differences. If tags reading Butch Bitch or Dyke Dog didn't alert her that she was a minority in new territory, then the fact that at the same booth she could buy Chachi flea spray and herself some UltraGlide drove the point home. Packaged in a variety of neon colors, in easy-to-open, single-use pouches, was an aquarium full of the personal lubricant. Rose was dying to pick one up to read the ingredients, but she didn't dare, not with Austin there, ready to make some humiliating comment.

A call for the vet came over the PA system, and he took off. Rose watched him jog to his truck. Austin was still her friend, wasn't he? Maybe one day they could move past this awkwardness and feel comfortable with each other. The guy working the pet products booth handed her a pouch of hot-pink lubricant. "That's okay," she told him. "I was just looking."

"Take it," he said. "They're free samples." Rose quickly shoved the pouch into her jeans pocket.

On her way back to the arena she was ambushed by two young men handing out condoms. In Rose's youth such items were scandalous. *Portalápiz*, the kids had called them in high school, which translated to something like "pencil boxes." Like the lubricant, the condoms were all racy colors. "Everybody needs latex," they said, dropping three into her hands and then racing off to find another victim in need of public embarrassment. The young men wore turquoise satin jackets with "Wrap that Rascal" embroidered in silver script across the backs. She tucked the condoms into her pocket next to the lubricant and wondered what someone might offer her next. She would have gladly accepted a free vibrator. It would be less nerve-racking to acquire one here than through the mail.

She arrived back at the bleachers just as the Goat Dressing event began. Two teams raced against the clock to a tethered goat and pulled a pair of Jockey shorts over its hind end, then raced back to the start. If the goat managed to extricate itself before the team crossed the finish line, they were DQ'ed. The goats quickly grew wise to this game and kept slipping through their tethers and escaping. They ran around the arena just out of reach and ducked under a loose section of fence, coming out right where Austin's truck was parked. Every time he brought one back the crowd went wild. The rodeo announcer proclaimed Austin a "goat tamer deluxe" and cries of "Hey, Doc, want to tame my animal?" filled the arena. Rose found herself laughing as hard as everyone else, and after awhile, even Austin could smile at the silliness. Then he needed her to hold a twitched mare while he took stitches in the animal's flank, where she'd torn herself open on the sharp edge of a trailer.

Rose held the halter and watched the needle flash as Austin did his work. The horse was nervous, and Rose tried to soothe her by speaking low, breathing into her flaring nostrils to help her relax. The owner was nearly hysterical, and repeatedly apologized for what clearly had been an avoidable accident. Austin didn't pass judgment; he tied his knots, and the girl whose horse this was stopped crying long enough to thank him. "Rita Mae is my life," she said. "This won't leave a scar, will it?"

"Not so anybody'll notice."

She impulsively gave him a hug before leading her horse away. "Hugged by a lesbian," Rose said. "You'll never be the same."

"Go watch the rough stock," he told her. "You're starting to feel like part of Eloy's sentence."

Inside the arena the bull riding was now underway, but Rose quickly wearied of Carmen Miranda drag queens getting pitched into the dirt. The whole thing sickened her, actually; bulls didn't want to be ridden, they wanted to stand around like Ferdinand and contemplate their lives. Instead they were prodded into this nonsense so people could enjoy ten seconds of heightened excitement. She returned to Austin's truck and sat down on the bumper. "You sewed that mare like you were performing plastic surgery, Austin. Such tiny stitches."

"Figured it was a chance to practice. Got a little sloppy there for awhile when I was tippling, didn't I?"

"Oh, not so anybody would notice."

"Except you."

There was truth in his words, and Rose had to acknowledge it. "You're right about me being too demanding. For years my children told me I was too hard on people. Lily says I expect a hundred fifty percent all the time. My father delights in telling me that I chase after everyone else's misgivings in order to ignore my own. If I treated you that way, Austin, I apologize."

The vet squirted water on his hands and wiped them dry with a towel. "I don't know that I'd call it a fault. More of a guaranteed method to stay dissatisfied. People are human, Rose; they screw up."

Nobody knew that better than she did. "So? Maybe the trick is to learn to love them in spite of their shortcomings."

"You really think you can do that?"

She didn't have to think of Philip to answer. "I know I can."

Austin looked surprised. "Come on, let's go watch the bull riders break a few legs. Anybody who gets hurt now needs the rodeo doc, not a vet."

Austin bet Rose quarters on which bull would throw the cowboy, and nine times out of ten, she won. They smiled at the lime green chaps and sequined shirts, the cowboy dressed like Judy Garland, and shot each other astonished looks when a bull rider's hometown was announced as Floralee. "I had no idea this many gay folk lived in the Land of Enchantment," Austin said. "This whole day has been one long eye-opener for yours truly. Well, it looks like things are shutting down for the night. I'm supposed to check all the broncs before I leave. Shouldn't take me too long. I have to say it, these people may dress strange, but they treat their animals humanely. Regular old rodeo could take a lesson."

The crowds began to filter out of the arena bleachers. Rose spotted the rodeo queen posing for a photographer. The red-haired woman was pretty, but she had about twelve piercings in her earlobes, which made Rose think of Amanda. The uncertainty of her children's whereabouts made worry her constant companion. At least Mami hadn't shown up, which made the day a whole lot more pleasant than she expected it would be. Austin's remark about the clematis vine intrigued her. Next spring she'd trailer Max out to the Philmont area and look for some, check to see if it indeed had a smell. She touched the lump in her pocket that was the lubricant and the condoms. First she wanted to look at them, in case she was missing anything, then after that she'd ditch them in the nearest trash can.

Austin leaned on the horn, and Rose hurried down the bleacher steps to meet him. She slid into the driver's seat and asked him if he wanted to be driven home or to the clinic.

"Let me take you to dinner. Make up for ruining your Saturday. I recall some important business about dyeing your hair. I guess I'm glad to have interrupted that. I like the way you can see glints of silver against the black."

"Sure, all men love gray hair. That's why all the supermodels have it."

"Rose."

The look on his face was hard to read. Austin was generous with his smile. Maybe he was gearing up to ask her to work tomorrow, too. "Know what? I'm not really all that hungry."

"Well, I am." He patted his belly. "You're losing weight, and I'm gaining it. I have a thirty-two inch waist now. I'm busting out of my jeans."

Rose reached over and placed her palm against his stomach. "You don't even know what a belly is until you've had babies. I don't want to hear another word about it. I'll drink some coffee while you eat. Where do you want to go?"

Austin stared out the windshield into the dusk. The long line of cars exiting the arena had just about dispersed. "Didn't realize how dirty I was. I guess just take me by the Chat 'n' Chew and I'll have another hamburger. Been eating enough of those lately I can tell when the night shift takes over cooking for the day crew."

Rose hesitated. "Look. I had the urge to cook this week, and it's hard to make anything that just feeds one. There's leftovers in my fridge that will rot if nobody eats them. Nothing special, just *ropa vieja*. We could stop by my place and heat some up. You could look at Max, too. After, I'll drive you home."

"It's been a long time since you cooked me anything. I'd be grateful for eggs and toast."

"Well, you're getting *ropa*."

"My lucky day."

"This is about food, Austin, pure and simple."

They drove in silence to the lane where her plain house stood, needing paint, the same way it had for the last five years. When the truck tires met the gravel, Max started in whinnying. Rose smiled. "He sounds the veterinary alarm whenever he hears you drive up."

"Then I guess I'll go throw him his dinner and give him an adjustment."

"Come in the house first. You can take him some carrots. They're just about on their last legs, but Max won't mind."

Austin stood behind her while she bent over in front of the refrigerator. Painfully aware of how that looked, at once Rose straightened up. He took the carrots, and she heard the back door shut. Chachi leaped at her legs while she opened a can of dog food and fed him. While the *ropa* bubbled in the saucepan, she heated corn tortillas, seeded and chopped tomatoes for *salsa fresca*, and set the small kitchen table for two. She lit one of the Eternalux candles and placed it in the center of the table. That looked too romantic, so she blew the candle out. Beer was the traditional beverage to serve with *ropa*, but lemonade was what they were having tonight. She tore greens for a salad, toasted a few *piñones* in a dry frying pan, scattered them on top of the salad and whisked up a balsamic dressing she had tasted once at the Apple Tree restaurant. Experimenting, she'd duplicated it at home in her kitchen. Fresh always tasted twice as good, plus it cost less to make than to buy.

Austin washed up at the sink and sat down at the table. He filled his plate three times and ate all the tortillas. Rose poked her fork around her food, remembering the casseroles she'd made over the last year that Austin had eaten by himself. A week would go by, and she'd walk into her office one morning and find the empty dish on her desk, washed clean. Back then, he hadn't possessed the vocabulary or the dignity required to say thanks. Now, sitting at her table, watching him eat almost made up for that.

"You should open a restaurant," Austin told her between mouthfuls.

Rose laughed. "No thanks. It can't be as much fun as cooking in my own kitchen."

"Still, you're that good a cook." He pushed his plate away and folded his napkin.

"You want a cup of tea? The water's hot."

"Sure." Austin got up and walked into the front room where he stood rubbing his arms. "Chilly tonight. Bet it snows early this year. I could light the fire. Get it going good so it'll last until morning."

"That would be nice."

She set the dishes into the sink and wiped the table clean. When she brought Austin his tea, he had the fire all set, and the smell of burning fatwood perfumed the small room. Rose sat down on the couch and stared into the flames. The fire would last long after Austin had gone home.

He moved aside her stack of romance novels and sat down on the edge of the coffee table facing her, his back to the fire. Since the night of the kiss in Taos, Rose no longer cared who saw her books. She certainly didn't need Austin's approval for reading material. In her opinion Ernest Hemingway didn't comprehend the first thing about romance or women. She thought he should have stuck to fishing, which he did seem to understand but made far too big a thing of. Austin sipped from his cup, then set it down and looked at her.

"Appreciate you coming with me today. And in case I don't say it enough, thanks for all your hard work, and the dinners."

He'd never said it until now.

"You're welcome."

"You mean a lot to me, Rose. Lately, I think about that."

"You could have fooled me."

"I know things are strained between us, and me acting distant hasn't helped. Getting sober's part of it."

She thought of the gentle sparring they'd engaged in all day long. Nothing new there, but something else lurked behind the teasing. A man didn't go out of his way to remark on a woman's perfume, real or imagined, unless she was on his mind. He'd worked eighty hours this week, easily, but he wasn't sleeping in his bed, he was sitting in her living room. "And the other part?"

"It's like stopping drinking's improved my eyesight."

Rose shifted uncomfortably. "You looked up, and I was the first female you saw, that's all. Maybe you're just finally getting over—" She had no intention of ruining this moment by saying Leah's name. "She whose name we will not speak aloud. She who deserves permanent acne."

He laughed. "Longest heartbreak story in history. Guess maybe I milked it a little."

"There's no timetable on grief, Austin."

"You got on with your life fairly quick after Philip died."

"I didn't have a choice. My children, work . . ." The image of her husband's clothes going into the washer flashed through Rose's mind. "You have no idea what goes on inside my heart, Doctor Donavan."

"That sad?"

"Sometimes, yes."

"Well, I'd give you a hug you right now if I didn't think you'd slap me for doing it. What the hell. I'll do it anyway. Aim for the right side of my face, Rose. The left's still pretty sore."

She shut her eyes. "Austin, don't."

His strong arms encircled her. She stiffened and held her breath, awkwardly patting Austin's shoulder as if he were the one who needed comforting.

"Rose," he said, breathing her name into her neck. The mutual shoulder patting developed its own evolution, at first slowing down, turning into friendly massage, then transforming into those long, slow strokes that all the way through sweaters and long-sleeved flannel spoke the insistent language of skin talking to skin. "I think you woke something up."

Despite all her well-intentioned defenses, Rose felt herself slowly catching fire, too. She knew she should pull away. Austin murmured into her hair. He laid her down on her own couch and began to move his lips against her neck. "I can't do this again," she insisted. "To you, it's nothing, but to me it's—"

"*Shh.* It's something all right. Let's just ride this horse awhile, see where he's taking us."

Where he took them was all the way down the hall to her bedroom. As she was walked backward, fueled by Austin's forward motion, Rose thought of the innumerable reasons why she shouldn't be doing this. She was just beginning to feel better, as if she could survive this, to jettison the embarrassment. There was no sense to starting up again, none, but the kisses Austin delivered in her own living room traveled farther than the two kisses in Taos, and she was greedy for them. Between her legs a pleasant buzzing began to warm her middle. Quickly that friendly fire turned to a deep ache. Austin urged her back against the mattress and down she went, wondering if she really could feel that almost imperceptible lump beneath her that was the forgotten statue of Saint Anthony, or if she only imagined she could. Austin pressed his pelvis against hers and she could feel how hard he was, how much he wanted her, at least physically. Maybe Mami was right, because this felt less and less foolish. He pulled her shirt loose from her jeans, fumbled for her zipper, but her pants were the button-fly style. As his hand grazed the pocket where the lubricant and condoms were, Rose reached down to stop him, but he'd already taken them out, and he sat up in bed to inspect what he'd found.

A half smile crossed his face. "For me?"

"Some guy at the rodeo was handing them out. I forgot I had them. I was planning on throwing them away."

Austin tilted her face up to his. "Lucky thing you didn't, or I'd've had to break my word to Eloy and drive a hundred miles an hour to the nearest liquor store and buy some. Say we're going to make love, Rose. Say you're going to let that happen because you know we both want it to."

She made a noise that caught in her throat, not sure what she wanted to say, and then she pulled away from him, sat up and took a deep breath. "Look. It isn't that I don't want to, it's just—"

"What?"

"I don't know how to explain it." But she did know. Austin was so newly sober he still got the shakes. What if he wanted inside her to ease that ache, to find another kind of high? All Leah Donavan need do was snap her fingers and her ex-husband would run to her like the trained dog she loved to torment. And Rose couldn't stop thinking of the face-less woman who'd taken Philip to bed without a second thought to what that ring on his finger represented. She wanted to make love with Austin, had wanted that for a long time, but everything felt wrong. Even the ticking of her bedside clock sounded out of whack.

Austin's fingers moved away from the buttons on her blouse. He sat back against the pillows, took one of the condoms and tore open the wrapper. At the sound of the foil tearing, Rose felt a shudder travel through her shoulders, move like hands across her breasts, then travel deep into her marrow.

"Last time I bought one of these things was in a gas station men's room over thirty-five years ago," he said. "I was so nervous I almost dropped my quarter. Don't even remember how to put one on."

"*Ven a mí*," she whispered, because asking him to come to her was easier said in Spanish. "We'll figure it out together."

He shook his head no and set the condom down on her bedside table. "Maybe some other time, Rose, but it ain't going to be tonight."

"Why not?"

"Because it isn't going to happen that way with you and me. Neither one of us is ready for this, so we're going to wait."

She pulled one of the pillows over herself, embarrassed to have Austin look at her. What he said was the truth, and having him point that out felt more humiliating than letting him see her naked. She waited for him to get up and leave, but he stayed. His body next to hers felt warm and solid. The sound of her own breathing amplified in her ears, quick and shallow from arousal and nerves. When she looked at him, she saw that Austin was undressing. He never once took his eyes from hers. His body was thinner than she had pictured it would be. His ribs were visible under his skin, and she wanted to trace each one with her fingers. As he kicked off his boots and stepped out of his jeans, she saw that he was wearing that funny Jockey underwear that reached halfway down the thigh. They looked so old-fashioned, but sexy, too. Things looked mighty crowded in there, but he didn't take them off. He stood at the foot of the bed looking at her.

"I can sleep on your couch," he said, "but I'd rather be in your bed. I'd just like to lie here and hold you, if that's all right."

She nodded.

When Austin sat down on the bed beside her, the plastic pouch of UltraGlide rolled toward his thigh. He picked it up and regarded it soberly. "Have to admit this is a new one on me. Do you require this stuff?"

"I'm pretty sure I don't."

Austin smiled. "Oh, Rose."

Her face burned, and she would rather have died that very second than know what lay behind his smile. Still, the Wilder in her had to ask. "'Oh Rose' what?"

"We have a little time here. It's not like we're trying to catch a bus."

He fell asleep in her arms, his face against her breasts, and Rose, surprised that he could relax while she felt so charged, held on and waited. No matter what, whether not making love to Austin was a mistake, or might kill what was left of their friendship, what she'd done tonight in terms of coming back to life felt massive. Lily wouldn't understand that, and neither would Mami, but Rose could tell. Like getting smacked in the head with a frying pan, realizations were coming to her at light speed: *You care too much about this man to ruin what's between you with one night of sex. He's fragile, maybe even more breakable than you are. And here he is, sleeping in your bed, minding his manners. He says he's willing to wait. That you both should. Maybe you can trust that, if any man can ever truly be trusted.*

When Austin was breathing evenly, she untangled her arms from his, got up, and walked into the kitchen for a glass of water. On the way back to bed, she stood in the living room looking at Chachi, who was crashed in front of the fire, his fat little body and stubby legs looking for all the world like a cocktail olive stuck with four toothpicks. She tried to visualize everything she'd felt while Austin had walked her down the hallway: Her arms locked around his shoulders, the way he thrust himself against her, so hard and certain, and the way he'd pulled back when he sensed her panic. She wondered why it was that the flood of sensations hadn't caused her to overcome her inhibitions. Good sense or cowardice? She had to smile, because at one point Chachi had come running from the other room and leaped on the bed, making his usual crash landing that announced he was ready to call it a night. The Jack Russell looked bewildered at finding the dreaded veterinarian in the bed where *he* usually slept, and caromed off the mattress without stopping.

Rose set the water glass down on her bedside table. Her marriage vows ended the moment Philip stopped breathing. In the eyes of God and the law, she was entirely free to do with her body what she wanted. That woman who'd bedded her husband hadn't had any rights, but she'd gone ahead and taken them anyway. Austin was a troubled man in the midst of a difficult transition. Forever was a word Rose applied to Philip's absence, nothing else.

Austin roused as she slid back into bed. He touched her arm. "Where did you go?"

"To the kitchen for some water. You thirsty?"

"I don't want water. I want you to promise something."

"If I can."

"Do not dye your hair."

She smiled. "I won't. For now."

He continued sleepily, "Or get a face lift, or apologize about your body. Just be Rose."

"And who is she?"

"Someone I can count on." He kissed her shoulder and cupped his hand against her elbow.

A few weeks ago she'd been willing to change her life for him, but now things were different. "Austin, I'm just hanging on from moment to moment."

"I know. The boys in AA would tell me this is too soon to get involved with you, that I need more time getting sober. They're right, but I couldn't let this time get away from me like all the others. I wanted to stay."

So it wasn't just her. He'd felt it other times, too. That eased her mind a little. "I'd walk away from you forever if that would guarantee you not taking another drink."

She heard his quick intake of breath. "That kind of devotion scares me. What happens if I let you down?"

"Go to sleep, Austin. We can't solve all the world's problems in one night. All we can do is try to get some rest and deal with tomorrow when it gets here."

"You're right."

He slept, and Rose looked out the window. She was bone-tired, couldn't stop yawning, and crazy dream images were coming at her, confusing her, blurring the boundaries between sleep and wakefulness. Somewhere in the middle of it all, she heard Mami's voice crowing: *Let it happen,* mija. *Surrender.* But Mami didn't know everything.

12

A Poco Loco

Shep halted his spotted horse at the fenceline. To Lily's eyes the man looked old and frail, but maybe it was the light this time of day, neither dusk nor dark, or coming down off the mountain she was nervous enough to seek out trouble where it didn't exist. "Hey, Shepherd," she said. "Come say hello to a blast from the past."

He leaned over the fence rail and shook Tres's hand. "Doctor Quintero. Heard a rumor you were back in town."

"Tres'll do, Shep. I'm no longer practicing medicine."

"Yeah, I heard that, too."

"Seen Mami and Pop?" Lily asked.

"Your mother took off in her plane just a little bit ago."

"Did she have the dogs with her?" Lily asked. "Did Pop make her get rid of the greyhounds?"

"One of them. The other's in the house, listening to the radio."

"What about Pop?"

"Trailered out early this morning with a fellow who wants to buy Matisse. He took Alfred. I expect they'll be back shortly."

"Well, poop." In Lily's mind the homecoming scenario had played out so beautifully—Pop and Tres clapping one another on the back, Mami inviting them in for drinks—a cozy Wilder welcome that would make Tres feel comfortable, included—and closer to her. For two people who ran a horse ranch, her parents sure didn't spend a great deal of time there.

"It's late," Tres said. "I'd better head back."

Lily took hold of his arm with both hands. "Stay awhile longer. Pop might come back any minute."

Shep cleared his throat. "If he does, he'll be busy trying to wear that buyer down so the poor fellow'll cut a check." He looked up at the sky. "Probably the last good ride anybody'll make before it starts in snowing."

"No way," Lily said. "It's October."

Shep chuckled. "Hear that, Tres? She's been in California so long she lost her weather instincts. It's going to snow, all right. If not tonight, tomorrow. I can smell it."

Tres took a small notepad from his back pocket. The spiral binding had been reinforced with duct tape. "Can you describe how it smells?"

"Guess if you put a gun to my head maybe I could."

Tres uncapped a pen, a fountain pen, Lily noticed. "Would you mind? It'd help a lot with this piece I'm working on."

"Sort of like copper. Or that could be due to the medicine my doctor has me on, which makes everything taste metallic."

"New copper, like you repipe with, or old, as in pennies?"

"Hey, don't mind me," Lily said. "I'll just duck in and say hello to my dog while you two work out the smell-taste issues of snow."

Shep dismounted and nearly lost his balance. He caught himself on the fence, and Tres hopped the fence and took hold of the horse's reins. "Real nice animal you've got here," he said, defusing what could have been a shameful moment.

The old man composed himself. "I like him all right. By the way, Lily, Rock Hudson managed to tear up one of your mother's ugly sculptures while you were gone. Can't wait to hear you explain that to her."

"You're exaggerating," Lily said. Buddy, when he was in the mood, tore up clothes—he had a particular fondness for panties—but she'd been gone long enough he might have switched vices. "Wait for me," she told Tres. "I'll only be a minute."

Just inside the front door lay the remains of a Deborah Butterfield horse sculpture constructed of birch limbs, its hind end entirely dismantled. Lily knelt and picked up a chewed-on branch. It could be glued back together, and turned the other way the damage would hardly be noticeable. Inside the kitchen Lily whistled for Buddy. No wild blue dingo came running out to meet her. Mami's Christmas cactus had bloomed while she was gone, and now tiny lipstick-pink flowers lit the end of every stem. The plant had begun its life as a four-inch potted promise, and with Mami's nurturing efforts, grown into lush green paddles. In this very chair Lily remembered debating her parents over why she should be allowed to study medical engineering, which was exciting, versus languages, which, granted, she had a flair for but bored her witless. Politics, religion, how to drive; nine times out of ten in these discussions Lily emerged the victor. She had reduced her mother to tears on more occasions than she could count. There was nothing she could do to take those times back. Her insatiable need to win every argument might not qualify as her most commendable quality, but it had driven her to career success. She wondered how much of her bullheaded personality had turned Rose into a doormat. The thing was, what Lily knew about Philip dogged her ten times a day. She imagined the inevitable scenario—and why not have it take place here, at the dinner table, where so much bad news had been delivered—*Rose, listen to me for a minute, and try not to kill the messenger. Philip wasn't the saint you think he was. Let me tell you why, and with who.*

Oh, it was pointless. Some truths didn't set a person free at all. She pulled a yellowing paddle off the cactus and threw it in the sink. Mami fed her houseplants like she did her greyhounds, weird herbal concoctions, she talked to them, played encouraging music, practically took them for walks. Lily put away the three bags' worth of groceries she'd bought with ATM money, whistling again and again for Buddy Guy. The food was more of a gesture than anything; she'd also brought Mami cash. When she leaned over the sink and looked out the window, she glimpsed the back of Tres's head and part of his denim jacket, frayed at the collar so that the red flannel lining showed. How safe it had felt to bury her face there and breathe deep, just wrap herself around that man. She wondered what he and Shep were chatting about as they stood by the fence, the showy Appaloosa between them. Whatever it was, nobody looked bored.

When Lily went to put away the grocery bags in the pantry, she heard a whimper. "Buddy?"

The blue heeler had dug a cave for himself beneath the back hall stairway, where Mami kept her mucking boots and the recycling bins. As Lily peered in she saw that Buddy, curled up tight, nose tucked under his hind end, had amassed quite a collection of chew toys. Among various items liberated from the greyhounds, there was also a pair of her panties, the expensive kind, *naturalmente,* or what was left of the thong portion. Also a metal food dish she recognized as belonging to Jody Jr., a ratty old pair of reins from her gymkhana days, and several uneaten dog treats. When she reached her hand out to pet him, Buddy growled but tempered the display by wagging his tail.

"You crazy nut," Lily said, as she sat down cross-legged on the kitchen floor. "Get over here and give Mama some dingo love."

The blue heeler's ears remained flat against his head. His lips were drawn up in twin "fake-out snarls," which was Lily's pet name for how his mouth sometimes accidentally curled up over his fangs. It made him look vicious but was actually nothing more than a result of saliva deprivation. When he was relaxed enough to let her, she loved to pull his lips way down over the fangs, which resulted in making the cattle dog resemble a bloodhound. This facial expression she called a "shamus."

Lily touched the breast pocket of Tres's shirt, which she was still wearing, inching the giant dog biscuit she'd bought in the gourmet section of the market upward so its rounded end was visible. "Now how did that get in there?" she said. "Maybe I'd better have a teensy taste, just to make sure it's not poison." She removed the bone-shaped confection from her pocket. Handmade by some hippie company in Dixon, the biscuit cost four dollars, which Tres told her was insane. Lily didn't care to snap at him so recently after the *serious* talk in bed, but however much she spent on her puppy was her own damn business. "Buddy's man's best friend, or in this case, woman's," she informed him. "I bet you'd spend four bucks on fishing tackle and not even blink." She bit a chunk off the end of the surprisingly soft, peanut-butter-flavored cookie. "Whoa, those hippies could be onto something," she said, studying the ingredient list on the cellophane wrapper. "This tastes way too good to be dog food."

In his heart, Buddy knew this was wrong, absolutely incorrect on every level. *He* was supposed to crave the people food, not the other way around. He cocked his head and studied her as she took a second bite, chewed and swallowed. Slowly he began to creep forward on his front paws.

Meanwhile Lily licked her fingers.

Buddy didn't take his eyes off her. By the time he reached her knees, he was once again besotted with love for his skinny princess magician with the remarkable hands that could scratch his back where he could not, open a fridge to reveal all manner of edible riches, and best of all, operate a can opener. He rolled over and showed her his spotted belly. Lily rewarded him with what was left of the biscuit. Delicately he grasped it in his teeth while she rubbed his chest. All around his treasured foodstuff, he groaned with pleasure. Pretty soon his lips fell back, exposing his weird pink-and-black speckled gums and his tartar-stained fangs. There wasn't a nickname for that besides overdue dental cleaning.

Lily knew she was supposed to brush his teeth every day. Getting Buddy in for regular dental attention was difficult because the moment he smelled a veterinary office he went ballistic. This was the perfect opportunity! She could check out the object of her sister's infatuation while simultaneously delivering the dog test. In Lily's estimation dogs were far superior to women when it came to spotting bad guys.

"Lily?" She heard Tres calling out her name.

"In the kitchen," she answered, and there he was, standing in the doorway, this walking, talking Hallmark card of a man who made her heart go as soft as her morning cereal.

She took hold of Buddy's front paws. "Meet the one, the only Buddy Guy. Buddy, say hi to Tres."

The blue heeler flipped his body upright and planted all four feet solidly on the floor. He let out a low growl, and his hackles lifted. The expression on his face was not fake-out anything. Buddy's introduction to Tres was starting out just like that time Buddy'd bitten one of Lily's dates. Out of fear of lawsuits, she'd had to date that particular loser for three solid months. "Buddy," she warned. "Be nice."

Tres stood still, not moving a muscle. "I don't get it. Dogs usually love me."

"Me either," Lily said. "He's probably feeling protective. "He doesn't like it when I travel. Actually, he goes mental when I drag out a suitcase."

Tres took a half step toward the table and Buddy lunged for his shin.

Lily grabbed her dog by the collar and got dragged toward the table in the process. "Buddy! Knock it off!" She looked up at Tres. "Maybe if you sat down or something."

"I'll wait for you outside."

He backed out of the room, and Lily heard the screen door creak shut. "Buddy. What in the hell's the matter with you?"

By way of answer, her dog began to perform the doomed helicopter dance of happiness. Mami's remaining greyhound peered in the kitchen doorway while Buddy demonstrated his vaudeville act. He seemed not at all threatened by the presence of the blue dog, in fact, the moment she walked into the room he abandoned Lily in favor of her.

She looks like an indoor deer, Lily thought. *I wonder why Buddy doesn't try to kill her.* Buddy raced circles around the greyhound, then rolled over to show *her* his belly. Finally Lily got it: Her dog was in love, which no doubt explained his behavior toward Tres. In that fevered, mine-all-mine state, one could hardly be responsible for one's behavior. The greyhound tolerated his affections for a few minutes, then resumed her state of majestic aloofness. Buddy slunk away. Poor old Buddy Guy. He didn't seem to fit in anywhere except here with her. Lily dragged her nervous doggie into her lap and kissed the top of his rattlesnake-shaped head. "Buddy," she whispered, "Pal-o-mine. I love you best and I always will. There's no man in the world who could take your place. But I really, really, really like Tres. Work on finding a way to be good with that, please?"

Buddy looked up at her adoringly. He pawed at her breasts and lapped her face with a hot, eager tongue. Overdoing it on the physical affection, making promises too good to be true, throw in a little jealousy that bordered on the insane: On Lily's bookshelf at home entire shelves were devoted to self-help, bestsellers that explained men were from other planets, how not to love the wrong kind of guy too much, too often, or too frequently. After the veterinarian drive-by, Lily intended to drop by Collected Works and pick up the newest book on dog training, something like that *Monks of New Skete*.

Tres clasped his hands over hers as Lily came up behind him and gave him a hug. "Relax, I left the dog inside. He'll be better the next time you meet, Tres. Sometimes Buddy's a little weird around men. Pretty soon he'll love you—" She bit her tongue before she was tempted to further embroider the sentence. "Let's saddle up Ansel and Georgia. I bet if we galloped a few miles we could catch up with Pop."

"Sounds great," Tres said, turning to face her. "But don't you think it's kind of late in the day to start out on trail?"

She didn't like that half smile on his face. "We could take flashlights."

"I need to pick up some things in town; then I really should get back up the mountain. I'm already a week behind where I want to be on the carving."

"All that sex I forced you to endure kept you from your chisels."

Tres sighed. "Lily, you know that's not what I meant."

"I could grab some clean clothes and come with you."

"Let's give each other a little breathing room."

Lily knew Tres was being sensible. He was probably as sick of seeing her ivory panties as she was of washing them out every night. "Well, fine. You have my cell phone number if you get lonely." She turned toward the house, and Tres pulled her back.

He kissed her forehead, evoking a momentary buzz of pleasure, but already Lily had felt her guard go up. It was going to take more than one kiss to bring it back down. "You're not upset with me?"

She smiled her seal-a-contract smile, showing just a flash of her chemically bleached teeth. Standing a little off her center of gravity, her hips jutted forward, reminding her that at one time, between the arc of those two bones, a part of each of them had existed, until she had it scraped away. "Good-bye, Tres."

She stepped deftly out of his reach, lifted her hand, and waved. He got into the truck and started the engine, still looking at her. She stared back, unblinking. As he drove away, Lily wondered if all she'd given Dr. Quintero was another journal entry.

Okay, so maybe he'd gotten to her, a little, enough that she stood there watching his truck until it was out of sight. It had a cracked right tail light, damage not bad enough to repair, but not intact either. Writing, carving, solitude—what made Lily believe she could coexist with that? She needed people, horses, Junior Wells on the juke box, nights at the ¡Andale! where somebody—it might be her—got up on the table and danced. Her eyes welled up with tears.

He's going to walk into his cabin, and the first thing he'll see is that unmade bed, the sheets with my scent on them, a stray hair left behind on the pillow. He'll think about washing the linen, but the Laundromat's a long ways back into town, so first he'll sit down at his computer and write: The approaching snow smells like copper pennies . . . *he won't write word one about me.*

Pop and his prospective customer rode into the arena. "Lily," her father called out. "Can I get a little help here with the horses while Mr. Lankford and I settle our business?"

"No problem." She jogged to the arena, opened the gate, and took hold of the reins of both horses. "I'll brush them out, see to their feet," she muttered, and her father whisked his buyer indoors.

Alfred stood patiently waiting in the crossties while she tidied Matisse, a dappled gray with stocky legs like all quarter horses used to have, and Rancho Costa Plente's get still did. "Tomorrow you're going to a new home," she whispered to the stallion while she haltered him. "Don't be afraid. You're going to spend the rest of your life making gorgeous silver babies. Won't that be fun?"

Shep appeared with a bucket and a rag. He turned on the hose and filled the bucket. "Is sex all you ever think about?"

"You happened to walk in at the moment I was discussing Matisse's future, that's all."

"Seems like a lot of those moments going around lately."

"Oh, shut up and help me clean these horses."

They worked side by side, using sweat scrapers and sponges, rubbing the horses dry since the hour was late and the temperature dropping too quickly for baths. "Doctor Quintero sure lit out of here in a hurry," Shep remarked.

Lily picked Matisse's hooves and applied thrush medicine as a preventative. "He had to," Lily replied. "The great snow essay beckoned."

Shep painted hoof conditioner onto Alfred with practiced strokes. "I'm guessing a first date that lasts five days needs a little recovery time."

Lily squatted next to the horses, the silver hoof pick in her hand. She stared at the curve of the blunt blade, thinking how it resembled a pirate's hook. "Probably so. Oh, poop. When's the last time you fell in love, Shepherd?"

"Fifteen years ago I had a thing for that woman who runs the Catholic church gift shop. She said I was worse than an old goat, and she gave me the gate."

"So that makes you an expert."

"Just seems to me you don't need to be in a hurry, Lily." He coughed, retrieved a lozenge from his shirt pocket, and stuck it in his mouth. "That's all I wanted to say."

"Well, I'll keep it in mind." Just as she was about to lead them to their various stalls, Shep tapped her shoulder. "Now what?"

He switched on the arena lights and pointed with the yellow plastic comb. It was snowing. Light flakes glittered in the amber glow of the lights, softly gracing the windshield of the ranch truck Buddy liked to hide beneath. Oh, the simple magic of changing weather. It lifted the spirit, reminded Lily of countless other seasons she'd been too preoccupied to appreciate. She stood out in it for a while, her arms lifted, bare palms up to catch the sting of each flake. Shep told her she was going to catch a cold, but Lily pretended she didn't hear him. When enough snow had fallen that there was a light crust on the truck's glass, she used her fingertip to trace the outline of a fat white heart. She stood there watching until the falling snow filled in the edges.

The next morning she was up early. The snow had melted, and it was definitely cooler than the previous day, but warm enough to work the horses. Shep was nowhere to be found, so she started without him. Her father readied Matisse for transport and loaded him into Mr. Lankford's horse trailer. "I'm going into town," he said.

"Where in hell's Shep?" Lily asked. "Does he expect me to ride all these horses by myself?"

"Had a checkup with the doctor, I think. Looks like you're doing fine to me, although I'd longe the chestnut mare before you ride her. She looks fractious this morning."

"No *duh*," Lily said. "She's thrown me every day I've ridden her."

"Better wear your hard hat."

Her father got in his truck and drove off. Lily saddled the mare and worked her on the longe line until the horse appeared docile. She unsnapped the rope and pulled herself up onto her back, and for ten minutes, they moved as one through her nicely developing gaits. She was responding so well to leg cues that Lily decided to try her over some Cavaletti poles. She wouldn't swear to it, but it felt like this one had the beginnings of a hunter-jumper in her. Lily dismounted, dragged out the red-and-white painted poles, situated them a horse's stride apart, and got back on the mare. They walked over, and she encouraged the mare to drop her nose and take a sniff. The next thing Lily knew, she was lying flat on her back in the sand, staring up at a cloudy sky. She'd fallen hard enough that the wind was knocked out of her, and she gasped while the mare ran a length of the arena, whinny-ing her victory, coming to a stop by the fence where Jody Jr. and her pack of unkind canine relations had witnessed the whole turn of events.

The horses and dogs seemed unimpressed by the string of curses Lily delivered. She looked at her watch: Eleven A.M. Enough of this crap. She went indoors, took a shower, fixed her hair, and sprayed her-self with Mami's most expensive perfume. She dressed in black jeans and a low-cut black silk pullover of her mother's and selected a *heishi* necklace from her jewelry box that was probably worth more than the sculpture Buddy'd ruined, which she fully intended to repair before that plane landed.

From the porch she saw Shep's truck, so she called his name but got no answer. She rapped on the bunkhouse door.

"What?"

"Sheppy," she said to the red-painted wood. "That freaking chest-nut mare threw me again this morning."

"You probably weren't concentrating."

"The hell I wasn't. Here's my plan. We tie cement blocks to her hooves or outfit her with a pair of wings. What do you think?"

He didn't answer.

Lily rapped on the door again. "I've been thinking about what you said last night, Shep. I have a question. Do you think maybe men are terrified of happiness? I mean, everyone goes on about all 'fear of com-mitment' like that's the core issue. What if that's—I don't know—some kind of distraction thrown out to keep women from understanding the real problem?"

The wrangler had no comment.

Lily pulled her gloves from her jacket pocket and put them on. "Oh, well. It was just a thought. You want to hear another one? Maybe that lapsed psychiatrist isn't worthy of what I have to offer. For exam-ple, he didn't buy a single one of the condoms."

Again, her words were met with silence. "Fine, then. Ignore me, you old fart. All that does lend credence to my theories. You all are on my list, every last one of you plus that nasty mare. I'm going to town. You need anything?"

Through the closed door came his answer: "Well, a little peace and quiet might come in right handy."

"Your wish is my command." Lily fetched Buddy and wrestled him past the ranch dogs into the Lexus. Jody Jr. snapped all the way up to the shutting of the car door. Lily guessed that maybe after they were weaned, dogs forgot they had children, which made her think of trying to find Second Chance again, an endless game of phone tag with various motorcycle magazines who knew of the lad but not where he currently resided. She loved her nephew enough that she'd rack up the long distance charges trying to find that out. What if she never got to have a baby of her own? Jeez. If the best she could hope for was being a stepmother figure to Leah from Stanford, it hardly paid to have ovaries.

The entire half hour it took to get to her sister's part of town she punched numbers into her car phone. The magazine in Arizona put her on perpetual hold, but the woman who answered the phone in Albuquerque said to try Mexico, a lot of the motocross riders went south for the winter and mutated into surfers. Lily thanked her and turned up the stereo. Buddy Guy's *Slippin' In* was permanently programmed disc number six on the CD player. The first cut was "I Smell Trouble," and the second, which she played three times in a row, was "Please Don't Drive Me Away." Lowering her voice to harmonize got her halfway to Rose's, but pretty soon the edges of her resolve crumbled, and she began to feel as friable as end-stage inflammatory bowel disease. While the blues tapped at her soul, Lily could swear the steering wheel was yanking itself in the other direction, up that mountain toward Dr. Q. Before "Love Her with a Feeling" was ten notes into the song she had to shut off the music entirely.

"Buddy," she said as they parked in the lot of the veterinary hospital, where sunlight struck the adobe walls, painting them a warm shade of russet, "a rawhide chew you don't have to share with anybody and decent treatment from the one man with whom I am sexually combustible—do you think we ask for too much?" Her blue heeler panted happily. She snapped on his leash and muzzle, dragged him across the parking lot, and into the clinic.

"Did you have a scheduled appointment?" the woman behind the counter asked suspiciously.

"I'm Rose's little sister," Lily explained. "I'm here to get my dog's teeth cleaned and take my sister to lunch."

The woman leaned onto her arms across the counter. "So this is famous Lily."

"I'm famous?"

"*Por supuesto,* but I thought you'd be taller. I'm Paloma. You'll have to fill out this questionnaire. Has your dog had anything to eat today?"

Only panties and a hippie biscuit. She couldn't say that out loud. "Even if we asked nice I don't think he'd tell the truth."

"He'll have to come back tomorrow, then. No food after midnight. No water in the morning."

Lily sighed. What was she supposed to do with Buddy while she and Rose ate lunch? "Couldn't I just board him and have you guys do it in the morning?"

"Is he current on his vaccines?"

"Yeah, of course. Probably. Call his vet in California. I have his card here in my purse somewhere."

"Without proof of inoculation, the doctor will have to examine him."

Lily pulled a handful of business cards from the compartment in her purse, laid them on the counter, and began shuffling through them. Surgeons, technical assistants, radiologists, not a vet in the bunch. "Any chance the doctor can see him right now?"

Paloma shrugged. "Have a seat. I'll let Rose know you're here."

"Why don't you wait and tell Rose after I've see the vet? I don't want to interrupt her work."

The woman picked up the phone and buzzed Dr. Donavan. Lily wandered around the waiting room. So, this was her sister's world: *Dog Fancy* magazines, old *National Geographics*, and on the wall above the benches, framed posters of all the known horse breeds and color variations. There was a stone statue of a dog holding a basket in his teeth. Inside the basket were folded-up flyers for tick medicine. Above the water cooler Lily spotted a little plaque with a framed Polaroid labeled "Pet of the Month." October's was some ancient palomino pony who reminded her of Sparrow. Maybe in exchange for a bill some artist had left framed sketches of a dachshund and two Siamese cats. Under the pictures a taped card declared that for a fee, he'd be glad to immortalize your pet on acid-free paper. Complimentary coffee in a pump thermos, a stack of paper cups, tiny packets of powdered fake cream, and the striped coffee stirrers Lily used to be addicted to chewing while she drove the LA freeways took up space next to the magazines—right here in front of her face was small-town Floralee, distilled into one of its larger businesses. Lily'd forgotten how the close confines got under her skin. *California has infected me with small-town-aphobia,* she thought. *If Buddy needed an endoscopy, would he have to be airlifted to 'Burque?* Mami *could fly him, if she was around, or I guess I could learn to fly a plane myself. How different can flying be from driving?*

The exam room door opened and a handsome, dark-haired man smiled at her. "I'm Doctor Donavan," he said. "Bring Buddy on back."

Lily returned the smile but reserved half the wattage of her total shine in case this skinny guy with the hippie glasses turned out to be unworthy. "I have to warn you, he sometimes bites."

"He looks friendly."

Buddy ambled on through the doorway, tail wagging. He seemed amenable enough, even blasé about the exam room smells. "I guess he's having a good day." Lily removed his muzzle.

"Let's lift him up on the table and check him out."

Lily held Buddy's collar and watched the vet work. Buddy allowed his heart to be listened to, his temperature to be taken, his belly palpated, and his ears checked, all without protest. This guy had the gentlest touch. She wondered what that translated to in bed, if such soft movements could tame her sister, because surely Rose was secretly as wild as Lily.

The vet peeled the dog's lips back. "I agree, his teeth could use a cleaning. How often do you brush them?"

"When he lets me. Well, I did it once. How am I supposed to when he chews up the brush? I feed him those hard biscuits."

Dr. Donavan patted Buddy's belly. "Could be Buddy's had a few too many biscuits in the name of dental hygiene. Ever thought about switching his diet to a lower-calorie formula?"

"You mean we *both* have to live on Lean Cuisine?"

The vet laughed. "Ms. Wilder, you don't look like you need to lose weight. Your dog, however, is obese."

"Why don't you call me Lily?"

"Okay." The vet wrote some things down in the chart he'd started for Buddy. Without looking up, he said, "The only resemblance I can see between you and your sister is your eyes. I've lived here all my life. Seems funny I don't remember you."

Lily tossed her hair back over her shoulders. "I'm five years younger than Rose. When you two were raising hell around Floralee, I was a barn rat in jodhpurs and mucking boots. I didn't even know boys existed."

He snorted. "That's not what I heard."

"What did Rose tell you? That stuff about the photographer is totally exaggerated. Those pictures were artistic, and they *never* appeared in *Hustler.*"

Dr. Donavan smiled. "Hadn't heard the photographer story, but as long as you brought it up, I wouldn't mind hearing it now."

Lily took out her lipstick and redid her mouth. "Not a chance. Forget I mentioned it."

"I'll try. If Paloma can't verify his vaccines, I'll have to give Buddy a new set. He can board here overnight and get his teeth done in the morning, be ready to go home by the afternoon. Where is home, by the way? California? Or are you back in town because you're considering relocating?"

Lily thought of Tres in his cabin, and this smart-mouthed veterinarian who was wearing a very nice watch, which indicated he made decent money or at least had good taste and a credit line to support it. "Haven't decided on that, Doctor. Why don't you come with Rose and me to lunch? You can pitch me the benefits of small-town life."

"Afraid I've got surgery this afternoon. And I think you can probably call me Austin."

Lily thrust her chin up. "Oh? Is that a small-town thing or a familiar thing?"

"Whatever you choose to make of it."

"Maybe Rose told you I'm in the medical field, too. What kind of surgery are you doing this afternoon?"

He tapped the file chart against the exam table. "Appaloosa gelding with focal dermatitis of the penile sheath. Removing the growths or leaving them alone offers roughly the same odds, but the owner wants them removed."

"Doesn't sound like it'll take very long."

"After that I have to check on some mules. That might take a couple of hours. They're a judge's mules. A judge who recently did me a favor."

"Well, Austin, if you ever have need of laparoscopic equipment, call me. I can get you the number of somebody who would cut you a dynamite deal." She handed him a business card with her various numbers and added, "I check my voice mail hourly."

He tucked the card into his pocket. "Thanks, but this is a fairly low-key practice. I'm pretty well set."

"How set are you with my sister?"

Austin fumbled the file he was holding and bent to catch it before it hit the floor. When he stood up he was tight lipped. "Excuse me, ma'am, but I don't see where that's any of your business."

"One simple question and we're all the way back to 'ma'am'? That must mean serious sheet time."

"Your dog'll be ready tomorrow."

Dr. Donavan hustled Buddy out the door so quickly Lily could feel the breeze in their wake. *Handsome,* she thought. *More Rose's type than mine. Damn that Tres Quintero anyway. I know I could have stayed quiet enough for him to type.*

"Order whatever you want," Lily insisted while the waitress stood, pad in hand, waiting. "This is on me, not the company, so you don't have to experience any corporate guilt. You love seafood. Have a shrimp cocktail. And save room for dessert."

Rose, who was dressed in nothing special—khaki pants, a navy blue turtleneck and an embroidered denim vest over that—pushed the menu aside and took a drink of water. "I only want a salad."

Even in baggy old pants and a vest that hid her tits, which were her best feature, Rose looked good today. "Why? Are you dieting? You don't need to lose weight." She turned to the waitress. "Do you think my sister's fat?"

"Jeez, will you stop annoying the waitress? I'll have the shrimp cocktail and the mixed greens salad. Bring my sister the Valium."

"Har-de-har-har, Rose. You have no idea what I want. You never did."

"Fine, then. Order. I have forty-five minutes, then I have to get back to work."

"He makes you punch a time clock?"

"No. I just don't take more than an hour for lunch."

Lily ordered the same salad, no dressing, and the fruit plate, from which she planned to eat only the melon. "Why do you work that job, Rose? It's beneath your intelligence. Do you do it to be near Doctor Cute? He was really good with Buddy, but I don't trust him."

Rose set down her water glass. "Let's see, I don't have a college degree, I need the money, plus I really enjoy the humiliation factor of having you point out to me that what I do for a living lacks status, importance, and a future."

"Come on, that's not what I meant and you know it."

"Do me a favor, Lily? Don't explain what you did mean. Let's just talk about something other than my job."

Lily leaned forward across the table. "You slept with Doctor Cute while I was gone, didn't you? You keep smiling for no reason. Plus, you were extra kind to the waitress."

"What if I did?"

"Let's hear the details."

Rose raked her hands through her hair. "Aren't we both a little long in the tooth for these dissections? You notice I didn't ask you what you were doing all last week with Tres Quintero."

"Oh, but you should have, Rose. It was the *Kama Sutra,* backwards, forwards, up the stairs, I lost track of how many times."

"You slept with him?"

"Used up two boxes of condoms."

"Lily, you just met him." The shrimp cocktail arrived and Rose unfolded her napkin and set it in her lap. "Never mind. It's none of my business what you do."

Lily watched her sister eat a few bites, then put her silverware down. "You think I'm immoral because I like getting laid."

"I never said that."

"The look on your face says plenty. Between you and Shep I'm ready to head back to California."

"What's the matter with Shep?"

"Hell if I know. He wouldn't even come outside and talk to me today."

"Maybe he wasn't feeling well."

"He was feeling well enough the night before to lecture me on my sex life."

Rose folded her hands on the tablecloth. "A lot can happen overnight."

"You did sleep with the vet!" Lily said. "I knew it."

Rose sighed. "Believe whatever you want, Lily."

"Why is it such a big deal? Why can't you tell me a few measly fine points and share like a sister?"

"I don't feel like it. Some things are private."

"I tell you everything. You're being stingy."

"You tell me far more than I care to know."

"Oh, and that's a sin, right?"

"What I do with Austin's none of your business, Lily."

The salads arrived, and Lily picked up her fork. She stabbed the tines into the glistening berries. She wanted to pick them up and one by one, throw them at her sister. "There's worse things in the world than me enjoying sex, Rose Ann. Lots worse. Murder, for example."

"We're in a public place, Lily. Lower your voice."

"Hey, I'm a paying customer, I'll talk as loud as I want to."

Her sister pushed away the half-finished shrimp and stared at the salad plate before her. "For crying out loud, Lily. I wish I knew what it is you're trying to get at."

"Do you believe true penance can put anyone back in God's graces?"

"Yes, I do."

"Even adulterers?"

Rose looked stricken. "Where did this sudden interest in morals come from? Is Tres married?"

"No, divorced. Maybe it's not my morals I'm thinking about. Maybe it's somebody else's."

"Lily, this subject is getting really old."

"Come on, Rose. I want to know. If you're not going to tell me what you did with Austin, at least answer my question."

"Even adultery, yes. I guess if I had to pin it down, there's only one sin I find unforgivable, and that's holding on to grudges. If we can't forgive each other, I kind of think we're lost as a species."

"Jeez, Rose," Lily said. "doesn't that strike you as *slightly* hypocritical, since you refused to talk to me for five whole years?"

Rose looked down at the table. She pressed her lips together, straightened out her napkin, and set her fork on top of it. Then she stood up and pushed her chair in. "Where do you think I came up with the idea?"

She left Lily sitting alone at the table.

Not too long after Rose's departure, the waitress came by with the check and complimentary toothpicks, packaged in tissuey white paper. Lily unwrapped one, stabbed it into the leftover shrimp and assembled a fruit and seafood kabob. She arranged the salad greens around it and sat there fuming. *I should have told her right then,* Lily thought. Sometimes Rose acted so prim and penned up inside it made Lily want to scream. Of course, that was the way a person's mind worked if she was having really great sex with somebody she loved, somebody who *loved her back.* Lily cut one of the berries in half and studied the pink, meaty flesh. She envisioned it infested with worms, which was basically how she'd stayed thin her whole life.

Rather than look for her, Lily let Rose walk the three blocks back to work. She dialed her voice mail on her car phone and was surprised to find no new messages. Next, she dialed her answering machine in California and other than a few hang-ups and a yet another telemarketer wanting to sell her the *Register,* there was no news. Out of desperation, and to make certain she still existed, she called Eric. "Just thought I'd check in," she said to her boss. "See what's up."

"I'm in the middle of something, Lily. Is this important?"

"Don't get nervous."

"You said you wanted to be left alone."

"So I did. See you in a couple of weeks."

"Whatever." He hung up.

She threw her cell phone onto the passenger's seat. First Tres, then the mare, then Rose, now stinky Eric. Apparently this was her week for rejections. She turned the heater down in the Lexus and drove up the highway to her parents' ranch. Sans Buddy, the ranch dogs didn't bother barking on her arrival, and Shep was nowhere in sight. She stood at the fenceline petting Rose's mare, who was turned out into the arena with a few of the older geldings. Winky was nothing special to look at. She didn't even sport a decent lineage. Rose had an instinct for such things, however, and Lily bet this horse would probably throw a beautiful gray colt. She scratched the mare's neck and tried not to think about how well everyone seemed to live their lives without her. The term "old maid" caromed through her mind. She started for the house, then turned. Once again, she knocked on Shep's door.

"Shep? You want to come up to the house and play backgammon with me? I promise I won't cheat. I'll fix you a steak for dinner, nice and bloody the way you like it. And a baked potato with sour cream and chives. I'll even throw in garlic bread. Pretty please, Shep?"

"Thank you, no," he said through the closed door.

Lily tried the knob. It wasn't locked, so she let herself in to the small room with the cot bed covered by a faded Indian blanket. Cowboy paintings covered the walls, and a braided rawhide whip lay on the table, where the old man sat writing out a supply list on a legal pad. So far it read, "Four-way, vitamins, hoof paint, thrush medicine, shavings, and painkiller." Lily wondered if the last item was for him or the horses. "Come on, Shep. It's insane for both of us to be here alone and sitting in separate corners. You've got to eat sometime, and I'm feeling lonely."

He set his pencil down and rubbed his forehead. "Go pet your fairy dog."

"Can't. He's in the shop. You're pissed at me because I ran off with Tres for a few days, aren't you?"

"Like I said earlier, your sex life is of no interest to me, Miss Loose Drawers."

"It used to be. We used to talk about everything. By the way, do you have a glue gun?"

"Not anymore. What in hell do you need to glue back together?"

"Mami's sculpture. You weren't lying. Buddy really did a number on it."

He rummaged through a drawer and retrieved a glue gun and replacement cartridges. "There. Now get lost."

"Sheppy," she wheedled, "don't be mad at me."

He looked her square in the eye. "I ain't mad. I'm dying of prostate cancer, and I'd like to do it in peace."

Lily's face went hot with shock. "Don't talk like that."

He looked up at her. The grizzled face seemed to be nothing more than tired skin lying slack against bone. His eyes shifted this way and that, as if he didn't quite know where to fix his gaze. "You rather come out here and find me dead some morning? That'd suit you better? What am I supposed to do, just shut my mouth on the subject until the night arrives? How in the hell do I know when that night is going to be?"

Lily set her purse on the floor and eased herself down onto his lap. She stroked his cheeks and touched his ears, grown long with age like a horse's. "Is that what the doctor told you today?"

He nodded.

"How long does he say you have?"

"Year maybe, if I do the chemotherapy."

She kissed the top of his head. "Come back with me to California. I know some doctors who are absolute magicians. You might not have to lose your hair."

Shep shook his head. "I don't have the right clothes for the great prune state."

The shock flooded her with adrenaline. "You're not going to do the chemo, are you?"

He pushed her away. "Lord, you're heavier than a stock saddle, and your butt is all bone. Get off me."

Lily knelt down on the floor next to him. "I love you, Sheppy. I don't want you to die. Please do the chemo."

He picked up a deck of cards, shuffled, and began to deal them out. "You're a spoiled brat, Lily. Always thinking of yourself. I want to hang on long enough to see your sister's mare through her birthing, then Saint Peter is welcome to this sorry old bag of stove-up bones."

Tears ran down her cheeks. "Are you in pain, Shep?"

"Not much."

"What are you taking for it?"

"Codeine or something. Upsets my stomach."

"There's no reason for you to hurt at all. Let me call your doctor. We'll get you a different prescription."

He laid his age-spotted hand over hers. "I never did much like swallowing pills. I could purely relate to the horses on that score. Now don't be sticking that lower lip out. You're supposed to be the tough one. Everybody dies sooner or later, just never when it suits you. Grab that other deck of cards and let's play double solitaire. Loser cooks the steaks."

13

More Snow

Rose's first thought as she opened the back door that morning was, *Oh, I've missed this,* and a fraction of a second later, *I wonder how long until spring.* All night long she'd listened to the wind blow, rattling the old windows in their wooden frames, a reminder that her house needed attention. Now, from halfway up the wheel wells of her Bronco to the mailbox on the post at the end of her drive, everywhere she looked, there lay a pristine white blanket of snow. It was six A.M., and Max was neighing for breakfast, so she began shoveling a path, working toward the barn.

If nothing else, her efforts expelled some of her anger toward her sister. She'd forgotten how peaceful—and insane—it felt not to be speaking to Lily. For example, Rose could feel grateful and amused by the simple things in life: a cartoon in the *Floralee Facts* that caught her by surprise, or Chachi's antics when he desperately wanted to finish the milk in her cereal bowl. That solitary way of looking at things had its pluses: Even this snowfall moved her. Lily, particularly when her poisonous tongue was in action, could cast a pall over the sunniest day, confusing Rose completely. Following their restaurant fight, Rose had immediately picked up the phone to call Mami, hoping to unload as well as gain an ally, but her mother was in California. Some dire dog business had beckoned, and off she flew. Paloma's sympathetic ear made a good substitute until her friend made a simple observation. "What do you expect?" she said. "Her purse is a mess," inferring that its contents belied Lily's carefully assembled exterior.

Maybe so. Which made Rose think of Austin—erstwhile handbag

inspector—who seemed to have caught whatever virus had infected Lily. Lately he nit-picked the orders she asked him to approve, and despite their sleeping together—and sleeping was all they did—couldn't have been more distant. When Rose made her bed in the mornings, taking hold of the sheets, she had to convince herself the vet lay there from time to time when he needed comforting. Words seemed unnecessary. Austin held her, and the shine of his eyes let her know that the horse he'd been trying to save from colic earlier in the day hadn't made it, or the surgery he'd performed on a dog that had been hit by a car wasn't enough to make a difference. When the vet got locked up inside himself like that, Rose was afraid to touch him, fearful she'd say the wrong thing. He never showed up with alcohol on his breath, but there were mornings at the clinic when he'd head upstairs without saying anything except, "Cancel my appointments," and sleep twelve hours straight on the futon balanced on top of his books. Oh, the idea of whatever this was between them moving beyond such nights seemed about as likely as the plot of one of her romance novels, which lately annoyed her with their outlandish masculine heroes. The only bona-fide hero Rose knew was Shep Hallford. Thinking of him made her stop shoveling, lean on the handle, and take deep breaths to keep from breaking down.

A couple of nights ago she'd driven up to the ranch to check on Winky, who was now entering her fifth month of pregnancy, almost the halfway mark, which meant time for another vaccine. Shep kept charts on every horse, almost as detailed as Austin's medical files, only Shep's handwriting was legible. She figured she'd double-check to make sure he'd already given the injection. Thankfully, Lily was elsewhere, so Rose was spared a face-to-face continuation of the morals debate. In the bunkhouse Rose had found her father's wrangler emptying whole bureau drawers into trash bags. His hair wasn't combed, he smelled like he could use a shower, and from the look of things he'd been at this "housecleaning" for some time, because his room furnishings were down to a few Spartan possessions. Rose had seen the same terrified look in Bijou's eyes the day the awful man brought him into the clinic. "Shep, there're storage boxes in the barn," she said calmly.

He acted as if he didn't hear her. When she noticed a leather-bound photo album and the treasured collection of his competition days clippings going into the mix, she held out a hand to stop him. "Let me help you organize this stuff."

"No," he said firmly. "It's all going. Every last bit of it."

"Shep, this is your history. You can't just throw it away."

"Yes, I can. I won't have it, Rose Ann."

"Won't have what?"

"Your pop wading through all my rubble after I'm gone. If nothing else I intend to leave behind a clean house."

The set of his jaw reminded Rose of Austin on one of his post-Leah encounters. So much pain locked up behind the steeled muscle that it bowed out from under his chin. Rose sat down on Shep's cot. He clung stubbornly to his task. For an hour things continued in that fashion until Shep stood up, swore once, dropped the bag on the floor and took off on his horse in the dark.

Rose watched him go. She carefully emptied each trash bag, separating the photographs and memorabilia into decades. Shep had been so handsome in his youth, raven-haired, stocky, that mischievous grin playing across his face in the majority of the pictures. Such a variety of women graced his arms it was impossible to recall all their names. What tore her heart was the handmade Valentine cards she and Lily had made for him, the crooked construction-paper hearts he'd saved all these years, with their crayoned messages, backward Ss, and childish declarations of love. She packed all of it neatly into boxes, marked them with pen, and stacked them in the barn next to a rolled-up carpet and the sled she and Lily had once fought over and Amanda and Second Chance had inherited, then grown too old to use. When Shep didn't return, Rose groomed Winky head to toe, administered the injection, and noted it on the chart. She stood awhile hugging her horse around the barrel, running her fingers through the thick winter coat the mare was growing along with her baby. As long as procreation continued she supposed hope existed. That evening, however, the notion didn't strike her as at all convincing.

She scraped her shovel down to earth, exhaling visible plumes of breath under the deceptively blue sky. In late October there had been subtle warnings of the coming season. The skies had gone dark, and some days the rain nearly blinded her as she walked from work to her car. As if fed up with itself, the sky delivered occasional momentary flurries that hit Rose in the face like a handful of sand, but the following days were generally sunny, burnishing Floralee's old adobe buildings to a rich, warm red. Every year the season fooled her. Rose never accepted that winter had arrived until she was forced to carve a path through it.

She leaned the shovel against the fence, catching her breath. In the barn she fed and groomed the old gelding, crushing three tablets of Bute in with his vitamins, mashing everything up good so he'd take the medicine he needed in order not to stiffen up in this bitter weather. She straightened some fallen tack, ran her fingers over the faded blue ribbons hanging on the wall, glanced at her son's shotgun that hadn't been fired in years, covered with cobwebs, looking more like an antique than a weapon. Amanda had won the blue ribbons back in a time when loving her horse was the most important thing in the world. Second Chance had earned a Scout's patch for his sash by shooting that gun—it was tangible proof of progress, and she wished she had some of her own.

She dragged out a fifty-pound sack of grain to replace the one she'd just emptied. A small tear at the bag's seam left behind a trail of corn and oats. Across her boot tops, fat brown mice scurried from old hiding places to new ones. Mice were supposed to be Chachi's detail, but in cold weather the Jack Russell ventured no farther than the back porch to relieve himself before retreating indoors to the woodstove. Rose hung up the shovel, walked out into the arena, and leaned against the fence. The bare branches of the trees glistened as the sun melted the ice from their branches.

She heard Max's whinnying before she saw Austin's truck pull up. The driver's door opened and he got out, holding two Styrofoam cups of coffee. Wisps of steam rose from the perforations in the lids. She had no idea what merited the early-morning visit, and whistled so he'd see her. Austin stepped carefully though the snow until he came to the path she'd cleared and handed her the coffee. "Thanks," she said. Isn't this kind of early for you? "

"Couldn't sleep. Figured I might as well get up and start my day."

They walked into the barn, where Austin placed his hand on the gelding's back. Max, thrilled with so much attention this early in the morning, trembled and nickered, lowering his neck in anticipation of the chiropractic adjustments he'd come to love.

"You Bute him already?"

"Yes." Austin lifted his cup to his lips. Rose saw the telltale shake visit his hands and set her cup down on top of the grain sack. "What's the matter?"

"Just a bad morning," he said, steadying his drink with both hands. "Following an equally vile night before. I'll be all right. I just need some caffeine in me and a meeting or three. " He tilted the cup to drink and spilled hot coffee down the front of his jacket.

Perhaps every cuss word Rose knew existed made its way into Austin's next sentence. She flinched as he hurled the cup across the yard. A swash of brown liquid arced across the snow. Rose let herself be pulled into his embrace and felt the shaking in his shoulders.

Austin had doubled up on his AA meetings, gone way past the thirty required by Eloy. He no longer drove all the way to Taos. These days he marched into the Floralee church carrying his *Big Book* around like Papa Hemingway had autographed it for him personally. He saw patients and kept on schedule, and those days he fell off the wagon, it didn't take more than a day for him to climb back on. The judgment he heaped on himself only seemed to increase, however, and nothing seemed to quiet him except moments like these. Rose laid her head against his chest and listened to the racing of his heart. Sometimes it felt as if they had skipped all the fun parts of courtship, gone straight to the ingrained habits of a couple married forty years. He kissed the top of her head, a chaste demonstration that deliberately held back what she knew lay hidden there. Austin expected her to wait forever.

She set her coffee down on a box of Philip's old power tools she'd been meaning to donate to the church rummage sale. Austin's neck smelled like shaving cream, his jacket strongly of coffee, and deeper still, his own unique citrusy aroma added to the blend. "This isn't fair," she said.

"What isn't fair?"

She pressed her fingers to the stain on his jacket. "You showing up after I've finished shoveling the snow. Got to tell you, doctor, coffee, a hug and a brotherly kiss no longer cuts it for this lady."

He pulled the snaps on her down vest apart, pushed her thermal shirt up far enough so that her bare breasts were exposed. She watched his hand move up her skin, take hold of one breast and squeeze hard. She gasped, her own shocked intake of breath surprising her.

"That any better?" he asked.

"You want to take this inside, cowboy?" she said, laughing nervously, but Austin didn't answer. He bent her back against the grain sacks, kneed her legs apart with his own, and the chill air against her flesh was beyond bracing. "That's enough, Austin. Stop it right now."

Rose shoved him away and pulled her clothes together. Her eyes stung with cold. She retrieved the fallen coffee cups and threw them in the trash. Inside at her kitchen sink she stood trying to remember how exactly it was one washed a dish, because in front of her the basinful she'd left overnight were still dirty.

The door opened and shut. Austin came up behind her. He laid one hand across hers, the hand that held the soapy sponge she now let drop into the sink. "Rose Ann, I'm sorry."

She straightened her back. "I know you're having a hard time, but sometimes you make me feel like I'm nothing to you but a place to stow all your anger. I'm not Leah. Why do I get the feeling that I have to spend the rest of my life making up for how she hurt you?"

"You don't."

"Bull. And that business in the barn? Good Lord, Austin, what were you thinking?"

He pulled her close, breathed into her hair. "I don't mean to put you through all that. I thought you wanted me to touch you."

She shut her eyes, embarrassed. "Yes, I do, in spite of how you went about it, but does that mean gentle and kind suddenly got outlawed?"

He let her go. "I feel god-awful. Last night she walked into the restaurant where I was eating dinner. She had some Texan with her. He didn't even look thirty years old. Hanging all over him, half in his lap, giggling. Waitress comes up and asks me if I want to switch tables. I swear, the whole damn town knows my business. What in the hell's wrong with her?"

"She's trying to make herself happy, Austin."

"Why's it make me so damned miserable?"

"Because you let it. Next time change tables."

He picked the sponge up and squeezed it dry. "I want a drink so bad I dream about it. I taste in my mouth when I wake up. I'm dizzy with meetings and talk about higher powers I don't believe in. I say the words, but they don't feel real to me, they don't drown out what I need. You're the one person I can go to who never calls me on my bullshit."

Rose laughed dryly. "Well, guess what, Austin, you just ran out of places."

He turned her face to his. His eyelashes were thick with tears. "Tell me what to do here. I don't think I could stand it if I lost your friendship."

Rose reached above the sink to straighten the metal crucifix from Chimayo hanging there. When the tiny church of miracles had been reroofed, some artist had bought the scrap metal and fashioned crosses from the worn-out roof, over a hundred years old. There were a lot of things about Catholicism that rubbed her the wrong way, but not this symbol of sacrifice. Lily made fun of her sister for praying, but Rose knew that if it weren't for her faith, she'd be in worse shape than Austin. She caught hold of his hand and laced her fingers through his, still damp from the dishwater. "We haven't lost our friendship, exactly, but things are different. It's time, Austin. Take me to bed."

He stood there looking at the weave of their fingers, squeezing hard. "What if I'm no good to you? What happens if I can't satisfy you?"

"Why don't you let me worry about that?"

The bedroom was cool. Rose wanted to dive into the tangle of sheets and bury herself behind the covers. Instead, she stood next to the bed, directing Austin's fingers under her clothes and up her flanks, where all her ignored nerve endings were jumbled up, so desperate for attention just the graze of his fingers made her excited. She closed her eyes and gave herself over to sensation.

When her shirt was off, Austin ran a fingernail across her inner arm, causing her to tremble. "Jewel quakes like that when a horsefly lands on her," he whispered. "Me, I practically have to get slapped in the face to feel anything. I keep telling you, I'm not ready."

"*Shh.*" She turned to face him, then moved her fingers down the length of his body and pressed against him with the palm of her hand. He was only semi-erect. All that guilt and rage inside him had locked up in one eternal fistfight.

Give up, Rose mentally commanded him, stepping out of her boots and pulling off the rest of her clothing. Every place she explored, she touched him as gently as she could. That business about needing to be slapped was so much manure. Yes, he was in pain, and she understood how that felt, how sometimes only more hurt allowed one to break through what already felt like agony. But familiar pain wasn't the only emotion one could feel. When his clothes were out of the way, she ran her fingers up either side of the fold in his groin and felt him shudder.

She knelt down and pressed her face against him, began kissing her way toward his center. Austin made a sound like a sob, and his fingers locked tight in the hair at the nape of her neck.

Rose could count on one hand the number of times she'd felt this close to Philip. In bed her husband had been a meat-and-potatoes kind of man, quick to inform her there was no need for her to "act that way" when she wanted to try something different, that he was just fine with "regular sex," which, of course, made her feel cheap and ridiculous for suggesting anything new. She imagined other women were expert, other women—say it, *Lily*—knew how to do all kinds of things, perform fellatio with a finesse that rendered a man speechless. Moving up his body, Rose laid her cheek against Austin's, and with her fingertips traced the whiskers on his chin. She waited for whatever would happen next, even for Austin to say he was leaving, because even if he said that he was never coming back, she understood he would be lying. They were connected in a way that never seemed to unravel. They lay down on the bed. Rose felt calm and quiet, deeply immersed in this, astonished by the power of love. All those years with Philip, and she'd never arrived at this place, not once. They were both going to be late for work. The coffee on the stove was probably down to an inch; any minute now it could burn down to a thick caramel and the house catch fire. The whole day in fact might slide down the drain. Right now, however, this quiet moment that elevated them both seemed more important than any of that.

She let the silence carry her like a jet stream, that long, meandering wind that blew in from the west, pulling inside it whatever was nearby, feeding itself in order to continue. His fingers began to explore her body, revealing the vulnerability he was finally willing to allow her to witness. Her own pulsing, unrelieved desires made her groan, and Austin hauled her to him, kissed her full on the mouth. "Rose," he said into her neck. "I don't deserve you."

She traced her tongue along the curve of his ear. "No, you don't."

He took hold of her upper arms, climbed up her body, pushing himself against her as if nothing had better try to stop him, a lost man in search of relief. It was the most eloquent prayer he knew, and the old Rose would have gone ahead and parted her legs for him, thrown open her heart, making believe the gift of her body was enough to heal him, but this Rose had a clearer head. "Austin," she whispered, "Slow down and let me catch up."

He stopped. "You're getting all nervous on me, aren't you? Next thing you're going to say you have to go bake a pie, just walk on out of here like you got better things to do."

She smiled. "There's always work to do in the kitchen."

He laid a finger against her lips. "And business to take care of here. Don't you leave me. Not yet."

"I'm not going anywhere." She flinched at the tickle of his hair against her face, his mouth moving across her nape, but after a few minutes there was no more important task in the world than arching her body to meet his hand, the middle finger pressing deep inside her where the slippery wetness let him know she was now ready. Rose bit her lip, trying to measure out all this sensation so that she wouldn't come as quickly as her body seemed to want to do. She circled her fingers around his wrist and pulled him away, placed his hand on her thigh, letting him know that she wanted him inside.

Everything he did to her erased her memories of Philip's touch. In quiet moments, she'd stop to think of the way Austin's hands felt against her body and compare that to twenty years of sex in her marriage, stunned that at forty, merely the *idea* that these slow dance steps they were taking could cause her to feel so alive. It was as if her body's edges were revising. Over the past two years, there were times she'd felt if not virginal again, so completely cloistered that she might as well be. And a part of her was comfortable with that, wanted to run out of the room, grab a bridle, and ride Max at a dead gallop as far as the old horse could go. But this was a morning of sacrifices, and to leave now would be to thumb her nose at this fragile man's taking the risk.

You listen, she scolded herself, deep inside where rational thought kept trying to intrude. *The horse won't die from neighing, and if me lying here allows a few mice to grow fat on spilled corn, so what?* She raised her arms and wrapped them tightly around Austin's shoulders. He thrust himself inside her. The bittersweet surrender caused each to look into the other's eyes, gravely acknowledging the significance of this moment.

Outside, thanks to a storm that had spiraled its way down from the frigid Gulf of Alaska, Floralee's temperature was dropping, snow flurries were swirling in white eddies across the yard, and in this bed a great heat spread over it all. As the weather gathered its forces, flakes began to cover the path Rose had worked so hard to clear. The falling snow obliterated the coffee stain from the yard. The old gelding turned his back on the day to retreat to the warmth of the barn, and nosed his empty grain bucket. Time passed lazily while Rose and Austin walked each other along a new path to the same old astonishing mountaintop. At the very peak, in the middle of all that ice, one waterfall still ran, determined, warm, and purposeful, eternally proclaiming spring.

When the new magazines arrived in the morning mail, Rose set them aside to put into their protective covers after she finished paying the bills. Imagine, December's issues, and it wasn't Thanksgiving yet. She didn't understand why retailers hurried the holiday season along. By the time Christmas arrived, people were sick of it. She entered invoices into the computer and backed up her files. Just before lunch she tucked the magazines under her arm and ran downstairs to ask Paloma what had become of the large manila envelopes she'd bought just a few weeks earlier.

Paloma was busy on the phone, so Rose took the opportunity to switch last month's issues. In *New Mexico*, where she flipped to the magazine's center so she could insert the metal bar that held the plastic cover in place, an ad for the Storyteller Indian Arts Gallery caught her eye. The three-quarter-page layout featured a dark-haired model standing with her legs splayed suggestively. Next to her stood an Irish setter, his tail a blurry red flag. The woman wore ankle-high tooled leather boots with silver toe caps. Around her sculpted shoulders she clasped a black suede cape, onto which various violet, bright orange, and crimson lightning bolts, Hopi-style sun faces, and abstract shapes had been appliquéd. All down the front, engraved silver *concha* buttons caught and reflected the light. Beneath the cape, it appeared as if the model wore nothing at all. Her straight black hair was blowing away from her bare shoulders into an attractively tousled mess, and on her face she wore a defiant pout that only intensified her sensuality. It was a fabulous garment, Rose thought, though what capes had to do with storytellers and art was beyond her comprehension. She started to flip the page, but Paloma slapped her hand down on top of it. Still on the phone, she tapped at the model's face and Rose tried to figure out what that meant. Cupping her hand over the receiver she whispered, "*Mira.*"

Of course. How could Rose have missed it? The model wasn't some anonymous face hired to look compelling in order to sell art, she was Leah Donavan. Rose had forgotten how truly beautiful the woman was. She turned the magazine facedown, put the others into their covers while she waited for Paloma to hang up the phone.

The minute she did, Paloma turned the magazine over. *"Que tu pensar?"*

"I think it's a beautiful cape. And I bet it costs more than my car is worth. Do you know where those large envelopes are? I need them to mail out some X rays to Doctor Zeissel."

Paloma tsked. "You have better *pechitos*, plus you can tell she's had a face-lift. Look at the chin. It defies gravity! *Perita en dulce*, that one. She has no shame showing her body like that, even in her hometown, and at her age, she should."

Rose studied the picture again. For a woman nearing fifty, face lift or not, Leah Donavan's looks ranked her in Mami's league. "She has the kind of body that doesn't have to feel ashamed."

"Rose! She's unhappy and a drunk, besides. Probably she posed for this only to drive Austin *loco*. It's not like she needs the money, since she took most of his. Quick, rip out the page so he won't see it. That would be all the excuse he'd need to start drinking again."

"No. If all it takes is a magazine to make him fall off the wagon, then Austin's really in trouble."

The reception door opened, letting in a blast of chill air. A woman entered carrying two gray kittens who couldn't have been close to weaning age. "Look what I found in my barn," she said. "I have no idea how long they've been there. I don't even own a cat. You can feel their little ribs, and they won't stop crying. I tried to get them to lap up some milk but they didn't know how. Do you think they're going to live?"

Paloma adopted a businesslike stance. "Cats are pretty tough. With bottle-feeding, there's every chance they'll make it. We can't take them, you know. We're not a shelter."

The woman smiled a sad smile. "I figured as much. I didn't think it would hurt to ask, though. Can you give me directions to the nearest shelter?"

"Those kittens are too young to go to a shelter," Paloma scolded. "We sell bottles and Kitten Milk Replacement formula. You can feed them yourself."

"I have to go out of town tomorrow on a business trip."

Paloma sighed. She handed over a sheet of paper and a marking pen. "You can make a sign and leave it on the bulletin board."

"People always want kittens at Christmastime," Rose offered. She took both babies from the woman's hands. Their ears were still crumpled like little seashells, and their paws were so small they barely wrapped around her thumbs.

The woman paused in her writing. "Can you tell me their sex? I think that should go on the sign."

Rose shook her head. "The young ones always fool me. Let me run them into the back and ask the doctor."

"Thanks."

In the surgical area, Austin was about to begin a spay on a golden retriever. Rose held up the kittens' tails. "Male or female?"

He squinted before he answered. "Both female."

"How old?"

"I'd say four weeks at the outside."

"Thanks." She started for the doorway.

"Rose. Who do they belong to?"

"Some woman found them abandoned in her barn. She's going to take them to the shelter."

"You tell her to leave the kittens here. They need bottle-feeding or they're not going to make it."

"Okay." Rose cupped the kittens close to her breasts and felt the rumble of the stronger one's purr. It was a common myth that cats purred purely out of contentment, but that wasn't true. They also purred when they were frightened or in extreme pain. She'd held an old calico for Austin once while he put her down. The cat was full of cancer, and her owner had tried every avenue to keep her alive and comfortable. It was time to let go, but she was too distraught to stay in the room for the euthanasia. Rose would never forget the strength of the cat's purring against her hands, or the moment when the vibration wound down, and the silence that followed.

Austin leaned over the dog and deftly made his incision. There would be no unwanted offspring in this dog's life. Tomorrow she'd go home to her owner with staples in her belly to live without the complication of motherhood. He kept neutering charges to a minimum, and on the Pueblos performed the procedures at no charge.

Rose took the kittens into the quarantine room, padding their cage with clean towels. After she told the woman that this was her lucky day, that Dr. Donavan was feeling generous, Rose opened a can of KMR and made a thin paste of formula and baby cereal. As soon as they got the idea, the kittens were gluttonous, crawling over each other to get to the nipple. Rose and Paloma took turns feeding them until the kittens' tummies were round and warm. Rose forgot about lunch. She got no more work done at all that day, and Paloma kept running back and forth from the reception desk to the quarantine room to see how they were doing. "Nacio will kill me if I bring home another cat," she said, "but these two *hermanas* should not be separated."

"Somebody will want them, Paloma. They're precious."

"*Sí*, and they need to be fed every couple of hours. They won't seem too precious at three in the morning, when they need cuddling the most."

"We'll ask Rey to feed them. He'll welcome a chance to sit around and play with babies. It beats cleaning cages."

Paloma held the smaller of the kittens in her wide, brown hands. "You think the mother cat got hit by a car?"

"Anything's possible."

"She wouldn't just abandon her babies. No mother does that willingly. Something must have happened."

Rose nodded. They never talked about it, but long ago Paloma had confided in Rose that she couldn't have children. Rose would never say so out loud for fear of hurting her friend's feelings, but sometimes it was the other way around, and kids abandoned the mother. All around her sacks of dog food were stacked up high, special diets and top quality feed, inventory that moved quickly in and out of the small room. The aroma of lamb and rice was strong. With dogs' ultrasensitive sense of smell, Rose always imagined that it had to be torture for whoever was lodged in the quarantine room. Today, however, all the other animals were in regular boarding or the hospital section. The phone rang, and Paloma reluctantly got up to answer it. Rose shut the kittens in the cage and washed her hands. She figured she'd better get on the road before the snow got too deep to travel through.

She walked past Austin in the operating room, totally immersed in his work. Bent over the table like that, his surgical greens pulled tight against his back, the vet looked deceptively thin. Sharp edges weren't the sum of Austin Donavan, though. While he slept, Rose trailed her hand along his back, lightly marking the placement of each rib, her hand coming to rest on the angle of his hipbone. For all that internal conflict, the man hardly moved once he lay down. Maybe she'd see him later, maybe not. She knew this was one of his meeting nights, and that sometimes he needed to be alone for a couple of days afterward. What they had seemed to be fairly solid now, seemed to have moved onto a level playing field. She wondered if Austin would automatically expect Thanksgiving dinner at her place, just the two of them together at her table, or if she should spend the holiday as she had the last few years, with her folks. Mami left her invitations open. Her feelings wouldn't be hurt if Rose didn't come. Various artists and writers spent a great deal of time and energy angling for an invitation to the Wilder ranch for Thanksgiving. As a result of that, their holiday fetes frequently became town legends. Should she invite Austin to go to her parents' with her? Was that assuming too much? Lily was back in California, working. Lily ignored holidays. Rose was ignoring Lily. For weeks now, neither sister had held out the olive branch. *File that under the big Oh Well,* Rose told herself, but she often thought about her, and missed her. It was unlikely that Chance and Amanda would show up, but the mother in her was already mixing the aromatic dough for cranberry-orange-walnut muffins, which Amanda loved, and filling the seasoned cavity of a turkey with sage-and-hazelnut stuffing, Second Chance's favorite.

Floralee enjoyed a week of balmy weather that melted the snow down to a thin crust. Only under the trees did the larger drifts persist. Then a second storm blew in, and the first blizzard of the year was officially announced. "You should go home early," Austin said as he leaned over Rose's desk signing checks. "You don't want to get stuck in this."

"I have four-wheel drive. You're the one who might have to call a tow truck. Why don't you come with me? I'll fix us an early dinner. Corn chowder and biscuits."

Austin slid the checks toward her. "I've been neglecting my horse, and Bijou's just about turned into a mental case. Think I'd better stay the night in my own place for a change. Besides, all your cooking is making me fat."

Austin, who had to have a third of the links removed from his watchband. It wasn't like she was forcing him to eat. "Okay." Rose tucked the checks into their proper envelopes and sealed them. The post office wasn't on her way home, but she didn't mind swinging by. While she was in town, she could pick up a few things, see some old faces, maybe buy a new paperback. She had grown up in snow like this. The best advice for driving in snow was to take things slowly. Only one time that she could remember had she gotten stuck, and that was in Philip's car. She took a breath and said, "Thanksgiving's coming up."

"Yeah, I guess it is."

"My parents are throwing the usual bash. Loads of guests, and Mami's making tamales. If that sounds like too much, you could come over to my place."

Austin flashed a quick smile. "Let me think on it and get back to you on Monday."

Monday? Did that mean she wasn't going to see him at all this weekend? Distant because he was struggling to stay sober was one thing, but this chill felt entirely different. She didn't like the way her stomach clenched. Gathering up the envelopes, she grabbed her coat and strode out of her office. "Well, I really have to go if I'm going to get these in tonight's mail. Bye, Austin."

He glanced at his watch. "I'm right behind you." And he was, until the parking lot, when he turned his truck in a different direction.

There was a line at the post office, and no available parking spaces, so Rose circled the block and came around again, parking next to the Sage Bakery and the ¡Andale! roadhouse. She shut the car door and, enticed by the mouthwatering smells emanating from the bakery, decided why not pick up a cinnamon bun for tomorrow's breakfast? Once she was inside, the small loaves of molasses bread looked perfect for toast. She took a number and waited her turn in front of the well-stocked cases, chatting with her old high school English teacher, remarkably sharp for a woman of her years.

Purchases made, she put her hand on the door handle and was about to depress the old-fashioned brass plunger, when she saw a familiar, thin man accompanied by tall, dark-haired woman entering the ¡Andale! Austin's hand slid across the woman's shoulders, and they turned their faces to each other, laughing in that familiar, intimate way that only lovers do. The Sage Bakery had a bay window, which—courtesy of the curve in the road—stuck out three feet farther than the

¡Andale!'s glass front. Rose had a clear view of them inside the bar. They sat down at a table near the door, right there, in plain sight of whoever walked by. For a moment the waiter blocked her view, but when he moved away, Rose saw Austin lift what looked like a longneck beer, toasting the woman across from him. She felt a shocky heat pump through her heart, cause the organ to beat double time for a few seconds as the realization hit her. Austin wasn't just drinking, he was drinking in the company of his ex-wife. Rose wished she could return the bun and the bread, because she knew she was never going to be able to eat them.

She walked in the other direction, to the post office, and dropped the letters into the slot. Then she returned to her car, sitting inside for a long time, not bothering to turn on the heater even when her face and fingers began to feel half frozen. She had to wait for them to come out of the bar. She needed to see for herself where they would go next. By the time they did, Rose was hugging her knees, hollow inside, feeling like she might be sick. Not fifteen feet from her Bronco—everyone in Floralee knew her old Bronco—she watched dry eyed as Austin and Leah hurried across the street to the Apple Tree. Hundreds of tiny white Christmas lights were strung in the restaurant's trademark trees. Combined with the softly falling snow, the scene couldn't have been more romantic. How easily they entwined their hands. Their bodies seemed to possess a memory that caused them to lean into one another as they made their way across the snowy street. They were a handsome couple. It was a shame they'd never had children, because any child born of those two sets of genes would have had to be beautiful.

She drove home and parked next to the barn. Chachi came flying down the gravel and leaped at her feet. She picked him up and rubbed her face against his familiar doggy stink. Max neighed and pawed at the snow, missing his exercise. She threw him his evening flake of hay but didn't linger. On any other Friday night, with the snow coming down so hard, Rose would have curled up on the couch with a blanket, an apple, and a pot of cocoa to lose herself in one of her novels, enjoying all that fabricated emotional triumph, perfectly willing to suspend her disbelief in the name of love. The most impossible of situations could turn out happy inside those pages. Tonight darker thoughts prevailed. Had Lily been there, she would have scolded her sister, told her how foolish it was to make love to any man without using a condom. "Six months of panic," Lily would say, referring to the amount of time to wait for blood tests clearing one of the HIV virus, if Lily cared to say anything.

Rose fed Chachi his supper and sat on the floor petting him while he scarfed down his food. Her house was still. She dredged up echoes of happier times, replaying them in her imagination: Second Chance running toy motorcycles across the kitchen floor. Amanda in her room, trying to play the guitar. Philip making a face at the noise and whispering, "Do you think our daughter's tone deaf?" None of that compared to the resonance of Austin's bootheels on the bedroom floor. Her house simply felt more like a home when he was in it. Not just when they were eating dinner or talking, but the way his body took up space in her life, and how when she was with him, she felt like her truest self. When they made love, it was as if a whole new possible life she'd never expected stretched out before her, beckoning. Loving Austin Donavan made her feel less alone in the world. But even before Philip had died, or she'd come to accept that he'd cheated on her, or the kids had left in search of their own lives, she'd been alone, too. It was always the animals she felt needed her most.

She hoped the kittens would get adopted, be loved as part of somebody's family, in a house with kindhearted children and merry noise and lots of spontaneous laughter. She sat on the floor of her kitchen for a long time, staring at the crumpled bag of bakery goods she'd set on the counter. With every passing second, they were turning stale.

That was where Lily found her, sitting in the dark in front of the stove. When her sister switched on the light, Rose looked up and blinked. It never crossed her mind that Lily standing there constituted the rarest of firsts: her sister coming to her to say she was sorry. Rose didn't give her sister the opportunity to apologize, because it seemed important that she tell her what she'd been thinking first. She cleared her throat. "Lily, did you know that if you add up all the years and multiply them by three—breakfast, lunch, dinner—I've cooked over twenty thousand meals here? Twenty thousand," she repeated, as if this revelation had somehow tipped her over, delivered her to a place where she was too far gone to cry. "Can you believe that?"

14

Welcoming El Niño

What I can't believe is how many dishes you had to wash," Lily said as she listened to the story of Austin falling off the Leah wagon. She sat down on the kitchen floor next to her sister. "I have a theory on heartbreak, if you care to hear it. Like taking algebra, it's one of those things nobody escapes. Anyway, factor in the amount of time you were involved with Austin, double it, and when that much time has passed, you'll be over him. Of course, that's discounting the first six weeks, which—no getting around it—are unspeakable hell. But I promise you, Rose, after that you'll at least be functional."

"I've known Austin my entire life. Define 'functional.'"

Lily reached for the bakery sack on the counter and peeked inside to glimpse the silver lining to her overcast winter day. She'd taken a six A.M. flight to Albuquerque and stood in on three surgeries before noon. She'd driven the four hours it took to get to Floralee without stopping. During the drive she'd rehearsed any number of scenarios involving the apology scene. She was determined they resolve things before the holidays, not just because Tres hadn't called, but for a lot of reasons it was difficult to articulate. A full itinerary for one day; however, she'd forgotten to eat. Should she have the bread first, which was technically good for her, or should she go straight for the cinnamon bun? Baked goods were tricky. No matter how healthy the bread appeared to be, it was likely to possess secret, hidden fat calories. "Just imagine yourself ambulatory," Lily said. "With a hardly noticeable limp."

"Great. Terrific. And how long before I get my regular life back?"

It had been so long since Lily had heard from Tres Quintero that she wondered if he'd moved. "Regular life is boredom interrupted by periods of intermittent devastation. Okay if I eat part of this cinnamon thing?"

"Be my guest."

While her sister pulled at a thread on her sweater, Lily unwound the cinnamon bun's snail-like spiral. Sugar, nuts, and butter oozed onto her fingers. When it came to grief, all dieting rules were suspended. Once broken, the female heart reverted to survival mode, and saturated fat provided the closest thing to Valium without a doctor's prescription. "If you ask me, happy endings and heartbreak both lurk in that first kiss. What was yours like with Austin? Awkward and shy? He seems like the type who'd bump noses."

Rose shook her head no. "I didn't know men could kiss like that."

"Like what?"

"Like how it must feel to shoot heroin into your bloodstream. I swear the rush took my breath away."

Tres kissed like that, too. Lily pictured him at his notebook computer, the pine boughs swishing at the cabin windows, and how Rose's simile would so captivate him he'd whip out that pad and write it down. "Oh, Rose. I'm telling you, when lips meet lips and everything feels that good, you might as well buy stock in Kleenex."

Her sister's laugh was fake and polite.

"Handsome as he is," Lily continued, "no two-timing veterinarian is worth your tears."

Rose sat up straight, and here came her real voice, the one that had survived losing her husband and raising two self-centered children. "Am I crying? Why would I cry when this is all my fault for being so stupid and blind in the first place?"

"Because you have to." Lily had finished half the cinnamon bun, but it hadn't satisfied her, and now she regretted not eating the bread. If she ate it, too, that would constitute a day and half's worth of allotted calories. She took a small bite of bread. "Loving somebody's not a crime, Rose. You just picked the wrong somebody. Every woman does it once or twice, or in my case perpetually. We start out with the best intentions. It's in our genes to caretake. You've been out of the dating game so long you didn't know what to expect."

Rose rolled the sweater thread around her finger. "We slept in my bed for weeks before finally making love. You wanted to know those details, Lily? Well, guess what? I had to talk him into it."

"You don't have to tell me anything."

But her sister went on. "He'd stopped drinking. He was leading meetings. Next thing I know he's in the ¡Andale!, in full sight of the whole town, drinking a beer with Leah. Was I somebody to waste time with until they reconciled?"

Rose let go a mammoth sigh, as if she wanted to exchange every molecule of air in her body for a disinfectant. There wasn't a woman on earth who didn't understand that particular exhalation of female breath. Women heard it coming from their sisters and welled over with compassion, all the while believing it would *never* pass through *their* lips. Never, could not, would not, but somehow it always did. Lily got up from the floor and filled the teakettle with water. She set it on the burner and turned on the heat. There was a teapot in the cupboard, an English import patterned with flowers—so typical of Rose to choose frilly china. Lily set two teacups in their matching saucers and, after sniffing all the boxes of tea in the cupboard, settled on peppermint, which she measured out loose into a strainer fashioned to resemble a schoolhouse. She stared at the kettle, waiting for the water to boil.

"It takes a pretty colossal hole in the security blanket to break people's hearts instead of loving them, Rose. You're going to live. You've survived much worse."

Rose looked up. "I'm ashamed to tell you this."

"Tell me anyway."

"It hurts worse than when I lost Philip."

Lily folded the hot pad in half. "I understand. Your first time out, and you got third-degree burns. But right now touching the wound is something to hold on to. Eventually you'll be able to let him go. You will."

Rose laid her head down on her knees. "I'd do it this instant if I knew how."

"Well, you can start by picking yourself up and building a shield out of all that hurt. There. I just saved you five years of therapy." She handed her sister the teacup. "Drink this, and write me a check for ten grand. Hey, I'm going to Mexico over the holiday."

Rose accepted the cup and took a sip. "That sounds fun."

The bracing scent of the tea permeated the small kitchen. It was pretty difficult to feel morose with mint steam in your face. After a few swallows Rose got up from the floor and sat in the kitchen chair across from Lily. She carefully placed her saucer on the table and touched a fingertip to the cup's rim, where a small chip marred the porcelain finish.

To Lily her sister's face had never looked more beautiful. All that sorrow did something to the facial bones, apparently, because even though Rose resembled Pop more than Mami, Lily could see their mother there now, too, maybe just the hint of her cheekbones, determination lurking below the surface. Way back in her ancestors' genes, struggle had been passed along to Mami. When life seemed particularly hopeless, when Lily got the urge to lie down and never wake up, it was generally her mother's attitude that rose up, and suddenly Lily was lifting life's metaphoric equivalent of the truck that had rolled over the trapped child. "Yeah, Mexico *sounds* fun, but my company will wrap back-to-back meetings around Thanksgiving, so I'll be too exhausted to enjoy my one day off. They'll pack us into airless convention rooms and tell us how if we sell more stuff, it'll only *seem* like we're making less money for more work. When I'm allowed outside I'll have to medicate on piña coladas so I don't die of boredom playing golf with the honchos. On the plus side, the beaches are packed with surfers this time of year, so many kids someone's sure to have seen Second Chance. I'll ask around, and maybe we'll get lucky. Want a shot of crème de menthe in your tea?"

Rose nodded yes. "It'd be a relief to hear he's okay."

Lily uncorked the bottle and poured. "Second Chance is fine. You'd hear if he wasn't. The only time either of them calls me is when they're in trouble. An auntie with a wallet is a favored relative."

Rose laughed the dry, polite laugh again. She was good enough at it to have fooled someone else.

"Cry, Rose," Lily urged her. "Just get it over with. Kick a brick out of the dam, and let the flooding begin."

Her sister covered her face with her hands. "I have a selfish heart," she said. "I don't want him to be with her, even if that's what it takes to makes him sober and happy. Someday I'll have to stand before God and confess to that."

Lily pulled her sister's hands away from her face. "God gets burned all the time. He's used to it. Austin's the one who should be worried. If he can make love to you one day and the next go back to Leah, the man is a cold-blooded reptile."

Rose looked at her. "Is that how you feel about Tres?"

"Trust me," Lily said, pouring more crème de menthe into her tea. "You do not want to get me started on that subject."

With the amount of energy we spend on seeking "closure," women could light up the whole damn state, Lily decided as she drove to her parents' ranch the next morning. She'd spent the night at Rose's, sleeping in Amanda's old room, which still had shelves of Breyer horses and posters of teen idols plastered on the walls. She'd called the airline and booked a later flight, packed her suit in her carry-on luggage and borrowed jodhpurs and a canvas barn jacket from Amanda's closet. They didn't exactly complement her high heels. "I look like National freaking Velvet, ready for trouble," she told her sister as she stood in front of the mirror.

"You're right," Rose answered honestly. "I don't suppose I could talk you into mucking the stalls before you go?"

Her sister's eyes were puffy and red. Lily knew she'd cried herself to sleep, because all night she'd heard her turning in her bed. Lily's stomach was upset from the liqueur, and she was exhausted from delivering the buck-up speech to Rose. Already this day felt like mud season, miles of road that would just as soon suck her down into the muck as deliver her to her destination. By any stretch of the imagination the jodhpurs were too much. She changed back into her suit but kept the barn jacket.

What in the hell is up with us women? she asked herself as she drove north. *We're intelligent. We've acquired financial independence, yet we remain willing to cook, and for sure we wear better lingerie than Donna Reed ever did. So why do the men we love choose their ex-wives or notebook computers over us? Come to think of it, Martha Stewart isn't married. Hmm . . .*

Since her last visit to Rancho Costa Plente, on the empty land near the arena where various horse trailers used to be parked, most of the space had been taken up with portable chain-link dog runs. The runs led to a newly erected metal shed, sporting a long orange extension cord that snaked over the gravel and into the barn. National Public Radio issued forth from the doorway. Lily recognized the program: *All*

Things Considered. A new batch of greyhounds had taken up residence, six or seven of them, it looked like, but she was unable to take an accurate head count because the moment she opened the door of her rental car Jody Jr. leaped onto her, leaving a smear of blood across the front of Lily's light gray Anne Klein skirt.

"Down!" Lily commanded, but Jody wasn't listening. The remainder of the ranch dogs kept their distance, barking at Lily or the greyhounds, it was hard to be sure when a fifty-pound blue heeler was trying to climb up her like she was a tree. Lily bent down and took hold of the old dog's front paws. The top of Jody's head was bloody, and her right ear hung at a funny angle. Automatically one of Mami's favorite endearments came out of her mouth: "*Pobrecita.* I take Buddy home to California, and they start in on you."

Jody needed veterinary attention, but Lily could imagine what would happen to the rental car's interior if she let the dog inside without first cleaning her up. Dragging Jody by the collar, she tied her to the wash rack with one of the old lead ropes hanging there. "Hold still," Lily said, "I'm doing you a favor."

She gently inspected the dog's wound, trickling the hose water over it, of course getting her pumps all wet in the process. It was so cold out that Lily's bare legs stung. As if Lily were beating her to death, Jody let out a series of pathetic yelps and struggled to get free. Eventually Shep came out of the bunkhouse to see what was happening. As soon as Jody saw the old wrangler she began barking in earnest, shaking her head. Drops of blood flew everywhere.

"I expect all that noise translates to 'Save me,'" Shep said.

"Look at her," Lily said. "What kind of dogs attack their own mother?"

The wrangler carefully peeled the torn ear back from Jody's hide. Lily noticed that Jody Jr. sat still for *him.* "Pissed-off ones, I reckon. Got a needle and thread in the tack shed if you want me to sew that up."

Lily turned off the hose. "That's okay, but you can fetch me a towel."

"Yeah, we could probably skip the stitches. Might heal a little bent, but hell, it ain't like she's a show dog."

"Shep, Jody Jr. deserves upright ears as much as you or me. Besides, I know just the doctor for the job."

Shep handed over an old bath towel that had seen better days. "Lily

Adrienne, don't you go sticking your nose into your sister's business. Let Rose fight her own battles. I mean what I say," he tacked on, as if she hadn't been listening.

Which was more advice than Shep had ever delivered at one time previously. Lily squatted down and rubbed Jody's coat dry. The ear wasn't bleeding anymore, but the cut was deep enough that Lily could see beyond the fascia. It really did need a vet. She didn't see why she couldn't get the dog repaired and at the same time smack the veterinarian with her lunchbox. "It's impossible to kick someone in the balls when he doesn't have any," she said, and then, given Shep's prostate situation, regretted her words.

"Oh, sweet Lord Jesus."

Lily threw Shep the wet towel. "Sweet Lord Jesus what?"

He shook the towel out, draping it over the fenceline where it might dry if the day warmed up. "You Wilder women ought to come with a warning label."

She kissed his cheek. "Don't worry about the fire until you see the smoke. Bye, Sheppy." Lily dragged Jody to the rental car and shoved her into the passenger seat. Buddy loved riding shotgun, but Jody, used to pickup truck beds, cowered and shook as if she were on her way to the gallows.

"It *is* an emergency," Lily said when Paloma tried to stop her from opening the door that led to the exam rooms. "Don't I hear your phone ringing?"

By the time she'd located Austin in the lab, where he was examining something under a microscope, Paloma had given up trying to stop her. When the vet looked up, Lily asked, "What are you looking at so intently?"

He pushed his glasses up his nose. "A canine fecal smear I'm checking for parasites. Want to take a look?"

"Sure." Lily pulled Jody Jr. to her side and looked through the eyepiece. At once she recognized the distinctive shape of ascarids. Dogs who spent time around horses eventually picked up the roundworm. In horses the larvae traveled through the gut wall, then by way of the bloodstream, entered major organs, including the heart. Via the lungs, they migrated up the trachea to the pharynx, where they were swallowed and developed to maturity in the small intestine. Turning the fine focus adjustment, Lily said, "I despise the life cycle of the round-worm."

"Hey," Austin said. "Unless he's had a sex change, that's not Buddy with you."

"Nope, it's one of my pop's dogs. Think you can fix her ear?"

"What happened to it?"

"Her own offspring turned on her. Can you imagine?"

"That can happen. Let's put her in exam room one," he said, taking the leash from Lily. She followed him, staring at his Dan Post boots, the leather toes worn but polished clean.

He examined Jody, beginning with the injured ear, then moving along, taking vital signs and noting them in a new chart. "Any idea why your sister hasn't shown up for work today? Paloma called but didn't get an answer."

Lily boosted herself up to sit on the counter next to a Sharps container for contaminated needles. "Any reason she should show up for work?"

Austin looked up from the dog. "How about it's her job?"

"What did you think she'd do when she saw you with Leah in the ¡Andale!? Throw you two a bridal shower?"

Austin retrieved needle and thread from the supply drawer, set them on sterile gauze, and readied a syringe. "We weren't doing any-thing wrong."

"Listen, I spent last night and part of this morning scraping my sister off her kitchen floor. Don't you tell me you didn't do anything wrong."

Austin sighed. "Fine. Take out an ad in the *Facts* and tell the world I'm a son of a bitch. I didn't do anything wrong, and she until she gives me notice, your sister has responsibilities to this office."

Lily gave the needle container a thump with her index finger. "Who's the lucky stiff who draws the job of emptying this thing?"

"It isn't Rose." Austin swabbed Jody's ear with disinfectant, and the dog snapped at him. He stopped and petted her until she was calm, then he muzzled the dog and shaved an inch around her ear. He injected the deadening agent into the wound, squirted water on it, swabbed it clean, and began to lay down beautifully even, artful stitches.

Lily was not surprised. *He wants me to say* Nice work. *Well, he can embroider hearts on Jody's ear if he wants to.*

Austin tied the thread off and snipped it close to the flesh. He filled an amber vial with pills and wrote out instructions on the label. "Amoxicillin for ten days, then the sutures can come out. In the meantime, if you notice any signs of infection, oozing, redness, or if she tears the stitches, bring her back." He fastened an Elizabethan collar around Jody's neck, and at once the dog began shimmying, trying to shake it off. He tossed the leash to Lily. "No charge," he said, and left the room.

Lily slid down off the counter. She pulled Jody toward the door. "*Adios*, Paloma," she called out to the receptionist and the roomful of waiting clients and various animals. "And hey—you might want to get the janitor in there to clean up because I just stepped in a big pile of bullshit wearing Dan Post boots."

Lily threw the collar in her backseat. She dropped Jody in the driveway of Rancho Costa Plente, tucked the prescription bottle into the mailbox, and drove directly up the mountain to Tres's cabin. If he didn't want to call her, fine, she'd call on him. She turned the stereo up as loud as it would go. The Forrester Sisters were talking about men. They knew whereof they spoke, and they had gone platinum in telling the world about it.

A red Geo Storm was parked alongside Tres's old truck. The same rental company sticker affixed to Lily's Oldsmobile graced its bumper. Only women rented teensy little gas savers like that. Probably drove straight from the airport, Lily figured, and wondered just who besides Tres fit in that one-room cabin, and judging from the snow on the car's hood, how long she'd been there. Lily gathered her resolve, got out of the car, and knocked on the front door.

Leah the stepdaughter opened it. She was dressed in jeans and one of her stepdad's flannel shirts, thankfully not the one Lily had borrowed. "Can I help you?"

"Well, I'm not selling encyclopedias."

The girl stepped out of the cabin and pulled the door shut behind her. She hugged her arms around herself against the cold and fixed her eyes on Lily's bloodstained skirt. Other than whatever spray from the hose had dampened it, Lily hadn't had time for cleanup. Leah's lower lip curled in disgust. "My father's writing. If you want, you can leave a message with me."

Lily put her hands into the pockets of Amanda's jacket, then took them out again. "Leah, right? Your dad told me you go to Stanford. That's a nice school. Do you like it?"

"So far."

"Good, because college is a long haul. The reason I say this is I was once standing exactly where you are and I remember thinking, *Jeez, this is too much, it's going to take forever to finish.* There's a few things I'd handle differently if I had the chance to do it over. One of them is be nicer to my elders. Really, Leah, it's not sportsmanlike to hate me this early in the game. So do you think you might find it in your heart to tell your father I'm here?"

By then Tres had come outside to investigate. He was wearing a wool sweater with chevron patterns woven into it, faded jeans, and brand-new Ugg boots. When he smiled at her, Lily forced herself to remember to be angry. "Hey, Lily."

"Hey, yourself." If Leah were suddenly to evaporate, Lily had a feeling she and Tres would have made tracks for his bed. Instead each stood there waiting for the other to make the first move.

"Leah, honey?" Tres said without taking his eyes off Lily. "Weren't you going to do some grocery shopping?"

"I thought you said it was going to snow."

"It is. Which is why you should go now. Here, take my truck." He tossed her the keys.

"Dad, I don't know how to work the four-wheel drive. What if I need it?"

"You won't, but I'll show you anyway. Excuse me a second." Tres got her situated in the truck and demonstrated the gear shift.

Lily stamped her feet, trying to stay warm. They waited until the girl had driven away before either one spoke. "What happened to college?"

"She's not sure if she's ready for college."

"So she flies to New Mexico to find out?"

"Debbie gives her a hefty allowance."

"How nice for Leah. Did she buy you those boots?"

Tres looked embarrassed. "Yes, she did." He put his arms around her shoulders and Lily stood there stiffly taking in his scent, aching to put her hands under his sweater, determined to resist the impulse. "You know, I take it personally when I spend a week with a guy and he never calls me again. Ever heard of a pay phone?"

Tres kissed the top of her head. "Leah arrived the day after you left. She's been a little needy."

Lily wanted to scream out, *I'm only in love with you, you idiot!* But she knew if she shut her eyes and said the words, by the time she opened them he would be half a continent away. "Tres, I have to catch a plane."

"Change your ticket," he said. "Leave tomorrow."

"Why? So the three of us can make S'mores in the fireplace and sing camp songs? Come with me."

"You know I can't do that."

Lily looked at him for a long time, not really certain who it was she thought she loved. If Tres Quintero was a ghost from her past, he was a powerful force; her body had never forgotten his touch. If he was using her, there had to be something in his style of lovemaking that rendered her bullshit detector useless. If he was backing off because he was scared, then the Wilder woman in her was responsible, and there wasn't anything she could do about that. Forgetting him a second time was going to be harder than the first.

"Come inside," he said. "Let me at least fix you something warm to drink. You're shaking."

All around them, cold wind swirled, reshaping the snowdrifts. Lily felt the chill in her cheeks, the icy air traveling through the jacket, which was designed for a spring or maybe a California winter, those few weeks when the temperature rocketed down to fifty and the population took it as a personal insult. Lily's blood had grown thin in a state that practically did without seasons. Tres however, hadn't so much as pulled up the collar on his shirt. What a mistake this was, them trying to reclaim the past. Lily kissed him good-bye, a nice, chaste, lips-closed kiss. She drove to the airport, turned in her car, and uttered a perfunctory thank-you when the ticketing agent automatically upgraded her to first class.

Lily scooped a healthy glob of Trader Joe's sun-dried tomato pesto onto the first Krisproll out of the package. The wonderfully oily mixture of basil, parmesan, pine nuts and walnuts, minced garlic, fine-grade olive oil, and tomatoes sank into the baked-in crevices of the cracker. Just 1.5 grams of fat in the cracker; an ungodly 18 in each tablespoon of pesto.

They'd been out of the low-fat kind. She inhaled deeply but hesitated before putting it in her mouth. One had to make the best of life's little moments, and sitting in her living room with a decent bottle of red wine newly uncorked and Buddy Guy on the CD player, just herself and her long-desired menu, was bliss, or it should have been. It was drizzling outside. After she got home from New Mexico, Lily had unpacked, answered her messages, taken the suit to the dry cleaner, and begged him to at least *try* to save it. She caught up on paperwork, finished her expense reports, and set appointments that stretched clear through December into January. She waited two whole days before allowing herself the reward of this meal. It was going to be heaven to taste her favorite foodstuffs once again—as soon as she could put out of her mind how much she missed that stupid non-practicing psychiatrist/fly fisherman/diligent stepfather/woodcarver/nature writer who knew the curves of her body like every synonym in his thesaurus.

This morning she'd stood in front of a roomful of surgeons at Cedars-Sinai explaining how much more efficiently their operations would go the moment they began using her company's endoscopes, laparoscopes, et cetera. Her smile dazzled them. Her delivery was perfect. When they hesitated, her calm, convincing assertions perked them up. Questions regarding cost and reliability were anticipated, her answers cogent and reassuring. She imbued these men with a budget-be-damned desire to own the entire line, she made her company some serious money, she shook their precious, gifted, irreplaceable hands, scheduled training sessions, and then later, on the drive home, she managed one-handed to shuck her pantyhose in traffic that was moving ten miles an hour through a smoggy haze that color-enhanced the California sunset like an animated movie. She wiped away her tears with the bunched-up stockings. Whatever the fat content, she deserved the pesto. She deserved Tres, too, but she no longer desired the pesto and she'd lost the man.

The first glass of wine went down like medicine. An Ansel Adams print titled *Autumn Storm, Penasco*, hung above her unlit fireplace. The spooky gathering of trees and moody sky reminded her of the northern boundary of El Rancho Costa Plente. Peeking through the foliage, the spired church in the photo's center seemed like a place so far from where Lily sat that it might as well be Mars. If they could find it, maybe she and Buddy could sit very quietly in the back of a pew, and if what Rose said was true, God would mend their broken hearts. But movie stars and rich people had bought up all the houses and land in New Mexico. The church probably didn't exist anymore. When you came right down to it, there was no *away*, really, only the representation of it in pictures like these. She wondered how Shep was doing, if he was taking something stronger for his pain, and if after he died dog runs would replace the horse stalls. Buddy laid his paw on her forearm and looked at her with liquid brown eyes. Lily knew pesto was bad for him, all those people-fat grams quintupled for doggies. His dish was still full of the high fiber, low-fat kibble she'd bought at the latest vet.

Floralee was the end of the earth, the boondocks, Hooterville unparalleled, no place for the college educated. It struck her as miraculous that in the northern part of her home state she'd stumbled across the one man she wanted. Lily never told anyone in the medical industry that she'd grown up in a town with a population of fifteen hundred. When pressed, she lied and said Albuquerque. A string of drool hung from the corner of Buddy's mouth. She fed him the cracker, wiped her hands on his coat, picked up the telephone, and punched in Rose's number. Her sister answered on the second ring.

"Hello?"

"Are you keeping busy?" Lily asked. "Busy helps."

"Yes. I baked for the church potluck this week."

"What did you make?"

"Bread, muffins, that curried vegetable dish with the carrots everybody seems to like. It doesn't seem right that anybody should go hungry on Thanksgiving."

Lily already had her travel suitcase packed for the upcoming Thanksgiving business trip. The modest bathing suit she would never find time to use lay folded next to the black and beige clothing that mixed and matched flawlessly. High heels and tennis shoes, too, plus a calculator and her notebook computer, which possessed more bells and whistles than the model Tres used. Only the bottle of sunscreen hinted that this trip was centered around a holiday. They began at Halloween and didn't let up until New Year's, relentless reminders everywhere from Santa at the mall to her neighbor's house all decorated with the irritating blinking lights. Lily managed by pretending they weren't holidays at all, but temporary madness, like the movies on the science-fiction channel that came free with her basic cable service. "Are you going to the ranch for dinner?"

"No, I'm going to work at the church dinner, go home, and pet my dog."

"Go to the ranch, Rose. Check on your mare. She needs attention, and so does Shep. You know he kind of gets lost in the shuffle around the holidays. Make sure he's taking his medicine. Drink too much. Maybe you'll sleep with somebody interesting."

Her sister laughed. "I think I'm a little ways off from all that."

"Seen Tres around town?"

"Oh, Lily. Hasn't he called you?"

"Lacks a telephone."

"And balls, apparently."

"Why, Rose Flynn, I'm shocked. Here you had a perfectly good opportunity to say 'nerve' and you deliberately chose the vernacular. I guess now you'll have something to confess in confession."

"Actually, I haven't been to church since you left."

Lily tucked the phone into her shoulder so she could pour a second glass of wine. "Of course, I take this as a sign you're coming to your senses, but that's only my opinion. You haven't missed church in forty years. Why start now?"

"I don't know. I just don't want to go there."

"Does Doctor Cute go to church?"

"He used to, when he attended meetings. I don't know about now. I really couldn't tell you what he does."

"How's it going at work?"

"I'm sort of pretending I'm on vacation."

"Good for you."

"Yeah, until next month when I can't make my house payment. I should hang up, Lily. This is costing you a fortune."

"I have Dime Line. Don't worry about my phone bill. Think about something for me, will you?"

"That depends on what it is. If it concerns Austin, count me out. I just want to forget I was ever foolish enough to think I loved him."

"Remember your algebra. The more you try to forget, the more you'll remember. What I was going to suggest was that you give Austin your resignation. There's plenty of things you can do if you need money."

Rose sighed. "I'll think it over."

"Do it, Rose. And keep an ear open for gossip. I want to know what in hell Tres is up to, if you hear anything. Don't you dare tell him I asked, just find out the details and call me back. Oh, I just love to rub salt in my wounds. It keeps everything so fresh and painful."

"Okay. Bye, Lily. Sell lots of those scope things."

"I always do."

It was eight o'clock in the evening in California, which meant it was what—nine—in New Mexico? Lily listened to the click that severed their connection. She shouldn't have said that to Rose about her job. It was projection—her wanting Rose to quit because she wanted to herself. Lily and Buddy sprawled together on the condo's living-room floor. Tomorrow she had to get on a plane to a city where the temperature was eighty. A jet from El Toro broke the sound barrier, and the fire-singed shake roof shook with the sound of freedom, which it would continue to do periodically until that base, like so many others, shut down. Buddy let go a mournful howl. Her neighbors started fighting, and the drizzly rain that had been falling since she got home turned to a downpour. *Lay out the welcome mat for El Niño*, Lily thought.

If he'd had a phone to answer, she would have called Tres right then, but her female pride was bionic even if her resolve felt like Jell-O. She thought of all those hours in front of his fireplace. Even if it had only been one kiss, it would still possess the same unforgettable power. She downed glass number two, poured glass number three, and toasted Ansel Adams, who knew how to shoot a picture so realistically that a person looked at it and would give anything to step inside. He must have been quite the man, she mused, brave enough to stand out in the middle of a storm and aim his lens with all that lightning flashing so close by.

15

Heart Like a Manatee

Floralee's annual Thanksgiving dinner was originally about feeding disadvantaged children, but over the years it had mutated into one of the town's larger social events. Various levels of town politics played out alongside the potluck dishes. Whoever was running for public office or reelection or simply wanted to mend fences used the dinner as an opportunity to shake hands and gain allies. Skipping the dinner was on a par with choosing not to vote, frowned upon by those who didn't get invited to exclusive parties, like the one Mami was throwing this very evening.

Much of the chatter Rose overheard as she scooped mashed potatoes onto plates in the serving line concerned the upcoming spring celebration of the four-hundredth anniversary of Don Juan de Onate's expedition from New Spain to San Juan Pueblo, a neighboring town. A high percentage of Floralee residents, including Eloy Trujillo, could trace a relative back that far. Rose watched the judge and his sons mingle with families seated at the long cafeteria-style tables. Two of Eloy's sons were attorneys, a third taught high school civics, and had in fact, tried desperately not to fail Amanda. However, Amanda, out to prove a point, earned her F to wave in Rose's face after all. Eloy held up someone's new baby and made silly faces so the child would smile.

Rose gave each person in line a generous helping. When Austin and Leah Donavan stood in front of her with their plates held out, Rose tried to make herself smile but couldn't quite pull it off. Then, just as she upended the scoop over Leah's plate and pressed the lever to release the potatoes, Leah pulled her plate away, and the buttery white mixture fell onto the crisp, clean tablecloth. Rose gasped, and for a moment it felt as if everyone in the room turned to look.

"Oops," Leah said. "Sorry, but I don't eat starches."

Already she was looking across the room, distracted by someone important who sought her attention. Austin had to touch her elbow to let her know it was time to move on. He helped Rose clean up the mess, then set his plate down on the table. "I need to talk to you," he said.

His face was difficult for her to read, but his accompanying Leah to this social event seemed to make things painfully clear. They were a couple again, and probably had been for longer than she knew. "You only *think* you need to talk to me."

"What about work, Rose? You can't just leave me hanging."

"I need a break." She set the serving spoon down, and before Austin could stop her she made her way through the noisy crowd and ducked into the church nave.

Aromatic pine garlands draped festively across every pew. Tied up in gilt-edged ribbons, the sprigs of red berries looked real enough to feed to the birds. Near the altar the heavy candelabrum with beeswax candles stood unlit. At midnight mass on Christmas Eve, with candles blazing, this church would overflow with parishioners. People were happy to stand during the long service just to bask in the comforting presence of a community praising the holy miracle.

Rose held onto the back of the last pew. She couldn't kneel. Her legs simply refused to bend. In this very church she had married Philip. No full mass, of course, since he wasn't Catholic, but they had stood in front of this altar to make their vows. She wondered how he'd managed such duplicity, if he had separate chambers in his heart, a pocket for each woman. It seemed that Austin did, too. Her own was so basic it could only concentrate on one man at a time. One thing she knew for certain, until she formally resigned things between them would hover in this uncomfortable limbo.

Rose couldn't recall the exact place where she'd sat, along with many other parents, watching as her son made his confirmation, but she remembered her gawky boy was dressed in a suit he could hardly wait to shed. She remembered swallowing hard against the lump in her throat so she wouldn't cry and embarrass him as he walked past her, his hands held upright in prayer. After making her First Communion,

Amanda insisted that church was crap and she wasn't going anymore. Philip said it was Amanda's right to make the choice—she'd been seven at the time—he said she was old enough to decide. Both Lily and Rose had worn the handmade white lace dress for their communions. The day she received the host, Rose's daughter looked angelic. Mami cried. Pop shot four rolls of film and gave Amanda a new saddle. The heirloom dress was tucked away into pink tissue paper in a box beneath Rose's bed. It struck her that her bed was like a layer cake of human failings: dust bunnies, because she needed to clean more often but rarely got around to it; the abandoned communion dress, its lace yellowing and fragile; the money-and-photo wrapped statue of Saint Anthony between the box spring and mattress—*I have to remember to get rid of that*, she reminded herself—the sheets newly laundered and redolent of fabric softener, but clinging unseen to the weave, the ghosts of the only two men she'd ever slept with.

In the morning she'd deliver Austin her letter of resignation, start looking for another job. It wasn't just the proper thing to do, she wanted it face-to-face so he'd understand that she meant it. Rose turned away from the altar, walking past the font of holy water without blessing herself. Outside it was snowing, and she turned her face up to feel the light, dry flakes land on her skin. At the far end of the parking lot, the windshield of her Bronco was rimed with frost. She climbed inside and turned the key in the ignition, nursing the pedal with her foot until the old engine caught. The streets were nearly empty.

At home she walked directly to the barn and fed the horse. Chachi didn't come out to greet her, and she wondered if the Jack Russell was parked indoors next to the woodstove. Probably he had peed on the throw rug, unwilling to venture forth in snow showers. *What a pair of hermits we make*, Rose thought, putting her key to the front door lock.

Inside, she set her purse down and whistled for the dog, but instead of racing over to beg for a treat, he merely looked up from the spot in front of the woodstove. She squatted down next to him and rubbed his chest, inspecting him for injuries, finding nothing unusual, no sore places, just a generally hyper dog acting aloof. "What's going on?" she asked. "Do you have the holiday lonelies, too? Tell you what, let's go to bed, Chachi. With a box of Milk-Bones and a pile of cheap paperbacks. Does that sound like a plan?"

* * *

The following morning she wrote out her letter and drove to the clinic. All the way there, her emotional side argued against leaving. She relived the casual banter she and Austin traded back and forth, and thought how every day she looked forward to the time when he'd end up in her office, sitting on a corner of her desk, telling her how his day had gone, which horse ran away with him, how far he'd gotten dragged this time, the two of them laughing, sharing jokes only they found amusing. The confidences they'd shared—like the time Rose found a Baggie of seeds in Amanda's room and, fearful they were some kind of illegal substance, gathered her courage and showed them to Austin. He'd planted them under a special grow light in the lab, and when the green shoots came up in the recognizable shape of wildflowers, they laughed, equally relieved. He dealt with the animal end of things; she kept the numbers straight. Their friendship was a precious by-product of shared work, but Rose couldn't help it that her feelings for Austin hadn't stopped there. Like the seedlings, her feelings had continued to grow long past the embryonic pair of leaves connected to the stem into the determined flower it was their purpose to support.

She rubbed her eyes, gritty from reading too late into the night. At breakfast Chachi remained subdued, which she wanted to blame on the weather, windy and cold. Any other time it would have ticked her off to see the explosion of tricolored terrier running toward her, glee-fully covered in dirt from his incessant hole-digging, or proudly drag-ging a rank, long-dead squirrel into her kitchen.

Paloma started crying the minute Rose walked in the door. Rose gave her a hug and patted her back. "We'll still see each other," she whispered. "It's not like I'm moving away."

"Yes it is," Paloma insisted, stifling a sob that sent her into the pri-vacy of the restroom until she could get hold of herself.

The roomful of clients and their pets looked up at Rose, as if they, too, deserved an explanation. She went in search of Austin, who she found setting a broken leg on a Jack Russell colored in almost the reverse patterns of Chachi, mostly black on her body, with occasional, haphazardly placed patches of white and brown.

"Whose dog?" she asked, laying the letter on the counter.

He continued winding the Vet Wrap around the splint. "Don't know. I found her in a ditch on Vega Road when I was driving to work this morning."

"She's awfully cute."

He showed her his hand, which was bandaged. "She has that Jack Russell spirit. There she was, dragging this leg behind her, I pick her up, and first thing she does is bite me."

Rose smiled. "Are you going to put an ad in the paper to try to find her owner?"

Austin turned over the dog's paws, revealing torn and bloody pads. "Looks to me like somebody abandoned her. I cannot fathom that there are people alive who still believe it's humane to dump a dog in the wilderness. I'll try to adopt her out when she's healed up."

Rose picked up the letter. "Here's my resignation," she said, handing it to Austin.

He pocketed the envelope without looking at it. "You really believe this is necessary?"

"Yes, I do."

"Mind explaining why?"

Rose sighed. "Austin, if it's your marriage you're trying to resurrect, that's an admirable thing. If it means you and Leah can fix whatever's broken, great, more power to you, but that doesn't mean I have to stand here and watch. I have feelings too. It's better for everyone this way."

He shut the Jack Russell into a nearby cage. "Will you come with me a minute? Will you give me that much?"

She sighed. "What's the point?"

He pulled Rose up the stairs into the supply room. Shutting the door behind them, he took hold of her upper arms. The look in his face was tender. "I don't want to lose you. I can't stand it if we're not friends. You're like a fixture in my life, Rose. Every day, rain or shine, drunk or sober, you've been there for me."

"Don't you see? That's the problem. I've been a fixture, all right, like a sink or a stove or a wastebasket."

He pulled her close to him and breathed into her hair. Rose marveled at how something so bad for her could feel so right, so necessary. The feeling lasted until she pictured him with Leah in the ¡Andale!, tipping the beer to his lips. She pushed him an arm's length away.

"Rose, what's happened between us scares me shitless. Leah's a known quantity. I know it sounds cowardly of me, but things are familiar with her, even when they're bad. We know how to do things."

Rose felt like she'd been slapped. "If you're with Leah because you're scared of me, then you aren't the man I thought you were, Austin, and you don't deserve either of us. Maybe you think you can distract yourself for a little while, and maybe that's true, but eventually Leah will do what she always does, which is hurt you and leave. And you'll be left with that dark little cave in your heart she always carves out and only I seem to fill. You can't have it both ways, my friend."

He stood there silently watching her.

When enough time had passed for her to count to thirty, Rose moved past him and up the stairs to her office. She shut the door and began sifting through personal things that had accumulated over time, making the desk hers. A mug in which she kept pencils, a scented candle she imagined took away the doggy smells but really didn't. A button Paloma had given her that read "Someday we'll look back on all this, laugh nervously, and change the subject." Most of it could go in the trash, but she was reluctant to abandon the donkey-tail cactus even if she couldn't imagine how to transport it home without breaking the long, green, carefully tended tendrils. She left it hanging from its ceiling hook and hoped whoever took her place would appreciate it. When she gathered the framed pictures of her family, Rose paused to look at the photograph of her husband. It made sense to her now, that look of surprise in his eyes. This picture was the closest she would ever come to hearing his confession.

Just for a moment, she told herself as she walked into Austin's office, but once there a kind of exhaustion overcame her, and she lay down on the bed, pulling his red plaid flannel pillow close to her chest. The whole place smelled of him: Oranges, a hint of sweat, antiseptic soap, unique smells, his alone. She switched on the reading lamp and looked out the window across the snowy lawn where the tattered American flags lay stiffly frozen against their poles. The futon sagged when she turned toward the window. The snow was coming down hard. It made everything look so clean and pure.

She thought about how beneath Austin's mattress lay all those books he revered, each one filled with a different story, each tale made up of labored-over sentences, each of those crammed with words, many of which she would need to look up in the dictionary to have them make sense. So much effort, when there was only one story, a poem she'd read it in a magazine she'd found while cleaning Amanda's mess of a room:

The oldest story ain't Jesus
but men and women
who once touched
and now ain't touching anymore.

Rose pulled back a corner of the mattress and pried opened one of the boxes. Hemingway, Steinbeck, Faulkner, Tolstoy, dead men whose worldviews belonged to past eras. She would be more likely to bungee-jump over the Rio Grande than understand what it was he saw in them. She switched off the lamp. If she shut her eyes, she could imagine the sound of his bootheels striking the risers. When she lay back against the pillows, she could feel his hands on her body, his mouth at her ear. It was time to go, past time, actually.

Downstairs she stopped in front of the cage where the Jack Russell was rousing from her treatment, trying out how to balance with the splinted leg. Rey was cleaning cages. "Spunky little cuss," he remarked.

On a portable TV in the background, she heard the sound of a Dennis Miller monologue, his precise intellectual rant against all the world's idiocy. Rey loved that show, often quoted from it. Rose found Dennis Miller funny, too, but essentially he said the same thing every time: Progress was impossible. It was disheartening news, particularly for a single woman recently unemployed who lived in a town so small it had to share a zip code. "Rey, can you come up with any reason this dog can't go home with someone who has medical skills?"

He set the mop down in its bucket of suds. "I don't think so. But you better ask the *jefe*. And watch yourself, he's in a real bad mood today. I'd hate to be whoever pissed him off."

Rose wrapped the dog in a towel and took the medical card with her. Austin was seeing a patient in exam room two. She tapped on the glass window in the door, motioning to him. "Excuse me for interrupting," she said when he opened the door. "But I've decided I want to adopt the dog, if I can take her with me now."

"She's all yours," he said.

"How cute," the woman whose pet rabbit he was examining said. "What are you going to name her?"

"Joanie, what else?" Rose answered before she shut the door.

* * *

Pop was sitting on her front step smoking his pipe as Rose pulled into the driveway. He brushed the snow from his pants when he stood up.

"For heaven's sake, you have a key. You could have gone inside," she scolded him. "I hope you don't catch pneumonia." She handed him the terrier and fumbled with her key chain.

"A man doesn't go into other people's houses uninvited. You just missed your mother."

"That's too bad. How was the party?"

"Festive enough that half the artists in this town are waking up with king-size hangovers. Heard you worked the church supper."

"That I did."

"Heard who you had to serve, too. Dammit all, Rose. I'd like to punch him in the nose."

Her face burned. "Don't, Pop. It was my mistake and I'm handling it. I've finally found the *courage* you so desperately want me to possess, and I'm dealing with the situation like an adult. To that end I just quit my job and adopted this dog."

He stared at her, the pipe clamped in his teeth. "Looks like she's busted up. What happened?"

"I don't know. Austin thinks she was dumped." She laughed. "I know how that feels this close to the holidays so I brought her home."

"Tell me something, Rose. Have I been so hard on you that you couldn't call your old man for comfort?"

"Every chance you get you remind me I'm weak."

"Hell, that's my shortcoming, not yours. That was wrong of me and I apologize. You know I'm not an educated man."

"As if that has anything to do with it. I'm no more educated than you are."

"Yes, you are. Educated hard by the adventure of your life. You've done all right, considering all your troubles. I admire the hell out of you."

"Lily's the one you admire."

He shook his head no. "Your sister talks a great game, but you're my rock. Always have been, always will be. Every night when your mother gets down on her knees to talk to the man upstairs, I tell her, 'Sweetheart, send up all the prayers you got for Lily. Rose Ann can take care of herself.'"

Rose put her hand to her eyes, pinching back the tears, feeling the ache of restraint vibrate in her jaw. Pop's kind words on top of having just quit her job were too much. Her father clamped his hand down hard on her shoulder and steered her inside. They placed the dog on the floor near Chachi, who growled once and then began to wag his tail and sniff her all over. When she nipped at him, Chachi rolled over and showed her his belly. "That's right, girl," Pop said. "You set the boundaries right from the start."

Rose inhaled the scent of pipe tobacco and yellow soap. Her father wasn't one for hair oil or cologne. The furthest Chance Wilder took things in the scent department was horse liniment. He cleared his throat.

"All summer long I've been standing back and watching you. I was so damn proud of you getting that mare bred, not giving up when she didn't catch the first time, and I've watched how you see to her on the weekends, making sure she's coming along on schedule. But that's only earned a small part of my respect. That's business. It's how you hold your head up with your kids acting so crazy that touches me, Rose. And this thing with Donavan. We live in a small town. Nobody gets to keep secrets. When you took up with him, your mother and I crossed our fingers and held our breath. He's a good man, but he's weak and he's troubled. That kind you got to give a little time to get clear on what it is they want."

She shook her head no. "I don't think so, Pop."

"I've been around the block, Sugar. Listen to me."

"This time you're wrong. I thought he loved me. I let him inside, Pop."

"Which took courage."

She took a breath and felt her voice crack as she exhaled. "Or stupidity. It turned out I was nothing more than a way for Austin to work something out—retaliation for how hurt he was, or like Lily says, something 'transitional,' but in the end, it was her he went back to. Not me, Leah."

Pop sighed. "Did you know that in Hebrew, Leah means 'old cow' and 'weary'?"

"It does not. It means 'gazelle.'"

He shook his head. "Not so. In the Book of Genesis, Leah was the elder of the two wives of Jacob. Her younger sister, Rachel, was the woman Jacob wanted. 'Leah had no sparkle in her eye,' but he married her anyway, with the promise that he'd acquire Rachel in the bargain. Took him seven long years to earn her. Rachel bore him two kids, Joseph and Benjamin. Joe was sold into slavery, and the tribe of Israel descended from Ben. Leah has been a losing name for damned near six thousand years. Rose, your mother and I named you and your sister after flowers, but of the two, you're the tough one. Rosebushes don't blow away in the first wind. They hang on to the earth, and they grow strong branches and tenacious roots. You are a good woman, temporarily bent by a foolish man who will come to regret his actions."

His pipe had gone out, and Rose watched him tuck it into his shirt pocket. Sometimes, when it was her turn to do the laundry, she'd turn a shirt right side out and into her palm would fall a tablespoon of ashes. She'd rub the sooty black grit across her skin creases to study her lifeline. Mami had caught her doing this once, and pointed out that Rose's heartline, which ran parallel to her lifeline, indicated that over the course of her time on earth, she would experience two great loves, two passions, but that only the second would endure. After she married Philip, Rose had forgotten all about the silly predictions. She expected she would grow old with her husband, that she would learn more about love by living than any fortune could predict. About passion she had learned that it was fleeting, and about marriage that its surface might seem binding but but that it could also be a well-tied knot with deception at its core. She wrapped her arms around her father and held on tight. Pop patted her shoulders, and for the first time since Philip's funeral, Rose cried in front of her dad, allowed the tears to run, let everything out.

"That's all right," he said. "You go on and let it all out, however long it takes you. I don't have to be anywhere but right here for the rest of the day. Of course, I might be getting hungry for a little breakfast pretty soon. You see, I woke up this morning just hankering for buckwheat pancakes. Your mother was busy with the greyhounds, mixing this supplement, feeding that coat conditioner, and had all these errands to run. She dropped me here on her way into town, and I never did get any pancakes. So you might keep that in mind while you're emptying your eyes—yeah, tuck that thought away for later—and don't mind my stomach growling. Consider that background noise. You take your time and cry now, go on, don't let me stop you."

Rose accepted his handkerchief. "Fine. We'll go have pancakes. I'm brave enough to sniffle into a tissue in public. But you'll have to drive."

He gave her a look of feigned shock. "In that old heap of yours?"

"Pop, I won't have you insulting my car. For your information, my Bronco's a classic."

"Weak birds fly south for the winter," Paloma said mysteriously into the phone. "Only some of them take America West instead of flapping their wings."

Rose yawned. Lately she had trouble sleeping nights and had taken to napping during the day. "I don't get it, Paloma. Did I miss the punch line?"

"She's gone. Vamoosed. My sister's brother-in-law saw her getting on the plane a week ago in Albuquerque. To Mexico. Of course *she* flies first class. Coach is beneath her." She trailed off into rapid-fire Spanish that Rose could only follow far enough to realize it was hardly complimentary.

"Who are you talking about? Leah?"

"*Sí*, who did you think I was talking about?"

Rose rubbed her eyes and yawned again. "So she left. What am I supposed to do about it?"

"Well," Paloma said. "You could make Doctor Skinny something good to eat. Lately I don't think he eats nothing but Chat 'n' Chew. If he don't got one already, he's going to get an ulcer."

"Good. While he's at it, I hope he comes down with herpes of the face. A permanent rash across his forehead that spells out her name."

Paloma made a shocked noise. "I can't believe you said that, Rose. Can we go to lunch? I'm worried about you."

Rose straightened the throw pillows and picked up the afghan that had slipped to the floor. Joanie and Chachi looked up at her from a wicker basket Mami had brought by the other day. Of course, as soon as her mother stepped into the house, she insisted on tidying up the place, and in the process of sweeping and changing bed linen, she succeeded in making Rose feel like a total slut. Rose gave the dogs equal pats, and Chachi licked her hand. Since Joanie's arrival he was a changed dog, always at her side. His devotion touched Mami, who said the basket would give the two dogs "something with corners to press up against." They sat in the basket while Rose took her bath, did the dishes, read novels, folded laundry; it was a portable, traveling, double dog bed, and sometimes Rose wished for one of her own. "Paloma, we can go to lunch whenever you want, but not to discuss Austin."

"I hate the girl he hired to take your place. Allergic to cats! And she don't even know how to use a computer."

"I thought you wanted nothing to do with computers."

"I didn't, when you were trying to make me learn them. But now—well, I feel different. And she's *vacio* in the head—don't even know her alphabet. She keeps asking me questions, like which comes first, the *M-a* names or the *M-c* names. You know he'd take you back in a minute."

Yes, Austin would. And give her a raise, and treat her with care and kindness and flatter her with well-placed comments that might even eventually land the two of them in bed, which would feel like heaven— for awhile. Then, little by little, their lives would slip back into the same predictable patterns. He'd stay sober, she would make him dinners. They'd walk the dogs together, watching for signs that Joanie's leg was completely healed. They'd ride Jewel and Max across the snowy fields, but winter lasted only so long, and after it came mud season, which was so awful to endure that even the soberest of drunks slipped and fell facefirst into the muck. When the weather warmed up, *la Leah* would return, and Austin would remember how well alcohol worked to dull the edges of the pain he felt at how badly she treated him. Having fulfilled her use, Rose would once again be discarded. "I don't think so, Paloma. Have to run now. I have a job interview. Big hug."

"*Y tú*, Rose. Call and tell me how it goes, okay? I'll see you in church."

Out of guilt she flipped through the classifieds. All the good paying jobs were out of town, mostly in Albuquerque. She supposed if she sold the house, got rid of the animals, she might be able to afford an apartment there, but Floralee was her home. She loved this house. The curtains, the tile she'd laid in the bathroom, even the dark spaces that Mami complained needed a good *limpieza* with lemon oil were hers. She owned this house, had earned it being married to Philip, raising the kids. Max needed her, and so did the dogs. Something in the way of work would turn up. She wasn't broke yet. When the foal was born in the spring, she could sell it, and in the next year or so, breed Winky again. There were other veterinarians she could call for mare care. Dr. Tracie Zeissel was young and hungry.

She studied an ad for a relief cook at a restaurant she'd been to once, with her sister. What were the requirements for that kind of job? Probably a degree from a culinary institute and ten years' experience. Forget it. She added another log to the stove and sat back down on the couch. It was time for Oprah, or that new show hosted by the smart-mouthed Rosie. Rose admired her spirit as well as her name. Rosie had no husband, either, but that didn't stop her from adopting two children, continuing with her life. Rosie took charge. To her, it was no big deal to set her show against the richest woman in television's long-running hit. Yes, if television remotely interested her, she definitely would have given Rosie's show a try.

16

California Slides into the Ocean

The rain continued steadily, and at seven A.M., two days before Thanksgiving, Lily rolled her commuter bag into the John Wayne terminal. Still half asleep, she stood in the ticket line for first class only to learn that her flight to Mexico had been delayed. With a cup of latte from the coffee vendor and the *New York Times*, Lily sat down to waste the half hour until the plane's rescheduled departure time. Halfway through her foam—why did the coffee people always overdo it on foam? Wasn't four bucks a cup enough of a profit?—an announcement came over the loudspeaker that all ticketed passengers on Flight 361 to Acapulco should see the ticketing agent. Lily groaned. That careful kind of directive could only mean the flight had been canceled outright. A fundamental incompatibility between Californians and rain existed—certainly they'd never learned to drive in it. For Pete's sake, it was a little *rainstorm*, not a hurricane. The *El Niño* predictions only served to feed the paranoia. As she mulled over her choices, it occurred to Lily that if this was how things were going to go all winter, she was not going to be able to hack it.

At the suggestion of the counter clerk, whose computers were "temporarily down," Lily boarded a commuter flight to Los Angeles, out of which there were sure to be countless available flights to Mexico City with connections to Acapulco. If she had to, she'd rent a car and drive the two-hundred-odd miles.

Despite crash statistics, Lily enjoyed flying turboprops more than the big jets. High above the gridlock traffic in her fixed leather seat, with her eyes shut and the plane occasionally bucking and battered by the rain, Lily felt right at home. This was how she'd assumed all flying should feel, thanks to growing up with Mami flying her plane. The Cessna was so insubstantial in comparison to commercial jets that Lily had learned air pockets and bumps were no big deal. In a weird way, turbulence comforted her. They'd logged a lot of airtime together, her mother at the controls, a bag of grapes between them to snack on, and usually a dog or two as cargo. At times the run from Floralee to California had felt like riding a roller coaster into one of those dark tunnels where twists and turns offered a thrilling, unknown quantity.

Lily missed her mother. She missed Pop, too, and her sister, Rose, but more than all of them put together, she missed Shep. His days were numbered, and she wanted to spend time with him, help with the horses, particularly if it was raining or snowing, which it probably was, and allow him his dignity. *Be honest*, she scolded herself. *Tres Quintero is a factor in your sudden desire to return home.* She imagined him wearing those fingerless wool gloves so he could keep typing in the unheated cabin. Surely by now he'd finished the carving he'd been working on and started another—a Nativity scene? This lapse into sentimentality could only be blamed on the holiday season. Forget the turkey decorations, Thanksgiving had already ended for the marketing and retail folk, and onto Southern California a plague of surfing Santas, cartoonish Magi, and red-nosed reindeer had descended. The mall parking lots were packed to capacity, and shuttle buses ran between them all hours of the day and night. Lily hadn't begun her shopping. She figured down in Mexico the hype would at least possess a folk-art flair, and she could find unique presents for her family in some charming local shop for practically nothing.

Her fantasy ended with two hard bumps on the slick, wet tarmac. Not the smoothest landing she'd ever experienced, but certainly not the roughest. Several passengers gasped, and all but Lily were muttering among themselves as they deplaned. She was unprepared for the chaos of the United terminal, where hundreds of displaced travelers swarmed in various lines, pushing, crying, punching cell phones madly, and cursing the weather. From what Lily could gather, it seemed that *all* United flights, not just to Mexico, had been canceled until late afternoon, pending improvement in the weather.

Usually Lily booked her own flights, either via the Internet or directly to the airline using her speed-dial, but she did have a travel agent. She put in a call and asked what other routes could get her to Mexico. "If you can drive to Ontario Airport I can get you on a ten P.M. flight to El Paso, where there's a connection to Mexico City. There you can catch a local flight to Acapulco."

"Great. Do it," Lily said, and flipped through her Filofax for her credit card number.

"One slight snag," the woman explained. "The El Paso to Mexico flight doesn't leave until tomorrow morning."

Which would mean she'd miss only day one of the meeting, the drinking-and-schmoozing party, announcements of agenda, nothing vital. "So find me a four-star hotel near the airport in El Paso," Lily said. "It sounds doable."

"I can get you a nice suite at the Hilton. What I can't guarantee is the flight."

"Why not?"

The travel agent sighed. "You're talking Thanksgiving Eve, Lily. The most traveled day of the year. The flight's overbooked as it is."

"Can you get me a rental car?" Lily asked.

"You're going to drive from LA to Acapulco?"

"In this rain? Of course not. I want a one-way from LA to John Wayne."

She reserved the car, and Lily, having decided to packed the day in, rolled her luggage happily to the Avis counter. *I ran into dead ends everywhere I turned,* she'd explain to Eric. *The rain was so bad I didn't dare fly in it.* A transplant to this precipitation-terrified state, her boss would understand.

"Nobody takes off the last two weeks of the fiscal year," he said, when she broached the subject of her December work schedule. "Especially somebody who misses an important conference."

"Don't try to make me feel guilty, Eric. We both know the only reason you only made it to Acapulco is because you left a week early so you could work on your tan. Besides, I met my yearly quota in October," she said from her living room couch, among the purple throw pillows and what remained of the *Los Angeles Times* that Buddy hadn't reduced to packing strips and strewn all over the carpet—symptoms of postkennel syndrome, which could last for a maddening length of time.

"When you were on *leave,* I might add."

She sighed into the receiver. "What difference does that make? My orders roll over like the dolphins at Sea World. Have I ever let you down? Reach into your memory banks for a moment and recall all those times I bailed your butt out, like flying to Denver when Ty blew it big time with Doctor Klein? Or how about wasting a whole day on the set of *ER* with *actors* just so our company name could appear in the credits? Seems like you have selective amnesia when it comes to my company loyalty."

He did pause, she had to grant him that much. During the brief silence, Lily imagined that Eric had undergone a heart transplant, and now he was going to tell her he was not only giving her a raise but a fat bonus as well.

"It would make me look bad if you weren't out there earning extra money for us."

"It's the holidays, Eric. No one's working but elves."

"Very funny, Wilder. You almost made me smile. No time off in the month of December unless you want to take off the rest of your career as well," he said, and hung up the phone.

Fine, whatever. She'd kiss doctors' stethoscopes, do whatever the munch-brain told her to, but she was filing this defeat away for later, ammunition for some larger battle. His attitude was just so much middle management posturing. From now until New Year's Eve, Lily intended to behave like Santa with a platinum AmEx card. Then in January, let Eric go into a Prozac overdose regarding her expense account. A Shep Hallford adage Lily had often heard her during her growing-up years came to mind: *You mess with the bull, you get the horn.*

Lily opened her collection of pricey gourmet catalogues. In a matter of minutes she'd earmarked the pages, consulted her list, and sat there on her couch, dialing 800 number after 800 number. Nice wine for each surgeon, yes, at forty-five dollars a bottle, that wasn't too shabby. Imported cigars for the smoker crowd, and Perugina chocolates for those who didn't drink or smoke. Certainly, the overnight shipping rate would be fine with her. She arranged to have lunch catered to the radiology department at Cedars, and marked the date on her calendar so she could put in an appearance. She knew her surgeons. They didn't want sales pitches and order sheets shoved in their faces in December, they wanted a year-end party. Lily's pet theory was that while the rest of the world was goofing off in high school, smoking pot, listening to the Eagles, trying to score in bed, their classmates destined to be doctors were busy studying. When college rolled around, and keg parties and driving all night to Palm Springs for spring break was the rage, premed students remained bolted to their desks. After graduation, when the partyers began making a living, fun was properly relegated to weekends; doctors, worn out from a decade and a half of shoulder to the wheel, suddenly realized what they'd missed out on, and from that point on, whenever possible, jumbo-size party hats and confetti showers were de rigueur. Adolescence could be postponed, but no one escaped it. Some people even got permanently stuck there, like Philip Flynn.

Lily remembered quite clearly the afternoon she had seen him coming out of the Taos Inn, and it wasn't because he'd been having lunch at Doc Martin's, either. On his arm was a dark-haired woman, too tall and thin to be her sister. At the time Lily didn't know who she was, only what she was doing, which was wrecking her sister's marriage. She had called out to her brother-in-law, forcing him to speak to her. The woman looked away guiltily, then made the excuse that she needed to powder her nose. Lily waited for Philip's explanation, praying it would make sense. "Please don't tell your sister," he'd begged. "It was a stupid mistake, a one-time thing. Promise me, Lily."

Whether she felt beholden to him because he'd helped her get started in sales and showed her how to fine-tune her pitches, or because at the time she and Rose weren't speaking, it didn't matter. Philip was right, the news would have ripped Rose apart. Lily had kept her word but Philip hadn't. Two weeks later he'd been killed in the car wreck in that same part of Taos. Lily's trips home had accomplished a great deal: horseback riding, the rekindling of her love affair with Tres, the subsequent pain of him not calling, which she wasn't quite ready to give up as a hopeless situation, and one other tidbit since the shopping day in Santa Fe. Lily now had a name to go along with the face of that tall brunette: Leah Donavan.

She didn't know who to feel sorrier for, her sister or the vet. Lily couldn't think of a thing to be gained by telling either one what she knew. This gloomy reverie served to remind her that once again, during the holiday season, she was partnerless. Lily always breathed a sigh of relief when the last New Year's Eve horn sounded, but just around the corner in February, Valentine's Day waited—a smarmy, leering, obese cherub armed with painful arrows.

She chewed on her thumbnail until the French polish flaked off onto her tongue. A one-day-old manicure, ruined. At fourteen bucks plus tip, that amounted to nearly two bills per digit. Before her Buddy Guy sprawled with his legs arched out in front of and behind him on the rug, asleep, in a position Lily referred to as the "Viking long dog." His lips were in a full shamus.

Lily clicked the television on to the channel that concentrated on Southern California news. The deeply tanned weatherman gesticulated madly at a map of the United States so grossly out of proportion so that California appeared twice the size of Texas. A slew of green swirls moved across the state, representing rain. Yes, it was raining. It didn't take a rocket scientist to note that. Now that there was finally some weather to report, he was trying to look like a meteorologist, a term that always made Lily wonder why he wasn't out in the middle of the desert, lying flat on his back looking up at the sky waiting to get hit by falling objects. She loved this channel. The anchor people reminded her of the paper dolls Rose used to cut out of Mami's women's magazine, *McCall's*.

It wasn't that Lily minded the showers, she rather liked them. However, that day after day of downpour sometimes triggered her headaches, and migraine on top of dismal holiday mood was nothing to be encouraged. She fetched herself a Diet Coke in hopes that a jolt of caffeine would stave off the slight throb in her temple. As she stood in the middle of her tiny kitchen looking around at the white enamel cupboards, the fake granite countertops, the gleaming linoleum she paid a housecleaning service to keep that way (paid them a fortune, due to Buddy's distrustful nature and their willingness to work around it), it struck her that hers was forever a single person's kitchen. The only family that could inhabit her condo and not bump into one another all day long would be a tribe of Lilliputians. The *Lilli* half of the word made her smile. Since it was too rainy to go riding, and shopping the crowded malls was out of the question, she went back to the couch to flop and watch more television, pulling the afghan up to her chin.

On screen a river of brown mud flowed through a seniors-only mobile-home park down at the beach. Massive old Cadillacs and Ford

LTDs stood in water up to their door handles. The car size Lily under-stood. Driving the California freeway system was taking one's life in one's hands. A bigger car might feel like a tank amid all those subcompacts designed to get sixty miles to the gallon. Firemen piloted inflatable boats around in the mock river that was once a road, rescuing people. Lily squinted to see if she recognized any of the firemen. It occurred to her that if sewage overflows due to flooding threatened the trailer park, her yard might be in trouble, too.

Already her terra cotta flowerpots were overflowing. The tiny redwood deck was an inch under water. Her lawn, small enough to cut with a weed whacker, was where the real problem lay. Buddy Guy's droppings were swelling up with rain, melting into the grass, creating an *E. coli* extravaganza. She wondered who picked up dog poop at Rancho Costa Plente. It didn't seem like she ever saw anyone do it, but probably Shep did. Horse manure, dog manure; what was the difference? Poor old Shep. She wanted him to live forever, but from cases she'd seen on her job she understood he was making the right decision, letting himself wind down naturally rather than doing a bunch of pointless chemo and having his last earthly act consist of vomiting. She knew Rose would disagree: *If you can pray,* she'd say, *there's always hope.* As if cancer trembled in the face of religion.

Next door, her neighbors had strung their Christmas lights across the back fence that graced the top of the steeply terraced hillside. When Lily drove up Santiago Canyon Road, she could see blinking lights from a mile away. Mindless of the rain, they flashed continually at a maniacal speed, redgreenwhitegoldblue. Her neighbors were fond of leaving the porch light on all night as well—a halogen monster so bright that from her living room Lily could read by it. She could have pulled the drapes shut had Buddy not recently done a number on them, leaving a ragged gap big enough for the lights to shine through. No, if Lily wanted darkness—and her throbbing head seemed to be pleading for it—she'd have to go upstairs, lie facedown, and put a pillow over her head. Oh, maybe this was just a sinus headache. She challenged herself to watch the lights for awhile, which seemed to blink at exactly the speed that made her blood vessels wonder: *Hasn't it been a long time since we've had ourselves a king-hell migraine? Let's consider it.* Her pills were in the zipper pocket of her purse.

But wait. On the TV now, more firemen. Dressed in their smart black uniforms with the yellow raincoats, asking for toy donations for needy children. Once a year people went soft-hearted, opened their wallets, all because of a date on the calendar. How did they stave off guilt attacks the rest of the year? *Merry Christmas, baby. But only on this one day. After that, you're on your own.*

From out of nowhere, a sob rose up and caught in her throat. "Tres Quintero," she said out loud, rousing Buddy enough so that he opened one suspicious brown eye, "You broke my heart. Damn. I had totally forgotten I had one."

He hadn't called, hadn't written, hadn't even hinted that she could loan him some frequent flyer miles for a free ticket (she was up to 150,000 on United alone). *You think men can't get along without you, Lily? News flash, here's one guy who can.* All the time some doctor or another invited her to dinner. But fatal flaws—the one who had breath that could stop a war, the one who liked to ride horses but was cute only if you liked redheads, which Lily did not—prevented her from accepting. The only doctor who remotely appealed to her sat in his one-room cabin content without her. She flung a throw pillow at Buddy, who snapped at it, missed, cast her a baleful glance, and slunk into the downstairs bathroom to sleep.

Next to her on the couch the cordless phone began to trill. For a half-second, she let herself imagine it might be Tres. "Hello?"

"Little Bit," her father said when she picked up, "you're harder to get through to than a mule. Who you been jawing with on the phone? Some new boyfriend?"

She had turned off Call Forwarding to order the surgeon's Christmas presents. "Just work stuff, Pop." She sniffled.

"You don't sound so good."

"I'm the same as I ever was. Is it snowing there?"

"Nope, but a few weeks back we got a foot and half. It's butt-cold, however, and rain's predicted. Likely that *El Niño* I keep hearing about. Floods and famine ought to be along any minute, thank you, California."

"Hey, you know what? I'm pretty sick of hearing everything blamed on California. *El Niño* didn't start here. Take a look at the ocean down near the equator if you want to view *El Niño's* birthplace. Incidentally, we've got rain like you wouldn't believe. Up until a few years ago everybody called that '*el* weather.' Tell me some good news."

Her father laughed. "Well, I'm standing at my desk, looking out the front window. The horses are all bunched up in the center of the arena, backs to one another. Even though I know they do it to keep warm, when they stand that way, I can't help thinking they look like the petals of some giant old sunflower."

Lily pictured the animals in her mind's eye and knew exactly what he meant. "How's Rose's mare doing?"

"Fattening up nicely, everything moving on schedule. I check her myself, twice a day."

"I miss you, Pop. How's Mami?"

"Just dandy. She's trimming the tree as we speak. We've got gold ribbons, silver pinecones, some fancy twigs spray-painted all to glittering, and I didn't know there were that many dog ornaments to be found in New Mexico, but your mother has rooted them out. She's got dog biscuits all tied onto the ends of the branches with twine, too. I keep telling her, 'Poppy, the dogs'll eat 'em right off the tree when you aren't looking,' but you know how much she listens to me."

"How about Rose? What's she up to?"

"Smack in the middle of doing absolutely nothing since she quit her job. I'm a little put off with her, to tell you the truth."

His voice had gone rough around the edges, and Lily's skin went to gooseflesh. "Why?"

"Holing up like that doesn't do anybody much good. Well, your mother's taking her out to lunch soon. Maybe she can snap Rose out of this slump."

Lily wanted to tell her father not to count on it. If Rose could hold a grudge long enough for it to grow lichen, the situation with Austin could sideline her indefinitely. "And my buddy, Shep?"

Her father was quiet for so long that Lily wondered if the cordless had cut out on her; sometimes it did that, never during a conference call, but usually in the middle of a conversation she really didn't want to end. "He isn't doing too well, Lily. I checked him into the hospital yesterday. I asked him if there was anything I could get for him, and he hinted around he wouldn't mind seeing you if you could spare the time. Do you think you can swing a quick trip? I know you've only been home a couple of weeks, but Christmas is coming. . . ." his voice trailed off the way it did when he was near tears, which for a horseman, took considerable provocation.

Lily had programmed the telephone numbers of all the airlines into the speed-dial function on her cordless. "There's a doc I can visit in Albuquerque next week. Can it wait that long?"

"Just how much do you know about Shep's problems?"

A sudden burst of rain beat so hard at the sliding door that Lily wouldn't have been surprised if the safety glass shattered. "Of course I know about it. I didn't say anything because he made me swear not to."

"It isn't like he's on the breathing machine yet. But I wouldn't wait much after say, Monday?"

Lily could have sworn she felt a cold hand close around her heart. "I'll be there as soon as I can make my reservation. I'll rent a car at the airport and drive up at light speed."

Her father's chuckle was one of the finest sounds in the world. It almost made up for being alone over the holidays. "Don't know if this will interest you, but I heard from the guy down at the feed store that Tres Quintero flew back to California. Guess he couldn't take the winter."

"Really?" Lily said, her heart pounding with excitement that he might be in the same state. But probably it was a Leah thing, some college-girl crisis only Stepdaddy could smooth over. "I guess if he can't handle winter in New Mexico he deserves to live in California. I'll make my reservation the minute I hang up. See you soon, Pop. Big sloppy kisses."

"Back at you, little girl. Fly safe. Hold a good thought for Shepherd, won't you?"

"Oh, Pop. It kills me that you thought you had to ask."

Shep in the hospital—and so soon. This was a family crisis, the real thing, not some manufactured spat between sisters. Weddings and funerals—at times like these the clan was supposed to gather. Lily punched Talk on her cordless phone and started trying to find her nephew again. She called the editor of *Dirt Rider*, which had offices in LA, NYC, Detroit, Chicago, and Atlanta. The Southwest was ingrained in Second Chance; it was in his lineage, his blood. Lily didn't think he'd veer any farther east than Colorado. The editor provided her with telephone numbers of various dirt-bike folk there, and in Arizona and New Mexico. Lily left messages with the numbers she'd been given and waited for someone to call back. "Tell him to come home," she told them. "It's an emergency." Now that she'd taken care of business, done all she could until the morning, she lay back against the couch pillows to rest. Out of the corner of her left eye, a purple-and-yellow glow shimmered. She was about to dog-cuss the neighbor's lights until she recognized the sparkly vision for what it was: incipient-migraine aura. She leaped to her feet to get her pills and at once buckled to her knees, humbled and dry-heaving at the vise-grip pain in her left temple.

After a series of long, slow breaths, she crawled to the bathroom, climbed over Buddy, and patted her clammy face with a damp wash-cloth. The nausea settled down to a tolerable queasiness, so she inched her way up the stairs in search of her purse. Two pills, another swallow of Coke, and she settled facedown on her bed. Her heart beat in time to the throbs of her headache. She shut her eyes and curled into the fetal position. When she first started getting the headaches, she'd been convinced she had an aneurysm. She'd talked one of her doctor pals into comping her an MRI. As she lay in the tomblike machine, claus-trophobia, her childhood bogeyman, descended with a vengeance. Rather than embarrass herself in front of a doctor, she concentrated on remembering the greatest sex of her life, which of course just hap-pened to be with Tres Quintero. Recalling his skill as a lover had taken her mind off the small space in which she was enclosed like some hastily bound mummy, but now calling Tres to mind just made her sad. The bones around her eye socket blazed. *Half an hour,* she told herself. *Then the drugs will kick in.* The pills always made her hands and feet go cold. She pulled the comforter up over herself and tried visualizing the pain being chased into a corner, the same way a good cutting horse could select and move a single cow from the herd. Sometimes, with the right horse, all you had to do was hang on. Nothing compared to the feel of a thousand pounds of horseflesh between your legs except—oh, what was the point of even thinking about it?

Buddy came trotting upstairs. Whenever Lily was sick, he stuck close to her side, as if his latent heeling instincts might be called into use should she become disoriented on her way to the bathroom. He lay down on the carpet next to her bed, licking at her hand. Lily dozed. She dreamed of riding Sparrow, her very first pony, shared with Rose, but secretly she knew the horse liked her best. Her feathery mane hair was colored the most wonderful shade of caramel. Lily laid her face against the mare's neck, smelling the sharp, distinctive odor of female horse, and noted how that smell was sometimes stronger than others, depending if Sparrow was in season. It was summer, they had trailered her out to the lake, and Lily rode her bareback into the water using only a rope halter. The moment the horse's hooves lifted and the mare transformed from a walking animal to a swimming one, her legs curving in the murky water like a carousel horse, Lily felt like she was flying.

Buddy snored, startling her awake, and Lily was overcome with the feeling of loss. Why did all that good stuff have to end with puberty? Why couldn't a girl go back, if she chose to, remain in that in-between stasis forever, brave enough to take off her T-shirt if it was hot out, tough enough to climb the tallest tree and—miniskirts be damned—risk scarring her knees. Simply possessed of a spirit so fierce she'd think nothing of lifting a fist to a bully, even if tucked away in his shorts somewhere, he was hiding a penis.

Lily remembered looking down at her breasts one morning and noticing her nipples, swollen and sore. They felt exquisitely painful to the touch, but the discomfort couldn't stop her from pressing her fingers against them, or all day long the awareness of them rubbing against her clothing. Boys she thought nothing of began to turn their heads, to look at her differently, as if they, too, sensed the change, and were just as uncomfortable in their skins. Lily had responded the only way she knew how—in competitive mode, putting her guard up—except with Tres. *We're doomed,* she thought to herself, flipping the pillow off her overheated face. *We'll keep on butting up against each other in search of love until we draw our last breaths. I can't take it that pretty soon Shep isn't going to be here. That I won't be able to tease him or shock him or just stand there and watch him doctor Pop's horses. Dammit all, it isn't fair that good people have to die.*

When her bedside phone rang, Lily expected one of two things: Pop to be calling to stay it was too late, or miraculously, that Second Chance might have gotten one of her messages. She pulled the receiver toward her, and the phone fell on Buddy's head, causing him to yip at an awful pitch. "Whoops," she said, her voice a little slurred from sleep. "Sorry, Buddy. I mean, I dropped the phone on my dog, Buddy. His name is Buddy. Jeez, whoever this is, sorry. I mean hello."

"Lily, it's Tres."

No way could this be happening. She rubbed her eyes. "I heard a rumor you were in California. Where are you? Leah's dorm room?"

There was a pause. "No, I'm standing at a pay phone in that very odd cowboy bar you told me about, in rather damp sawdust. You're right about the couples wearing matching shirts. It's awfully loud in here."

Hall and Oates throbbed in the background, and Lily's migraine waved from a far-off corner. "I never lie."

"Your subdivision is like some three-thousand-piece jigsaw puzzle with no edge pieces. I've been driving around trying to find Palomino Street for what feels like hours. I'm soaking wet. I thought it never rained in Southern California. And people around here are not terribly friendly when you ask for directions. Right off they assume you're a serial killer."

Lily smiled and rolled over onto her back. "Blame *El Niño*. Everyone's paranoid. Around here they don't know fly fishermen from the Unabomber. Too bad you're not a flood insurance salesman instead of an unemployed shrink. Or an umbrella distributor. You could clean up."

"I'm filled with regret."

"You know, Tres, I'm not sure how to respond to this phone call. I think I remember that I'm kind of pissed off at you."

"I'd like a chance to explain in person."

Naturally. As if they were equipped with sensors, men called the moment women were beginning to accept the loss. She should hang up the phone right now, this moment. Her fickle mouth opened right up. "Got a pen?"

"Yep. A little cowboy napkin to write on, too."

She explained the twists and turns and told him where to park. He said, "Thanks." Lily said, "You're welcome." They listened to each other breathe for a while, and Lily said good-bye first, but she didn't hang up until Tres did. Then she turned to Buddy and, using both hands, took a firm hold of his muzzle. "Do not blow this for me," she warned. "I mean it. Take a doggy Valium and let whatever is supposed to happen happen."

17

The Table Nearest the Door

---

1. Take the feed store job, working the counter. It paid only minimum wage and meant lifting grain sacks all day; still, a 10 percent discount on hay was something to consider.
2. Crawl back to Austin and find a way to endure the humiliation of spending eight hours a day around a man she'd once slept with, who now desired only her accounting skills.
3. Decide nothing and keep the lunch date with Mami.

Rose flipped through the hangers in her closet for anything she might have overlooked. She was now down almost 20 pounds from her original 130, and everything she owned hung on her. It wasn't that she didn't eat, she ate half a cup of oatmeal in the morning, a cup of soup and carrot sticks at lunch, maybe part of one of those frozen entrees for dinner. She put a hand to her cheek and felt the distinct angles of the bones through her skin.

Finding nothing satisfying in the way of wardrobe, she braved Amanda's bedroom. Despite recent cleaning efforts, a musty smell met her nose the moment she opened the door. Echoes of unresolved arguments lingered in the static air. Her daughter's lightning-quick departures always caused her to picture Amanda in midspin, turning on her heel to flee something her mother had said. If Amanda were to have a baby of her own, that might cause her to settle down, maybe even change her ideas about parenting. Maybe.

But if Rose continued to follow this thread, she knew she'd have to stand Mami up, lock herself into her bedroom, and spend another day hiding. She pushed aside the mess of shoes and rumpled blue jeans that lay at the bottom of Amanda's closet. In the middle of the rack she found a nearly new outfit that had come from Chelsea Court down in Santa Fe. Even with Ginny's courtesy discount—Mami had placed a greyhound with the shopkeeper—the clothes had cost as much as a week's worth of groceries. Amanda begged, promised to muck stalls, repaint the barn, anything. Only these clothes made her feel pretty. If she were dressed like this, that boy she liked at school would notice her, and if she had a decent boyfriend then she'd study, make good grades, go to college—the possibilities were endless. Rose had tumbled right down that slippery slope and written out the check. Amanda wore the outfit twice that she could remember. The top was a stretchy black lace pullover, embroidered with autumn-colored flowers and leaves. The slacks were heavy black twill, Capri-style, with a hidden zipper up the back, something only Barbie dolls or women with flat bellies could pull off with grace.

Rose stripped to her bra and panties—her good bra from Nordstrom's—after Lily's crack she'd thrown the white cotton one away—then dressed in her daughter's clothing. She shut the mirrored closet doors to study her reflection. That area of gray growing out from her part had widened. In a strange way its presence felt comforting, as if the outward and visible change reflected how she felt inside where no one could see. Amanda's shirt hugged Rose's breasts, outlining her rib cage. The fabric was semisheer, too revealing. If not for the strategically placed roses, it looked almost as if she wasn't wearing any undergarments. Her hipbones stretched the pants fabric tight across her stomach. *Good golly, Miss Molly,* Shep used to say when she or Lily walked out of the ranch house dressed to impress, or he'd let go one of those primal male sighs that meant language was too much of an effort. Remembering that made her smile. Rose ran her hands from her pelvic bones up her breasts, curious how it was she could present this sort of pared-down, utterly sexual persona yet feel absolutely nothing. Maybe that one night of lovemaking with Austin was her body's swan song. Oh, for goodness sake, the clothes would do for lunch with Mami. She pulled her black Jones New York blazer over the blouse and her black overcoat on top of everything. So much black. On Georgia O'Keeffe the color provided a neutral background, showcasing her remarkable face. "I, on the other hand, look like I'm headed for a funeral," Rose said to Chachi, who whined as she ordered him back in the house. "Old pal, I'm sorry. They don't allow dogs in restaurants. Go sleep with your girlfriend. I won't be gone very long."

The Jack Russell assumed the begging position, cocking his head so pathetically that Rose finally decided she'd take them both, crack a window, and leave them in the Bronco.

But the driver's door was frozen solid, and she had to go to the barn to find an extension cord, and once there, feed Max a pail of sweet feed to ease her guilty conscience at having ignored him lately. She ran back into the house, fetched her blow-dryer, and aimed it at the lock until the ice melted so she could fit her key in. If there had been a garage door, this wouldn't have happened, but Philip had never gotten around to building one. A carport was sufficient for a man who drove a sedate company car. Back when they were all close and friendly, Philip had so much time to spare that he kind of took Lily under his wing. Yet when Rose stopped speaking to her sister, Philip supported the silence, even seemed to encourage it. In his eyes, that probably meant more attention for him. Looking back, it seemed that Philip's needs had been the focal point of their marriage, and it had to be Rose's fault for constantly adapting. The wind bit at her cheeks, and her nose ran. Had there been a garage door, she'd be down on her hands and knees thawing that out, too.

As agreed, Mami met her in front of the Apple Tree, but she didn't want to eat there after all.

"Let's go to La Calaverada. They hired a new chef, and I heard they're serving six different kinds of tamales. If I can talk him into giving me some new recipes," she said, "my spring equinox party will be unforgettable."

"It doesn't matter to me where we eat," Rose answered. She planned to order salad. "Let me put the dogs in the car."

"The maître d' of this restaurant also is a fine black-and-white photographer," Mami said as they stood on the sidewalk, talking. "He's recently divorced, the poor man, and very understanding about dogs since he adopted a greyhound and discovered what rewarding companions they can be. I imagine you can bring your little dogs into the restaurant with no fuss." She took a deep breath and exhaled, a smile spreading across her face. "It's such a beautiful day, let's walk instead of drive."

Beautiful? The wind chill felt like a deep breath blown southeast from the Arctic. In her Pledge-polished boots, Rose's toes felt numb. After holing up for so long, this venture out into the world made her tired. She plodded along next to her mother, who in her not-so-subtle fashion seemed to be trying to fix her up with this photographer/restaurateur/greyhound rescuer. Honestly, the woman did not know the meaning of quit. but her heart lay in the right place. Today she was dressed all in white, an ecru-and-rust shawl cloaking her shoulders. Her silvery-streaked black hair was knotted up into an intricately braided bun. For makeup she wore only a swipe of red lipstick, exactly the right shade, with just a hint of gloss. Rose wondered how she coordinated everything.

Chachi trotted alongside Rose, who carried Joanie in her arms. The new dog had learned to make her way around just fine at home, but here on the street the snow and muck would present a challenge to her splinted leg. Whenever a passerby remarked what a cute doggy she was, or made a move to pet her, Chachi raced protectively around behind Rose's legs, and she got all tangled up in the leash.

"It's good you adopted her," Mami said. "I think Chachi's been lonely since Buddy left."

"He has me for company."

"Yes, but you never go out of your house. It can't be much fun to watch a grown woman sit on the couch all day. Honestly, Rose, why you find it necessary to hide this way is beyond me."

Rose stopped on the narrow sidewalk. A half block away, the Catholic church lunchtime AA meeting was just about to start, and people were filing in, Austin among them.

Her mother saw, too, and made a sad face. "You have to trust that what is supposed to happen will happen," she said, touching her daughter lightly on the elbow.

Rose walked quickly toward the restaurant, her dog trotting beside her. La Calaverada's saloon-type swinging doors were for decorative purposes only in winter. The snow door behind them was closed to keep in the heat. "I don't want to discuss him," Rose said. "That's over and done with, and here I am, out in public, so I don't need to hear about staying home too much, either."

Of course, the moment the words left her mouth, she heard how false they rang. The sight of Austin on the church steps was all it took to erase her brief period of comfort. No advice from her mother was going to change the facts. Eventually, Rose figured, enough time would pass that she could find a slot in which to file this sorrow, the same way she had done with her children's behavior, her grief over her husband's death, and admitting his infidelity to herself.

"Look," Mami said. "If you want to live the rest of your life *patas arriba*, I cannot stop you. Let's go inside and eat something good and talk of other subjects. I'm telling you, it's okay to bring the dogs. Benito loves dogs."

Benito. So, not only was this man artistic, dog friendly, and unattached, he possessed the added bonus of Spanish blood. Rose sighed. They chose the table nearest the door.

The restaurant's adobe walls were painted a terra-cotta, decorated with photographs, some of which featured early Floralee during a time when a rider could trot up the main street of town and feel the earth beneath his horse's hooves. Each table was unique; it looked as if somebody had decorated the place aiming for the "almost antiques" look, decor so comfortable diners couldn't help but relax. Rose admired the way the coffee cups were all different shapes and sizes and the plates didn't match. A restaurant sure enough of itself to use secondhand crockery undoubtedly felt confident regarding its efforts in the kitchen. She fanned her face. They certainly kept the place warm enough. She took off her coat, then her jacket, draping them across the back of her chair. Her mother's eyebrows lifted.

"What?" Rose said.

"The blouse. Different for you."

"It belongs to Amanda."

"Very nice, but you're getting too thin. It doesn't suit you to get bony. Your shoulders are broad, you can support a little weight. You need to eat more."

People at nearby tables were listening, because whenever Poppy Wilder opened her mouth it was hard not to. "Mami," Rose whispered, "that's enough."

Her mother made a face, but she did not stop lecturing. "I know a thing or two about eating disorders."

The man Rose assumed had to be Benito came over with menus, kissed Poppy on the cheek, and they exchanged a few sentences of rapid-fire Spanish.

So, this is the daughter you were telling me about?

Sí. And a wonderful cook; you should hire her to work here.

Maybe I will. We're still looking for help.

Rose blushed. Did they think she'd forgotten all her languages? "My mother tells me you take photographs," she said, in what she hoped was a neutral, conversational tone. "Any of your work hanging on the walls here?"

Benito smiled and laid the menu open in front of her. "No, but Two Moons Gallery carries a few of my pieces. They're not everyone's cup of tea, but you might find them interesting."

"Interesting?" Mami laughed. "Imagine Miguel Martínez with a camera instead of a paintbrush."

"I'll stop by and take a look," Rose said. She felt absolutely no attraction to this man. He wasn't obese, he didn't have facial warts or a hunched back; it was just that the stocky, barrel-chested body type reminded her of wrestlers, and wrestlers made her think of displays of machismo and dripping sweat. She'd married a man like that. Benito's eyes loomed huge and kind in his face, a warm shade of coffee brown, but Rose favored skinny men who needed glasses and flaunted their arrogance like wearing a suit with wide lapels.

"I'll have a salad," she told Benito.

Mami clucked. "You didn't even look at the menu."

"I don't have to. A salad is what I want. With whatever your house dressing is, which I'm sure is wonderful. And some bread."

Benito nodded. "We make a fine house salad, Poppy. It's very generous. Our greens are locally grown in the Embudo basin. Have you decided what you would like?"

Her mother had a choice; smooth down her hackles or make a scene in front of a man she was trying to impress. "Well, the mushroom/leek tamale with the mango salsa sounds good, but you know what, Benito? I'd *love* it if you could talk the chef into making me a sampler plate of all your tamales. Do you think that such a thing is possible?"

Benito smiled so widely Rose could see a gold crown on one of his molars. "Certainly. But I feel I must warn you, that's a lot of food."

Mami smiled. "Rose will help me eat them. What we don't finish, I'll take home."

Benito squatted down to pet the dogs. Joanie startled, but tolerated the man's hand on her back.

"She's nervous," Rose said. "I've only had her a little while."

"It's okay," Benito said. "She can tell I'm a dog person. Would it be all right if I brought them something?"

"Bring whatever you like," Rose said. "Chachi's never been picky, and Joanie could use the weight."

"Like you," her mother put in. "A broken leg and a broken heart are not so very different."

When he left with their order, Rose breathed at her mother, "Do you think you could you be any more blatant?"

Mami sat up straight in her chair and looked directly at her daughter. "All I want is for my daughters to be happily married. Is that a crime?"

"No, Mami, but love isn't something you can engineer, like one of your parties. It happens or it doesn't. I had a happy marriage."

"You did not. You kept on adjusting yourself to whatever Philip wanted. That's not happiness. And certainly not passion."

Rose gasped. "How dare you say that?"

"Because somebody needs to shock you back into living."

"You won't even give me time to get over—" Rose stopped herself, cornered by her own words, not having intended to say that much. "Never mind. We'll eat and then we'll go home."

"We're going to talk, Rose."

When Benito brought her salad, Rose bent her head and dug in.

Mami carefully pried apart each tamale, studying its ingredients. Rose, grateful for the distraction, relaxed.

The lunch crowd was beginning to wander in just as Rose was finishing her salad. The AA meeting had ended, because she recognized several of the people she had seen going into the church. Chatting animatedly to another man, Austin did a double take when he saw her, of course catching her looking back at him. Dr. Donavan waited for his companion to finish his sentence, then excused himself and came over to their table.

"Mrs. Wilder," he said, nodding to Poppy, then at Rose. "And Mrs. Flynn. How are you ladies?"

"Fine." If Austin wanted her to ask after his health, he could wait until next spring.

"That's good to hear."

Rose could think of no response to that. Under the table she pressed her boot against her mother's.

"People ask about you at the clinic," he said. "You're missed."

"You can tell them I'm fine."

"Are you really?"

"Why wouldn't I be?"

Austin looked at her, his face wide open. People knew each other's business in Floralee, so she imagined her staying in her house for a few days or weeks, however long it had been, was rumored to be full-blown agoraphobia. He looked sad in a way that made Rose want to slap him, then press her lips to the mark her hand would leave on his cheek.

"Well, nice to see you." Austin shook Poppy's hand, but before he could reach for Rose's, she quickly put hers in her lap. There was a moment of awkwardness, and then Joanie emerged from under the table, her tail wagging. "Hey there," Austin said, bending down to scratch the dog's chest. "How's she doing, Rose?"

The polite thing to do was answer the question. "Coming along. She and Chachi are great friends."

Austin stood up. "Be sure to bring her in if there're any problems. Otherwise I'll see you when it's time for the cast to come off."

"Right," she said, hoping he'd leave things at that and walk away.

But of course Mami went whole hog into her charming mode, placing a hand on Austin's forearm, laughing when her diamond ring caught in the weave of his sweater. "The next time you're seeing to my daughter's mare, Doctor Donavan, stay for dinner. You look like you could use some fattening up. I'm curious. Are you and Rose in some kind of competition here? What is the prize for starving yourself to bones? Sainthood?"

Austin laughed out loud. It was such a rare sound coming out of his mouth that the unexpected pleasure it evoked in Rose surprised her. "My weight's a by-product of bachelorhood and an unwillingness to learn to cook for myself, that's all. I can't speak for your daughter's, but I will admit she's looking thin. Maybe we should both take you up on that dinner, Mrs. Wilder. Now, if you two ladies will excuse me."

His skinny legs, bowed slightly from years of riding, moved in sure strides across the dining room. Just up the road from those legs was his butt, and Rose could feel the memory of those taut muscles against her hands as she had pulled him close, felt the hardness of him enter her softest place, and the thrill in her blood as he began to move inside her. She let out a breath. Longing like this tethered the spirit. Austin sat down at a table with three other men. They bent their heads and said a prayer. Austin looked away, uncomfortable. If he was trying to get sober, he wasn't there yet.

"Such a handsome package," Mami said. "Too bad about his drinking. Best to forget that kind."

Rose felt the hair on her neck bristle. "It's not easy getting sober. He'll find a way if people can be patient."

Mami pursed her lips as if she was giving that idea some thought. "We can always pray for that kind of strength, but I wouldn't count on anything like that happening until Austin wants it." Her mother sipped at her water, set it down, then poked the wheel of lemon with her index finger and set it spinning. "You see, *mija,* when you want something for a man more than he wants it for himself, you burden him with your wishes. Years ago, I did that to your father. It was only when I stopped caring, and another man suddenly found me attractive, that your father could give up his drinking. You know, I almost left him for good to marry that professor. I'll bet you didn't know that about your mother. I thought that life with a sober, intelligent man would bring me the happiness I ached for. But it wouldn't have. From the first moment I saw him, it was always your father for me. Even if he hadn't come after me, I would have gone back to him."

Rose sat there stunned. The forbidden subject, and Mami had brought it up, casually discussed it, and revealed her heart, all in a matter of minutes. What did she say? Thank you? "Are you giving me advice?" she finally asked.

"Not exactly."

Her mother reached across the table and touched the white streak in her daughter's hair. Self-consciously, Rose reached up and gently pulled her fingers away. "Do you think I should dye it?"

"Your hair is your flag, Rose Ann. The decision is up to you. You're going gray the same way I did."

"How is that?"

"Every shock that hits you from now on will travel through body and be revealed in your hair. I think it's going to be *maravilloso* when it's entirely silver. You weren't a pretty child the way Lily was, but you are going to make a striking older woman."

It was just like Mami to temper a compliment. Rose looked at her plate. The leftovers from the tamale sampler would make a second meal. Rose couldn't have eaten a bite more, whether Mami made a scene or not. Joanie and Chachi noisily licked the plate Benito had brought them until Rose reached down and took it away.

Mami chattered about the tastes of each different tamale and made notes on a napkin. "These are the best," she said, pointing to the mushroom tamales. "But the sun-dried tomato one has too little texture. Corn isn't enough."

"What if you added olives?"

Mami nodded excitedly. "Maybe some peppers, too."

In a few weeks' time it would be Christmas. As she did every year, Mami expected Rose to stand alongside her in the kitchen and mix up huge batches of masa and lard into paste. Then, with the back of a wooden spoon, Rose would spread the paste across a corn husk and send it along to be filled with shredded pork, chile verde, mushrooms, whatever, and tied with thin strips of husk. The idea didn't make her mouth water like it usually did. Maybe she should go to the doctor, ask for B_{12} shots. She looked up and saw her mother fold her hands on the tablecloth. The posture was unmistakable: imminent lecture.

"You know, Rose, when you and Lily mended your fences I was thrilled. I try to stay out of you girls' business, no one can say I don't. But I feel that I just have to say this one thing."

"Mami," Rose warned.

"No, I must. Then I have something else I need to tell you. Something serious."

Rose pushed her plate away. "Fine. Say it. Get it over with."

"Your sister Lily isn't as strong as you think."

"Give me a break. Lily's like some unstoppable force of nature. You ought to have named her after an element, not a flower."

Mami nodded. "There's truth in what you say. Lily's spirit is strong like quicksilver is strong. When you two quarrel, she's trapped, with no outlet. If the climate gets cold enough, she cannot be more remote."

Rose spread her hands. "And this is supposed to mean what? Mercury can be poisonous. I'm getting a headache trying to follow you. Just tell me, and let's ask Benito for the check."

Mami pressed her lips together. "I should think that being older you could find it in your heart to be the bigger person here, to overlook Lily's shortcomings. To be there for her."

"Be there for Lily?" Rose sputtered, her voice rising in pitch. "*I'm* the one whose children turned into thieves and motorcycle fanatics so thoughtless they can't even be bothered to telephone home and say Happy Thanksgiving to the woman who gave birth to them, who gave up any hope of a sex life to raise them to adulthood after their father died, and I'm the one whose husband was screwing somebody else, not that anyone gives a damn, and I'm the one who picked the wrong man again, and Lily—" Rose ran out of steam and breath at the same moment, looked around and saw that half the people in the restaurant, Austin included, were looking her way. She clapped her hand over her mouth. The dogs pawed nervously at her ankles. "Oh my God. I have so little sleep under my belt I just blurt out every thought that comes into my head. I could curl up and die."

Her mother looked out the window at the cars in the parking lot. In the afternoon light, her face showed the strains of age. She reached across the table and patted Rose's hand. It was such an unexpected, tender gesture that it made Rose ache for a whole lifetime of that kind of kindness.

"Shepherd's in the hospital, Rose. I think he's going to die soon, maybe this week, if the doctor your father hired knows what he's talking about. I'm going to need you to help me with the arrangements. This is going to be very hard on your father. Those two go back almost fifty years, Rose Ann, not to mention hundreds of horses. It's going to be a sad time for all of us, but I'm most afraid of how it will affect Lily."

Benito chose that moment to set the check down on the table. "So how was everything?" he said, smiling tentatively.

Rose burst into tears.

"*Lo siento,*" he said, handing her a napkin, as if the application of linen to her overflowing eyes would quell the outburst. "Don't worry about the bill; this lunch is on me. Maybe next time we can feed you a better meal."

"Benito, listen," Mami said. "Rose just got some bad news, and it hit her hard. The food was wonderful, really it was."

He let out a sigh of relief. "I still won't let you pay for it." He touched Rose's hand. "Maybe this isn't the best time to ask, but if you want a job here, we'd love to have you. Only part time, I'm afraid—prep work, salads, and soup—and the hours are terrible, but if you decide you like the work, it could turn into full time. If you're interested."

To embrace good news so soon after hearing about Shep only made Rose's tears flow that much harder. All she could do was pat her cheeks with the napkin and shake her head yes. Mami laid a tip down on the table. "It seems that we've solved two problems today. That's wonderful. But she'll have to start next week, Benito. Right now Rose is needed for family business."

There were times all you could do was walk past a church, quickly, without stopping, and Rose knew this was one of them. The sanctuary of an empty pew was too tempting. Yes, they provided comfort, a space for reflection, but avoiding the hospital room was the wrong thing to do. After Mami left, Rose drove to the veterinary office and dropped the dogs off with Paloma, who gave Rose a quick hug. "Go be with your family. If you don't make it back by closing time, Rey will make sure they get supper. Nacio and I will feed the horse tonight. Just go. And Rose? When all this is over, try not to be such a stranger."

"*Gracias*, Paloma." Rose hurried to the client parking area, found her car keys, and a flush of shame burned her skin. She'd been so focused in on her own troubles she'd neglected her friend. She didn't have such a surplus of friends that she could afford to do that. *Just let me get through this business with Shep*, she prayed, *and instead of behaving like some self-obsessed idiot, I promise I'll start acting like a human being.*

Floralee's hospital boasted 125 beds, an emergency room, two ORs, a radiology department that shared space with the hematology/pathology lab, and a volunteer-run gift shop that sold yellowing get-well cards, slipper socks, playing cards, and breath mints. What it didn't have was the kind of state-of-the-art equipment Lily was used to selling, or renowned physicians able to work miracles. Its doctors were down-home specialists. They set broken ankles in casts so that a cowboy could still go riding while his bones knitted themselves back together. A workingman's lacerations, or trauma caused by an excess of beer and country-and-western music, were stitched up neat, but it wasn't plastic surgery. The hospital held free vaccination clinics for children whose parents couldn't afford their shots, delivered a couple of dozen babies a year, and dried out the occasional drunk who generally went back out there and got wet all over again. Anything more complicated they sent by ambulance to Santa Fe or to Albuquerque via helicopter. Rose walked into the reception area, received a sincere smile from the woman working the desk, and kept moving, checking the brown plastic signs on the wall to find the wing Shep was in. Beneath her boots the shiny linoleum was polished to a glare. A warm, clean-soap-safe smell filled the hallway. Rose passed two doctors dressed in blue scrubs and a nurse who still wore those old-fashioned rubber shoes that didn't make any noise. The nurse told her which room was Shep's. Rose hesitated only a moment, her palm flat against the laminated wood door. As soon as she opened it, this crisis would be real. She steeled herself, gathering her resolve, calling on every last bit of composure. All the way over here in the car, she'd cried her tears. Now was the time to put them away.

A nurse was checking Shep's vital signs when she pushed open his door. Hat in hand, her father was standing at the foot of the bed looking down on his oldest friend, whose skin bore the unhealthy pallor of those who are fundamentally tired and on their way out of this world.

Rose touched her father's shoulder. Without looking, he reached up and laid his hand over hers. She whispered, "Tell me what you need me to do, Pop."

"I wish I knew. Just stay here with me, I guess. He's going downhill so fast."

The nurse finished her work and left the room. Shep was hooked up to various machines, but not a respirator. There had been one of those in the room when they let her in to see Philip. Someone had cut into his neck in order to fit in a tube to help him breathe. In the end, what was one more hole in his mangled body? At the time her faith helped her believe his spirit had already departed.

Rose sat down in one of the chairs. Her father stood between her and Shep's bed. For long minutes they said nothing at all. Occasionally her father squeezed her hand, and Rose felt its age as strongly as she did its warmth. It was hard for her to raise her head, to look up and acknowledge that Shep's death was coming, because she knew that it wasn't going to be the last one she'd experience. Someday she'd be standing at her father's bedside, and that was going to hurt ten times more than this. Eventually she noticed that her father's other hand was clasped around his old friend's. He and Shep weren't blood, but they didn't need to share DNA to feel a bond. She rubbed her father's knuckles with her thumb, wondering how long he'd been standing vigil. "Pop? You want me to get you some coffee?"

"Thanks, but I don't think I could stomach it. Let's just stay put until your sister arrives. Just before you got here she called from the airport. The way she drives, it shouldn't be long now."

"Yes," Rose said. "I imagine." Lily would be here soon. After all, she was the one Shep loved best. Losing him would rock her world. Mami had a point there, but surely when he was on his deathbed, Lily could manage to hold herself together.

18

Recalibrating the Human Heart

"Allowing you back in my heart was harder than leaving my job," Tres said when he'd shaken off the rain, left his shoes on the welcome mat, and settled in at the foot of Lily's bed.

She wanted to argue, *Look how easily you love Leah*, but, stoned on pain relievers, for once she was able to hold her tongue. "Maybe if I knew the reasons you left I could believe that," Lily answered.

Tres took a breath and let it out slowly. "I had this patient, a middle-aged woman, moderately depressed but certainly not suicidal. Been seeing her a year, and it seemed like she was making progress. Turned out she'd saved up the pills I'd prescribed for her anxiety and taken them all at once."

Lily sighed. "That's awful, Tres. Every doc I know shoulders his failures, but it's the decent ones that don't forget them."

"Maybe you're right." He got up and touched the framed print of the white coyote. "Veloy's work?"

Lily nodded, and the movement made her already spacey brain feel like Jell-O bouncing inside her skull. "Every time I look at it I miss being home so bad I can feel it in my chest. Why do I get the feeling you're not telling me all of it?"

He smiled. "Because you know me too well. After I lost that patient, I told myself it was a fluke: I'd never let it happen again. Then this teenage boy, whose major problem seemed to be nothing more complicated than adolescence and being the object of his parents' custody battle, cut his wrists and bled to death in a swimming pool. He left a note saying he 'didn't want to make a mess.' I still don't know how I missed the clues."

Lily didn't need to hear any more, but she knew it was essential for Tres to tell her.

He shoved his hands into his pockets and looked her in the face. "I'd lost my instincts. How could I continue practicing if it meant risking a single client's health? So I took the leave, and I still don't want to go back. Whenever I think about it I come up against a wall."

Several times Lily wanted to interrupt, but she petted Buddy instead. Her blue doggie was being remarkably calm, but she knew him well enough not to trust outward appearances.

"So maybe you can understand why I'm gun shy," Tres said hopefully, "even though around you I swear it's the last thing I want to be."

Lily held out her arms. Tres went into them gratefully. She held on to his shoulders and ran her hand up the back of his collar, which was damp from rain. She bent and smelled the skin at the nape of his neck, which smelled like campfires and cloudy days, and faintly of detergent. She kissed him there, and he ran his fingers through her hair. After a while of that they got naked, but with every incremental motion of increasing passion Lily's migraine pain returned, so fiercely that she started to cry. "Damn!" she said. "I'm going to have to take another pill. This hardly ever happens."

"Migraines are often symptomatic of underlying conditions," Tres warned when he looked at the prescription label of her medicine. "When's the last time you saw a physician?"

She laughed. "Depends on your definition of 'see.' Far too often, if you ask me. I've had the tests, Tres. I let this one go on too long. By morning it'll be history. Come on, let's try it again. Just don't make me move too much and I can probably—"

He cradled her gently against his chest. *El Niño* beat at the windows. "*Shh.* Lie quiet and let me tell you a story."

She looked down at his penis, which was no longer firm and eager for her. How strange to study a man's equipment at rest. She couldn't imagine what it felt like to carry such an unpredictable appendage around twenty-four hours a day, never certain when it was going to act up. "What story is that?" she'd asked, terrified it was the I-love-you-but-I-just-can't be-with-you story she'd heard so many times before.

"This is the story of a man who got smart late in his life. So smart he was allowed a second chance with someone he never should have let go in the first place."

"This isn't one of my grandmother's stories, is it? Starts out great, but then somebody drowns the children in the river and they mess up your dreams every night for the rest of your life?"

Tres laughed. "No, this one might have a happier ending. It all depends. The man's going to have a hard time of it, because she makes more money than he does, and he's in the middle of redefining himself, never a pleasant task. It means financial sacrifices, for one thing, and probably going back to school."

"What about the woman?" Lily asked. "Does she just go to sleep and believe the man's going to be there in the morning? I think she'd be more comfortable with a guarantee."

"Come on, Lily. You know the best stories don't have guarantees."

She wanted to buy it. She wanted him inside her. She wanted her headache to sprout wings and fly out the window into the storm. "But tonight was supposed to be their big reunion. Memorable."

"It already is. She can sleep right next to him, and her headache is going to go away."

"But these two characters in your story, they still make love, right? And it's glorious, for a lot of years, like say at least until they're eighty?"

He patted her shoulder and brushed his lips against her skin. "Yes, Lily. Mountains are moved, but they don't have to do it six times a day to prove the mountain exists."

Just like that, believe him? Before they had fallen asleep, Buddy Guy had heaved himself onto the foot of the bed. Tres had taken his right hand from the complex curve of Lily's breast and slid it down the bedsheets until it rested on Buddy's diamondback-rattler-shaped skull. Her bad blue dog growled a warning but did not snap. Lily shut her eyes and fell asleep in Tres's arms. If he got bitten it was his own fault.

The day after a headache she always felt a little weird. Taking those pills was the equivalent of having her brain sucked out of her skull with a straw. The gray matter grew back, but never as quickly as she hoped it would. Her thoughts puddle-jumped from one rock to another as she packed her carry-on and tried to remember everything she needed to take along. As her ability to move through the world at Mach 1 returned, fragments of the evening returned to her in the form of mood swings, filling her with regret when she thought of Shep, and uneasy triumph when she thought of Tres. Instead of taking him in out of the rain like that, maybe she should have told him she had other plans, to try back another time, and made the man wait and wonder the way he'd done to her. But didn't there come a point when a woman could quit the games, just ask for what she needed outright? Lily told herself she had been too preoccupied with her migraine to manage female diversion tactics, but that was a lie. She didn't want to take the chance Tres wouldn't come back. She made a quick sweep of the condo before it struck her that she'd forgotten to make a boarding reservation for Buddy Guy.

She could leave him home, but what if she was gone longer than a few days? Southern California had enough kennel facilities that Buddy hadn't yet been banned from them all, but she'd miss her plane if she stopped to find a new place right now. Maybe Tres . . . ? Bad idea, no way. Fear of lawsuits kept her from trusting Buddy on an individual basis with anyone except Mami and Pop.

Tres walked into the kitchen, where Lily stood eating a cracker slathered in jelly. "I'll watch the dog if you need me to," he said, and reached into the sack for a cracker of his own. "It's not like I have to be anywhere soon."

He drove Lily to the airport, too. As she stood by the curb listening to that dreadful recording, "The white zone is for loading and unloading of passengers only, no parking," she handed him the various keys he'd need. Car key—well, that was obvious, it was in the ignition. The condo key presented a slightly different matter. She had to take Blaise's old key and lay it in another man's palm. The cool metal against her fingers reminded her of how much he'd hurt her, and that only hours earlier she'd dismissed Tres's weeks of silence with a blanket forgiveness. Was this the right thing to do, just hand over her life? At her core, even without Shep's reminders, she knew she could be foolhardy, at best a tempestuous idiot. However, what happened in her bed last night had dramatically altered her definition of peak sexual experiences. Dr. Quintero was now five across the board, and every other guy was history, but the strangest thing was they hadn't even made love.

As anxious as Lily had been to feel that pelvic reassurance, Tres hadn't made a move other than to hold her in the crook of his arm, stroke the hair from her face, and kiss her—she wouldn't have let him get away with anything less—and he had *talked* to her, sometimes in

Spanish, other times in English, until she was asleep. Migraine medicine definitely loosened her pins, but painkillers didn't have the power to make Lily surrender her heart. That she'd done all by herself.

He'd wanted to park the car and walk her inside the terminal, but Lily said no. She hated good-bye scenes, and airports only made them worse.

"Have a safe flight," he told her, waving *adios* at curbside. "Call me if you need me."

John Wayne had the best takeoffs in the world due to their noise abatement procedures. Lily shut her eyes and enjoyed the moment of weightlessness as the engines cut power before they throttled up again over the Pacific. She looked out over the water, visible only for moments through patches of winter clouds. It was a pretty sight, all that water, home to whales and so forth, but it sure wasn't the Sangre de Cristos.

As soon as the seat-belt sign dimmed, Lily hit the ground running. "Ladies first," she said, pushing past the pokey businessmen with whom she'd ridden in first class. She intended to be up the jetway and into the terminal proper before the coach passengers had time to sort out their carry-on luggage. The chill December air fingered its way through the bellows, but Lily didn't stop to pull on her coat. She ran all the way to the escalator toward the rental car counters. Hoping to endure the least amount of red tape, she had prepaid by credit card, said yes to the insurance package, which came free with her Chairman's Club membership anyway, and had given her card number to the clerk on the other end of the line. She wasn't some first-time tourist out looking for bargains, she wanted a solid car with four-wheel drive and a CD player. The clerk suggested a Ford Expedition, and Lily said, "Now you're talking."

At the top of the escalator, she slowed down while a woman folded up her jillion-dollar baby stroller and tried to manage the flotsam that went along with having an infant as well as the kicking, squalling baby itself. Lily examined the baby with mostly a scientific interest. They were poorly designed packages that took far too long to evolve into an appropriate level of self-sufficiency. She tucked her pull-along suitcase handle into its disappearing pouch and opted for the stairs between the escalators. At the bottom the Avis Preferred Customer line was mercifully short. She tapped her foot, waiting for the people in front of her to finish. While she waited it occurred to her that for once in her life, she'd left a man without worrying there would be no man to come back to. When the woman with the stroller and the baby got in line behind her, Lily decided maybe the baby was tolerable now that the crying had stopped, but a long way from cute. All that drool—ick— but still, a baby would be someone to talk to in the middle of the night. When the Avis clerk snapped her gum and asked whether Lily wanted to stick with the Plymouth Neon or upgrade to an Oldsmobile, Lily patiently unfolded her faxed confirmation for the Ford Expedition and waited for the retired rodeo queen to catch up.

She drove out of the airport and picked up I-25. She chewed the polish off two more fingernails, found a rhythm in the traffic, set the cruise control for eighty, and tore the annoyingly efficient sticker and cellophane off a Susana Baca CD. She slid it into the player, heard the chime of the Dolby calibration tone, then cranked up the volume. All it took for the singer's heart to be filled with longing after her man left was a simple rainstorm. Tres had come back to Lily in the rain. What a song that would make. She drove on, pondering the questions of *ritmo y nostalgia*, praying she'd make it to the hospital in time to say good-bye to Shep.

Out the driver's-side window of the Expedition, she charted her home state's famous blue sky, which had not taken the winter off. No amount of scientific explanation would ever convince Lily that those blues songs she loved, heard constantly playing in her head, felt moving through her veins, charging her forward, were not the exact same shade as northern New Mexico's upper atmosphere.

"Okay, what are we dealing with?" Lily said as she pushed open the door to Shep's room, a pitifully equipped private room, one of five, in a dinky part of the hospital they designated the ICU. Rose and Pop wore the pinched faces of an already grieving family. "Where's Mami?"

Rose spoke first. "She went home to feed the horses."

Yeah, it was about feeding time. The horses at El Rancho Costa Plente were fed three times a day, rarely off schedule. Neighbors would be more than happy to lend a hand, but Lily knew her father was too proud to ask for help. "What's Shep's condition?"

"Twice we thought we'd lost him," her father said, "but his heart started beating again. I guess he's stronger than he looks."

"Has he been conscious?"

"Not in the last couple of hours. I swear, Lily, he was talking to horses been dead twenty years. Didn't forget a single one of their names. Talking to them like they were right here in the room. I guess that doesn't mean anything to you girls, but it gives me the shivers."

Rose put her arm around his shoulders. "We understand, Pop. There isn't a day that goes by that either of us don't think of Sparrow."

"That old mouse-colored pony? I clean forgot her name."

"Sparrow rivaled Black Beauty as far as we were concerned."

Lily eyeballed the various machines Shep was attached to: cardiac monitor, spitting out his heart rate, steady as a metronome, and the thermal paper lead for the EKG. He had an IV with a push-button morphine drip, utterly ridiculous, since the man was incapable of regulating his needs. Hopefully the nurse came in every couple hours and injected painkiller into the tubing. A Foley catheter snaked from beneath his sheets and emptied into a bag containing urine the color of a cheap Bordeaux. Taped above his bed were the letters *DNR* in black marking pen across a sheet of notebook paper. The handwritten scrawl of the "do not resuscitate" order brought Lily close to tears. Then Shep groaned, an ocean-deep sound coming to the people standing in the room from so far away that they might as well have been on another planet. Pop grimaced. "I know it's selfish of me, but I don't see how much more of this I can take."

Lily pressed the morphine pump trigger six times. Still the man's face remained twisted into a rictus of pain. "Excuse me a minute," she said.

At the nurses' station she plucked Shep's chart from the rack and flipped through the pages, reading quickly, committing the important information to memory. Two nurses stood behind the desk and, sitting in a swivel chair, a bearded man she supposed was a doctor.

"You can't do that," the younger nurse told her.

Lily gave her a look that could level a building. "Appears like I already did."

"Charts are for doctors only."

Lily handed the chart to her. "Fine, get the doctor for me. I have some questions I'd like answered."

"I'm not sure where Mr. Hallford's physician is at the moment."

"Find out. I doubt very much he'd like his patient moved without notification, but I'm telling you if he doesn't get his ass over here in about two and a half seconds, I'm calling a damn ambulance and hauling Mr. Hallford home so he can die in peace."

It always amazed Lily how easy it was to send the medical help into panic mode. The unhappy nurse dialed, and the page for Dr. Simons echoed in the hallway. "Thank you," Lily said. "I can't tell you how much I appreciate your cooperation."

The nurse kept her distance. "Are you family? He's not going to tell you anything if you're not family."

Lily mustered up every bit of restraint she possessed. "I'm *so* family you cannot imagine."

A few minutes later the doctor showed up and lazily picked up Shep's chart. Chin thrust forward, he stared at Lily. Calmly she introduced herself and shook his hand. "Mr. Hallford's condition is ominous," he told her.

Which basically told her nothing. Lily didn't falter. "I noticed on his chart you have him listed as preop for a double amputation of the legs. Surely that's a mistake. There's a signed directive to die right here in the admit papers."

"The blood supply to his legs is so diminished that we can't manage his pain unless we operate."

"Why would you cut his legs off when he's going to die anyway? He doesn't want or need surgery."

The doctor's face remained unruffled, but Lily had dealt with enough of them that she sensed the palpable rage lurking behind it.

"Perhaps you don't realize how intractable this kind of pain can be," he said.

"If it hurts so much, up his morphine."

"Only so much morphine is allowed."

"Oh, horseshit!" she exploded. "He's going to die. We both know that. Quit trying to do a mind trip on me and up the dose. You're not cutting on him and that's final." Lily took a breath. If it was going to take hardball, this white coat was about to learn how well she could pitch.

The doctor flipped through the pages of Shep's chart so fast Lily expected to hear them rip. Pop and Rose came out to the nurse's station and stood watching.

"According to your notes, doctor, his heart's stopped three times. We're talking a matter of hours, aren't we?"

"His heart has also started again three times."

"Of course it has! Mr. Hallford's got the finest pacemaker money can buy. In fact, I suspect that's the only thing standing between him and heaven. Turn it off so he can die without anymore fuss or—God forbid!—too much morphine. That's what he'd want."

The doctor's temples pulsed. "Once the pacemaker's in place, it cannot be turned off." Another page came for him, and he turned and strode off down the hallway.

"Explain this to me," Rose said. "The pacemaker is what's keeping him alive?"

Her father pinched the bridge of his nose, and tears threatened in the corners of his eyes. "Does that mean we have to sit here and watch Shep get jump-started back to life until one of us gets brave enough to hold a pillow over his face? I promised him when I checked him into this godforsaken place it wouldn't happen that way. How am I supposed to live with myself?"

"They can be turned off, Pop," Lily said, patting his arm. "I know they can. Just give me a few minutes to figure this out." She pulled her cell phone from her purse, dialed the 800 information number, and got the main number for the pacemaker company. She told the operator who answered the model number of Shep's pacemaker, and wrote down the telephone numbers for both technical information and engineering on one of her business cards so in case they lost her while transferring the call she wouldn't have to find her way through the maze twice. "Hi there," she said to the person answering the phone. "I'm in the biomedical industry, selling laparoscopes for ten years now. I need your help. A pacemaker of yours is inside my oldest and dearest friend's chest. From what I can gather from his physician, it appears to be tuned to parameters that cannot be turned off. My friend's terminal, and it's time for him to go. But the damn thing keeps kicking him back to life. Any suggestions?"

"Is this the model number?" the tech asked, and rattled off numbers that matched the ones Lily had copied from Shep's chart. "If so, blame the nicad battery. Top of the line. Those mothers'll run for years."

"Yes," Lily said. "That's the one. If I'm ever in the market, his is the model I'd choose, but we're talking end-stage prostate cancer here. Also his leg circulation is obstructed, and I've got a surgeon here telling me he wants to amputate."

"Sounds like your basic Medicare ripoff."

"Yeah, I thought so, too. Couldn't those parameters conceivably be recalibrated?"

"Absolutely. Every lab in America's got the equipment for that. What you do is set them to a range so far apart that they're unable to recapture a heartbeat. Takes maybe two minutes."

"We're dealing with some distinctly unhelpful staff here. How is it accomplished? Is there any way I can do it myself?"

"Look, if the hospital won't do it for you, we can send a rep out. Where are you?"

"Floralee, New Mexico. We're a couple hours north of Albuquerque."

"I've got a rep in Albuquerque who could be there in as long as it takes to make the drive."

"Give me the specs," Lily said, "and I'll have one more go at the doctor. Call you back in fifteen minutes if he's still being stubborn. Thanks for your help. Anytime you need anything laparoscopic, you call my voice mail. I'll make sure I take care of you personally."

She gave him her number, hung up the phone, and tucked it into her purse. Rose had both arms clasped around their father, who was studying the linoleum. Chance Wilder could put a colicking horse out of its misery, he could shoot a dying ranch dog, but saying good-bye to his friend exceeded his reach.

"Here's the way it's going to go down, Pop," she said, laying things out logically and without emotion. "I'm going to have to get in that doctor's face if we're going to do right by Shep. You might want to take Rose and go out for coffee or something, because it's probably going to get ugly before I get my way."

Rose hooked her hand through her father's arm and rubbed his sleeve. "Hot coffee, Pop," she said softly. "Doesn't that sound good? We'll call Mami from the pay phone, and she can come back and sit with us."

Pop pulled away. "I'm not going anywhere. If what you say is true, and that doctor won't take care of it, I'll kick his ass from here to Durango."

Her father was true to his word. Lily turned to the nurse who'd been listening to them since Lily made the call to the pacemaker company. Her face was drained of color. "Hate to trouble you," Lily said, "but I need to talk to the cardiologist again."

"May I tell him what this is regarding?"

Like she hadn't stood there listening to every word. "That's probably better discussed with the doctor."

Dr. Simons wasn't any happier being hauled back the second time around. Half a BLT wrapped in a napkin stuck out of the pocket of his lab coat.

"Admit it," Lily said. "You have the power to turn this son of a bitch off. I'm not leaving until you do. I'm going to be in your face and in your sandwich until the deed is done, so which is it going to be? You want me to call out the company rep or will you do it? I have the instructions right here. And a number you can call if you doubt my word."

Lily knew how to focus her energy so intently that her blood raced through her veins. She could win whatever argument she set her mind to, but winning wasn't always the prize it seemed to be. No matter how necessary her actions, it troubled her conscience to be an instrument in Shep's death.

The doctor turned to the younger nurse. "Have Mr. Hallford's pacemaker reset."

She looked up, stunned. The male nurse, who had up until this moment quietly observed while filing papers and cataloging Lily's cuss-word vocabulary touched her arm. "I'll do it," he offered, but the older nurse stepped in front of him.

"Pardon me, Doctor Simons, but I certainly didn't receive that order in writing, and neither did Cathy or Damien here. If you don't write it down, it doesn't get done. Those have been the rules since this hospital opened, and I've worked here twenty-seven years. " The nurse thrust the chart onto the counter, where it clattered between them.

Lily turned to Rose and Pop. "You both just became witnesses. We'll give him five minutes, and if he doesn't take action, I'll call the pacemaker company again. Shep won't suffer any longer, I promise."

The doctor moved his pen across the chart.

"Is that the order?"

He didn't answer.

"Excuse me, I asked you a question."

"Ma'am, there are papers that must be filled out."

"Good. Let's make sure we dot every *i*. And one more thing. In the future I'd like to suggest that you respect the patient's wishes, not stand there angling for a way to milk a few grand more out of his insurance coverage by performing unnecessary surgery."

Dr. Simons finished his paperwork and looked at her. "You technical representatives are all alike. A couple of years' education and you can't wait to challenge the physician's authority."

"And you guys are understudies to Mother Teresa. Let's get this show on the road. Move Mr. Hallford out of ICU into the hospice unit."

"Floralee doesn't have a hospice unit."

"Then move him to wherever it is you put people who aren't going to last the damn night, unless you can give me a good reason we should pay for this room and the equipment he's not going to use."

The doctor retreated back down the hallway with his BLT. Inside her jacket pocket, Lily felt the 800 number, right there at her fingertips. One way or another, this ridiculous scenario was going to end with Shep being allowed to die in peace.

Within five minutes a technician dressed in a lab coat and khakis wheeled a cart into Shep's room. Lily, Rose and Pop followed her in. "What's going on?" Lily asked, and the woman set her jaw.

"I'm not supposed to talk to you."

She held up a metal disk that reminded Lily of one of Rose's pie tins. It was about fourteen inches in diameter, shaped like a Frisbee, and she held it over Shep's chest and began to punch some numbers into what looked like a computer keyboard. "If you're resetting the parameters, thank you from the bottom of my heart," Lily said. "This man is like a second father to my sister and me. I don't want him to die, none of us wants that. But if he has to go, we don't want him to suffer one second longer than he absolutely has to."

The woman was about her age. Apparently Lily's words made a dent, because she looked her straight in the eyes and answered, "Well, if I *was* resetting the parameters, which you understand I'm not that saying I am, the process would look just about like this."

It took about three minutes for all the buttons to be pushed. The tech tucked her equipment into the cart and wheeled out of the room.

Two Hispanic orderlies were waiting. They wheeled Shep's bed to the south wing of the hospital. Pop, Rose, and Lily walked alongside. The new room looked exactly like his old one, but friendlier somehow, with a yellowing Formica bedside table and a plastic water pitcher and matching emesis tray. Once the commotion ended Shep's face relaxed. The same cheeks Lily had rubbed her little-girl face against had lost their muscle tone. Also, the catheter looked as if it might be blocked, but maybe Shep was just all done peeing. It didn't matter. Nothing did except to stand here and remember how much she loved this cranky old man, his restrained commentary on the stupid things she and Rose had insisted on doing with their lives, his wit that was as dry and hard to cross as a streambed in summertime. She pulled up a chair and sat down next to the bed. She stroked his forearm, remembering the day he'd taught Buddy Guy to ride that old gelding. One last trick, and it was a beauty. She talked to him in a normal tone of voice, though she wasn't convinced he could hear her.

"Shep? You can take off now. We're all here, Rose, Pop, and me, and we'll never stop loving you, I promise. Are you worried about Pop? Don't be. Rose and I'll be just naughty enough to keep him busy. And the horses are going to be fine, I'll see to that personally. Rose will be all right once she finds a job. I'll be fine, too, Shep, because you know what? I love Tres Quintero, and I'm going to find a way to make him marry me even if I have to get myself knocked up again to do it. But I'll always love *you* most of all, Shep. Forever and ever and ever. You say hi to Sparrow for us. Say hi to all the horses, and feed them all the carrots and sugar they want."

In the background Lily could hear her father weeping. What an awful sound it was to hear a man cry. Probably Rose had cried with the same despair when Philip died, so overcome with loss she couldn't control herself, but she wasn't crying now. *Keening*. Sometimes a word couldn't be understood until it was enacted.

Within fifteen minutes, the heart monitor began to throw irregular beats. Shep's breathing became deep and slow, like snoring, and though Lily knew to Rose and Pop that probably appeared to be restful sleep, it was Shep's worn-out body shutting itself down for the rest it craved. When his heart stopped for the last time, Rose cried out sharply, and even Lily—braced for it—felt the shock in her whole body. Pop put his hand around his friend's and held on tight until the buzzing monitor began to show a flat green line. "You old horse fucker," he said in a strained voice. "Now you can ride all day or you can play cards with the devil, it's your call. I'll see you by and by, my friend. *Que te vaya bien.*" He put on his hat and walked out of the room.

Lily and Rose stood staring at each other. The two sisters awkwardly embraced. Lily chewed her lower lip so she wouldn't break down. When they came apart, Rose said, "That was the most heroic thing I've ever witnessed in my life. Thank you, Lily, for saving Shep from all that pain."

"Oh, poop," Lily said, her voice shaking. "This one time I knew what to do. All the other times I didn't. Sometimes I did the wrongest thing."

"What do you mean?"

"Never mind. Let's go find Pop. Surely by now Mami made it back."

In the hallway Rose stopped the doctor. "Doctor Simons? I appreciate you finally respecting our wishes."

He was in the company of two men in suits, whom Lily suspected were hospital lawyers. She handed them her business card. "There isn't going to be any lawsuit," she said. "Although if he hadn't done what I asked, you can bet your bedpans there would have been. It's funny, but I guess I expected a little more humanity from a small-town hospital. This is the kind of crap I expect to find in Beverly Hills, not Floralee, New Mexico."

The men said nothing. All their hands had found their pockets. Lily and Rose walked away.

The family embraced in the hospital entranceway. Mami kissed Lily's cheek, smoothed her hair, mumbled in Spanish. Once again Rose said, "You should have seen her, she behaved like a hero," and Lily wanted to cry out, *Stop believing everyone is inherently good; your husband sure wasn't!* She'd have to tell her, beg Rose's forgiveness for being the messenger, even if it meant her sister never spoke to her again.

19

Leaving Cheyenne

When Mami and Pop left the hospital hand in hand, Rose couldn't help envy them having each other to hold on to, a warm body to help this long, sad night pass more swiftly. She thought of all those evenings Austin had slept next to her, and wished for one of them back so she could truly appreciate it.

Lily pulled at her sleeve. "You're thin. Are you sick, or back on the Doctor Done-It-Again diet?"

"Neither. Just not very hungry. Please, no lectures. Mami's already counseled me on eating disorders."

"Mami's nuts. You look terrific in that shirt. Did you lose weight everywhere but your tits?"

Rose glanced toward the snowcapped mountains in the distance. The scene in Shep's hospital room wouldn't leave her mind. "I guess."

Lily made a fist and gently bumped Rose's arm. "You luckout."

Rose smiled faintly. "Guess we should go to the ranch."

Lily sighed. "Guess so, but I sure don't want to."

The parking lot of the hospital was damp with rain. The snow packed along its edges was dirty, but winter wasn't even halfway over yet, more would come and cover the grime. "You know what kind of evening lies ahead for us," Rose said to her sister. "Mami will whip up some wonderful stew, and harp at me when I don't eat it. We'll tell our favorite memories of Shepherd and try to maintain a dignified composure, but eventually each one of us will break down. I'm so tired of crying, Lily. It's like Shep used to say whenever one of the animals died, 'Weeping won't get you your horse back.'"

Lily nodded. "Know where I really feel like going?"

"The ¡Andale! for a drink?"

"No," Lily said. "Chimayo."

"There's a church three blocks over. Of course, you walking inside voluntarily might give the priest a heart attack."

"Ha-ha. I just want to sit in the church and smell the beeswax candles burning. I want to touch all those crutches hanging on the wall and remind myself that even if miracles don't happen anymore, they did once. Do you think I'm nuts to want that, Rose, even if I don't believe in it?"

Rose hitched her purse up on her shoulder. "Whenever I mention church, you race back to California as if faith's contagious."

"This is different. I can't explain it. It's just where I feel like being right now."

"Not me." Rose exhaled, her breath silvery in the cold air. "Here's a little update for you, Lily. Your good Catholic sister? Since Austin, and well, a couple of other things, she doesn't know what to believe in anymore."

"Nonsense. Your faith's unshakable."

"Not anymore." Rose put her hands into her pockets and looked up at the sky. "It dried up." She shivered. "I think it's going to snow again. Wherever we go, let's find somewhere warm."

It was dusk, that witchy hour when depending on one's mood, the purple shadows could turn romantic or dangerous. Lily said, "Let's do it. Let's get in the car and drive over to Chimayo."

"What about Mami and Pop?"

"They'll go home to a houseful of neighbors and brandy. Besides, we've never in our lives minded our curfew. Why start now?"

"It'll be dark soon. All those thieves and heroin addicts. You've heard the stories about Chimayo."

Lily opened the door to the rental car. "Shep just died. What else can get us? I have a cell phone, four-wheel drive, and this car's costing me fifty stinking dollars a day, so let's drive it fifty stinking dollars' worth. We can listen to my new CD. Nobody'll dare mess with us. We're Wilder women."

Not to mention sisters, Rose thought.

Out the window of Lily's rental car, snowy trees and ice-covered rail fences cast sharp profiles. Smoke rose from the chimneys of well-tended adobes, and every once in a while they came across a roadside cross marking the spot where someone had lost his life and someone who remembered him had left a clutch of artificial flowers. *I'm never going to leave Floralee*, Rose told herself. *I'll take the feed store job if the restaurant doesn't work out. This is my home, and it will be until I die, too.* She realized Lily had been talking for a while, and tried to catch up with the conversation.

"So even though I had a four-star migraine and we didn't do anything, Tres stayed, he didn't leave. I never knew how intimate not having sex could be. And he tells me this bedtime story! Have you ever heard anything so romantic?"

"I guess not."

"Come on, admit you're impressed. When's the last time anybody told you a bedtime story?"

"When I was a kid, I guess."

Her sister made a right turn, and they were on a narrow, twisting road with occasional patches of ice. Lily had to slow down and switch over to four-wheel drive. "Never mind. I don't really feel like talking much either."

She turned up the CD player, and a woman's voice sang to them in a plaintive, smoky Spanish. The leather upholstery smelled like new saddles. Rose twisted her index finger inside her curly hair the way she used to when she was a little girl. The music was husky, emotional. Usually Rose listened to whatever happened to be on the radio, to the station the kids had it on before they left.

They began to pass dimly lit single-wide trailers and shaggy horses pastured in fields of dry, brown winter grasses. The occasional adobe storefront offered chile *ristras* and crudely carved statues of the *santos*, or local weavings. "There was no reason on earth Shep had to die in that much pain," Lily said as they navigated the hairpin turnoff for the church. "If he'd croaked anywhere but America, he'd have done it pain-free. Freaking AMA—at their core they're Puritanical Calvinists, and on the outside they dress in worse suits than Republicans."

They'd never see him alive again, but Rose knew that wouldn't stop her from finding Shep everywhere she looked around the ranch. "At least it's over."

"Yeah, but it'll take me three weeks of solid bitching before I can stop thinking about it. I'm going to write that hospital a letter."

They parked the Expedition in the empty lot, and Rose pulled her coat close as they hurried across the cracked asphalt toward the adobe archway. The headstones in the churchyard were rimed with ice. One nice thing about Catholic churches was that their doors were always open. Rose's heart thumped as it did whenever she tried to tell a lie. She felt ashamed to enter a place filled with such history and hope. "Maybe I shouldn't go in."

"Why?" Lily said. "What's the problem?"

She stopped and looked around her, as if the graves and statues might accuse her out loud of the doubt she felt at her core. "Because I don't know if I believe anymore."

"Rose, this place is a tourist spot. Do you think they tell the Japanese to stay out because they're Buddhists? Quit fretting and let's go inside where it's warm."

Lily struck a match and lit vigil candles. Rose stuffed her spare change into the offertory box. When the match burned low, Lily singed her finger and cried out.

"Stick it in the holy water," Rose suggested.

"Oh, leave me alone," Lily said sharply, and turned away from her sister.

Standing at the altar, Rose wondered if Lily would ever truly recover from Shep's death. Her sister was tough on the outside, but inside was a different matter. Shep had been Lily's compass. Not even Tres back in her life could replace that. Rose wandered into the tiny chapel where those who'd made the pilgrimage had left behind crutches, braces, casts, photographs, handwritten pleas, holy cards, artificial flowers, rosaries, *milagros*, and candles—all manner of candles—wax and wick burning so fervently that even in winter, the room didn't need a heater. The doorway was so low she had to stoop to pass through, to get to that room with the hole dug through the floor. The indentation was nearly two feet deep. Rose got down on all fours and put her hand into the hollow. The red earth felt cold and ordinary to her fingertips. It wasn't the original earth supposedly responsible for the renowned cures; too many miracle seekers came here and scooped up Dixie cups, Baggies, and film canisters of the stuff for a souvenir for that to have lasted. But over the fill dirt the priests said blessings, and they believed, deeply enough to commit their whole lives to God.

After scooping out her handful, she tucked two dollars into the donation box. By candlelight the soil appeared silky and dry, and felt to Rose almost as if she was holding a part of last summer in her palm. She fingered the grains, about a tablespoon's worth. Clasping her fingers tight so she wouldn't spill any, she slid her fist up under Amanda's shirt until her hand rested just above the swell of her left breast. She opened her fingers and let the cool grainy dirt fall against her skin, slipping inside her bra cup and down her ribs. As she rubbed it in, she imagined that all its elements could travel through her pores, part the tight muscle beds and soften them, finally arriving at her sore heart in some perfect and pure form at the molecular level. She massaged until the infinitesimal grit began to abrade her skin, and then she removed her hand, wiped it on her pants leg, and walked back into the chapel, stopping at the altar for the *Santo Niño*.

She knelt to say a prayer for Shep's soul. But the sight of the peeling statue lit by candleglow and the bouquet of artificial daisies in the white Easter basket alongside it awoke a question in her that she couldn't ignore. What was she doing here, really? Shep had been a truly decent man, and if heaven existed, he was already there. Remembering the dead was an act of respect, but it hardly took courage. Rose rummaged through her purse, looking for paper. All those freebie real estate scratch pads left on her doorstep, and all she could find was a couple of old shopping lists: *milk, bread, dog food, cheese, tomatoes, Tampax, fabric softener* on one; *the bank, post office, library, office supply store* on the other. The idea that she had ever planned such an orderly life on a weekly basis seemed positively archaeological. These days she bought stamps one at a time. She turned the lists over and scribbled quickly, filling every inch of one paper before going onto the next.

God, if you're there, please take Austin Donavan out of my heart. Help me move past this into some place where I can at least function. I've tried to make sense of all this, but if there was a lesson for me to learn by in falling in love again, I must have missed it. Austin belongs to Leah and he always will. Now help me let him go.

At the edge of the paper, she paused, reading over what she'd written, trying to make certain the words she offered up were honest. Chimayo was legendary; one didn't trifle with such power. Deep down Rose knew she wasn't saying all that needed to be said. She had to put the other part down, too.

She picked up her pen and began to write, in smaller script this time, directly over the words on her lists. *If, on the other hand, what I feel for Austin was meant to be*—there came that song into her head again—*then I'm kneeling here asking you to send him back to me in whatever form you care to see fit. I love him as much now as I ever will, and that's not going to change just because he doesn't love me back. I'll take him back in my life even if it means we only get to be these awkward friends who always bump up against the memories of what once happened in my bed, even if only that. Yes.* Then, not because she felt a connection to her heritage, but simply because certain phrases of Spanish beat English hands down, she wrote this too: *Regresame la otra mitad de mi corazón*—return to me the other half of my heart.

She folded and tucked the notes into the basket of artificial flowers. A film of dust coated the *milagros* scattered at the *Santo's* feet, among them a heart stuck through with a sword, a leg bent at the knee, kidneys attached to the spinal column, and a set of hollow pelvic bones. At the moment she let the notes drop out of reach, Rose vowed that no matter what happened, from this moment forward, she was going to be okay. It was her choice. She understood that now. Prayer seemed appropriate, but none of her Catholic devotions, so committed to memory she recited them by rote. The words that came to her she'd heard recited in AA meetings: *God, grant me the serenity to accept the things I cannot change, courage to change the things I can, and the wisdom to know the difference.* Who could tell, maybe that same minute, Austin was standing in a circle in one of those meetings, saying it himself—in a way, saying it along with her?

Lily sat in the third pew, sucking on her sore finger, looking pensive. Rose scooted in beside her and moved aside a dog-eared Spanish missal somebody had forgotten to put away.

"You were gone so long," her sister said. "Did you say the rosary twice?"

Rose shook her head no. "I was being incredibly selfish, asking for my own miracle."

Lily looked surprised. "About freaking time."

"Do you think you could not talk like that in church?"

"Rose, I think God's probably got more important things to worry about than my vocabulary."

"So you admit He exists."

"I admit nothing. Rose, I believe in *good.* That's "God" with an extra vowel. I've got as much right as the next person to say what's on my mind, and to say it the best way I know how. That's the stuff of faith, Rose. Not the hokey-smokey God-box stuff, but belief in *doing* good."

"*La pasionara.*"

"Yes, I'm passionate, and I've decided to stop apologizing for that, too. Tres can take me as I am or he can hit the road." Lily pulled her knees up on the pew and hugged them. Tears gathered at the corners of her eyes. Rose could see her sister's ankles under the designer jeans, the expensive socks with the Ralph Lauren logo peeking out like a tattoo. The heart bore its own sort of ritual scarring, too, even if nobody but a sister ever saw it. "There's something I need to tell you," Lily said. "I don't want to, because it's going to hurt you to hear it."

Rose felt her pulse speed up. "Then don't tell me."

Lily pressed her lips together. "I have to, Rose. I think not telling you is why we fight all the time. It's chewing on my guts. I don't want to go the rest of my life carrying this around even if it means you never talk to me again. It's time you knew. It concerns Philip."

The hair on the back of Rose's neck tickled uncomfortably, and she had a feeling she knew exactly what Lily was going to tell her, as soon as she could force her tongue to move past the fear stopping it. Oh, she didn't want to hear this any more than Lily wanted to tell it. Her sister was going to tell her that she knew what Philip had done, that other people knew. Rose's face went hot, and she fought the urge to run from the church into the darkness, because anything out there felt safer what was happening right here. "I already know. I know what he did." She picked up the Spanish missal again and flipped through its impossibly thin pages. "Being his widow makes me sort of like a permanent wife. I wanted to live out this fantasy that my husband loved me, and that part of that love included fidelity, except for maybe one tiny slip. What an idiot I was."

"You're wrong," Lily said. "Philip was the idiot. I'm sorry if I hurt you, bringing this up, but I should have years ago."

"You didn't hurt me. Philip did. All the way from the grave. I think I felt it was my fault, being so naive to assume he was faithful. It's been bothering me a lot lately."

"Why didn't you talk to me about it?"

Rose shrugged. "I don't know. After Austin, maybe I felt I had to prove I was strong. The Widow Flynn routine."

Lily placed her hand on her sister's arm. She rubbed it up and down for a moment. "Rose, he didn't sleep with just anyone, he slept with Leah Donavan."

Rose turned her head to look into her sister's face. Lily stared back, unblinking.

"I saw them once, in Taos. I confronted him, and he made me promise not to tell you. It was easy at the time, since you weren't talking to me anyway. Funny, isn't it? The one time I have something important to tell you and I couldn't. I intend never to let that happen again."

Rose looked up at the altar with its gilt statuary glinting in the candlelight. Somehow the idea of Philip's infidelity had been so much easier to bear when the woman involved was faceless. Leah Donavan— that made his cheating something else entirely, like learning your parents had adopted you but never told you, or leaving the scene of an accident that was your fault—acts that were harder to forgive. She thought of Thanksgiving night, the stupid incident with the potatoes, and Austin cleaning up after Leah—one way or another he was always cleaning up after her. Rose wished she'd flung the potatoes in Leah's face. It struck her as absurdly funny that yet again, as if their lives had intersected in some Gordian knot, this knowledge tied her more firmly than ever to Austin. "You probably know what to do next," she said to her sister. "How to put this in perspective. I envy you, Lily."

"Don't. All my life I was so jealous of you. You had this perfect life, two babies, your own little house, all the things I said I never wanted but ached for. When I figured out what Philip was doing, it hurt me, too. I felt like he was cheating on all of us. But not even that stopped me from wanting what you had. I still want that."

Rose closed the prayer book and ran her thumb down its leather binding. "Excuse me? You had college and a career, and you got to travel all over the world. You make your own way, and you're a better rider than I'll ever be. If there was any envy involved, it was *me* wanting to be like *you*."

"Stop it! I'd've traded all that in one single heartbeat to have what you had. I felt like I wasn't allowed, like Mami didn't want that kind of life for me, that only you deserved it."

"Lily, I felt exactly the same way! Keep Rose in her little house, working menial jobs; don't let her step outside that definition. Only Lily gets more. You don't know how many times I hated you for your successes."

They were quiet for a few minutes. Rose didn't know what else to say, and every time Lily opened her mouth, she shut it. The repressed emotions eventually transformed into giggles. "You know what our problem is?" Lily said. "We know how to fight, but we can't figure out how to get along."

Just then it became very cold inside the church. Rose could hear the wind rattling outside, determined fingers working their way through the walls, as if the adobe were full of chinks. One of the doors bumped open, and both sisters jumped. An eerie howl of wind followed the blast of cold air, and the candles in the wrought-iron grate guttered. All but one of them blew out.

"Shep!" Lily cried out. "I can feel him here, can't you?"

The skin on Rose's cheeks felt prickly. For a fleeting moment it almost felt like fingers touching her face. Then the wind moved on, and the single candle remained, burning, in a church that had been built more than a hundred years ago by Spaniards who believed in their religion enough to leave behind this architecture as a testament. They were two sisters whose blood, however diluted, connected them to that. No more secrets remained between them. Rose took Lily's hand and squeezed it tight. "Are you positive it was Leah Donavan?"

Lily nodded. "She really gets around, I guess, because Tres told me he slept with her once himself. Busy lady."

Rose sighed. "Well, that's going to take a while to sink in. Maybe I'd better light another candle to keep Shep company." She got up and did just that, stood at the altar awhile, watching the wax puddle around the wick before she sat down in the pew and took her sister's hand again.

Long ago Mami had told her daughters that the dead could see light, that lighting candles provided a medium through which some people could communicate with those who'd departed this earth. Perhaps because of that, or innately, both girls grew up adoring candles. They lit them for meals, during baths, and set birthday cakes ablaze whenever the opportunity arose. Rose closed her eyes and forced from her mind the image of Leah Donavan with Philip. She remembered Shep in a dozen different ways: Cutting the clinches on various horses' shoes, mending fence felled by bad weather. Dog-cussing the fact that nobody had invented affordable post-and-rail, let alone something that would last ten years. At her wedding reception, she'd witnessed Shep and twenty other cowboys performing the "gator," that silly all-male line dance fueled by beer and bravado, in which they snaked across the dance floor in some kind of cut-loose brotherhood they would deny as soon as the sun came up. She thought of the proud way he'd insisted on taking care of himself after his pacemaker operation, the utter dogged-ness of the machine, and how Lily'd had to scream to it get discon-nected in order for him to die. Even after he'd had the contraption installed, Shep still worked horses, but Pop usually managed to be alongside. He had taken CPR classes. He was always watching Shep out of the corner of his eye. How he must have worried. How much this must hurt him. It was like losing your brother, only worse, because Shep was more loving and faithful than any brother could be.

And she thought of Philip, too, taken from her in an instant by some drunken skier who probably had all manner of rationalizations for the "accident" and had tucked that unfortunate little episode into his past. How only now, after Lily telling her, she was able to under-stand what in the hell he was doing in that part of Taos when it wasn't even his territory. Leah's father had a furniture store there, and some-times she helped out—or in this case, helped herself. Anyone but Leah Donavan, and the whole thing wouldn't seem so ludicrous. She let go of Lily's hand, which she had been grasping so tightly that her fingers tingled. "Maybe someday I can grow a big enough heart to forgive Philip, but I doubt I'll ever forgive myself for being that blind. Like Shep used to say, 'Fool me once, shame on you; fool me twice, shame on me.' I am going to miss him so much."

They put their heads together and cried, trading Shep's dopey old sayings back and forth because it seemed important to share that, and to leave their tears in a place used to sorrow. They swabbed their faces with all the Kleenex Rose could scrounge from her purse, and exchanged tentative smiles. Whatever happened after today, the things they'd said to one another had made them equals. At the holy water font on their way out of the church, Rose dipped her middle fingertip into the water. Touching Lily's forehead, between her breasts and each shoulder, she made the sign of the cross. "Even if you don't believe," she said, "What harm can come from a blessing?"

Lily responded by dunking all her fingers—her thumb, too—then flicking the water in Rose's face.

Rose gasped. "That's sacrilege."

"No, it isn't," Lily said. "This is how bad girls bless themselves. I'm sure it says so, somewhere in the Bible."

Shep's body was to be released the following day, to Mami and Pop, who in the few hours since his death had managed to get hold of both a plain pine casket and a friend with a backhoe who owed them a favor. Lily and Rose spent the night at El Rancho Costa Plente, beginning in their old bedrooms, and then around three in the morning, sleepless and hungry, they bumped into each other in the hall on the way downstairs to the kitchen for a snack. They ate crackers on the couch by the fireplace, which was still burning and, with the addition of another log, began to blaze. They intended to sit by the fire and keep each other company only until they could face their pillows again, but the next thing Rose knew, she awoke with Lily's arm around her, both of them flopped back against the couch hugging throw pillows, eye level with two inquisitive greyhounds who had very cold and equally wet noses.

"Oh my God," Rose said, bolting upright. "I totally forgot Joanie and Chachi!"

"They won't die one night on their own," Lily said, rubbing her eyes. "I leave Buddy alone all the time."

"They're not alone. I left them at Austin's clinic. It's Max. Somebody has to give him his morning Bute. I better drive home before he goes so lame he can't stand up."

One of her mother's neighbors stuck her head into the doorway. She was a ranchwoman all the way—short, blond, with leathery skin and heavy-duty turquoise jewelry. She stood there towel-drying a Nambé platter Rose remembered Mami using for every major holiday. "All that's been taken care of by people who rise at a decent hour. Look at you girls. Sleeping like puppies, at your age. Get showered and dress. There's a lot to be done before tonight, and your mother needs help."

"Where're Mami and Pop?"

"Went to the hospital to pick up the body. There's rolls and coffee for breakfast, and somebody brought by a real nice honey-glazed ham. One thing for sure, girls. Nobody ever starves at a funeral."

* * *

Around noon she and Lily pulled on boots and jackets to watch the men dig the grave. Pop and a few of his buddies dismantled the fence that surrounded the family cemetery, and then Denny Wayne drove his 416V CAT backward through the snow, stopping just short of where they planned to bury Shep. The ground was frozen a good twelve inches deep, so he hooked up the chisel attachment and hammered until the earth was tillable. Then the men removed the chisel, reinstalled the bucket, and he dug the grave.

Lily held Jody Jr. by the collar. The scent of dirt was strong in the air, and the mother of all the ranch dogs seemed bewitched by it.

"She wants to help dig the grave," Rose said.

When the men got to the hand-shoveling part, Lily let Jody Jr. go. "I think Shep would have approved," she said.

It hurt Rose's eyes to behold that red earth, so out of season in December. Railroad ties separated the individual graves, which went back further than the Wilder family, to long before Pop had inherited the land. Out of respect for those buried here who weren't his family, he'd fenced off the older section in chain link. When they were kids, it got Lily all spooked—*Think of all those dead people!*—but Rose kind of enjoyed walking around over there, though Pop had forbidden her to do so. He'd take off for town, and she knew the exact spot where the chain link sagged, just how far to pull it away without bending it permanently, how to slip under the fence and explore without anyone finding out.

The gravestones were so old that many of the inscriptions were no longer readable. The ones that were bought tears to her eyes: HIJO MIJO (little son of mine); ADORADO MADRE (beloved mother); NUESTRO QUERIDO (our dear). There were two, side by side, bearing the Montoya cattle brand, which went clear back to the time of land grants. And MOTHER OF NONE: MOTHER TO ALL, that one made her throat nearly close up. But some of them were so funny she couldn't help but laugh, like DUN LOGGIN, DUN COWIN, TOO. And others were so plain and poignant that Rose could only imagine the whole, sad cloth of the stories that accompanied them, like the old rotting wood pieces that lay in the dirt in an unmistakable crib shape surrounding a pint-size headstone bearing the words PRIMOGENITO HIJO—firstborn son. Her absolute favorite remained the pink marble headstone etched with clouds, a single bird winging his way across the words: GONE HOME.

Leaning against the pile of shovels was a crucifix that would mark Shep's grave, constructed of horseshoes welded together to form a cross. Rose wondered if the farrier had finished assembling it last night, if the silvery seams might still hold the torch's heat. Later on her father would order a headstone similar to the other Wilder graves, and Pop would know just the right words to put down, or maybe it would simply be Shep's name, the dates, and a design of a man on horseback. Then, on November the second of every year, like she always did, Mami would come here to decorate the final resting places, to leave behind some earthly token of what Shep had loved best, probably a paperback copy of *Leaving Cheyenne*.

"Rose!" someone called, and she turned away from the business of sober-faced men lifting shovels, aiming them at the broken earth, huffing out hot breath into the cold air as they squared the corners, and went to see how she could help.

"Don't you wonder how Shep could have stood this?" Lily asked as they made their way through the crowd gathering at the graveside. Everyone was dressed in Sunday clothes, which for many meant flannel shirts that had been ironed. "Not the horsemen—he would have expected them—but all the others."

Rose nodded. An endless trail of artists, musicians, photographers, not to mention the mayor of Floralee, Judge Trujillo, those few among the bedrock of Santa Fe—neither the new-money people nor the elite—but the old-time cattlemen, Hispano shopkeepers whose families went way back, the few journalists who still cared enough to write the truth about the state, even several priests were in attendance. "I didn't realize this many people knew Shep."

"Me neither."

Mami shushed them. "Girls, this is the holy part of the service!"

Rose noticed Paloma and Nacio in the crowd; then, standing a few people away, Benito, the restaurant manager—her boss, she guessed, if things worked out—and next to him, Austin Donavan, who held on to dog leashes, which must have meant Joanie and Chachi were in attendance. Benito held up his hand in greeting but didn't smile. Rose fluttered her fingers in return, and she saw Austin turn to take in the scenario. He didn't look happy.

A light snow was beginning to fall. Hard to imagine that Christmas was coming, that anyone would ever feel like celebrating. Maybe she'd fly out to California and see Lily's place, or maybe they'd both go someplace warm, Texas or Mexico. Maybe she'd just stay home and put her feet up. The sound of a motorcycle broke her reverie, and she wondered who was foolhardy enough to ride one of those machines in such bad weather.

Lily took hold of her arm. "Try not to cry," she advised. "Bite the inside of your cheeks; that always works for me."

"Lily," Rose hissed. "I'm perfectly composed. Stop ordering me around."

"Sure, right now you are. But you won't be in a minute. Here comes your son."

The priest was speaking. So far the service was in Spanish, and she knew she had to be quiet or appear disrespectful. Later on the eulogies would be delivered in English, friends would share memories, and people would relax, even laugh, but Shep had strong ties among the community, as well as some Spanish blood that rated him this service. Nevertheless, the sight of Second Chance after so many months of not knowing where he was proved to be too much for Rose to hold herself together. Great soundless sobs began to shake her body, and she pulled away from Lily to go to him. So handsome—that dusky olive skin, the dark hair shaved close, the cheekbones that echoed his father's—she had loved Philip, she *had*, for a long time, and Leah Donavan couldn't take that away. That ridiculous skull-and-crossbones earring, however, had to go. Despite his screw-ups, her son had somehow managed to grow into a man.

"Mom, why are you crying?" he whispered, putting his arms around her shoulders as they embraced.

"Because I'm your mother and I love you."

Mami came over to them and took hold of Second Chance's gloves. Pop smiled from where he stood between the priest and the shaman, who was intent on getting his two cents' worth in, smiled, too. The Wilder family stood up straight and did right by a man who had always done right by them. "*Achaques quiere la muerte,*" the priest intoned.

"What did he say?" Second Chance asked.

Lily's beeper went off, and she thrust her hand into her pocket to silence it.

Rose opened her mouth to tell her son she wasn't sure, but Mami spoke right over her. "That death needs no excuses to take the corpse. It's shameful that you've forgotten your languages. If this weren't an important part of the service, I'd box your ears."

Then everyone was praying, the first of many invocations that would be said today: *Hail Mary, radiant splendor, intercede with Christ for us and the soul of Shep Hallford . . ."*

Rose bent her head to recite the words. When she looked up, her gaze wandered over to Austin. He was still staring at her, and he didn't look any happier than he had the last time she'd looked. Chachi was pulling on the leash. Austin had picked Joanie up and held her in his arms. Her sleek coat looked newly laundered, and she was wearing one of those ridiculous dog sweaters that they had on sale on the rack across from Paloma's desk. Nobody ever bought them. It was unfair, him using the dogs like that. He had to know how much that got to her.

The man who ran the hardware store and eight of his cronies all removed their cowboy hats and held them over their hearts. After calling out a single note that seemed to lift and take wing in the chilly air, the others joined in and began singing "The Cowboy's Lament," which was neither a hymn nor particularly resonant of Shep's life, but had been his favorite song. If you had a heart, and mostly everybody here did, this was the moment that tipped you over into tears. Even Austin was blinking. The light snow began to fall more thickly now, a thin crust building up on the pine casket. Her father gestured, and the singers skipped the last verse and went straight to the chorus. Six men took hold of straps attached to a large canvas on which the coffin rested, and lowered the box into the ground. After the Wilder family walked by, throwing in yellow roses, every person attending the service scooped up a handful of dirt and tossed it into the grave until the casket was covered. Rose watched her father, his shoulders dusted white with snow, cross his arms in front of him and clear his throat as he stood at the foot of the grave. Without faltering once, he said, "Your foot's in the stirrup, your pony won't stand; good-bye, old partner, you're leaving Cheyenne."

Next to her, Rose heard Lily snuffle and say, "Now *that* Shep would have loved."

* * *

It took about half an hour before the party got into full swing. Lily and
Rose stood in Mami's kitchen, taking hot dishes from the oven, opening drawers, searching for serving utensils, mopping spills when the
room got too crowded and people bumped into one another. Second
Chance sat on the counter eating a two-inch-thick peanut-butter-and-
cheese sandwich.

"That is beyond disgusting," Lily told him. "If you had any idea
what that crap does to your arteries, you'd throw it in the trash."

"I'm young," he countered. "I burn twelve thousand calories a day.
I can eat like a caveman, Aunt Lily."

"How on earth does riding a motorcycle burn calories?"

He winked. "I didn't say riding motorcycles was all I did."

Rose held up a wooden spoon. "Hold it right there. If we're ventur-
ing into any discussion of your sex life, let your mother leave the
room."

Second Chance and Lily stared at her blankly, obviously waiting
for her to do just that.

"Just let me get this platter, and then I'll be out of your way."

The enchiladas she carried into the living room were immediately
taken from her hands by Benito. "Those look wonderful," he said. "Did
you make them?"

"No. I think one of the neighbors must have. I make my own red
sauce. The store-bought stuff is too salty for me."

"I agree. I'd love to try yours sometime."

Rose helped him clear a place on the table for the tray. She felt that
distinct discomfort of the double-entendre lurking in his words. Even
if it was unintentional, how could she go to work for a man who had
the hots for her? "Maybe I'll bring some by the restaurant."

"Or you could teach me to make it in your kitchen."

"Maybe," she said, looking for a graceful exit. "I'd better get back to
the food."

"*Uno momento, por favor?*"

Rose stopped. "What is it?"

Benito took the hot pads from her hands and led her into the
foyer, where Mami's best Navajo rug hung on the wall. "I brought my
camera. I was hoping you'd let me take your picture."

"Some other day, Benito."

"It won't take long. I had this idea the day your mother brought you to lunch. Of how I could shoot you to bring out your cheekbones."

"Not today. I look awful. I cried off all the makeup I was wearing. I have mascara ground into my cheeks, plus I'm not wearing any lipstick."

"Most of the magic happens in the developing, Rose. Just let me stand you against this blanket like that. I promise, when I'm done with the portrait, you'll look beautiful, not that you don't already. Just a couple of quick shots."

Now she couldn't take the restaurant job. Office romances never worked into anything except a real bad deal: Witness Austin. People walked by, headed in either direction, and rather than create a scene, she decided to make the best of things. "All right, but do it quickly."

Benito posed her in a three-quarter view, stepped back, then reached over and gently rearranged her hair, tucking some of it behind her left ear, pulling a few tendrils down so that they touched her eyebrow. It felt no more intimate than being touched by a hairdresser. Then he was all business, shutter clicking away, and it was as if she were no more fascinating than the pattern in the rug. Rose forced a smile.

"I don't want you to smile," he said. "Relax your face."

Austin walked into the foyer, Joanie still in his arms, though he'd removed the dopey sweater, thank God. He stood behind the photographer, and Rose felt her breathing quicken.

"Yes, that expression exactly," Benito said. "Whatever you're thinking of, don't stop. Just a few more pictures, Rose. I can't quit when it's this good. Let me finish the roll."

Austin allowed him to fire off six or seven more shots, then he moved in front of the camera and grabbed her hand roughly. "I think you're done, pal," he said, pulling Rose outside onto the porch, where several men stood drinking from coffee mugs. Rose could smell the spicy odor of cinnamon schnapps, and she wondered if that scent made Austin's mouth water.

"That was polite of you," she said, taking her hand from his.

"What kind of manners does it take to act like a cover girl at a goddamn funeral for somebody who was close enough to be your uncle?"

"Shut up, Austin. I hate it when you swear. Give me my dogs."

He stepped back. "No. I'm holding them ransom until you start behaving yourself."

Rose sighed. She folded her arms across her breasts. He'd yanked her outdoors before she could put on a coat, and the black dress she wore, one of Mami's, was thin and low cut. She shivered. "Austin, do you think this is funny?"

"Never said I did."

"You're really starting to piss me off."

"Ditto back at you, Mrs. Flynn."

A part of her wanted nothing more than to step right up and slap his handsome face. But Joanie had seen enough trauma, and she didn't care to make a scene. "Fine, whatever. Tell me what you want so I can go back inside before I freeze to death."

He pushed his wire-rimmed glasses up his nose. She could see the vein in his temple pulse. "I want you to come back to work."

"This is why you behave like a boor and yank me outdoors? This couldn't have waited for a phone call? No." She took hold of Chachi's leash and grabbed for Joanie, but Austin stepped back before she could reach her.

"Please, Rose."

"I said no. I found another job."

"Does it provide you with insurance benefits and a decent enough wage so you can make your house payment and buy a new dress now and then? Does it come ready-made with animals who appreciate your kind touch and people who care about you?"

"All I need is a paycheck." She was lying, and Austin knew that, too, but that didn't stop either of them from pretending that this argument concerned employment.

He sat down on the porch swing and nervously twisted Joanie's collar. "I know I don't deserve it, but I want another chance, Rose."

"When was the last time you were at Chimayo?"

"Hell, I don't remember. What's that got to do with my question?"

"Nothing." Rose looked him over, trying to see him objectively. Other women wouldn't find that thin, angular face and little beard compelling. What was he? Sober a week? Two? Aching to get laid, and Leah out of town? Leah, who'd bedded her husband, and Lily's boyfriend, too. "I think we had our chances, Austin, and they passed us by. Give me back my dog, and let's get on with our lives."

After awhile he nodded. "Guess I was a horse's ass to ask."

Rose set Chachi on the porch and looped his leash around her right hand while she took Joanie in her arms. "Oh, I don't know if I agree with you. Actually I think you were a horse's ass a long time before today."

Austin put both hands on his waist, as if bracing himself against her words. Then he stood up, his mouth drawn tight, and pulled her to him, hard, close enough so that Rose could feel the sharp protrusions of his hipbones, the curve of his hand against her waist, his fingers opening and closing there in deliberate familiarity. He kissed her once, on the forehead, then pushed her away. "Please accept my condolences on your loss," he said. "If you can stand to."

He hurried down the steps and made his way through all the pickup trucks and four-wheel-drive Jeeps and the few sports cars parked there toward his own truck. Rose listened to his boots crunching in the snow, each footfall coming down so hard it broke through the thin crust and met the gravel. He opened the driver's-side door, got in, and slammed it twice as hard as he needed to. The engine caught, and, like a teenager, he spun his wheels in the snow before he drove away.

She pressed her face against Joanie's coat and stood there watching the space where his truck had been parked for God knows how long, when she noticed a girl making her way up the drive. She was dressed in a green cape, her face obscured by the hood, and she was waving. Rose squinted. It was Amanda, a day late as usual.

"Some freak in a truck just tried to run me down," she said.

Just once—it wasn't as if it would kill them—Rose wished one of her children could start a conversation with "Hello."

20

CC: The World

"I can't believe how mean I was to Austin just now," Rose said as she led her daughter into the kitchen. "I'm thoroughly ashamed."

Lily abandoned the mushrooms she was slicing and rushed forward to give her niece a hug. "If he smarts a little, maybe he'll learn some manners," she said to Rose over Amanda's shoulder. As she pulled back to look at her niece, her expression softened. "Amanda the panda. You're hell to track down, you know that?"

Behind the China girl pale makeup and the black lipstick, Amanda was still the same kid Lily remembered, snapping her gum, riding horses through the center of town, getting into trouble just like her aunt had. "We're always on the road, Aunt Lily. That's life with a band."

Second Chance laughed out loud. He'd finished his big cheese sandwich, and now he was eating cocktail olives out of a jar. He looked at his sister for a few moments. "Jeez, Mando, whatever happened to your hair, I'm really sorry about it."

Amanda protectively cradled the dreadlocks with her fingers. "Screw you, Chance. They're called dreads."

"A man we all loved has just died," Rose quietly reminded them. "Do you think maybe you could watch your language?"

"It wasn't me swearing," Chance said. "Anyway, they look more like deads, what's left of the roadkill when the buzzards are done."

Lily put her arm around her niece. "Kids, here's an idea. If you're going to get into a knock-down-drag-out, at least do it in the living room so our guests can enjoy the show."

"There isn't anybody out there under forty years old," Second Chance said.

Lily smacked him on the knee with the spatula she was holding. "Excuse me? I'm not forty yet."

"You know what I meant."

"*I* happen to be forty," Rose pointed out.

"Mother," Amanda whined. "Make Second Chance say he's sorry about my hair."

Rose gave her daughter a weary look. "Amanda, if that was all it took to get you two to behave peaceably, I'd've done it years ago."

"The two of you stop acting like brats," Lily said. "I hate to tell you, Amanda, dreads will make your hair fall out. It's true; this doc I know from South Africa tried it. Ended up having to shave his head, and when it grew back, the hair was all thin and different. Not even Rogaine helped. He ended up having to get hair plugs. His was more damaged than yours, though, so if you got rid of them right this second you might be okay. You might want to try combing them out with this conditioner I've got. It costs fifty dollars an ounce, but it's worth every penny. Hey, Rose, remember what Mami always said about our hair?"

She and Lily put their arms around each other's shoulders and recited the line as if they were saying the Pledge of Allegiance. "Your hair is your flag."

Amanda touched the ropy strands. "Caleb thinks my hair is cool."

"Caleb?" Second Chance said. "What kind of dopey name is that? Sounds like a rap singer. No, I take it back. It just sounds made up."

Amanda tore her cape off and threw it on the table, just missing the pasta salad, into which Lily was sliding some roasted peppers. Underneath the cape she was wearing a shapeless gray dress not even an Amish woman would be caught dead in, and tall black boots that needed resoling. "Like 'Second Chance' doesn't sound about as pathetic as your life is? How many bones have you broken this year? How many of your teeth are capped? You suck as a brother. I don't even miss you."

"Same to you, rat-hair."

"Mother!"

At the stove, Rose emptied a can of chopped tomatoes into a pot. "You'll notice the only thing I'm paying attention to is my spaghetti sauce."

Lily watched her niece and nephew escalate from chop fights to childish faces to mock blows and finally end up in mutual friendly laughter. She and Rose had been the same way. The bond between these two spoiled children would carry them a long way. Someday, when they'd weathered enough road, they might even be nice to each other, and reap the benefits of family.

Second Chance slid down off the counter. "So, dogface, you want to see my bike?"

Amanda shrugged. "Why not. There's nothing else to do."

"Put the lid back on those olives, please," Rose said as she stirred the mushrooms Lily handed to her into the pan.

Lily inhaled the comforting aroma of Rose's spaghetti sauce. Her sister grated carrots into the tomato puree, tempering the acid with sweetness. Seconds before she ladled the sauce onto the pasta, she'd bunch up fresh basil, coarsely chop it, and sprinkle it in. Like an arranged marriage, those disparate flavors had no choice but to fuse passionately. The end result was a close enough cousin to pesto that Lily could eat it on Krisprolls. All she'd had today was coffee and a piece of bread. The fact that there seemed to be no end to the food made her nervous, because no matter how full people became at this party, somewhere out there another person was hungry. When the music started, and the dancing got under way, Shep's funeral would transform into a typical New Mexican hoedown. Lily ached for some time alone, so she could take in what had happened to her world, not to mention the horses'. First chance she got, she planned to sneak away on the pretext of feeding them.

"Your boots are fine, but you'll have to lose the skirt," Second Chance said. "And the Elvira face has to go, too, or I'll ditch you in the first snowbank deep enough to hide your body. You got jeans in that skanky backpack, or just ganja?"

"Of course I have jeans, but I'm not changing my makeup. It took me an hour to get it to look this way."

Rose turned to say something, apparently thought better of it, and clamped her mouth shut.

Lily knew if she were the one to suggest helmets, the kids might comply. "No way either of you're riding in this weather unless you're both wearing brain buckets. I mean it, Second Chance. I've seen emergency room carnage like you wouldn't believe. Brains coming out peoples' noses. Faces scraped down to bone plastic surgery couldn't repair."

The dirt-bike king remained unfazed. "I've only got one helmet with me."

"Then she can wear a riding helmet. There're dozens in the barn. Come on, Amanda, let's go find you one."

Lily pulled on her coat, and they sidled through the partygoers to the outdoors. The snow had stopped. The horses meandered around the arena, anxious about the ruckus taking place in their normally quiet world. They lingered by the fence, hopeful that the number of people increased their chances of handouts. Lily spotted Winky, paired off with another pregnant mare, and wondered if mare talk, that almost imperceptible exchange of nickers between female horses, intensified during the gestational period. She was curious if their conversations focused on the developing foals they carried or if—like most women—they spent the majority of their time discussing stallions.

In the tack room she and Amanda stamped their feet at the cold coming up through the floorboards. Second Chance lingered by the fence patting the necks and blunt muzzles of curious horses. "Hey, look," Amanda said. "That's my yellow schooling helmet from when I used to show Max. What's it doing up here?"

"I don't know," Lily said. "Your mom probably left it. Sometimes she trailers Max up and rides with Pop. Maybe it fits her better than any of the others."

"Lame," Amanda said, as if once claiming ownership made a thing hers for life. "She could buy her own."

Lily bristled. "Hey, your mom is living on a budget, ska girl. And speaking of money, what is the deal with you swiping her grocery funds? That was a perfectly rotten thing to do."

Amanda's face reflected total innocence. "Aunt Lily, I swear—"

Lily held up a hand. "Please. Anytime you start a sentence with 'I swear,' I'm sure you're lying. Jeez, Amanda. How old are you now? Twenty? Twenty-one? You could go to jail for that if you did that to anyone but your overly understanding mom. Cop to it for once. Pay her back. She's had a pretty rough couple of months."

With her sleeve, Amanda rubbed a clear spot into the old mirror that hung on the wall alongside bridles and spare bits Shep had carefully arranged with the name of each horse penned in marker beneath.

She pulled the helmet down over her awful hair, and except for where the ends stuck out, she looked like Lily had always remembered her: attractive, insecure about it, feisty, because she had Wilder blood running through her veins, and intelligent—so smart she hadn't yet scratched the surface of what she could do with her life if she ever settled down and followed just a few of the rules.

"What happened? Was there a crisis at the church potluck? Somebody forgot to bring the green beans and not all the food groups got represented? Unthinkable."

Without a moment's hesitation Lily gave her niece a slap across the face. Not hard, not mean, but to get her attention, the way she sometimes had to give Buddy Guy a whack or he'd amputate the legs of the UPS delivery man. Amanda cried out in shock, pulled the helmet off and touched her cheek.

"As a matter of fact, there were a couple of personal crises thrown in there along with constantly worrying about you two. It just kills me how you and Second Chance think Rose will always be there, like she's some endless freaking well you can dip into for a meal, a few dollars, to pay your parking tickets, never once giving a thought to putting anything back. When's the last time you remembered her birthday? How about Mother's Day? Not to mention Thanksgiving, when normal families at least call each other."

"We'd probably still have a family if she'd paid Daddy more attention," Amanda said, pouting.

"What's that supposed to mean?"

Amanda scuffed the toe of her boot against a sawhorse. Her eyes glittered with tears. "Just that if she had, he wouldn't have needed to look for it elsewhere."

Lily sighed. She guessed maybe the whole town knew about Philip's wanderings, which let her off the hook as the unwelcome messenger, but somehow that wasn't much of a comfort. "Take it on faith, Amanda, you do not want to get me started on your dad, not while I'm feeling this raw. Do not say one more word. In ten years we'll talk about this, and believe me, you'll see it in a different light. For now, you go ride the damn motorbike with your brother and zip your lip. Don't either of you get hurt or I promise, I will hunt you down and hurt you worse. And as soon as you get back, meet me in the upstairs bathroom and we'll do something about your hair."

Lily stomped out of the tack room. She knew she'd better take a walk and cool down. Faintly, in the distance, she heard Amanda say to Second Chance, "God, Aunt Lily's on the rag today."

Shep's studio adjoined the tack room. Lily opened the door and walked inside, intending to stay only long enough to forget how badly the kids were behaving. His room was so cold. Somebody had turned off the heater. Well, of course. Why waste electricity if there was no one to warm? His iron-framed cot was covered with a faded red-and-green trade blanket that had been there since time itself. All the corners were tucked, and the pillow case looked crisp, fresh from the laundry. Leave it to Shep to make his bed before he went off to the hospital to die.

A deck of Bicycle playing cards sat on the table, waiting for someone to shuffle and deal, get the pants beaten off him, and lose a week's wages. On the small bookshelf were three choices of reading material: the King James Version of the Bible, *Xenophon's Illustrated History of the Horse*, and Larry McMurtry's *Leaving Cheyenne*. Lily picked up the hardcover novel, which was a first edition, inscribed to Shep from the author. One Christmas her father had gone to Texas and found Mr. McMurtry. God knows what he'd paid the man, but he returned with the autographed book, and on Christmas morning, Shep sat in the living room of the main house, running his hands over the cover, so tickled he couldn't speak. He kept paperback reading copies galore, buying them five at a time, because he liked to give them away, but this particular book he kept in its original jacket, taking it down from the shelf only when he wanted to savor the story in its purest form.

Lily opened the cover and ran her finger across the inscription in black ink. *To Shep Hallford, horseman.* "Oh, Shepherd," Lily said to the empty room. "Already I miss you so bad I can't stand it." She sat down on his bed and pulled the blanket folded at the foot of the bed up over herself. She lay there hugging the book to her breasts and staring at the ceiling, done up so well in pseudo viga that matched the main house and looked nearly authentic.

Maybe slapping Amanda was overstepping her boundaries as an aunt, but the gesture was long overdue. This year had been rough on Rose. That heartbreaking business with the vet, coming to realize Philip had been unfaithful—and with whom—Lily couldn't wrap her mind around the irony there. Maybe someday Rose would stand up to her kids, but somehow, in her heart of hearts, Lily knew that the essence of her sister was and always would be a mother rocking an infant too helpless to lift his head. Lily tried to imagine what it would have been like to hold her own baby. How watching her daughter grow into her own person would have been as fascinating as it was terrifying. A day of rocking a baby versus power-lunching with surgeons? Bliss, probably. She reminded herself of the statistics for birth defects. She'd never be able to erase medical worries from her brain. There would be amnios and sonograms, and she'd have to eat real food and gain so much weight and get stretch marks, plus it would ruin her breasts. Tres would run for the hills if she so much as broached the subject. Well, aunthood was better than nothing. Maybe it would sustain her if she didn't think about it too much.

Remembering the beep she'd gotten during the funeral, she reached into her jacket pocket and dug out her pager. Lily had just about all her docs' numbers committed to memory. The area code was Orange County. She figured she'd better return the call now, before she forgot, so she dragged the blanket with her to the table and used Shep's phone.

It was Dr. Help-Me's hospital. Lily asked the woman who answered the phone what was up. "I got a page," she said. "Does he need technical assistance?"

The woman said she'd take a message. Lily gave her all five numbers: cell phone, voice mail, 800 number, Pop's house, and once again the pager. "I'm at a family funeral," she explained. "But if there's a physician who needs assistance with any of my company's products, absolutely go ahead and interrupt me."

She hung up the phone, shelved the McMurtry, and walked outside toward the house. The horses spooked at the sound of her shutting the door, performing the nip-and-bite cha-cha for her attention, which made her miss Buddy something fierce. The amount of squealing and fence kicking showed just how deeply the loss of Shep affected the horses. The transition was bewildering for her, too, but in equines the fight-or-flight response ran deep. It was the first thing a trainer learned to respect about the horse; then he spent the rest of his life learning how to work around it. With luck some horses came to trust that the human in charge would see the inherent danger in situations and calmly work a way out of whatever terror that might be. Laundry hanging on the line or mountain lions, it made little difference to the animal. The danger was there in the dark, waiting. Any horse trainer worth spit could tell you that the way to a horse's trust didn't mean "whispering," for Pete's sake—he needed to *listen* to what the horse was trying to tell him. Hollywood, glorifying that crap, was responsible for generations of equestrian ignorance.

Lily wondered if Pop would hire somebody young to take over as wrangler right away, and they'd continue business as before, selling horses and breeding a select few; or if Pop might begin selling off his stock, slowing down, aiming toward retirement or whatever Mami had on the back burner. *Please, not yet,* she sent out to Rose's God and beyond, into the universe. *If Pop gets old, then we all do. I'm not ready to be old. I have twenty more years before I want to even start to feel like that. I haven't done* half *the stuff I want to.* T.C., lonesome for attention, whinnied from his stall. The sound rattled Lily's bones. "Hang on," she told him. "I'll be right back."

Inside the tack room, she measured out individual buckets of bran mash, adding molasses and vitamins, following the detailed instructions designated for each horse. Then, patiently working her way through the snowy arena, one by one, she haltered the horses, taking them into the barn, letting them enjoy the rib-warming treat alone and unrushed. While they ate, she spoke soft and low into long, shaggy ears, notched ears—all kinds of different ears that needed to hear the same story: *Everything's going to be okay. Tomorrow morning, flakes of rich, green hay will arrive, on time, and yes, I promise, there will be enough to go around.* When the last horse had been fed, she felt as calm as they did, and for the first time that day, she too felt hungry.

"Benito wants your body," Lily said as the sisters stood by the fireplace sampling tiny portions of all the desserts. "Looks like he wants it bad."

"Tell me something I don't know," Rose said, then spooned some coffee soufflé into her mouth. "This is so good," she said, "it's almost illegal. I wonder who made it."

The string quartet her mother had hired began to tune their instruments to the violin's pure, solid *A*. People quieted for a moment, then continued talking. Benito, cameraless, his hands in his pockets, walked over to the fireplace. "How do you like my soufflé?" he asked. "It requires eight eggs."

As unobtrusively as possible, Lily elbowed her sister.

"It's wonderful," Rose said, setting her plate on the fireplace mantle. "I hope it's on the menu at the restaurant."

Pride blazed in his dark eyes. "It is."

"Well, then. That's lucky for the people who eat there."

"I'm glad you think so."

"Let me have a bite," Lily said, and took a taste off Rose's spoon. "You're right, this is great."

"Is that your daughter?" Benito said, pointing across the room where Amanda and Second Chance were filling plates with food.

"Yes," Rose said. "And my son. I'd probably better go catch them before they bolt." She smiled and set the soufflé dish down on the table. "See you later, Benito."

"What am I doing wrong?" he said straight out to Lily as Rose hurried across the room. "Is it my suit? My breath?"

"Who do you take your greyhounds to," Lily asked, "when they need their shots and so forth?"

"Doctor Donavan. Your mother says he's the best."

Lily patted his shoulder. "There's your problem, pal."

"My veterinarian?"

"Yep. A definite dating impediment. Will you excuse me? It appears I'm needed to perform a miracle on my niece's hair. Wish me luck. And Benito? About my sister Rose. She doesn't fall in love very often, but when she does, she gives it her whole heart. She also makes a great friend."

He nodded soberly. "I'll keep that in mind."

Upstairs, they sat on Mami's bed, combing conditioner through the ratty mess of dreadlocks. It was taking forever, and Amanda was growing more impatient with every pull of the comb. "What if I hate it?"

"Then you can knot it right back up again. Just give it a try, Sweetie, for one day," Rose said. "That's not too much to ask. Come on, Lily, you do this side, and we'll finish twice as fast."

Slowly, patiently, the two sisters worked their way through Amanda's tangles. "This reminds me of that time in kindergarten when your whole class caught head lice," Rose said. "You were so horrified."

"That was gross," Amanda said. "I still have nightmares."

Rose laughed. "It's just something that happens. You survive it."

"Yeah," Lily said, setting down her comb. "Wait until the first time you catch crab lice."

Amanda laughed. "Already been there."

Rose sighed, shook her head, and ducked into Mami's bathroom for a clean towel. "Guess I missed that particular rite of passage."

"Now that you're dating again," Lily pointed out, "anything's possible. Could still happen."

Rose unfolded the towel and draped it around Amanda's shoulders. "Let's hope not."

"You really *date*, Mom?" Amanda said. "Like, he picks you up and takes you to a movie?"

"Something like that."

Lily laughed. "Tell us the name of the last five movies you've seen, Rose. I dare you."

"Hush. I think we're ready to shampoo this."

They scooted Mami's dressing table stool up to the sink, and Amanda sat down and leaned her head back. They rinsed the conditioner out, washed her hair with baby shampoo, and then Lily towel-dried it. She rubbed a handful of leave-in conditioner into the chestnut hair, then went after it with a brush and a blow-dryer.

Meanwhile Rose gave her daughter a "facial," basically rubbing cold cream into her skin to remove the ghostly makeup. She used a facecloth to wipe it off, then blotted her skin with some costly toner that Mami had sitting on the edge of her sink. The label on it said 10,000 Waves, the spa Mami frequented.

"Someday we have to go there," Lily said. "Imagine all the Wilder women in our own private tub. The water would boil."

When Lily finished, Amanda looked into the mirror. The two sisters leaned down so that they could put their faces alongside Amanda's. Rose's smile was the first to arrive. "*Damn*, we are good-looking women," Lily said. "And I think very soon we deserve a four-star shopping trip."

"Yeah," Amanda said, touching her pink cheeks. "I could use some new makeup."

The next morning, when the funeral get-together had dwindled down to a hard-core few—alcoholics, artists, single men with nowhere more interesting to go and horsemen so fueled by good food and spirits felt they had to stick around and help with chores—Lily got a phone call from Eric.

"Where in the hell have you been?" he demanded, and before Lily could say, "Right here," he was off and running, frothing at the mouth about how she'd embarrassed the company, let Dr. Help-Me down, and worst of all, made him look bad.

"Bring me up to speed here," she said calmly. "If I'm going to lose my job over this, I want to hear what I did wrong."

Dr. Help-Me, killer of gallbladder patients, pathetic dropper of laparoscopes, had apparently had a sterilization patient on the table when he had some trouble with the scope. It rarely happened, but it wasn't out of the realm of possibility. He claimed he'd tried Lily at her pager, but when he didn't receive an immediate callback, he bypassed all the other numbers he could have tried, instead calling the company headquarters back East. The technical-assistance people talked him through the problem—it was a simple tubal ligation, women could practically perform it themselves—and thankfully, everything turned out fine. But before he could embark on his Christmas holidays in Cabo San Lucas, he just felt he had to call her boss and tell him how badly Lily'd let him down.

"He said, and I quote, 'If I can't count on her to be there when I need her,'" Eric said. "'I want a new rep—somebody who'll be there all day, every day.' You know, Lily, we're dealing with human lives here, not lab rats. The man has an oath to uphold."

Lily stopped taking notes in order to digest that last comment. Truly, her boss had to think she'd been struck with the convenient amnesia that frequently overcame soap opera characters if he expected she'd forgotten one single patient that had died while she was in the OR alongside a surgeon she'd personally trained. "I'll give him a call," she said, forcing calm into her voice.

"Whatever you do, don't make a bad situation worse."

"Not to worry, Eric. We all want the same thing here."

"Suppose you remind me what that is."

She held her hand out and studied her chipped nails. Manicure today, no doubt about it. "Profits for you and me, laurels for the surgeons, and cures for the patients. What else is there?"

He hesitated. "I don't feel good about this. E-mail me later, and let me know what happened. I expect a full report. And you get your butt back to California by tomorrow."

He hung up without saying good-bye, yet another nasty little social ill that made Lily's arm hair lift. She'd e-mail him, all right. But first, damage control. She poured herself a cup of coffee, added a shot of Amaretto, yawned, and stood looking out the window at the men feeding her father's horses. Floralee might not boast a multiplex capable of showing ten newly released films at the same time, but it did have a Good Samaritan policy. She drank her coffee, took a shower, dressed in her jeans—funky by now from all that travel, plus the kind of sweat one produces when fear boils in the veins, but the closest person to her size was Amanda, and her clothes looked like they ought to be burned. She swiped one of Pop's flannels from the dresser and tied the shirttails around her waist.

She telephoned Dr. Help-Me first. "I understand I've let you down," she said. "I've come up short as a rep. I hope you'll accept my sincerest apology, because aside from the success of your surgical procedures with my company's laparoscopes, maintaining a good working relationship is my primary concern."

"What are you talking about?"

"Eric explained about the surgery last night. I wish you'd tried my cell phone. I carry it with me everywhere. I was at a family funeral, and I apologize for not returning your page immediately. Even if it were Christmas Eve, I'd drop whatever I was doing if you needed me."

"I don't know why you're making such a big deal out of all this, Lily. Are you trying to make me miss my plane?"

Dr. Help-Me also hung up on Lily without saying good-bye, which provided further opportunity for reflection. Lily pulled the door to the study shut, sat down at Pop's desk, and plugged in her laptop. While she waited for the computer to cycle through its various menus, she inventoried the misery required to earn her yearly salary. An exorbitant car lease was a peripheral concern. The amount of hairy M.D. buttock she'd had to kiss was not. She once recalled receiving a Christmas card from a chief surgeon at the hospital all the stars used for their plastic surgeries. "Hark the herald angels high, my dick's thicker than your thigh," it read. She told herself, *Just smile, and tuck this puppy into a file for later.* And eventually the card had friends. The medical world was hard at work on an AIDS vaccine, and had recently identified the gene on which Alzheimer's disease was located. Giant strides were being made on a daily basis. Believe it or not, there were still doctors who tried to cop a feel in the scrub room. And the constant innuendo—unrelenting comments regarding her breasts, or out-loud speculation on how well she could perform fellatio, or the reason she was working in the first place, had to be due to some kind of hormonal imbalance—she wondered why these men felt the need to go out of their way to make it difficult for her job to be about providing innovative medical equipment that helped them save lives.

Finally the AOL link connected. Lily'd intended to get in on the group lawsuit thing regarding the inaccessibility of on-line hours but had been too busy to fill out the forms. The only new mail she had was from her corporate headquarters. She sighed. It had to be more Dr. Help-Me fallout. She might as well get it over with. She double-clicked on the first message and learned she had been named top salesperson for the fiscal year, beating out even the midwestern sales rep who'd won it eight years running. For her effort, she would receive a cash bonus, more stock options, and another week of vacation Eric would never let her take.

She paused a moment before she clicked on Reply and typed: "I resign."

Just for fun, though she had no intention of mailing it, she CC'ed every administrative person and surgical doc in her address book, sending it to the Mail Later queue. Next she scrolled through her personal address book. Most of the names were old boyfriends who'd dumped her for a variety of reasons. One guy actually told her that her breasts were too small, as if somewhere there existed a chart denoting acceptable sizes. Another pointed out that horses would never be equal to mountain bikes, and Lily hated mountain bikes and those stretchy black pants with the fanny pads, which she thought men looked particularly childish wearing. She clicked on the address of one guy she'd believed had such great potential that she had actually looked at a *Bride's* magazine while standing in line at the supermarket. He had left because her "opinions were too strong." Blaise, the only man she had ever told to leave first, had frequently pointed out that he felt Lily was too forward in the bedroom. What he'd said had shamed her down to her bones, at least until this moment. One thing they all had in common (in addition to telling her she used words they had to look up in the dictionary) was that they felt the inevitable crumbling of the relationship lay with *her* shortcomings. Lily supposed it *was* her fault, in a way. She'd chosen them. She'd used them as much as they used her. Maybe the true impediment to intimacy wasn't their fault but hers, for comparing every one of them with Tres, who might end up saying the exact same thing and leaving. There were no guarantees. When she arrived at Blaise's address, who was still blocked from sending her mail, it surprised Lily to discover that the pain she'd felt she'd lug around for a year had dwindled down to a small twinge. She wrote:

Dear Blaise,

How strange life is. A few months pass and the world changes so profoundly I can't believe you ever made me cry. We had some good times, I know we did, and I'm grateful for them. It's funny, but I didn't realize until now that when you called me names and told me how to cook or that I wanted sex too often that you were giving me a gift, too. As I sit here typing, I tell myself hate doesn't do any good in this world, what we need to aim for here is progress, not perfection; one infinitesimal nudge up the evolutionary chain for the both of us would be something to name a new holiday after. To that end, I want you to know I forgive you. But I also want you to know you're the one, the first man who made me see that I'd be better off alone rather than settling for less. So, thanks. I hope you have a happy life, you win all your softball games, and your beer never goes flat.

> *Good-bye forever,*
> *Lily*

She knew what Rose would say: *God sets people up to fall in love.* Despite losing Philip and Austin, even the bizarre way Leah Donavan figured into their lives—not to mention their beds—Tres was connected to her as well, Lily reminded herself—Rose would insist it was all part of some higher plan that shouldn't be questioned. Mami would take that a step further and throw some magical hoodoo into the pot, and get that gleam in her eye that went all the way back to the Martínez family, but Lily believed love had more to do with biology, that pheromones plus a primal desire to better the gene pool was what drew people together—that if love was meant to be, even briefly, two people in a room of a hundred would sniff each other out and fall in love. Like she had with Tres, twice now, which had to count for something.

She stretched her arms above her head, took a deep breath, thought about how maybe she had potential as a writer, too, and absently, with one careless finger, hit Send. But instead of delivering Blaise his message, she had e-mailed her client list and everyone at the company, too. Immediately she broke out in a cold sweat. *Good Lord, what have I done? Well, calm down, Lily, this is fixable.* Quickly she opened the Check Mail Sent menu, *.*ed the list, and hit Unsend, but she soon learned that AOL was so retarded one could only Unsend to another AOL user, so a few of the messages had already gone out into cyberspace. The majority hadn't, though, and one by one, Lily deleted them, double-checking, triple-checking that she'd gotten them all— that she hadn't burned her employment bridges just because her smart mouth had chosen today to travel all the way down to her fingers. She was heaving a sigh of genuine relief when her father opened the door and came into the room.

"Sorry. I didn't realize anyone was in here."

She turned away from the computer, embarrassed. "It's okay, Pop. I was done anyhow. *Boy,* was I done."

Her father was dressed in his work clothes, faded Wranglers and the mustard-colored Carhartt jacket that had seen a lot of trail. "What were you working on so intently?"

Up until that moment she hadn't known exactly how to answer him, but the minute she opened her mouth, that changed. "My letter of resignation. I want to come home, Pop. Let me take over the work Shep did with the horses. You know I can handle it."

Her father thought it over. "These are workingmen's wages, Little Bit. I can't afford to pay the lease on your Lexus."

"So I'll turn it in. I want to drive ranch trucks, Pop. And get my riding muscles back. I want to breathe clean air and break up dogfights and listen to Mami tell me how to live my life, I'm that ready."

Her father scratched his chin. "What about Tres Quintero?"

"If any man wants me, he'll have to come to New Mexico. As of right now that just became part of the package."

Chance Wilder wasn't one to take weeks to make a decision. "All right," he said. "Looks to me like the stalls could all use a good mucking. Call and have the feed store deliver some decomposed granite and cedar shavings. Dig them down a good six inches, mind you. Shep kind of let that stuff go when he started getting sick."

He paused for a moment, and Lily saw the sorrow he was carrying, that almost palpable weight on his chest. It still wasn't the time to hug him, because comforting would only make him sadder, but there were other things she could do to ease his pain. "You bet, Pop. See you at lunch?"

"I don't see why not, if you're finished by then."

Lily jumped up and did the helicopter dance of delight. Her father's smile spread slowly around his pipe stem, and he shook his head, bewildered at her behavior. Lily turned back to the computer and still dancing, typed the real thing, the letter she had written so many times in her mind that it flew out of her fingers in a matter of seconds.

To HQ, CC: the world

Herewith find my intent to provide two weeks' notice of my resignation of my position with the company. I deeply value the relationships I have made while a part of this family and all that I learned while in this position, which I depart only to pursue other interests. My heartfelt thanks for the wonderful working opportunity.

It was essentially the same message she'd sent earlier, only now it was dressed in a presentable outfit. This time she hit Send with a deliberate click of her mouse, and felt a thrill when the little box announcing "Your message has been sent" popped up in the center of the screen.

"*Adios*, pantyhose," Lily said, and went gleefully to muck out thirty-six stalls in record time.

21

Scorned-Woman Salsa

"Y ou *have* to come in and help, Lily," Rose pleaded. "Two of our waiters called in sick. Benito says he'll cover the tables if you'll do the
wait list and seat people. I had no idea so many people went out to
dinner on Christmas Eve."

"But I only just now finished unpacking," Lily grumbled. "Plus
Buddy's all freaked out about the snow, and Tres is coming in around
midnight."

"I know it's not the best timing," Rose said. "I wouldn't ask if I wasn't
desperate." In the end Lily said she would not dress up, she would not stay
all night, but she'd help out for a couple of hours so La Calaverada could
serve its customers.

Rose hung up the phone, looked out through the kitchen toward
the dining room, and waved to get Benito's attention. She nodded her
head, and the man she'd recently begun dating looked relieved. Then
she went back to work, chopping tomatoes into a bucket-size container of what would eventually become *pico de gallo*. People were
going through the stuff quicker than they could make it.

Within her first week of employment, Rose's position as prep chef
for salads and soup had been upgraded to include appetizers, and
twice a week she was responsible for creating the daily special. She
made *ropa* the first time, and the dish was so popular Benito added it
to the permanent menu. When a customer requested her recipe for
Mexican potato salad, Benito insisted that Rose go out to the table herself and talk to the woman. Rose had stood there blushing and feeling
absurd while the tourist waxed on and on about what seemed to Rose

a matter of a few fresh chiles and black beans. Benito typed up the recipes on his computer, and now whenever someone asked she could just hand a printout to the waiter and stay in the kitchen, where she felt comfortable. The job was working out splendidly, and movies with Benito weren't so awful. Rose wouldn't go so far as to say she felt happy, but her life felt so tolerable that occasionally she found herself laughing. She knew where her children were, Joanie's leg was healing, and she had gainful employment. Everything seemed to be moving along—at least until Austin decided to make La Calaverada his nightly dining spot.

The first time he came in, Austin ordered the *ropa*. He tasted one forkful, stood up, and looked toward the kitchen. Rose immediately hid behind Ruben, the chef with all the formal training. Ruben was huge, garrulous, great fun to work with, and continually inventing new twists on old dishes. When things got quiet, he revealed to Rose all manner of culinary secrets, like using his fingers to separate eggs so the yolks never broke, and how much elbow one needed to put into grating the zest from a lemon—very little, it turned out, because the secret was more in the wrist. Rose made notes on the kind of pad reporters carry around, which she began keeping in her apron pocket, and pretty soon she was making suggestions to Ruben.

Eventually Austin had sat back down and finished his meal. When he left, Rose asked Dolores what he'd ordered to drink. "Iced tea," the waitress answered, and told the busboy to hurry up and clear so she could seat people at that table. Rose made mental notes of all his drink orders, but so far he'd ordered nothing more dangerous than the occasional nonalcoholic beer.

Gallons of *pico de gallo* later, she washed her hands and immediately took down a clean cutting board to slice lemons, oranges, and apples to add to the spiced cider. They kept running out of that, too. It was a cold night. People needed something hot to warm themselves up, and coffee didn't cut it for everyone. Though not as fancy as Santa Fe's Christmas at the Palace of the Governors, with countless *farolitos* and *luminarias* illuminating the portal and courtyard, Floralee possessed its own small-town allure that was quietly becoming a tourist draw. As in Santa Fe, *bizcochitos* and cider were staples, plus a blend of strong, hot coffee liberally doused with imported Mexican vanilla. Downtown there was storytelling going on in the old library building, and after that was finished, over at the church the elementary schoolkids would reenact *Las Posadas*. No matter how bitter the weather outside, the church doors would stay open until two things happened: Satan made his frightful appearance, and the Holy Family arrived, triumphing over the fallen angel's evil with the hope of the newly arrived baby Jesus. Rose had seen the play before, and tonight it was enough to stay busy working. La Calaverada was the first job she'd ever had where she felt creative and appreciated. All night under her breath she hummed Christmas carols.

Benito ducked into the kitchen and took the tureen of cider right out of her hands. "Better start another batch," he said. "People are standing in line."

Rose nodded and went to the cold room for more fruit.

Lily arrived wearing skin-tight jeans and a pair of gorgeous black knee-high cowboy boots that somehow made the jeans look formal. She'd thrown on a black velvet shirt cut low enough that her cleavage was duly advertised. "I figured this was expected in a hostess," she said. "Tell me what to do, and get me out of here by midnight. I have a date with the man of my destiny, and I don't want to keep him waiting."

"Nice boots," Rose said. "Did you buy them local?"

"Santa Fe, all the way. I used a little bit of my bonus. Well, a lot. It's my Christmas present to myself. You like?"

"Oh, Lily, I *adore*. Someday I want a pair with bucking horses and rows of stitching and the whole nine yards. *If* I can ever afford it."

"*When*," her sister insisted.

"Maybe. You look happy."

"The funny thing is, I am," Lily said, as Benito dragged her back to the entrance, where customers were waiting to put their names on the list. "I don't miss wearing high heels at all."

Rose figured if things got too crowded, Lily would seat people with perfect strangers, introduce them, and like the communal table at Pasquale's in Santa Fe, they'd have a memorable dining experience on this holiday eve and walk away with new friends as well as full bellies.

Shortly after Lily arrived, Austin showed up, working his way through the tables, obviously intent on finding Rose. While Rose peeked at him over the tall counter that separated the kitchen from the dining area, Ruben took her by the shoulders. "You want me to throw that *pendejo* out in the snow, Rose Ann?"

Was he drunk again? It seemed he'd been doing so well. "No, it's okay, Ruben. Probably he just wants a cup of coffee."

Lily seated him square in the middle of the restaurant. Austin sat there staring into his mug, sipping slowly. Rose continued working. Sweat beaded up on her forehead. The smell of roasting corn and chili was thick in the close air. Mountains of dirty dishes had piled up, and the dishwasher was off somewhere smoking a cigarette. Rose's calves ached. If she had a Christmas wish it was for two minutes to stop and drink some of the aromatic cider herself while she put her feet up, but the break never came; they were just too busy.

About ten-thirty Benito came back into the kitchen and stood behind her, rubbing her shoulders. Rose groaned and said thanks. Out of the corner of her eye she noticed that Austin hadn't moved from his chair. The restaurant was three-quarters full, but it was nearly time to close. They didn't want to make a bunch of entrees that had to be thrown away, but they didn't want to come up short, either. "How about we shut down the entrees and serve only dessert?" Rose suggested.

"Can't not have salsa," Benito said.

"Then we'll keep making salsa until our hands are raw," Ruben said, and he and Rose returned to work, seeding tomatoes and chopping onions.

When Benito left, Rose lifted her hands to show Ruben. "Mine already are."

"Catch," he said, and threw her a pair of plastic gloves.

A few minutes later, Austin stood up. He'd finished his coffee and the refill Lily had poured him. He left the cup at the table and called out, "Rose! Cut a man a break. It's Christmas."

The restaurant went silent. People froze in their conversations. In a few seconds, Austin had dismantled the merry ambience and replaced it with a sense of impending dread.

"I have to take care of this," Rose said to Ruben. She stripped off the gloves, straightened her apron, and hurried out, hoping to quiet him down without too much of a scene.

"Hallelujah!" he announced to the restaurant as she approached the table. "Mrs. Flynn graces me with her presence!"

Rose tried to steer him toward the exit, but he refused to go.

"Austin, lower your voice."

"Why should I?"

"You're making a fool of yourself."

"I don't give a damn. I'll stand here and yell all night if that's what it takes to make you to listen to me." His words weren't the least bit slurred. Rose was the one making the effort to keep steady.

She folded her arms across her chest. "You don't have to shout. I'm here and I'm listening."

He threw his hands up in the air, and Rose shied. She could see Lily and Benito frowning over by the entrance, where they were stacking up menus. Rose held up her hand to let them know she was okay.

"What the hell do I have to do, Rose?"

"I guess that depends on what it is you want."

"You know what I want."

"No, Austin, I don't."

"I told you at Shep's service. I tried to tell you a bunch of times. All damn winter I've been . . ."

"Screwing your ex-wife," Rose said evenly, and the man at the next table laughed softly.

Austin made a dismissive gesture, and the man stopped laughing. "Leah's out of the picture. You can forget about her."

"You're the one who can't seem to forget."

He pointed a finger at her. "You want to know what your problem is, lady? You expect too much. You always have. You want things a man can't deliver."

"Like what? Fidelity? Honesty? Sobriety?" She pulled out the towel she had tucked into her waistband and rubbed her face with it. It stank of lemons and onions, and somehow that combination not only made her eyes start to run, it just royally pissed her off. "Since when did you become the expert on what I want?"

"Since you took me into your bed."

The people at the next table were laughing as if this were dinner theater. Rose's face burned with shame. "You were never interested in what I wanted."

Austin crossed his arms across his chest. "Maybe I wasn't then, but I am now."

"It's too late."

"The hell it is, you're just too afraid to tell me."

She took a deep breath. Back then, she'd been so sure of what she had wanted—his mouth on hers, and the feeling of him inside her, the beads of sweat cooling on their bellies to be the only thing separating them. She had ached for his hands on her, and to share the rest of his life, however long that might turn out to be, since nobody knew when a car might cross the double yellow line. She had wanted Austin to let down his epic guard for longer than it took for him to take a drink and to tell her, just once, how it was he really felt about her, Rose. What had he felt? A mild attraction? Thankful for the convenient way she picked him up when he'd fallen? Eager to work out the hurts of his past on somebody who loved him too much to set proper boundaries? Rose had learned the hard way what that led to the day she saw him walking out of the ¡Andale! with Leah. Was it too much to ask that Austin be honest enough to tell her he wasn't done with his ex-wife? That was what she'd wanted once, but she didn't want it anymore. She turned to go, but Austin reached out a hand and stopped her.

He stood his ground. "I'm asking you please to tell me what you want."

"I want you to stop showing up in public places drunk and acting like an idiot. You're embarrassing yourself and those who for some unfathomable reason continue to care about you." She held out her hand. "Give them to me."

"Give you what?"

"The keys to your truck. I mean it! Or I'll call Ruben to wrestle you to the floor, and then I'll call Eloy Trujillo myself. Watch me."

He handed them over, and she pocketed them. "I haven't been drinking, Rose. I haven't had a drink since before Thanksgiving. You can get the cops to give me a blood test if you don't believe me."

She flung the keys back at him and turned on her heel. It felt as if flames were shooting out the top of her skull. It wasn't until she was nearly in the kitchen before it dawned on her that the rushing noise inside her ears wasn't rage, it was the sound of an entire restaurant full of people applauding her exit.

Lily followed her back to the kitchen and did a little dance.

"What?" Rose said.

"A spine is very becoming on you. I'm leaving now. See you tomorrow at the ranch. Merry Christmas. I hope you got me a really good present, because the one I got you is so cool I might have to keep it myself."

However good a spine might have looked, it was difficult to get used to. Rose's hands were shaking. Ruben threw her an onion, and she caught it lightning quick, surprising herself. After that she sliced peppers with the accuracy of an assassin, assembled salads in record time, scattered chocolate flakes atop desserts that turned out too beautiful to eat. At midnight Rose and Ruben slapped their sore hands together in celebration of such incredible teamwork, and for managing to not run out of food. At Benito's insistence, they left the kitchen cleanup for the busboys and janitor. In the dining room Benito opened a bottle of champagne, poured everyone a glass, and they toasted the holiday. "Rose," he said, "You're the best Christmas present La Calaverada could ever hope for. Me, too." He kissed her on the cheek, and Ruben whistled.

Embarrassed by the attention, she gave both men a quick hug, then walked out in the darkness to the Bronco. On this painfully clear night, with perfect white stars poking through the inky sky, the smell of woodsmoke strong in her nostrils, she was far too energized for sleep. *"Feliz Navidad,"* she said to herself, and drove home to where the neigh of an old horse and the yaps of the terriers were waiting to greet her. She gave them snacks and saddled Max. Together they rode across the snowy fields in silence, which was a Christmas gift to each other.

On New Year's Eve, Austin had that look in his eye again. "Return of the dog mechanic," Ruben announced on his way into the kitchen.

"Maybe we're just a pit stop on the way to a party," Rose said hopefully, looking at her watch. It was eight-thirty, and another scene, while amusing to locals, would drive away tourist business. "I'd better nip this in the bud," she said, peeling off her apron and stomping out to the dining room. "What is it this time?" she fairly hissed when she got to his table.

Austin held out a bouquet of roses. They were an uneven number of red and white, bracketed by greenery and a satin ribbon. "Can it be my turn to tell you want I want?" he asked quietly. Rose could feel every eye in the place on the two of them. "This won't take up too much of your time, I promise."

"Fine. You have two minutes."

"More than I deserve."

"Just remember you said that, not me."

"I don't want to start the New Year with you hating me. Tell me what I have to do."

He thrust the roses forward, and what could she do but take them? She abandoned the heavy bouquet on the nearest table, which happened to be occupied by her parents, who had come into town to see a movie, stopping at La Calaverada before the show started. Her mother looked at her and smiled. Rose felt the compassion and the courage Mami was sending her way bolster her spirit. "I don't hate you, Austin. I hate what you did, and I don't know how to get past it. But I don't hate anyone, not even the drunk who killed my husband. No, wait. I take that back. I do hate one thing in this world. Your drinking."

He pulled an AA keychain from his jeans pocket. "What do I have to do to convince you I'm sober? I'm making meetings every day. You want me to check into rehab? If it makes you happy, I'll take those pills that make you vomit if you take a drink. Tell me what you want me to do."

Oh, *why* was it that the moment you'd found a plan where you could live without them, men came marching back into your life with muddy boots, messed up the rug, and rearranged all the furniture? Even Philip had managed to, just when Rose was beginning to think she'd survive losing him. She felt her resolve beginning to slip, and it made her so furious she wanted to stamp her feet like a child and scream out loud. "I guess you'd probably have to crawl a hundred miles on gravel every day for the rest of your life. And I know you, Austin—you'd die before you'd ever humble yourself for someone ordinary like me. Leah, on the other hand—"

He turned his face as if she'd slapped him. "Rose Ann, Leah's gone. We're divorced. That day you saw us together we were working out her alimony over a nonalcoholic beer. I took her to dinner, that's all. I swear—"

"I have to get back to work."

"Rose?" Her father stood up, a good six inches shorter than the vet, but Rose knew that if called upon, Pop would escort him from the restaurant in a matter of minutes, and that any number of people here would be delighted to assist in the task. Mami put a hand on Pop's arm. "*Sientate*," she ordered him, and he sat back down. "Rose can handle this."

This time it was Austin who walked away first, but nobody applauded his exit. Pop gave Rose a hug and squeezed her shaking shoulders. She held back the tears until she was safe within the confines of the kitchen. She tried to muffle her sobs by crying into a towel. Ruben politely turned away. It was Benito who came to comfort her, the bouquet of roses in his hand.

"Nobody gets to pick the people they love," he said sadly. From one of the water pitchers, he poured her a glass and set it in front of her. He placed the roses into the same pitcher he'd poured from. "Believe me, I know what I stand to lose here, but maybe you should give him another chance."

For the first time since they'd begun dating she put her arms around him. He'd been patient, but she knew he was anxious to touch her. "No, Benito."

He pulled her hands away. "Rose, how can it work for us if you're still tied up with him?"

"Because I can't let my heart be broken a second time," she said.

Benito touched one of the roses, fingering its delicate petals. "If you can't take that kind of risk, how can you truly love anybody?"

She knew he was right, but every fiber of her being didn't want to believe it. In a ramble she confessed about the *curandera*, the *polvos*, the plea she'd left at Chimayo, all of that foolishness, including the statue of Saint Anthony which was still beneath her mattress. "Oh, no," she said, her face hot with the craziness of it all. "Do you suppose that's the reason we can't seem to let each other go? Because I forgot that stupid statue?"

"I don't know," Benito said to her in Spanish. "But it seems like that heart of yours is barely scabbed over. It's not ready to love anybody else just now."

Austin ate at the restaurant every night, choosing various tables, ordering the special on the nights Rose made it without inquiring what it was. He left generous tips and behaved himself. Between filling orders, Rose leaned over the counter where she and Ruben set the plates for the waiters to catch and studied the vet sitting there alone. There was more gray in his hair now, which he'd let grow longer. His face looked drawn, as if the light that had once sparked the man was fading and would someday render him ordinary, plugging along from day to day in a job that no longer felt like a calling. Rose took Joanie to Dr. Zeissel and had her remove the cast and x-ray the terrier's leg. She'd healed well enough to join Chachi in his eternal pursuit of digging to China in the yard. Snow didn't prevent them from creating a few ankle-breaking chasms.

"It's not a crime," Ruben said, joining Rose at the counter. "The man has to eat somewhere. Why not where he can get some of your cooking but none of your lip?"

Rose snapped him with her towel. "I rarely give lip."

"*Sí*, but when you do, it's memorable."

"I think he's trying to prove to me that he's staying sober," Rose said. "The only trouble with that is, he could walk out of here every night and empty a bottle before morning. I have no way of knowing that isn't exactly what he does. Or who he's sleeping with."

Ruben picked up the latest order from a passing waiter and began to sauté baby squash and julienned carrots in butter and lemon. Shaking the pan, he flipped the vegetables, and Rose admired his certainty. "No, you don't," he said, adding herbs as he stirred. "Unless you're where he is all night long, you can never know for sure." He winked.

"Spare me, Ruben." Rose went to check on her custards, which were baking in glass cups in a water bath. After caramelizing the tops, she carefully lifted the dishes out one by one and set them on the cooling rack. Her feet ached a little bit, but when she soaked them in the bathtub before going to bed, they were always back to normal by morning. Austin finished his dinner, took his wallet out of his back pocket, and left the money for the bill on the table. He didn't look toward the kitchen, but he did stop at the doorway to chat with Benito. The men were smiling, and Austin seemed to be telling Benito a story, but Rose couldn't make out what he was saying.

Benito still took her out, but usually he invited other people along. Only once in the dark of the movie theater, during a romantic moment on the screen, had he touched her hand with his. When Rose looked up, he had already pulled it away, and pretended he'd been reaching for the box of popcorn they were sharing. When she related this incident to Lily, her sister said, "I have no idea what you should do except get your butt up here and help me ride these horses. I'm only human, you know."

Rose bent her head and put together the same mixed green salad she'd eaten here with Mami the day Shep died. It still made her cry to think of her father's wrangler. She concentrated extra hard on giving the salad her undivided attention, keeping the presentation simple, because creating a good meal meant giving it your all. When she got it right, it felt like serving up a piece of her heart, something that regenerated each time she chipped off a piece. She had to admit, when she knew it was Austin's plate she was preparing, every step of the way she felt awed by the knowledge that the food her hands prepared would feed his body.

Then, in March, he stopped coming into the restaurant.

"I guess he got over you," Ruben said. "Come over here and let me show you the trick to *carne asada*. Many people believe it's in the seasoning, but you look at how I cook it in the pan here and you'll learn something special."

Over me? Rose thought, and wondered where he was eating his dinners, and with whom.

On her birthday she trailered Max up to Pop's, deciding to leave him there until the snow had melted. Like a kept promise lurking in the air, she could smell spring pushing up through the inevitable mud, but it wasn't here yet. Max seemed delighted to see Winky again. The mare's barrel was spreading so wide and round from the pregnancy that Rose couldn't help but run her hands over it and grin. Winky stood placidly enduring the attention. Dr. Zeissel was here, working on T.C., who had an eye infection, and she'd said she wanted to check Winky before she left. Without Rose saying a word, Pop had switched his primary veterinary care over to Dr. Zeissel. Rose knew that had to make a dent in Austin's practice, but the last time she'd called Paloma, her friend said Austin was in Iowa for some chiropractic seminar and had turned the practice over to Tracie and a part-time vet from Farmington who wanted some extra cash. At least that explained his absence from La Calaverada.

Lily helped Rose unload the trailer. "I hope you're spending the weekend," she said. "My butt's got blisters, and I need a break. I hope your job's going terrible and I can talk you into quitting to become my assistant."

"Sorry, Lily. I still love it. You're going to have to hire someone else. How about Tres?" Rose asked, reaching down to pet Buddy Guy, who never strayed far from her sister's side. "I imagine the days would pass more quickly if he rode alongside you."

Lily smiled wickedly. "The other night Pop comes out to the bunkhouse and hammers on the door. 'You two don't keep it down; that mare is likely to slip her foal,' he says. I'm on the bed laughing, and Tres is pacing the floor, practically hysterical over how he's going to fix this; no more fun for me that night. I told him Pop was only kidding, but I guess it's a guy thing. Anyway, he won't work for me now that he's got that clinic job in Albuquerque counseling teenagers. He swears he was born to do that kind of thing, and the reason he gets along so great with me is that teenagers and I have the same level of maturity. Smartass. I don't care. On the weekends he's mine, all mine. And he's not half bad with the horses, so things're going okay."

A part of Rose couldn't help but feel a pinprick of envy. "Think you'll move in together?"

"Jeez, Rose, no. Not for a long time, if ever. I like taking things slow for a change."

"I wouldn't call spending all weekend in bed taking it slow."

Lily smiled. "Hey, I don't know which math book you studied, but in mine two days out of seven constitutes taking it slow. Seriously, you know what I mean. We're taking it slow in the *other* stuff. His daughter might come out for the summer. Makes me nervous even to think of it. I guess whatever happens is meant to be."

Rose wondered if that phrase would ever stop echoing in her life.

"Is Doctor Cute still your most reliable customer?"

Rose brushed the dirt from her hands. Austin had turned out to be a forever thing, it just hadn't turned out to be the kind of forever she envisioned. "He's not here. Before he left he'd put on some weight. I guess I should start making low-fat dishes for the specials if he comes back. That's what he always orders. It was strange how he came in every night but never talked to me. I miss it."

"Seems to me you both said what you had to say at Christmas. Rose, I don't know when I've ever been more proud of you. Floralee will be talking about this holiday season for years to come."

"Maybe," Rose allowed. "Floralee will take her high points wherever she can find them."

"And Benito?"

She closed the trailer door and bolted it. "Just friends."

"Good. I think that's for the best. You're not ready for anything more complicated than that."

"Hey," Rose said, pulling a letter from her pocket. "Look what I got from Amanda a couple of days ago. The first letter she ever wrote me other than to tell me she was running away from home."

"Let me see."

Rose smoothed the paper. "'Dear Mom. Caleb quit the band in Boulder on account of this girl he met named Heather he's decided he's in love with, the freak. I might come home for the summer. Here's a money order for twenty bucks on account of what I borrowed without asking you first. Love, Amanda. P.S. If you see Aunt Lily tell her I get what she meant at Shep's funeral.'"

Rose folded the letter into the envelope. "Do you have any idea what she means by that?"

Lily shrugged. "You know kids, it could be anything. Probably something I said about hair conditioner. Where's Second Chance?"

"Wherever there's a dirt track and challenging speed bumps and cute girls, I imagine."

Dr. Zeissel called the sisters over and gave them instructions for Winky's diet. "We're in the countdown, ladies," she said. "A few short months now. Are you getting excited?"

Mami came walking over from her greyhounds to catch the last of the conversation. "The new foal can't come soon enough for me," she said. "A baby around here is just what we need to put the smiles back on everyone's faces. What a long winter this has been."

"I'm actually looking forward to sleeping next to the birthing stall," Lily said. "It'll be like camping."

Rose felt a little pang of jealousy. If she didn't have the restaurant job, she could stay here as long as she wanted, and she could sleep in the stall.

"Probably she won't deliver while I'm there," Lily said. "She'll wait until I'm in the shower or loving on Tres so she can interrupt me."

Mami got a faraway look in her eyes. "Shep always knew when a mare would drop her foal, didn't he?"

Rose nodded. "He had a sixth sense."

"Well," Lily said, "I may only have five, but I work the sons of bitches overtime."

* * *

By the last week in May, Rose was so anxious about her horse that she started dropping things at the restaurant. The weather was fickle, business wouldn't pick up until school let out, and even secondhand crockery cost money to replace, so Ruben and Benito told her to take off. "We'll say extra prayers for the mare to deliver early if that's what it takes to get your attention back on food, Rose. Just go."

The old Rose would have argued and continued working, but this time she just said thanks. Benito handed her an oversized envelope along with her paycheck.

"What's this?" she asked.

"*Abrelo*," he said, and looked away while she lifted the flap.

At first Rose thought it was a photograph of her mother, taken twenty years ago, but Mami had never worn her hair like that, cut to fall against her shoulders, layered in curls. Rose put a hand to her throat as she recognized the Navajo rug in the background, the day of Shep's service, the expression on her own face made as vulnerable as she felt seeing it this moment, because she had been staring at Austin Donavan.

"Oh, Benito," she said, unable to stop looking at the portrait, seeing something different in it every time she looked. Mami was right; his work was painterly, dimensional in a way that mere photographs were not. "This is magical. You're so good. Can I pay you something for this?"

"You could let me photograph you again," he said. "Someday I'd like to shoot your mother, too, and that sister of yours."

Rose laughed. "There are plenty of days I'd like to shoot them myself." She gave him a hug, and she could feel his desire for her to be more to him than a model, his employee, more than the friend she had quickly become, still there, very much alive. The moment her heart was her own, she knew he'd act on the impulse. She felt bad about not being able to return his ardor, but she would not lie to such a decent human being, and she would never again get romantically involved with someone she worked alongside. "I'll have this framed by a professional. Then I think I'll hang it on Mami's wall of fame. In a very special place, so everyone who comes to the house will see it. *Gracias*, Benito."

He said, "*De nada*," and then he opened the door so she could scoop up Joanie and Chachi, their traveling basket, and head north to El Rancho Costa Plente.

* * *

It rained all day, and Rose had a feeling that this would be the night the mare would deliver. Just a steady, light drizzle that was good for what grew in the earth, but it made mud season seem like never-ending shoe-sucking hell. For two nights now, Lily and Rose had slept rolled up in sleeping bags just outside Winky's stall, passing the time whispering to each other, trying not to make too much noise, but so itchy with anticipation they couldn't settle down. Dr. Zeissel said to page her the minute Winky started in with the typical behaviors, the general restlessness, lying down and looking at her hindquarters, those signs that were just ordinary enough that it made the girls scrutinize the mare's every movement, see things that weren't really there, grow cross with one another and argue. From dusk to nine P.M., the mare picked up mouthfuls of hay, chewed uninterestedly, let the bulk of the food drop, and paced her bed of shavings, which Lily zealously changed on a daily basis. After nine, she stood there dozing. Ten o'clock came and went, and around midnight Rose fell asleep. When Lily woke her at three, she pointed to all the uneaten hay. "That's not like her," she insisted. "Winky is a regular Hoover."

"She's stuffed as full as a sausage," Rose said. "Maybe she just isn't hungry. I didn't eat the entire week before I had Amanda."

"How can you remember what it was like when you had your babies?" Lily asked. "That was over twenty years ago."

"You never forget," Rose answered. "The pain isn't so real to me anymore, but the sensation of them sliding out of me, and the first time I held them in my arms, all slippery and new? Feels like it only happened yesterday."

Lily doubled up her pillow and rested her chin on it. "Amanda cried like she was pissed off beyond words."

"Yes, she did. We should have taken a hint."

"How come Philip wasn't there when she was born? Was he working?"

Rose smiled a sad smile. Maybe he was, maybe not. "You were there, Lily. You'll never know how much it meant to me, holding your hand, hearing you tell me I could do it."

"You're so freaking sentimental," Lily said, and threw a handful of shavings at her. Rose sneezed robustly, twice.

"There go my girls," Pop said, from where he stood in the tack-room doorway. "Sneezing like the horses they are. Settle down. You two are going to fret that mare into another week of hanging on to her foal."

Lily patted her sleeping bag. "Come sit with us, Pop."

He held out a thermos. "I'm simply delivering the cocoa your mother kindly fixed for you. Then I'm going back to bed. I'm too old to wait up for babies. Good Lord, it'll be light in a few hours. Get some rest."

"Stay just a minute," Rose begged. "Lately I'm so busy we hardly get to talk."

"Okay," he said. "But only for a minute."

From the bunkhouse Lily fetched the Bicycle deck, and they dealt out cards under the glow of flashlights, aiming to cream each other at hearts. After three hands, Pop shot the moon, won, and then tucked the cards back into the box. "I wish Shepherd could have lived long enough to see this foal born," he said. "I think he felt he'd let you girls down by not hanging on until spring."

"That's nonsense," Lily said. "He's here. I can feel him. Sometimes when I'm in the bunkhouse, it feels as if he's sitting right there at the table, frustrated that I haven't picked up my clothes. He kept the place so neat."

Their father looked away, and Rose could tell he was close to tears. She reached out and took hold of his rough hand. That hand had fought in Korea, lovingly touched her mother, spanked her only a few times that she could remember, and patted her shoulder when things were so bad that words didn't make a difference. She gave it a kiss and squeezed it.

"Look," Lily whispered, and pointed at the mare, who was lying down, nipping at her rear end, where something that looked a whole lot like a hoof was protruding from Winky's rear end. Lily picked up the cell phone, speed-dialed Dr. Zeissel's exchange, and punched in the telephone number so she'd know it was time to come out. "I told you it was time," she said. "I knew it, I just knew it."

All three of them sat still, watching the gush of birthwaters, the first exploratory poke inside the emerging amniotic sac, the unmistakable blunt baby face pushing from the muscular uterus toward their world. Rose felt her skin chill to gooseflesh, her nipples harden, and deep in her own pelvis, the faint echo of something she'd once known herself.

The baby was three-quarters out now, encased in the translucent amniotic sac. "So long as we move real quiet," Pop said, "I think it's safe to get up."

Winky's bound tail arced stiffly away from her body. Certain horsepeople believed in pulling the foal, especially with thorough-breds, but Chance Wilder believed in letting nature take its course, and he had taught his daughters to embrace the same tenets. Rose could tell it was killing Lily to wait, but her sister stood by the stall door and chewed her nails.

When the mare stood up, gravity tore the sac, forcing the foal to take its first breath. All three moved into the stall. As the colt moved to free himself, the last few pulses of blood traveled the umbilical cord, and it, too, snapped, and then Winky stared at her firstborn as if asking, *Where did you come from?* They stood with their backs against the railing and let mother and son get acquainted, smiling and crying because the whole ordeal had taken eleven months and change, and in eleven months so much had happened to their lives that this was a wonderful cherry to top such a difficult year.

Rose heard the sound of the vet's truck. "I'll go," she said.

But it wasn't Dr. Zeissel getting out of the driver's side, it was Austin, looking sleepy but determined. "Sorry," he said when he saw Rose's stunned expression. It was the first word he'd spoken to her since New Year's Eve. "Tracie got hung up in Pojoaque with a bad case of colic, and I was on call. Winky doing okay?"

"It's a colt. Everything looks fine so far. How was Iowa?"

"Educational." Austin gathered up his paraphernalia and headed into the barn as if he'd never been banned from it. "Well, I'd better go earn my call-out fee."

"Do you want some coffee?" Rose asked.

He gave her a half smile. "If you made it, I won't turn it down."

Rose and Lily sat on the porch watching the sun come up. Austin and Pop were still in the barn. After seeing to the mare, the two men got to talking, Pop handed the vet a hammer, and they walked the perimeter of the arena, mending fence along the way. Only part of it was literal, it seemed, because the longer the talking went on, the more they were laughing. Rose wondered what they found so amusing. At Pop's request, Austin took a look at the rest of the ranch horses. Now he stood in the arena demonstrating how well chiropractic adjustment worked, using Max as an example. Max was more than happy to assist.

Rose watched as the lanky vet laced his arms around her old gelding's neck. It was too far from the porch to see the way he shut his eyes, the bond that both man and horse leaned into, but the image was burned indelibly into her memory. Austin had gotten the same look on his face that one time he had leaned into her body, seeking another kind of bond. It made her shudder to remember how that felt, to acknowledge just at this moment how much she missed it. "I'm starving," she said to Lily, getting up from her chair. "Are those chips still around here somewhere?"

"They're right on the table where I left them," Lily said without looking up from filing her nails. "You know, the only thing about Shep's job that truly stinks is my hands always looking like crap."

"Wear gloves," Rose called out, fetching the chips and tearing open the cellophane. She held the bag out to Lily, who took a handful, ate one, then looked at her sister with a frown on her face.

"What?" Rose said.

"It's just that without your *pico de gallo*, they taste like, well, ordinary chips."

Rose gave her a look. "Lily. I've been up all night. There is no way on God's green earth I am going into Mami's kitchen to make you fresh salsa because the chips don't taste *special*."

Lily tipped her handful back into the bag. "Fine. There's a whole bunch of jars of salsa in the pantry. Grab one. All I want is something to dip them into. You know, like pesto."

"You and your pesto! You could learn to make it, you know. It's not so difficult. Pine nuts, oil, basil, mortar and pestle."

Lily smiled. "How could I ever remember all that?"

"This from a woman who taught surgeons!"

"*Used* to teach surgeons," Lily said. "I'm a cowgirl now."

Rose went into the pantry and found the jars Lily was talking about. They were pretty six-sided glass containers, each with a gold label that read "Scorned-Woman Salsa." She took one with her, twisting the lid, which was on very tight but not enough so she was going to ask for male assistance getting it open.

At the screen door, she carefully stepped over a sleeping greyhound and shouldered open the door. Just as she put her right foot across the threshold, Lily called out, "Rose!"

"You don't have to yell—I'm standing right here."

Lily pointed down the circle of gravel-covered driveway. "What do you suppose is the significance of Doctor Cute crawling around on all fours? Did Winky kick him? I mean, he's getting a little old to be playing Twister, don't you think?"

Rose stepped through the doorway just as the lid popped under her fingers. The spicy smell of salsa cleared her sinuses. She remembered how in his most frustrated moments, when diagnosis eluded him, Austin dropped to all fours and tried to think like the animal, to better understand the source of its pain, to come at the answer from his patient's point of view. She held on to the jar, looking down the driveway at Austin making his way across the gravel toward the main house. He was sober; he had been for months. Every once in a while he lifted his head and looked up at her. What was this all about? Rose felt her mother's strong hands on her shoulders and the wet nose of a greyhound tickle her fingers.

"*Escuchame,*" Poppy whispered in her daughter's ear. "As badly as you want to go to him, you must stand here and wait for him to come to you. You have the rest of your life to come when he calls."

Slightly delirious from lack of sleep, Rose handed the salsa to Lily. Maybe Mami's second sight had finally infected her, because just now, beyond this moment, she thought she could see quite clearly into a lifetime of ordinary days she would do her best to cherish, one by one, for as long as they lasted. The images were so real, and they just kept coming. Austin was moving slowly, but he did not stop. He would always have to go to AA, but that wasn't the worst thing, was it? From time to time, they would butt heads, but they'd go to sleep in the same bed, their stubborn *cabezas* on adjoining pillows. If either of her children ever settled down long enough to have babies, there would be no more wonderful grandfather in the world than this man. Wherever they lived—his place, hers, or somewhere entirely new—neglected animals would enjoy a second chance at life; they'd fill up the barn, provide a chorus of barking and neighing through every season. She swore she could smell barley soup simmering on the back burner, the simple aroma of whatever she'd baked fresh that morning adding to the rich mix of flavors in that life, that now seemingly possible other life.

Less than three feet from the steps, Austin got to his feet. The knees of his pants were filthy, but he didn't reach down to brush them clean. Rose knew how to get stains like that out. She supposed it was backward of her to admit, but she liked doing laundry. Under the denim, where his bones resided so close to the flesh, she wondered if the rocky gravel had cut or only bruised him. Austin held out his hand, and she stared at it.

It seemed as if this moment had taken forever to get here, this whole hard year of the two of them coming together, finding their way, like one long mud season—but wasn't that how life was for everybody? All good things took their sweet time arriving—new horses, forgiveness, laying to rest old griefs, and just now, the first touch of his fingers on hers—each in their own particular way, she believed, left a permanent impression.

Down the road from the ranch, a little less than a half hour's drive away, in the cool, dark stillness beneath Rose's mattress, something else was happening. The photograph of Rose Mami had secretly placed there, tied in string face to face with Austin's, curled lovingly toward his likeness. Embracing the two of them was the statue of Saint Anthony, the patron of harvests, who had his own bread, and among whose special attributes was the ability to find whatever it was one thought was lost.